GOLD

An Ogmios Team Adventure

Steven Savile

GOLD

An Ogmios Team Adventure

Steven Savile

ONE
FUNERAL FOR A FRIEND

Ronan Frost stood beside the open grave.

He leant on the shovel.

It had taken him an hour to dig the hole.

It would take a lot less time to fill it.

Lethe stood under the shade of a weeping willow.

They didn't have a coffin, and they didn't have a headstone.

They had a body in a bag.

Maxwell, the Old Man's butler. He'd taken a bullet to the head during the attempt on Sir Charles's life. The Manor, their base of operations, looked like the loneliest place in the world in the rain. Frost, along with Jude Lethe, Noah Larkin, Konstantin Khavin, and Orla Nyrén had joined the Old Man to pay their respects to their fallen friend. It was the first time the team were together in the same place since this whole nightmare began.

They each brought their own unique skillsets to the team.

Lethe was the technical guru, though he was more of a ghost in the machine than a hacker. Wiry and pale, Frost wasn't used to seeing the kid outside. He'd always figured Lethe would burn up in direct sunlight, leaving ash and a pile of 90s grunge shirt, ripped jeans and black-rimmed glasses where once a genius had stood. Lethe was the deadliest weapon in their arsenal. There wasn't a computer system in the world safe from him. He could shut down entire countries if he chose to— or if the Old Man asked.

Orla Nyrén was the sole female at the graveside, but no one would dare use the word token about her. She was coldly beautiful but broken in ways that would take all the kings horses and all the kings men forever to put together again. She took refuge in killing. She was tall, with brown eyes and black hair. She'd spent time with MI6, specializing in Middle East Intel. She was fluent in a dozen languages and, Frost had no doubt, was more than capable of killing everyone else here if the need ever arose. The question was if she'd break a sweat in the process. Frost wasn't so sure she would.

Noah was the rogue element. Cheap, self-destructive and more often than not reeking of whisky, Noah Larkin could be relied upon to explode any given situation. He wasn't subtle. He wasn't even stable. Why the Old Man kept him around baffled Frost. Sure, the ex-sniper had a talent for violence, but he was far too unpredictable and unprofessional in a world that demanded tact and diplomacy. But he had his uses, and weirdly, Frost had come to love the maudlin bastard.

Then there was Konstantin Khavin. Koni. The big Russian kept things close to his chest. He spoke little of his past. In fact, he spoke little of anything and smiled even less. He was a dominating presence in any room. Konstantin was a man you wanted on your side, because if he wasn't you were already dead.

The last man at the graveside was considerably older than the others. Confined to a wheelchair, Sir Charles Wyndham was closest to the grave, in more ways than one. The Old Man was their saviour. He'd put the team together under the aegis of Secret Service Mandate 7266, otherwise known as the Ogmios Directive, which sanctioned the formation of an elite team under his command. Their orders were to do anything and everything necessary to preserve the sovereignty of the British Isles. What that actually meant was often difficult to pin down. The truth was that they were deniable. They acted outside the law, removed from the security of the State. If something went wrong they were on their own. If something went right no one ever said thank you. It was enough that when things went to hell, they were there. Sir Charles, known affectionately to his people as the Old Man, called them the Forge Team, but their nickname amongst themselves had always been the Lost Cause.

The Old Man reported to a faceless bureaucrat in the upper echelons of government known only as Control, though no one with the power to would ever admit that.

The people gathered around the open grave were often the last hope.

"First, I need to thank you all for coming home." Sir Charles shook his head, trying to come to terms with the weight of what was happening. "Max would have appreciated it. He was a good man and didn't deserve to die." The words were simple and seemed to be adequate, because the Old Man didn't follow up with anything more meaningful.

The fact that they were together was a miracle on the scale of loaves and fishes, not least because in the eyes of the world out there beyond the walls of Nonesuch, Konstantin Khavin was a wanted man. The Pope was dead and the world was in mourning. Konstantin didn't do it, but what did innocence matter when there was video footage from multiple angles, and hundreds of eye witness accounts swearing they saw something they didn't?

Counter that with Orla's successful mission to Israel and Frost's own liberation of the wives and children of many of those forced to do the bidding of a madman, and you could have been forgiven for thinking the death of a Pope and the wrongful accusations against Koni were troublesome, but not the end of the world. But Noah had suffered that crushing defeat in Rome. So close. Frost didn't know how the drunk had managed to get himself home given what he must have been going through inside. He'd failed to stop the slaughter of the cardinals as they gathered to decide the upon dead Pope's successor. Every last holy man had died in the conclave, Noah arriving seconds too late. That wasn't the kind of shit you came back from, even if you'd started on a strong footing.

Konstantin was in the biggest trouble, no question, but Frost wasn't worried about him in the same way that he was about Noah. Koni had lived through worse and emerged on the other side with the same stoic gaze and practicality he'd always had. Noah, on the other hand, was one flat tire away from disappearing into a bottle and never coming out. That he had made it back to Nonesuch at all was something, though he'd muttered something about just coming back to collect his car.

It wasn't as though Noah and Max were exactly close but getting here in time for the burial wasn't a coincidence.

"Where did Koni go?" Orla asked.

Frost had to smile. The big Russian had slipped away without any of them noticing. He could move like a ghost when he wanted to.

"He couldn't stay, not with half the world looking for him," Lethe said. "Amazed he came at all given how many people are after him. This is the first place I'd expect them to come looking."

"I'm not sticking around, either," Noah muttered.

"I'm afraid you must. We have new management coming," the Old Man said. He let out a long, laboured breath. "I fear I may not be in control for very much longer."

"In that case, I really can't stay," Noah said.

Frost placed a hand on Noah's shoulder as he turned to leave.

"What?" Noah snapped, shrugging away Ronan's hand. There was no apology for the curt reply. Frost didn't take it personally.

"This isn't over."

"It is for me."

"It doesn't work that way, Noah. Do you think Solomon will just let you walk away?"

"I don't give a flying fuck what he thinks. I'm not his puppet."

"Still."

"Still what?"

"Solomon."

"What about him?"

"We need to find him and we need to do it quickly. More people are going to die if we don't."

"Do you think I don't know that, Frosty?"

He knew he irritated Noah. From his chipper Irish accent to his immaculately tailored steel gray suit. His background with 1 Para in Kosovo and then the SAS didn't seem to endear him that much to the scruffier man. But they weren't here to be friends. Ronan wasn't about to blame Noah for what had happened in Rome. It could have happened to any of them. But he wasn't about to let him off the hook, either. Not with so many lives on the line.

"So?" Ronan prompted him. "We haven't talked much since it happened. You got anything that can help us? We're pissing in the dark here."

Noah reached into his pocket and pulled out a small bag, which he tossed to Frost. "Knock yourself out," he said. "That was left in the media van outside the Vatican after the Cardinals died. Now, if you'll excuse me, I have a date with a vintage single-malt and a hooker who loves my money."

As Noah trudged to his 1966 Austin Healey, a classic car in classic racing green, Frost opened what he saw was a drawstring purse. He opened it and tipped several silver coins into his free hand.

"Let me guess," said Jude Lethe. "Thirty, right?"

Ronan didn't need to count them.

There was a message in the purse too, written in blood on a scrap of paper. Ronan read it aloud.

"All debts paid back in full."

"What does that mean?" Lethe asked. He was drowned out by the roar of the Austin. The tires kicked up a spray of gravel as Noah spun the car in a half-doughnut before tearing off along the driveway.

"We need to clean house," the Old Man said, wheeling himself back towards the manor. "That's what that means." But he was talking to himself.

"I'll look into this," Lethe said, taking the note and the coins from Frost. He followed his boss.

"Then I guess it's you, me and a shovel makes three," Orla offered.

Ronan thanked her and handed her a second tool. Together, they plunged the shovels into the pile of earth beside the grave and set about filling the hole. Little by little, Maxwell's body disappeared under a rain of dirt.

TWO
THE FAMILIAR AND THE FAITHLESS

FIVE DAYS AGO

Lael Kelly Logan clasped his hands together.

It was difficult to accept that they had become strangers to him over the last twelve months. No, not just strangers; strangers was too gentle a word. They were traitors. Their betrayal was at the heart of everything bad that had happened to him. He could trace it all back to his hands and that first involuntary twitch. They were like the wings of a shadow puppet thrown up against a wall, and he was the wall. It was hard to believe he had been happy eleven months ago. He couldn't understand what he had done to deserve it.

Denial was supposedly the first stage of grief.

Anger was meant to follow, then bargaining, depression and finally acceptance. But he had known anger from the first twitch in his little finger, and no matter what, he was never going to accept it.

Never.

People like Lael Kelly Logan didn't meekly accept, they got angry and stayed angry. And in their anger, they struck back. To quote the poet, they raged against the dying of the light.

He lowered his head. Thinking. He did a lot of thinking these days. Black thoughts.

He watched his hand dance. It was a spastic movement. The medical word for it was dyskinesia. *Levodopa-induced dyskinesia*, to be precise. That crappy pop song was right; eventually the rhythm had got him. Now his entire body moved to music he couldn't hear. Talk about dancing to a different drummer. Lael clenched his fist. Sometimes that helped, if only momentarily, like he could use his anger to cheat the disease. It didn't last long. Nothing did.

His life had effectively ended on Christmas Eve last year when he woke up to his body's betrayal. Over the course of the year the twitch had spread to his other fingers, then worked its way down the length of his arm while starting in his other hand and working to meet somewhere in the middle. He had lost weight. Lots of it. It was an inevitable symptom of the disease. Part of that was down to the fact that he couldn't control a knife and fork anymore and refused to be spoon-fed like a baby. For a while he had used a Spork – stupid word that, Spork, why not call it a foon? That was equally apt, and if anything even more humiliating– but even that was beyond him now, hence the uncanny resemblance to Tutankhamen he saw in the mirror.

Amyotrophic lateral sclerosis was the official diagnosis.

ALS.

Give the demon a name and you weakened it; that was the theory, at least. But by giving it a name the doctors had given his demon wings and transformed it into the enemy he could not kill. It was an unremitting bastard of a disease. Not content with his hands it had worked its way into his chest, making breathing difficult, and into his throat, making it difficult to swallow and causing him to slur his words. Day by day it had robbed him of everything that made him Lael Kelly Logan, including the better part of him, Elsa. She couldn't stand to watch him die day by day, she said. What a crock of shit. She said he'd pushed her away. She had panicked and run. He wanted to blame her but he couldn't. Would he have stood by helplessly and watched her die if the roles were reversed? Maybe. He didn't know. There's no way anyone could know, not without going through it. He'd seen statistics about divorce rates in cancer survivors being considerably higher than in non-cancer couples in the same demographic. People didn't like being reminded of their own mortality.

Beside him, the phone rang.

He didn't move.

It was cordless. Elsa had liked to walk and talk. A permanent bundle of energy. She couldn't sit and watch the TV without flicking through the channels. It was as though she lived her entire life in fear of missing something – and it didn't matter what that something was, just as long as there was the possibility that it was out there and she wasn't experiencing it, that was enough. He hated the phone. If he tried to lift the receiver the chances were he would fumble it and the handset would end up on the floor and then he'd have to spend half an hour trying to pick it up. It was better to just leave it there and let the battery run out. He willed it to stop ringing. For the caller to just leave him alone. He didn't want well-wishes and he wasn't in the mood for sympathy. The only other type of call he got these days were from telemarketers and they could rot in call-waiting hell for all he cared.

But the phone wouldn't stop. With no machine to pick it up, it rang off the hook.

Lael had been wheelchair bound for the last six weeks.

It had been the straw that finally broke the camel's back, or in Lael Kelly Logan's case, the devout man's faith. Because he had been faithful once, not so long ago. He had believed. Now he had no time for God.

His damned hands twitched and jerked like he was conducting some invisible orchestra, and there wasn't a damned thing he could do to stop them. Doctors had given up on him, basically. They didn't say it to his face, but it was only a matter of time. There was an inevitability to ALS. People didn't recover. Not once it was inside their muscles. Pray? What was the use of praying to a God he no longer believed in? Why bother sinking to his knees, clasping his hands and bowing his head. It didn't feel right. What felt right was looking to the sky and screaming his rage at the heavens. There was no God worth his devotion. This wasn't a trial of faith. This wasn't the new caring Christian God he had given his life to; this was either the vengeful Old Testament one who smited first and asked questions later, or a complete absence of divinity in the world.

But Lael Kelly Logan had done nothing to deserve that wrath. He had been a good man. Observant. Faithful. And God, his God, mocked him for it by taking away everything he had. And not merely possessions; things didn't matter, they could be replaced, all that took was money. He took everything; relationships; friendships; self-respect, even pride. So to Hell with Him.

He reached for the phone with both hands, cradling it even as the trembling worsened. He almost dropped it.

It rang and rang and rang incessantly, demanding he answer. He wanted to scream, "Leave me alone!" at it.

But the phone didn't care. He could rant and rave at it, it would still ring and ring until he answered. The only way to silence it was to answer it.

Lael's clumsy fingers pressed six keys before he could push his thumb down on the one he wanted. Still holding onto the receiver with both hands, he lowered his head towards it, aware of the irony that it looked as though he were praying. It was a laboriously slow process but finally his lips were almost level with the microphone.

"Yes?" he rasped, his voice raw. "Who is this?"

There was silence. No, not silence, he realised. Breathing.

"Who's there?"

In. Out. In. Out.

Lael felt his temper rising. He embraced it. "You've got two seconds. If you don't tell me what you want, I'm hanging up."

In.

Out.

In.

He hung up.

The phone started ringing in his hands instantly. He didn't answer it. Not immediately. But it wouldn't stop. He screamed and threw the receiver across the room. It hit the wall, but didn't break. It just rang and rang and rang until he wheeled over to where it lay, angling the chair and leaning forward, trying to snag the receiver with his fingers, until the chair tilted precariously. Unbalanced, he fell and was reduced to crawling on his hands and knees. He curled up in a shivering bundle on the floor with the receiver pressed to his ear.

"The time has come for you to rise up, Lael Logan Kelly. The time has come for your name to ring out on the lips of the faithless." Hearing the voice stirred something deep inside Lael Kelly Logan. Something he had never thought to feel again. It took him a moment to grasp what it was: fear. "This is your destiny," Solomon told him. "You know what you must do. Are you with us?"

Was he? Of course he was. There was never any doubt. Not once in three months since the man who called himself Mabus had come to him. He was their creature. He had met Mabus in Regents Park, on the island where the heron stood immobile, waiting for the moment to scoop up a bill full of fish from the brackish water and fly away. He remembered thinking at the time that they were the ultimate predators. They didn't waste their energy flapping around like so many of the other birds. They simply bided their time. Girls from the nearby Catholic school ran laps, alternately sprinting and walking between lampposts before sneaking off for a sly smoke behind the trees. So young. So full of life. Brimming over with hypocrisy. He doubted more than a handful of them prayed of their own accord at night, or believed, deep down in their bones, in the thing they were praying to.

The more he thought about it the more it infuriated him. He had started yelling at the nearest girls – one far too well developed for her age, with breasts that belonged in blue movies, not on Catholic school girls… or maybe that was exactly where they belonged: on Catholic school girls in blue movies – earning himself a finger and a stream of obscenities in return.

That was when Mabus found him.

He sat down beside Lael Kelly Logan on the park bench and opened up a bag of stale bread and started to feed the birds. For a moment he didn't say anything, then, watching the birds fight over the scraps he turned to Lael and said, "Savage little blighters aren't they?"

It was such an incredibly English thing to say, but the man didn't look English with his olive skin and black eyes, and he didn't sound English with his thick accent. "Just watch them. In thirty seconds they offer a perfect snapshot of the civilized world. They're at each other's throats and all because they want what the other has got and think they've got a right to take it."

Lael Kelly Logan wasn't in the mood for idle chatter with a stranger. He grunted. But he couldn't help watch the birds, and true to Mabus's words, in thirty seconds they were bickering and trying to snatch the stale bread out of each other's beaks. Only the heron seemed to be above it all. It wasn't survival of the fittest; it was survival of the biggest and most intimidating. They squawked and unfurled their wings in a primal dance, showing off to intimidate the smaller birds and drive them away. In a few months' time Lael Kelly Logan would be one of those smaller birds. It would only be a matter of time before someone bigger came along and snatched away from him everything he had worked so hard to accumulate. Mabus was right; the story of humanity was there for all to see, played out by a bunch of squabbling birds.

"Those who God wants to destroy He makes truly bloody miserable first," Lael Kelly Logan said, watching the birds fight.

That was when Mabus offered him an alternative.

"There is no God," Mabus had said. "Not yet. Not in the way you think you understand it, Lael." He didn't question how Mabus had known his name. It didn't surprise him, particularly. "We are all part of Him. He is not a part of us. He shall only come into existence at the end, when all of us are dead and have returned to Him, sharing our consciousness, our memories, our experiences and everything we have become. Only then shall He live and breathe. Imagine Him in all his glory, Lael. Imagine Him knowing everything because He is everything! Just not the way we ever thought. He didn't send his only child to us. We are not His children; we are His fathers and mothers." Did that explain why his God would abandon him to this Hell? Because he wanted to experience it for himself, to understand it, when finally He came into being? "You have a destiny, Lael Kelly Logan," Mabus had promised. "It is in your hands – those same hands that even now betray you with their shaking – to help us, Solomon and I, to bring God to life. Are you willing?"

His first instinct had been to say, "Why should I?" But there was something about the man, something charismatic, dangerous, and he found it impossible to say no. For the rest of their time together Mabus fed his anger, stoked it, planting the seeds he would need later to ensure his sacrifice. The simple truth of the matter was Lael Kelly Logan hated the world for what it had done to him. He was more than happy for the world to hate him in return for what he would do to it.

Another man had turned up at his door a week later with an envelope and instructions that it wasn't to be opened until the appointed time. He didn't say when that would be, only that Lael Kelly Logan would be made aware of it, and would know what to do when the time came. The only instruction they gave him was to store it in a cold place, so he kept it in the fridge and forgot about it.

A month after that the phone had rung. This was two days after Elsa had left him. "Hello?" He said, hoping that it was her. Hoping that she was calling to say she was wrong, that she wanted to be there with him to the end. He knew who it was immediately. Solomon. His question had been simple: "Are you willing to make your death mean more than your life?" There was no preamble. No introduction. It wasn't needed. He thought about the padded envelope in the refrigerator and asked, "What do you want from me?"

"The envelope you were given contains an ampule and a syringe. The ampule contains a pathogen. A disease. It is highly contagious. When the time comes you are to inject yourself with the virus and in doing so you will become Patient Zero. You will have six hours left, but there will be no time for goodbyes if you want to teach the world your name. Believe me, if you follow our instructions they will remember you, Lael Kelly Logan, because yours shall be the first death of the new plague. *And I looked, and behold a pale horse: and his name that sat on him was Death, and Hell followed with him. And power was given unto them over the fourth part of the earth, to kill with sword, and with hunger, and with death, and with the beasts of the earth.* You shall become Death. Are you willing?"

"Yes," he said, almost hungrily. "How will I know when it is time?"

"You will know."

And now he knew. It was time.

"Yes," he said into the mouthpiece. "I want to teach the world my name. Tell me what to do, Solomon."

*

He gave the taxi driver a generous tip, knowing, even as he did, that he had killed the man and no amount of money would make up for it. They had talked the entire way, about nothing in particular. The man's ability to keep up on constant stream of mindless chatter was a gift: football, freedom of religion, the useless lump that had won the Labour Party leadership race, and how he'd set back Socialism fifty years with his watered down brand of Conservatism, how actually they were all much-of-a-muchness, these politicians, and, of course, as they'd left the M25 at the Heathrow off-ramp, the terror attacks in Rome and Berlin, and how, thank God, even if it happened here we'd just dust ourselves off, stick two fingers up to the terrorists and get on with it because that was just the British way. The man didn't need to breathe. Lael Kelly Logan listened to all of it, wondering if the taxi driver would feel the same way in a few hours as his throat began to close up and the fever-shakes and vomiting set in.

Lael Kelly Logan stared out of the window. England's Green and Unpleasant Land, he thought to himself. There was nothing poetic about it. It was wretched; an industrial wasteland, abandoned shops and derelict houses, boarded up windows and barbed wire fences, belching smog and the pollution.

"You sure you want Terminal Five, Guv? If you don't mind me saying, I reckon you'd be much better off going for Terminal Three. Got to be ten times the amount of people going through there every day. More bodies means more money, right?"

More bodies. Lael Kelly Logan could not hide his smile. What a horribly apt way of putting it. He had thought about making a statement, grounding the new plague in the flagship terminal of the most famous airport in the world, but the taxi driver was right, more bodies meant a global tragedy. "Where'd they fly to from there?" It was a strange question, but if the taxi driver noticed he didn't mention it.

"From Terminal Three? Everywhere, mate. You've got Air India, Air Canada, Air China, Emirates, SAS, Qantas, Virgin, you name it. Japan, Iran. Pretty much everywhere in the world."

Which was exactly what he wanted. He made a show of thinking about it, licking his lips. He looked down at his hands fluttering excitedly in his lap. "I think you're right."

A few minutes later the black cab pulled up in one of the drop-off bays outside Terminal Three Departures. There was a unique energy to the place – the cab wasn't hermetically sealed, he could feel it through the glass. There were a hundred or more cars and cabs lined up along the curbside drop-off. Holidaymakers dressed in their garish vacation colours wrestled with suitcases that seemed to have a mind of their own. Lael Kelly Logan watched them from the anonymity of the cab for a moment, enjoying the barely controlled chaos as it played out around him. He saw people of every creed and colour. In no more than two minutes of sitting there he saw Muslim women in hijabs, Orthodox Jewish women in their *sheitels* and their men hiding their heads from heaven beneath their Kippah's. He saw face-painted girls with their crucifixes nestled between pale breasts and the accouterments of a dozen more religions walking boldly toward the check-in desks while twice as many languages offered travel information across the Public Address system.

A young family emerged from the taxi in front of him. One look at their luggage told Lael Kelly Logan that their weekend away had turned into an expedition with all of the junk they needed to drag along with them just in case. Baden Powell would have been proud. They were most certainly prepared for all eventualities.

Their daughter, a young girl of no more than five or six, stared at him as the taxi driver helped him out of the black cab and into his wheelchair. He grunted, clinging on to the taxi driver's shoulder as he sank down into the wheelchair. It was humiliating but there was nothing he could do about it. Lael Kelly Logan smiled at her. She looked away quickly, burying her face behind her mother's skirt.

"You need help getting inside, Guv?"

"No, it's fine. Thank you. You've been very helpful."

"You sure? It's no bother."

Lael Kelly Logan smiled again. By his count he had four hours left to live. He could think of everything in terms of lasts now; this was the last taxi ride he would ever take, the last time he would be helped into his chair by a stranger, the last time he would look up at the sky. He bit down on his lower lip. His right hand was shaking again. Soon enough that too would be happening for the last time. That was the beauty of entering the Kingdom of Last Times. Everything must end.

For these last few hours his world was reduced to the bucket he had written 'Children In Need' on, and 'Hugs A Pound!' beneath, and a practised smile. That was all he needed. He didn't need help. He looked at his watch. In two hours he would come into contact with tens of thousands of people who would drop their loose change in his bucket, hug him, thank him for what he was doing for the children, whilst paying, essentially, for their own murder.

A huge Boeing 747 thundered by overhead, its down-draughts beating at the concrete below. He wondered where it was going. And then, a fraction of a second later he wondered if they knew how lucky they were. They would see tomorrow.

Solomon was right; the world would remember his name.

"It's fine," he said.

"Okay, well, have a good one. Hope you raise a bucketful, mate."

Lael Kelly Logan balanced the bucket on his lap and used the small joystick in wheelchair's armrest to guide him toward the building. The doors opened for him. He steered his way inside.

Snakes of people lined up dutifully, some for the different airline desks, some for the left luggage, some at the hire car desks, returning their keys, some for the cafés and shop checkouts, others for cash machines. There were dozens of self-service check-in machines that would ask if they'd packed their own bags or if they had any liquids or sharp implements in their carry-on. There were machines between them and the planes that would check if they were lying. Machines had taken over.

He looked around for a good place to set his pitch. He wanted somewhere central, but not so intrusive as to draw security and have him evicted from the terminal. In the end he chose a place close to the up escalator across from the Virgin Airlines desks. Within a few minutes of setting his bucket down he had collected fifteen pounds, and a big kiss from a Flight Assistant on her way to Lagos. She had whispered in his ear what a good thing it was he was doing. Lael Kelly Logan squeezed her hand as best he could, savouring the closeness of her body as she leaned in, all the while thinking, even as he tried to look down her blouse, that this was the last time he would feel a woman's body press up against his.

For the next two hours, until the blisters broke out on his face and his strength gave out, Lael Kelly Logan smiled and hugged people through the ALS tremors and laughed and joked like it was the best day of his life. He rattled the coins in his bucket at girls and boys, and urged them to come over and give him a hug. More than once he said, "It doesn't matter if you haven't got any money, I'll make an exception just for you, a smile for a hug." And they always smiled.

He knew some of them looked at him and saw only the ALS. He knew they pitied him. He could see it in their eyes, but for once, it didn't matter. He just rattled his bucket and urged them to cough up any spare change they had in their pockets, reminding them that it would only set the metal detectors off. It worked more often than it didn't. They came to him sheepishly, throwing pocketfuls of loose change into his bucket. In return he shook their hands or hugged them or simply smiled.

Lael Kelly Logan didn't know the name of what was killing him. He didn't care. All that mattered was that in his own way he had beaten the ALS. He had taken control of his death. By the time the paramedics loaded him into the back of their ambulance it was too late, the virus was airborne, quite literally.

Lael Kelly Logan died before the ambulance reached Hillingdon Hospital.

The paramedics who had tried to save him died four hours later.

It took another forty-eight hours for the world to learn Lael Kelly Logan's name.

And even then they couldn't quite comprehend the horror of what he had done.

*

Marietta Jahr felt sick.

That wasn't unusual. She had been suffering bouts of sickness for almost two weeks now. She hadn't taken a test yet, but she knew she was pregnant. Morning sickness at thirty thousand feet was no fun.

The passenger in 24F reached up and hit the Call

Attendant button. It was Marietta's turn to answer it. She checked his name on the passenger manifest. Aiden Smith. It was part of the airline's personal touch policy, it was meant to make passengers feel more welcome if you said things like "How can I help you, Aiden?" instead of less personal banalities like "Thank you for choosing to fly with Virgin Atlantic," as though the price of the ticket had nothing to do with their decision. She was in a foul mood. Her head was throbbing. She was coming down with something, which was just perfect. They were still a couple of hours out of Lagos' Murtala Muhammed airport.

The plane hit a pocket of turbulence, juddering. Marietta rolled with it. She was so used to the ground shifting beneath her feet she didn't even think about it anymore. She touched her forehead. She was burning up. She poured herself a glass of iced water and swallowed it thirstily. 24Fs light flashed annoyingly. She didn't care. She washed it down with two more but couldn't slake her thirst. Then her stomach began to cramp. Something was wrong. Her first thought – a stabbing fear – was that it was the baby. She put on a brave face and took three steps from the galley toward 24Fs seat. She had already forgotten his name. All she could think about was the knot of pain tying itself in her stomach. She marched up the aisle to 24F and flashed Smith a smile as she reached in and turned off the Call Attendant light.

"Hi, how can I –" she had been going to say help. She didn't need to ask. There was nothing she could do. 24F was a mess. He was slumped in his chair, eyelids fluttering like he was having some sort of seizure. His fingers clawed at the armrest. Marietta grabbed his wrist. His pulse was erratic. She saw the blisters ringing his mouth. Several of them had ruptured and wept into his neatly trimmed black goatee. She peeled back his eyelids. His pupils had rolled up into his skull. Only the whites showed. Only they weren't white, they were red. That was when the convulsions started.

Marietta hit the Call Attendant button and pushed down on his shoulders, not to restrain 24F but to prevent him from hurting himself. Holding on was hard. The spasms intensified as he started coughing. His entire body bucked against her. "Can I get some help here?" Marietta shouted as phlegm hit the side of her face.

She wiped it away and looked back over her shoulder as another spasm twisted her stomach. This time it doubled her up in pain. Something was wrong and it had nothing to do with the baby. She touched a finger to her lip and felt a blister forming there. She tried to stand and felt her stomach clench again. It took her a moment to realise there was a wet stickiness spreading between her legs. Her head reeled, threatening to betray her balance. She was bleeding. It took every ounce of willpower to straighten up, and she needed the seatback in front of her to stay on her feet. The first splash of blood hit the lighting strip that ran the length of the aisle. Her fear had a name now. Miscarriage. She didn't know why it was happening to her. She wanted to scream. But years of training kicked in. She couldn't give in to panic. At 30,000 feet panic was a killer. She needed someone to take care of 24F so she could take care of herself.

But she couldn't take care of herself.

It was only then that she realised 24F wasn't alone. There were 416 passengers on board. The old woman in 25C and her neighbour were slumped unconscious in their seats. Marietta staggered down the aisle towards the cockpit, looking from face to face. She saw blisters and red eyes in every seat. She stumbled forward, reaching out again and again for the seatbacks in front of her to stop herself from falling. Across the aisle she saw two of the flight crew holding down another passenger. They looked like they had staggered out of the Zombie Holocaust.

The door to the cockpit was locked. IATA regulations. The phone was the only way she could communicate with the pilot. It was the same phone that governed the Public Address. Marietta fumbled it out of the cradle and for a moment forgot to hold down the button that would put her call through to the cockpit. Instead, her panicked voice crackled through the cabin, turning into an anguished cry as another spasm wracked her stomach and she buckled. The receiver swung from its cord, a metronome ticking down the moments to impact.

Marietta cradled her stomach and sank down against the door.

*

Thirty minutes outside of Indira Gandhi Airport, Delhi, Captain Tim Bekker knew he wasn't going to be able to land the Learjet. He pressed the button on the headset and called, "Mayday!" It hurt to talk. He couldn't swallow enough breath to force the word out above a barely audible rasp. Beside him Cully was dead in his chair. They weren't getting out of this alive. Now it was all about minimizing the scale of the tragedy.

Air Traffic Control crackled in his ear. "Flight VS300, please repeat."

But he couldn't. He had to conserve his strength. Working off memory, he punched in the co-ordinates for DEL into the Instrument Landing System and activating the APP to hold the approach. It wasn't an autopilot landing system; it was ground-based, and used localizers to lock the glide path and glide slope, with course deviation indicators that would trip adjustments in the autopilot routine, including auto-throttle and deviations due to meteorological conditions. He didn't know how long he would be able to hold the aircraft on the ILS centreline. He was just going to have to trust the Nav Indicator to follow the marker beacons. He wouldn't be able to maintain separation or anything else. He just had to trust Air Traffic Control to do their job. He programmed in a glide slope for a standard 3° rate of descent. Indira Gandhi International ran a CAT III B ILS system, the only one of its kind in India. The CAT III B system negated the standard 200 feet Decision Altitude whilst allowing autopilot to control taxi-speed, meaning, with luck Tim Bekker could land his plane one last time from beyond the grave.

*

Lights flashing, fire engines and ambulances raced alongside the jumbo jet as it hit the runway hard. No one on the ground knew what to expect when flight BA0486 reached the end of the runway; was anyone in control? Would it simply stop dead in the middle of the hardstand or would it go to its assigned gate? Would it thunder along the tarmac and plough on into the security fences and the fields beyond? Or would it topple, unbalanced, and spin, its wing tip dragging on the runway before forces tore its frame apart and turned it into a fireball? Had BA0486 been hijacked? Were they going to be greeted by terrorists with guns and demands? Was that why Air Traffic Control hadn't been able to raise the cockpit since the plane came into Spanish air space? They'd run every scenario in simulation, and drilled emergency protocols every month, but this was different, this was happening to them and all the statistics and eventualities and scenarios went out the window the minute their call hit dead air.

The flaps came up and the airplane's huge Rolls Royce engines switched into reverse thrust, roaring as they kicked in and arrested the plane's groundspeed. It was a textbook landing, save for one thing: the cabin lights hadn't been dimmed, which was standard procedure for a night landing.

The plane thundered along the runway, engines shrieking, rubber burning as the brake pads locked in. It seemed for a moment that it wasn't going to slow in time before the runway ended.

Sirens blared and lights strobed as the emergency services vehicles struggled to match the plane's momentum as it sped towards the end of the landing strip. They shadowed it all the way. Miraculously, the engines cut out before the plane careened into the fields beyond the runway.

It idled at the end of the strip, engines whining.

Again, the tower tried to raise BA0486 only to be met by dead air.

There was something horribly wrong about Flight BA0486. Everyone knew it. They could feel it in the air. It was a palpable thing. A presence. Each one of the emergency service workers remembered the terror attacks of last week, the poisoned water in Rome, the sarin gas on the Berlin subway, and closer to home, the image of the martyr in Plaça Catalunya burned indelibly into their minds. None of them believed Barcelona would be spared. Not when the promise was for forty days and forty nights of fear. Not with over

36 million Catholics in Spain. It was inconceivable that one burning man was the only horror they would face.

Out in the cold night they knew on some primal level that it wasn't a plane that had just landed in their lives. It was the fear Solomon had promised.

Nacio Soto, a paramedic on the third week of his airport rotation, was the first man up the metal stair the ground staff rolled up to the plane. He was the first to peer in through the windows of Flight BA0486 and glimpse the horror a simple hug had wrought in a few short hours, though it took him a few moments of complete disbelief to grasp what was wrong with what he saw. Behind him people shouted, "¿Qué ves?" *What do you see?* "¿Cuál es el problema, Nacio?" *What's the problem, Nacio?* "¡Hablenos!" *Talk to us!* "¡Díganos!" *Tell us!* It was a babble of sound and questions and he didn't know how to tell them that row upon row of dead men and women and children were still in their seats with their seatbelts fastened. He didn't know how to describe the ruin of their faces, the blisters that had wept and run down their cheeks, or the looks of sheer terror and desperation that locked into their faces in death. He didn't have the words. He backed up along the steel stair, shaking his head as his legs threatened to betray him. Behind him, someone else breathed, "¡Oh Dios mío!" and the dam that had held the fear back broke.

It was still forty-eight hours before the world would know Lael Kelly Logan's name, but already Flight BA0486 was being called *El Avión de Cadáveres*, the Corpse Plane.

THREE
THE DEVIL'S DEBT

YESTERDAY

Solomon finished the prayer and looked up, straight into the camera. The spotlight was uncomfortably bright but necessary. Instead of the fundamentalist's lair, the backdrop painted behind him was one of the single most recognized monuments in the world: Mount Moriah. The Noble Sanctuary, as it was known in Arabic. Temple Mount to most. The place where God gathered the dust to create the first man, and where Abraham bound Isaac for sacrifice, and the site of the first temple, built by Solomon, son of David.

It was the most holy site in Judaism, the place God had chosen for the *Shekhinah*, the Divine Presence, to rest, and where Muslims believed Muhammad had ascended to heaven. It was where, even today, the faithful believed the word of God would come out to reach all nations.

The gold cupola of the Dome of the Rock defiled the mount.

Beneath the dome lay the foundation stone, *Eben Shetiyyah*, which according to Judaism marked the spiritual centre of heaven and earth, and beneath that, the Well of Souls. It was all about what lay beneath.

Always the unseen. And so it was with the message he was about to impart. It was there, before *Eben Shetiyyah*, that the last judgment would be delivered to the dead souls that had gathered in the Well of Souls awaiting damnation or salvation. And it was before it Solomon chose to deliver his first message to the masses since the deaths of the Cardinals. Forty days and forty nights of fear he had promised them.

It was all part of his carefully constructed act, the persona he had decided to show the world. What you saw and what was were not necessarily one and the same. It was nothing more than misdirection, but it worked just as well whatever the cause of the limelight. It was all about manipulating perceptions, feeding into preconceived ideas. The world expected fundamentalism. It expected violence. But the truth normally hid in the dark places beneath the known and expected.

"These are the last days," he pronounced, measuring his words out slowly. It was good that they think of him as some religious fanatic. Let them imagine the fire of madness in his eyes. Let them see a Bin Laden or a Khomeini. It would skew their psychological profiles and lead to a million and one different jumped-to conclusions. "The good souls are gone. Only the corrupt survive. Men and women who have traveled so far from the path of right they have lost their way. Like Icarus we have flown too close to the sun. We have fallen in amongst the liars, cheats and thieves. We live in a world that worships money and machines over people. The mark of the beast is not something we are born with, but a branding we willingly accept and carry in our wallets. It is the mark of greed and corruption. There is no place for the spiritual in our lives, only the fiscal, the financial. But what happens when we cannot trust our money? What happens when our machines fail us? What then? Who do we turn to? What other false gods do we look for in our Time of Tribulations? Do we turn to the Holy See, filled with its own host of sinners and corrupt souls? Do we take guidance from those tortured priests who struggle with their own afflictions and perversions?

"Or do we find another path to God?" He wanted to shout at the camera then, to mock them, to yell: *There is no Hell! There is no Paradise. There is no God. There is only me!* Instead he paused, the only sound the regular inhalation and exhalation of his breath as he let the question hang there unanswered. He had told Lael Kelly Logan that God was the sum of all men, all knowledge collected at the end. He didn't believe that. The Devil was the sum of all men. He closed his eyes, as though falling into a meditative state, and listened to his breathing. He counted to ten in his head, then he presented his alternative.

"Wisdom says the only way to God is through man, but you are wise enough to reject this. I know you are. We can communicate directly with the Compassionate One. The Torah has taught us to pray. Moses, Aaron, Miriam, Deborah, David, Isaiah, and Jeremiah all talked to God. HaShem is close to all who call upon Him, to all who call upon Him *sincerely*, regardless of creed, colour, or nationality.

"The House of our God has many rooms.

"There is a word you should learn, those of you listening to my message, and that word is Chassid. It is an old word. It means anyone who is dedicated to the service of our Creator and His creation. Only a Chassid may enter the Gates of Paradise.

"God will not need to judge by what His eyes see nor decide by what His ears hear. He will judge the destitute with righteousness, and decide with fairness for the humble of the earth. He will strike the world with the rod of His mouth, and with the breath of His lips He will slay the wicked. Righteousness will be the girdle round His loins, and faith will be the girdle round His waist.

"I am His Voice. My deeds are his Words. I am his tool.

"Our faith demands the future redemption of Israel, God's Land, but it is not only Israel whose redemption rests upon the restoration of Zion. The entire earth thirsts for redemption. And so we wait for the arrival of the Messiah who will lead us through enlightenment and unity to Paradise. Will this Messiah be a King? A holy man? A warrior? Will he be a simple man?

"Answer me this, does the vessel matter?" Again he paused, seeming to weigh his own words.

"I do not claim to be your Messiah, that is for you to decide. My message to you though, no matter what your belief, will not change: the redemption of the world is a gift of hope, and through these acts of violence we are paving the way for our entry to paradise. Only the repentant, the humble, those who have returned to the one faith, shall know heaven. We cannot wait passively for salvation. Now is the time we must rise up and strike these false gods down. We must purge the mark of the beast from our flesh. Melech Israel."

Melech Israel, King of Israel.

He looked down, his message delivered. The spotlight went out, returning the room to a more natural light. He had sermonized. Preached. And most importantly, he had hidden the truth of his threat beneath his words. The news agencies would focus on apocalyptic tone of his opening words, of last days and only the corrupt surviving. Only in retrospect would they grasp that he had been telling them the truth from the very outset. He was like Cassandra, offering his warning but doomed to be disbelieved. The thought made him smile. Even so, he was careful to make sure the camera was off before he did.

"You can leave me now," he told the man behind the camera, then waited for him to close the door behind him before he reached for the telephone and dialed a number he knew off by heart. It circumvented switchboards and personal assistants at Devere Holdings, avoided the denials that they were in anyway affiliated with Humanity Capital despite the corporate world of paper trails and paper tigers and paper houses, and went through directly to an Elizabethan-style study in the heart of a rambling mansion, itself in the heart of Sherwood, Nottingham, the forest that covered the ancient heart of England, where an old man sat waiting for it to ring.

He had been expecting the call ever since he had seen the news footage of the corpse plane in Barcelona and the crash footage from a dozen other airports across the globe.

"Frasier Devere," he said into the mouthpiece.

"Are you ready?" Solomon asked.

"I have been ready since the moment they murdered my son. What do you need me to do?"

"Do you trust me?"

"No, but I will do what you want."

"As it should be. A fool trusts blindly, no matter what ties bind him. We are neither of us fools," Solomon said.

"I want to hurt them," Devere said. He sounded old and tired down the long distance phone line, but Solomon was not so naïve as to dismiss the man's usefulness. Solomon had taken the time to study prospective allies. He knew both their weaknesses and strengths, and what they would respond to. It was how he differed from most men. He was methodical. A planner. A schemer. He saw the long game. People were always the key – the weakest and strongest links in any chain. And he knew people. He knew what to say to them. He was like some Grimm Brothers' fairy tale shapeshifter. He became what the listener most needed. He let them hear want they needed to hear in his words. It was more than just charm.

And just as he had told Lael Kelly Logan what he had needed to hear to make him take up arms, he offered Frasier Devere exactly what he most needed to strike back at the world he hated. He offered Frasier Devere a way to avenge his son. Devere was many things, but first and foremost he was a family man. The murder of his only son had broken part of him, but it hadn't broken him. There was a difference, and that difference hinged on one irrefutable fact: Frasier Devere was consumed by the notion of vengeance. He wanted a name. It was as simple as that. He wanted to crush one man. A life for a life.

Solomon knew the identity of that man.

Konstantin Khavin.

The Russian who had brutally murdered Miles Devere.

He was not about to give Khavin's name to Devere senior, though. Not without some quid pro quo.

"I know you do. I am counting on it, my friend. And believe me, you will hurt them, I promise you. But you are merely one piece in a long game. It is time for you to make your gambit. Now, listen carefully, Mister Devere, do this, and only this, and you will have your revenge on the man who killed your son, do you understand?" and Solomon explained how, precisely, he intended to use the reach of Humanity Capital and Frasier Devere's millions to hurt the world, and kill Konstantin Khavin in the process.

FOUR
ONLY HAPPY WHEN IT RAINS

TODAY

Noah Larkin held the Queen's head in his hands.

She looked old now, even on the back of the money. Worn out. And it wasn't just the fact that the note had been in circulation for the best part of its eighteen month lifecycle. Every line was etched in. The artist showed no mercy. Supposedly they were security features, but as far as Noah was concerned they were just disrespectful.

He didn't consider himself a royalist. He had no particular preference if Charles or William followed Elizabeth. As far as he was concerned she was the last of her kind anyway, the last true Queen of England. This new breed of Royals were clueless; if it wasn't the father calling landmark buildings carbuncles on the face of his country or phone-tapped sex tapes of calls to his lover, it was the sons dressing up as Nazi officers for fancy dress. Like many things, it seemed to him, the Monarchy were ill-equipped to survive the Age of Invasion.

Noah remembered when the Treasury had finally replaced the youthful Elizabeth on the notes with the old woman that life had made her. Had that happened to Caesar? Had the senate switched out his noble nose for an aged version of the same when they decided the old coins just didn't cut it? Nothing in this life was sacred, like the song said, that much was true.

It was late. He was tired. He hadn't slept well since returning from Rome. He had an entire army of new ghosts now to keep him awake. So instead of sleep he sought solace, company. What he couldn't do was stop his mind from chasing strange thoughts down the rabbit hole of his mind, like: how did Her Majesty feel about being used to pay for a sleaze-pit by-the-hour hotel room around the back of Paddington Station? And that led him to think about all the other things her face paid for. She was an accessory to sex trafficking, drug dealing, smuggling, and other back alley trades, but her reach was more pernicious than that because it was legitimate. Her face was linked to deforestation, CFCs, Third World exploitation at the hands of multinationals and conglomerates all the way down to street level with sweatshops in seedy SoHo and Chinatown back alleys. It paid for guns on the streets in Chechnya and the IEDs that took out convoys along the Kurdish borders. It bought blood diamonds to adorn pretty models' necks. All of it, every bad thing he could think of, and, by extension he could find a way to apportion the blame for the fast food culture, Reality TV and everything else that was ending civilization as we know it. After all, it all came down to money. Day by day the Queen's face was party to the destruction of her subjects. If he really put his mind to it he could probably come up with at least a dozen ways to link her to the spread of disease, war, famine and death, making her all four horsemen in one. It was like playing a game of Six Degrees of Separation from Lizzie. About the only things he couldn't pin on her were tsunamis and earthquakes. Everything else was fair game.

Money was the new god, and it was one they all worshipped.

He handed over the crumpled twenty to the night clerk. Given the room rate, that would take him through to six in the morning. Come six he would find somewhere else to rot. The guy took it and handed him a key in return. It had a long Perspex fob with the number 13 engraved on it.

"Unlucky for some," Noah said.

"That'd be you," the clerk said, going back to the sports page.

"A friend will be joining me in about fifteen minutes. Send her up."

The clerk nodded without looking up. There was no sermonizing. If he had any moral objection to 'friends' coming to visit he would have been working at a different hotel. He simply said, "That'll be another tenner then. Double occupancy." He pointed vaguely toward a plaque on the wall behind him that ran through the tariffs.

Noah paid him, and then climbed the narrow staircase to the third floor landing. The only thing he had that might have been considered luggage was a Tesco's carrier bag. The room itself was small; a double bed dominated it along with a wardrobe that looked like it might have doubled for a doorway to Narnia in another life. The woodchip on the walls was yellowed with nicotine. A bare bulb hung from a length of flex. There was a single bedside light on the MDF unit and a copy of the Gideon Bible beside it. Were they still trying to save his soul after everything he had done?

He crossed the room, putting the carrier bag down on the far side of the bed, and then stood by the window for a moment looking out across the city. The view was anything but spectacular. He might have walked through a time warp as he climbed the stairs. He looked out over Victorian London at its most industrial with the intricate iron and glass structure of the station dominating the view. Hundreds of pigeons had settled on the glass roof. It was streaked yellow-grey with the crap from a billion birds. He looked up at the rest of the London skyline. It wasn't Manhattan or Paris or Rome, but it was beautiful just the same because it was home.

The drum and bass pounding of an unseen nightclub rattled the window in its frame. It sounded like the blood thumping through his temples given a voice of its own.

Noah threw himself onto the bed without taking his shoes or coat off, crossed his legs at the ankles and his hands behind his head, and lay staring up at the Artex swirls and spirals for the fifteen minutes without moving so much as a muscle until Margot knocked on the door. He had called her because she was the one person he could face. He hadn't called the old man or Ronan or even Orla, despite wanting so badly to hear her say she was all right. He didn't want to see them. Not until he could face his reflection in the mirror and look himself in the eye. The cardinals had been dead less than four hours by the time he arrived at the departures gate in Rome Ciampino. With all the possible destinations the airport offered, the last one he expected to choose was Stansted, but he needed to be there to see off Max, and that the one person he wanted to talk to – the one person who wouldn't judge him – was Margot.

He called her after he'd walked out of Nonesuch.

They had a peculiar relationship, complicated by the fact that he paid her by the hour for her company.

"It's open," he called.

As she came into the room he turned the bedside light out. The street light turned the room an eerie amber. Its shadows did her no favours as they stretched across her face. She reminded Noah of the Queen then, her face painted by a disrespectful artist trying to make a point of his irreverence and edginess by transforming her into a hag.

"Hello handsome."

"Hello yourself," he said, patting the bed beside him.

Margot took her coat off and at a loss for somewhere to put it, risked Narnia and opened the wardrobe door. She hung it on a wooden hanger and started to loosen the buttons of her blouse, getting as far as the lacy red fringe of her bra cups before Noah said, "No. Don't. Just come lie here next to me."

"Whatever you want, handsome."

"Noah. Call me Noah. Like we are old friends."

"We are old friends, honey." She sat on the bed and started to unzip the side of her knee-length patent leather boot. She was the definition of mutton dressed as lamb. She was also his oldest friend. The fact that he paid her by the hour for companionship didn't change that.

"No, don't," he said again. "Keep them on. Keep everything on. I just want to talk."

"That's what friends do," Margot said, settling down beside him. Noah enjoyed her nearness. It wasn't physical. There was no arousal. It was the simple presence of another human being beside him. For the first time in weeks he didn't feel lonely. "Pity there's no minibar in this high class establishment. You sure know how to treat a lady."

Noah laughed at that, rolled onto his side and hoisted up the Tesco's carrier bag from beside the bed. "Always be prepared," he said, emptying the bag of its few contents: a cheap bottle of blended whisky and a cone of plastic cups. He tore off the cellophane wrapper and twisted off the bottle's cap, pouring three fingers of rocket fuel into the two cups he'd balanced awkwardly on the mattress, then handed one to Margot.

"To us," she proposed, raising her plastic cup high.

He grinned. It felt like the first time he had smiled since that day in Rome.

The day that he had failed.

It wasn't as though it was the first time he'd screwed up, and it sure as hell wouldn't be the last. He was Noah Larkin, that was what he did, at least as far as the Old Man was concerned, but that image he'd seen on the monitor as he'd broken into the RTL mobile broadcast trailer had been indelibly burned on his mind. He couldn't shake the image of the cardinals, some on their knees staring down into the pits of Hell as their last prayer fell on deaf ears, others lying on their backs, blindly staring up at Michelangelo's painted heaven. Solomon's message rang in his ears as if someone had spoken it aloud to him. All debts paid back in full. But like the Devil, Solomon lied. That much Noah knew beyond a shadow of doubt. Debts weren't paid. The account had barely been opened.

"To us," he echoed, clinking plastic. He downed the whisky in a single deep swallow. It burned like a bastard as it went down, lighting a fire inside. He savoured it. It was the first time he could remember feeling something in days. "So, talk to me. Tell me something good. I could do with hearing something good right now."

"What's to tell? We're both here, both still kicking, which is about as good as it gets in my book. Plus, you bring me to all the best places."

Noah sank back down into the thin pillow. How many heads had it cushioned? How many sad men had it sustained? He thought of the dog days of summer and the long hot nights where the lack of air-conditioning in the room would have turned it into a stuffy little sweat-box. His mind found another rabbit hole. How many men's and women's sweat had soaked into these pillows? How many had stained the sheets? If he fell asleep would he hear their trace memories, the lovers and losers, the hopeless and the hateful?

He rolled over onto one elbow. "One day I'll take you to a nice place. How's that sound? A nice restaurant maybe. Somewhere in the city. Then a nice hotel for the night."

"It sounds like you are lying through your teeth," she said, but not unkindly. "I like it when you lie to me, Noah. It makes me feel special."

"You're a strange woman."

"Maybe that's why you love me?"

"Maybe."

He leaned forward and kissed her. There was no hunger to the kiss. It was tender. Surprisingly so, given the nature of their friendship. He broke the kiss to brush a stray lock of hair away from her face. It was only then that he saw the bruise on her cheek. The amber light and the heavy shadows had hidden it until then. Noah traced a finger over it, recognizing it for what it was immediately. Someone had hit Margot in the face. He eased back the edge of her blouse to expose her neck. There was nothing erotic in it. He found more bruises. The marks were old. Fading. But there was no mistaking what they were. They hadn't just hit her; they had tried to strangle her. There were thick purple finger-shaped bruises around her throat. "Who did this to you?" he asked.

She didn't answer him. Not immediately. And when she did it was only to say, "Don't," just as he'd said to her twice already since she entered the room. "Please."

"I'm not going to leave it," Noah said, softly. He knew what he was doing. He was looking for something he could do. It didn't take a bunch of letters after his name for him to know that after Rome he needed a win. "Who did this to you, Margot?"

"How about some more of that whisky, handsome?" she said instead.

"Who did this to you?"

"You can ask until you are blue in the face, I'm not going to tell you."

"Who did this to you?" Noah repeated, pulling at more of the buttons of her blouse. The entire right side of her ribcage beneath the lacy bra cup was a mess of fading bruises. She had been battered, but the bastard had barely touched her face. He knew what he was doing. Only a particularly twisted punter would pay money to sleep with a whore who looked like she'd gone ten rounds with Mike Tyson. "I'm going to ask you one more time, Margot, who did this to you? They don't deserve your protection."

"I don't want you making it worse," she said, and she meant it. Beyond the window the bass beat changed to something far more urgent, matching the mood in the room. It was relentless. It would have been a good strong rhythm to have sex to, Noah realised.

"This is what I do. Trust me."

She shook her head. "I don't," she said. "No offence."

"Someone hurt you, Margot. That's not right."

"It goes with the territory, Noah. Just leave it. Please. I'm asking you as a friend."

"See that's just not playing fair. There's no way a friend would expect me to walk away. They'd know me better than that."

"What are you? Some bloody white knight that comes rushing to save the damsel in distress?"

"Something like that."

"Well, last time I looked I didn't exactly fit the definition of damsel. They tend to be pretty young blondes, not saggy old brunettes."

"But you're dead on for a woman in distress. That's the part of the description that matters."

"It'll just get out of hand if you go after –" She caught herself before she said his name. "Him."

He touched her cheek. "Look at me," Noah said, softly, challenging her to look him in the eye. She couldn't. That was when he knew he had to do something. She reached up and grasped his wrist. Not tightly. Her red nail polish was chipped, the nails themselves bitten down to the quick. He didn't fight her. He needed her to trust him. She lived in a world where men came in two varieties; they paid her for sex because it made them feel powerful to think their money could buy anything, including her, or because there was something fundamental missing from their life and they thought she could give it to them. It was a simplistic way of looking at the world, but being simple didn't make it wrong. Predators and prey was another way of classifying the men in her life. Noah's relationship with Margot fell very much into the latter category. It wasn't love. That wasn't what bound them. Or if it was, it was the kind of love that didn't come with the potential for hurt. They both knew what they were getting into when he called. And if he didn't call, his absence wouldn't tear a hole in her heart. "Some people can't help themselves. Either they don't know they need help or they're just not in a position to stop what is happening to them. Look at me, Margot," and this time she did. "You need help and I want to help you. Let me."

"I like you better when you want to get drunk," she said.

"I like me better that way, too. But stop changing the subject. All I need is a name. I am not asking you to say anything else. Just a name."

"What are you going to do to him?"

Noah cupped her cheek in his hand, and then traced a line from her jaw down to the lacy cup of her bra. He was tracing the outline of the bruises. He undid two more buttons, this time leaning in closer to kiss her neck and leave a soft trail of butterfly kisses all the way down to her belly. When he looked up, he said, "Nothing he doesn't deserve."

"His name is Jordan," Margot said. "Jordan Walker."

"And where can I find this charming man?"

"I don't know."

"What is he to you?"

She didn't say anything.

"A regular?" Like me, he wanted to add, but didn't.

She shook her head. It was a barely perceptible denial in the jaundiced light.

"Family?" Even as he asked he realised he didn't know her name. She was just Margot. He'd never asked Margot what. So much for a special relationship.

She shook her head again.

He was running out of options, but he hadn't said the obvious one yet. "Is he your tout?" He knew he was right even before he said it. "He is, isn't he?"

She pressed a red-nailed fingertip to his lips and shushed him. "Make love to me, Noah. I want to pretend we're lovers, in love, like normal people.

49

Please. Let's just pretend the world outside the window doesn't exist. Just for tonight. We can worry about Jordan tomorrow. But tonight I want to fall asleep and lose myself in dreams like lovers do."

He never could deny a woman. She didn't have to be beautiful. She only had to be damaged. He was a fool for a damaged woman every time. In that he was Cupid's toy every bit as much as the next man.

*

Love came in all sorts of shapes and sizes. It could be romantic. Grand gestures. It could be the comfort of routine. Familiarity. The little things shared day after day. It could be just about anything. Did he love Margot? Not in any fairy tale sort of way. She wasn't a *Pretty Woman*. There were no happy endings that didn't cost fifty quid a toss as far as she was concerned. But he did love her. He just didn't want to define it. Putting a label on it would just turn it into something dirty.

He eased himself out of bed. The entire mattress shifted as though under the pressure of some huge tectonic shift. He sat on the edge of the bed for a few minutes, head in hands, elbows on knees. He knew what he had to do.

He put his jeans on, buckling them, and then slipped his plain white tee-shirt on over his head. He stuffed his feet into his Reebok's and took one last look around the room. The bottle of blended whisky was half empty. He couldn't remember having drunk that much. But then he'd been doing a lot these last few days that he couldn't remember.

He let Margot sleep. She snored. There was nothing delicate about it. The chainsaw buzz didn't disturb him in the slightest. This was one of the few precious moments he had in his life, watching Margot sleep. There was an intimacy about it. Trust. She felt safe enough to sleep with him. He liked that. It was just another reason why he wasn't going to let a no-mark like Jordan Walker raise a fist to her ever again.

He took a handful of notes out of his wallet and put them beneath the whisky bottle. He didn't bother counting them.

Noah kissed Margot on the forehead, causing her to shift slightly. She didn't wake.

He stood there for a few more minutes just watching her.

As though she sensed his scrutiny, Margot rolled onto her back, stretching her hands up over her head. The movement caused the thin blanket to slide away from her, leaving half of her body naked. Noah covered her up again. She looked up at him sleepily, not really seeing him. "Shhh," he whispered. "Go back to sleep."

It was five in the morning when he left. He had a full hour left on the room. He left the night clerk another twenty pounds to keep the room until lunch time. The man seemed happy enough to take his money. He didn't ring it up; it went straight in his pocket. A good night's business. How much of the money that went over the counter ended up in his pocket? More than half, most likely. Who was going to complain? The hotel owners? They could hardly go to the police without Vice getting involved. It was a lucrative little sideline. It also helped Noah stay invisible. The city was full of low rent places like this that charged a pittance, offered the barest essentials in terms of amenities, and didn't keep a register. He could drift night by night, invisible. For all his gadgets and gismos Lethe couldn't find him. And for that reason alone cash was king.

And yet, as he stepped out onto the pavement into the fine mist of rain that had begun some time during the night, he dialled the one number that guaranteed his days of hiding were over. The dial tone cycled three times before Jude Lethe's groggy voice asked, "Do you have any idea what time it is, monkey boy?"

"I need you to do something for me."

"Isn't that always the way?"

"You know I love you, Jude."

"Well that makes everything all right then."

"I need you to find someone for me. Jordan Walker. That's all I know. Can't be a common name though. I'm doubting he is best friends with the Tax Man and he doesn't strike me as the kind of guy who'd fill out his census form."

"So, you think this is going to be challenge? Seriously Noah, how long have you known me? This is what I do."

"Then shut up and work your magic."

A black cab cruised toward him, its yellow light on. He stepped into the road to flag it down but it just drove on by, splashing up a sheet of water. Noah stepped back onto the pavement, barely avoiding a soaking.

"May I ask why you are in such a hurry to find this guy?"

"What you don't know you can't tell when called to testify," Noah said, only partially joking.

"Oh, it's like that is it?"

"Very much so."

He started walking down the street. The Austin Healey was parked some way away where nobody would find it. He didn't really want it sitting outside when he did the deed. It was not exactly inconspicuous. He hadn't driven the car much since jetting off to Rome in search of Nick Simmonds' ghost. The image of the burning man in Saint Peter's Square was another one branded onto his mind's eye. *There is a plague coming. Forty days and forty nights of fear.* That threat still tormented him. The Pope, the Cardinals, they couldn't be the end of it simply because there was still almost a month of those promised forty days to go. It didn't make sense for it to just end now. Noah didn't like threats that didn't make sense. They had a habit of escalating until they did.

"Is this what the old man means by doing something stupid?"

"I'd say it's the very definition of it. As of about three hours ago Mr Walker became a dead man walking."

"Oh good, I'd hate to get in trouble for using my powers for good."

"What have you got?"

"How did you know I was digging?"

"You started to sound excited. It's a dead giveaway."

Jude Lethe laughed at that. "Okay, here we go: Jordan Walker. Pillar of the community he isn't. Age 33. In and out of detention and care homes for most of his teens, graduated to violent crime aged 21, when he served six months of an eighteen month stretch in Wormwood Scrubs. Let out for good behaviour only to break the terms of his early release when he got caught during a raid on an armored car in the Docklands three months later. Most notable about that failed heist was the death of Steve Tanner, one of the three men driving the armored car. Tanner died as a result of his injuries sustained in the attack, but not immediately. In fact it he didn't die until almost fifteen months after the fact. What makes this interesting is the fact that it's before the 1996 Year and a Day Law Reform. Walker quite literally got away with murder, but was sent down for the robbery and served the full term for that."

"Sounds like a charmer."

"Oh, it gets worse. Believe me. Tanner's death obviously gave him a taste for the darker side of life. He's been linked to sex trafficking from the Balkans. There was that shipment of girls smuggled in the freight cargo they picked up a couple of years ago at Felixstowe, half of them starved to death, the others barely alive?"

"I remember."

"That was our boy Walker, not that they could ever prove anything. Slippery son of a bitch. But that's the problem with the law, sometimes it just can't act. It can't help the people it's put in place to help." Lethe's observation echoed Noah's own thoughts eerily. He'd never thought of Lethe as a kindred spirit, but something had changed in him since the attack on Nonesuch.

"So what you are saying is he deserves what's coming to him."

"No one deserves it more, mate."

"Tell me where to find him."

"Patience grasshopper. Walker owns a place on the Riverside, down behind the Oxo Tower. That's some pricey real estate."

"I guess that's what sexploitation and human trafficking buys you these days. Address?"

"Well, I could give you that, or I could go one better and tell you where he is now."

"You frighten me, Jude. Do you know that? How the hell do you know where he is right now?"

"Mobile phone triangulation, my technically retarded friend. I can tell you the name of the shabby little shithole of a hotel you've just walked out of, if you like. I'm looking at his car right now thanks to the wonders of London being the most surveilled city in the known universe. So, do you want me to tell you where he is?"

"What do you think?"

"No need to get tetchy. You're going to like this. Thanks to the marvels of modern technology I can tell you that right now our friend is in Delamere Terrace, London, W2."

"And for those of us who aren't walking A-Zs?"

"Little Venice. About fifteen minutes' walk from you. Down on the canal to be precise. Our boy has got a houseboat moored down there. *Wet Dream*."

"Classy," Noah said. Little Venice. Two or three minutes in a taxi: along Bishops Bridge Road, onto the Harrow Road, under the Westway, follow the road around and take a right down into Maida Vale. But he wasn't about to hail a cab. The fewer people who knew about his nocturnal visit the better. He was already thinking about the clean-up. As Lethe said, he could basically walk it in fifteen minutes, run it in considerably less. But running through the streets of London before 6 a.m. was going to get him noticed. Walking he was just another early riser or late night reveler and the city was full of those.

"Thanks, Jude. I owe you one."

"Break a leg. And with that, I'm going back to sleep until the old man drags me kicking and screaming back to consciousness in a few hours. Are you going to grace us with your presence later?"

"That depends," Noah said. "Let me know what the new management is like and I'll think about it. In the meantime, sleep well."

He hung up. The newsagent's on the corner was already open. Its dim bulb barely held back the night. The owner was outside on his knees straightening out the morning's headline beneath the wire trap that was supposed to hold it in place. Great streaks of rain had already smeared the black ink. Not that it mattered. In this age of 24 hour reporting it was already yesterday's news.

Noah nodded to the guy as he straightened himself up and offered a friendly, "Morning," as he walked past.

The rain didn't bother him. It felt right. It should be raining. Part of him wished the heavens would really open up. It would make walking away so much easier when the time came. They didn't. It was still the same mist-drizzle as he took the turn off the Harrow Road onto Delamere.

It was barely 5:30.

Noah walked along the side of the canal reading the names painted along the sides of the boats. Some tried to be funny, like *For Sail, To Sea Oar Knot to Sea, The Other Woman* and *She Got the House*, some were sweet, and others just made no sense to him. The *Wet Dream* was moored about half way down the terrace. Noah scanned the rows of windows on either side of the canal. The houses were the same white-fronted clematis-suffocated townhouses all along the row. Each had its own unique and very expensive personality while contriving to look exactly like the ones on either side of it. A few lights were on but most were still bathed in darkness, the curtains drawn, keeping whatever secrets they harbored secret. He hopped down onto the narrow tow path, looked around once more to be sure no-one was out walking the dog, and then made the small jump onto the rail and dropped down onto deck, landing lightly. Any nosy neighbours who'd taken it upon themselves to do the whole neighbourhood watch thing through their twitching curtains would have thought he had every right to be there. And that was the secret, looking like he belonged.

Noah didn't waste time trying the door.

He'd learned a thing or two from hanging around with Konstantin. And at 5:30 in the morning it came down to fear. It was all about explosive violence. The military called it Shock and Awe, but it came down to the same thing: raising hell.

He kicked the door down.

His foot hit the centre of the wooden doors, about two inches across from the metal plate that housed the flimsy lock, splintering the entire thing inwards. The door's scream as it exploded inwards was bestial.

Noah stood silhouetted in the doorway, looking like some Night Angel or Dark Avenger or other vigilante straight out of the pages of a comic book. He took it all in in a split second: the galley kitchen was narrow, with plates and bowls stacked up. Ashtrays were yellowed and overflowing with more than just cigarette butts. At the far end of the galley kitchen was the bedroom. Really it was little more than the dining area with the stowaway table flipped over and a mattress laid on it. Walker wasn't alone. He was in bed with one of his girls, but she was out of it, loaded up on her drug of choice. It looked as though her Emo-eyeliner had been drawn on with black magic marker.

Startled awake, a naked man – Noah assumed it was Jordan Walker – scrambled backwards, kicking at the sheets as he tried frantically to untangle himself. He wasn't screaming. Noah had to give him credit for that. In fact he was doing everything humanly possible to drag his arse out of bed, eyes darting between Noah and the counter, where Noah assumed he'd left his gun when he'd crawled into bed with Smack Girl.

Noah didn't wait for him to free himself.

Amped up on righteous fury, Margot's bruises all he would allow himself to think about, Noah burst into the narrow boat, taking the three steps down into the galley in a single leap and charging down the gap between them. He was on Walker before the man was half way out of bed, dragging him the rest of the way clear by the hair. He slammed the side of his head off the corner of the stowaway table, taking all the fight out of Walker in a single blow. The skin ruptured, blood pouring down the side of the pimp's face. This time Walker did scream. He screamed and babbled and begged and pleaded, going through all the stages of denial in about three seconds flat.

Noah stood over him, judge, jury and the proverbial executioner all in one.

"What do you want from me, man? Whatever it is, whatever you need, mate, anything, it's yours. Just name it. Anything."

"I want you to suffer," Noah said flatly. He didn't give Walker the chance to say another word. He went to town on him. It was brutal. He wasn't just beating seven shades of shit out of the pimp. He was beating the hell out of Solomon and Mabus, each brutal kick was for the bastards who had beaten Orla. Each crunching blow was for the dead priests he'd failed. For the thirteen martyrs who had been forced to burn themselves alive, and the commuters on the Berlin subway and the tourists who had drunk the water in Rome. All of them. He crouched down over Walker, hammering his fist over and over into the side of his face until he'd beaten him bloody. Walker could barely hold his hands up to cover his face; there was nothing he could do to protect himself. Noah was relentless. Possessed. He drove his fist in again and again and again and again, each time harder, until Walker's head rolled on his neck, blood and spittle streaming down his chin and his eyes rolled up into his head.

And still he hit him.

Punishing him.

And he kept on slamming his fist into his jaw and nose even when he had to hold Walker's head up to do it and there was more blood coming from his torn knuckles than from Jordan Walker's ruined face. Still his bloodlust wasn't satisfied. It wouldn't be until he'd had his win. And Walker slumped unconscious in the corner wasn't a win. It was just the start.

Noah stood up again, and took in the mess of the galley kitchen and the makeshift bedroom. Jordan Walker was a slob. No two ways about it. The place was infested. Aphids crawled over the plates in the drainer. The food on the plates had crusted and shriveled and started to mold. Bottles of cheap Russian Vodka and no-brand Gin lay on top of the rubbish and there were enough cigarette butts scattered around the place to make a life-size effigy of the Buddha. Noah found the kettle, filled it from the tap and plugged it in. It took less than three minutes to bring it to the boil and in that short time Walker showed no signs of stirring.

He found the radio while he waited, and turned it on, fiddling with the dial until he settled on a tune as inappropriate for his purpose as any ever recorded: Deacon Blue's Dignity. There was nothing dignified about what was about to happen.

Noah unplugged the kettle and stood over Walker, kicking him once with his foot to see if he would stir. When he didn't Noah dribbled a steady stream of boiling water down the side of the pimp's face until he came around kicking and screaming as his skin seared. Noah upended the kettle, pouring its entire contents out over Walker's head. The boiling water scalded the entire right side of his face, blistering even as the skin burned red raw. Walker's screams were sickening. He couldn't speak. His jaw worked but there were no words. Just shrieks and the coarse rasps as the screaming lost all coherence.

The cramped cabin stank of burned meat and, beneath it, shit. Walker had lost control of his bowels.

Noah waited until they faded inevitably to hoarse whispers, and then said, "Consider this a public health warning, Jordan. Margot's protected. Lay a hand on her again and I'll kill you. There's nowhere you can hide. Believe me, my friend, you'll never be safe again. Understood?"

Tears streaked the pimp's face. The blisters had already begun to weep. His eyes were full of hatred.

"This is going to go one of two ways. You nod or I kill you here and now. It really is that simple. And if you don't sell it to me, if you don't make me believe you really will keep your word, I'm not going to take any chances, I'll hit you once, in the throat, crushing your windpipe and walk out of here while you suffocate, unable to make so much as a sound. So what's it going to be? Do we have an understanding or don't we?"

Walker nodded frantically, his eyes bulging out of his face. The burns were bad. He'd be scarred for life. Noah had been very careful to match the burns to Margot's bruises. It was symbolic. Symmetry.

"I'm not sure I believe you, Jordan. I think the minute I walk out of here you're going to try and take it out on Margot because that's the weak piece of shit you are. Convince me I'm wrong."

"Please," the pimp said, his throat barely capable of sound. It was pitiful.

The Smack Girl on the bed still hadn't moved. She could well have OD'd for all he knew. Or cared.

"Are you begging?"

Walker nodded desperately wanting Noah to believe him. And the truth was Noah did believe him. But the thing was the fear would only stay sharp for so long and then it would start to fade and Walker would forget how he felt with Noah standing over him and would just remember it being Margot's fault, and he'd want to hurt her for it. He knew men like Jordan Walker. So he couldn't just walk away. Not this time. Not if he was going to have his win.

He crouched over Walker, grabbing a fistful of his hair and, ignoring his screams as he found his voice again, yanking his head back. He clenched his fist and stared at the pimp's burned throat and the blisters that had started to cluster around his Adam's apple. It would only take one punch, but when it came right down to it he couldn't do it.

Noah Larkin was many things but he wasn't a murderer.

He shoved Walker backwards, sending him sprawling across the cramped floor. "I believe you," he said. "Don't disappoint me, Jordan. She's not your property anymore. If I hear that you've so much as crossed the street to talk to her I'll be back to finish this."

The pimp wept.

That was enough for Noah.

He left him there huddled up against the side of the stowaway table and returned to dry land.

The rain had stopped.

He thought about heading down to Nonesuch,

but he couldn't face the Old Man. Not yet. Instead he walked the half mile back to the flea pit hotel behind Paddington because that was the only place in the world he wanted to be. He wanted to lie down beside Margot and tell her all was well with the world, that he had protected her. One little victory in a world of body blows and defeats. Twice on the walk back to the hotel he thought about turning back and finishing what he had started. Oddly, thinking about Margot stopped him.

When he opened the door, she was gone.

She'd taken the money and the bottle.

She hadn't made the bed, so he crawled in and lay in the shape her body had left in the rumpled sheets. He fell asleep breathing her smell in from the damp sheets, and for the first time in a week didn't dream of horrors, burning men or dead cardinals.

Yes, there were lots of different kinds of love.

This was just another one of them that defied classification. That didn't make it wrong. Just different.

FIVE
FRIENDS IN LOW PLACES

Konstantin Khavin looked over his shoulder.

Just once. That was all he needed.

He wasn't alone.

There were hundreds of people shuffling towards the next checkout along the street, heads down, bulging carrier bags in hand. But the big Russian wasn't worried about shoppers. He was being followed. They were sloppy. He was aware of at least three people strategically placed to keep him in sight. He couldn't be certain, but he suspected there were at least two more shadowing him.

He didn't need to be certain.

He just needed to be aware.

He kept his pace measured, even. There was no point in pretending he hadn't seen them, but equally running wasn't an option. When it came to a choice between the two there was only ever going to be one choice. It was the Russian way. He would just wait them out. Let them make their move.

Konstantin measured his breathing, keeping it in time with his footsteps.

Logically, they wouldn't try to take him here; the potential for collateral damage was too great. Which meant for now this was the safest place in the city, making it exactly where he wanted to be. For now, at least.

But that would change soon enough.

He counted to eleven and stopped to look at the window of the next shop in the street, but not at the mannequins dressed in cheap copies of the latest designer-label fashions. His gaze didn't penetrate the glass. He positioned himself at an angle to the window and used the glare on the huge plate of glass to study the reflections of the street behind him. It took Konstantin a second to locate the ghostly shape of the nearest watcher. It was indistinct at best. But he didn't need details. He wanted to see how they adjusted to unpredictability. That would be the benchmark for just how serious they were. It would also give him an idea of just what he was up against. Professionals would adapt. And quickly. With the minimum of fuss.

So he watched for tells through the glass; anything, a little look or signals that passed between the watchers, could be the difference when it came to how this was all going to play out.

It was all about shifting perspectives. Right now he was the rat in their maze, and they were ringing the bell. The trick was in ignoring it, in not going for the cheese. But, and here was the hard part, still leaving them with the impression they were in control while he transitioned from being the watched to becoming the watcher.

He resisted the temptation to call Lethe, back in the sanctuary of Nonesuch, though no doubt he could co-opt the street cameras to give him extra eyes or work some other magic. And as far as Konstantin was concerned it was magic.

He could do this alone.

It was surprisingly easy to do.

Just knowing they were there shifted the balance.

People were sloppy when they thought they weren't being observed. It wasn't about making mistakes – everyone made mistakes, it was how they reacted to them that mattered. No, it was even more basic than even that. It came down to thoughtlessness. A disciplined team never would have dared acknowledge each other if they thought there was even the slightest risk that they might be seen, but when they thought they were unobserved the playbook was replaced by human nature. More often than not people resorted to the simplest of silent communications. They didn't disappoint him. As it was, the nods were barely perceptible through the glass. Two distinct nods, meaning two men on his tail. Five in total. Five against one. They weren't great odds, but they could be shifted in his favour with a little cunning and, when the time came for push to become shove, an explosive burst of violence.

He had no desire to start a fight, but he wasn't averse to finishing one if he had to. That was the Russian way. Always finish.

He turned his back on the shabbily dressed mannequins and started to walk down Oxford Street again.

It was a little after lunchtime. The huge doors to the shops were open, each one offering a different enticement to lure the shoppers in. Konstantin was assailed by the smells of leather from the shoe shops, the overpowering scents of soaps and perfumes from Lush, and music, lots of music. Between the space of fifty feet and four doors he was bombarded by, mindless pop songs, an '80s riff, hip-hop and some indie disco tried to drown his senses. He had no time for any of it.

Something was happening inside the shoe shop.

He was going to walk on by but an argument at the counter caused him to glance sideways. A big woman who had no right dressing in the stretch-Lycra leggings she had forced herself into was up in the face of the checkout girl. The assistant was doing her best to placate the woman in her Pidgin English. It was like something out of a West End farce. He couldn't catch the words but the gist of it was plain enough – the woman's charge card had been refused but she was having none of it. It was all about her rights, how the girl was humiliating her and she wanted the manager. Now. The fat woman was getting more and more irate and self-righteous as the argument escalated. Her face was flushed and turning purple as the blood vessels in her temples bulged out and the thick vein in her neck pulsed angrily towards heart attack territory.

He would have thought nothing of it, except for the fact that the self-same argument was going on next door. Once was unfortunate, twice was the beginning of a pattern, but he had other things to worry about.

Konstantin sidestepped an old woman, moving straight into the path of a beautiful Arabic girl who scowled at him from beneath her hijab. She had the most incredible melted chocolate eyes, but there was no warmth in them. Like too many other people in the city, her world revolved around inconveniences, and he was one of them. He turned side on to slip between two fat, balding men wearing football shirts that stretched tight across their beer bellies. "Hey, watch it, mate!" the bigger of the two shouted at his back, but Konstantin ignored him. He quickened his pace, moving determinedly through the crowd, knowing that the watchers would be cursing his sudden burst of speed. He had been in their position often enough to predict exactly what they wouldn't want him to do next, which meant, of course, that was exactly what he intended to do.

He pictured the city in his head.

He knew it well enough not to get lost, but not necessarily well enough to plot an elaborate escape route through the warren of back streets and alleys. This part of London was laid out like a crucifix, with Regents Street intersecting Oxford Street at the Circus, about a quarter of a mile in front of him. There must have been twenty thousand people between him and the Underground entrance there. More. It was in constant flux, bodies in motion. Evening Standard sellers barked out the headlines, handing over dozens of papers every few minutes now that they were free. Road works around the Circus had transformed it from a bottleneck into a blockage, the only people negotiating it with any confidence were the city slickers in their sharp suits and sharper elbows who treated it more like Circus Maximus than Oxford Circus. There was Tottenham Court Road and Centre Point behind him and a warren of smaller side streets to his left, down around Liberty's and Carnaby Street, to Kingly Street and Bridle Lane that were like one large maze all the way down the hill to Eros and his poisoned arrow. Alternatively, he could cross Oxford Street, and duck between the shops towards the rich houses of Cavendish Square to the slums of Paddington, or cut back towards the brownstones of Fitzrovia, or Marylebone, the other way.

He wanted a quiet place, not too much in the way of passing traffic or pedestrians. Somewhere secluded without being enclosed because the last thing he wanted was to be herded into a corner and trapped with his back against the wall. Ninety-nine times out of a hundred survival came down to having your exit strategy in place before your back hit the wall. There were a dozen department stores he could disappear into. It wouldn't be particularly difficult to get lost within the crowd, but turned him back into the rat. No, he wanted to know *who* was following him. And why. Which meant finding another exit strategy.

Red double-decker busses crawled down Oxford Street beside him, managing twenty feet before they had to stop for the next set of lights, meaning he was out-pacing them walking along the crowded pavement. The black cabs weren't fairing any better. The tortoise and the hare might work as a parable for life, but it was pretty much useless in this situation. There was the Underground, of course. But it went against every instinct he had. Going underground meant tunnels, confined spaces, and dead ends. Plus, after Berlin, he had an aversion of subways.

Konstantin watched the traffic, judging the ebb and flow between the lights, the slow-downs for the constant stream of people crossing back and forth, and the points of absolute standstill. He timed his next move carefully, looking down the line of busses for one of the old ones with the open back, then stepped off the street, into the road, as one approached. He could feel the displaced air against his face, it was that close. Konstantin reached out to catch the steel pole at the back and hauled himself aboard. It didn't matter that it was barely crawling, it made things difficult for them. They needed to get an operative aboard in case he stayed on it beyond the logjam at the Marble Arch end of Oxford Street and lost them up by Hyde Park. If he made it that far they'd never see him again. Not that he had any intention of staying on the bus that long. It was all about making it difficult for them so he could see just how good they were before he turned on them. Because he knew just how good *he* was.

He went all the way to the front, and sat down in one of the worn seats. The stuffing had been picked out through the threadbare weave and burned with cigarette butts despite the fact that the downstairs on the buses had been no-smoking for as long as he had been in the country. He watched the street. Sure enough, before the bus had made it through the next set of lights one of the watchers had boarded and taken up one of the seats between Konstantin and the door. He slumped down in his seat, this time using the driver's panoramic mirror to watch the back of the bus. The man had his hand up against the side of his face, and whispered into his cuff. He wasn't even trying to hide the fact that he was reporting in.

There was a particular brand of arrogance in that: it smacked of authority. Government. Though which government, he couldn't tell. He had no way of knowing, not just by looking at them. But it wasn't unreasonable to think that they had to work within rules, and rules only served to handcuff people in the same way that morals did. Again he thought about calling in Lethe's extra pair of eyes, knowing that face recognition software would almost certainly identify the nature of the threat he faced, but just this once Konstantin wanted to do it the old fashioned way.

He wanted to break some heads and send a very definite message back to whoever needed to hear it: Konstantin Khavin was not constrained by any such moral code or handcuffed by the rules of polite society. *If you want me,* he thought, *you'll need to send a damned sight more than five men to bring me in.*

He had to hide his smile.

The next few minutes were going to get interesting.

He watched through the window until he saw the flags of Selfridges a short way ahead, and then pushed himself out of his seat and made his way to the back of the bus. The watcher called it in. Subject on the move. Only he wasn't. There was nothing quite like the adrenal thrill of the hunt, whether you were playing the part of quarry or sniffer dog. He sat down in the seat beside the man, nodding to him as he did. Konstantin was enjoying himself. He was close enough that he could smell the sickly sweet tang of the man's sweat, but more importantly he was too close for the watcher to call in the change of plan without blowing his cover.

As the bus started to accelerate away from the traffic lights, Konstantin turned to the man beside him, letting the smile spread slowly across his face. "Time to dance," he said, and pushed himself out of his seat. He took three steps and launched himself out of the bus and hit the ground running. The man came out two steps behind him, but didn't land so gracefully. His legs tied themselves in knots and he ended up sprawling in an ungainly heap half on the pavement, half in the road. Konstantin resisted the temptation to walk forward and help him up. He made sure the man was watching, then turned and walked away down Gees Court, the narrowest of passages between high street shops, leading to St James' Place with its crush of overpriced restaurants offering pizza, pasta, mixed meze platters and crepes. Each restaurant spilled out into the street and had people standing around waiting to be seated. It was anything but quiet or secluded, but one street on, less than two hundred paces, across Wigmore Street, he cut down Jason's Court, a narrow alleyway that ran beside the whitewashed façade of the old Svenson Hair Clinic, held up now by huge Atlas-like construction braces, nothing behind the wall, and onto Marylebone Lane, but, for the space of about forty feet, he was completely hidden from the view of passing traffic. He wouldn't find a quieter place in all of central London.

It was perfect for what he had in mind.

Marylebone village was full of old Victorian streets with deep-set doorways and glass-globe lights that the new city of polished glass and steel had grown over. The tarmac that had replaced the cobblestones was quite possibly the only thing about the lane that had changed since Dickens' day. But Konstantin didn't care about the architectural features or the quaint relics of Victoriana, or shops with names like The Button Queen that might have been lifted off the pages of Grimm's fairy tales. He'd chosen this particular lane because the doorways in these old houses were deep enough for him to hide in. Most had a short flight of two or three steps up to them, but several didn't. Black and green rubbish sacks were piled up at various points along the street, waiting for collection. It was obvious no bin man had been around in weeks – the stairs leading down to one of the basement flats was stuffed to overflowing with torn sacks giving the entire lane the ripe reek of rotten food and soured milk. It was no wonder there were more rats than people living in the city.

Konstantin glanced over his shoulder. The lane was empty. He hurried on past the iron railings that barely contained the rubbish sacks, and found what he was looking for; a doorway deep enough to hide him from anyone coming up the lane until it was too late.

He stepped back into it and pressed up against the brick wall trying to make himself invisible in the shadows as he waited, listening.

It didn't take long for him to pick out the slap of hurried footsteps coming his way.

He counted out their meter in his head.

Five.

Four..

Three...

Two....

One.....

Roaring, Konstantin launched himself out of the shadows and took the man down in a full-body tackle, barrelling him to the floor before he could react. There was nothing pretty about it. They hit the ground hard, but instead of rolling with it Konstantin grabbed the man's face and slammed his skull down hard, cracking it off the curb. His entire body spasmed once, a great involuntary shudder, and his eyes rolled up into the back of his head. It was over as quickly as that. There was blood on the street where the skin had ripped as he'd fractured the man's skull. Konstantin pressed his fingers to the man's throat, feeling for a pulse. He was alive. It was only a matter of time until that particular detail would become academic.

Konstantin patted him down, looking for an ID. He untucked his shirt and tucked the man's Browning 9mm, a functional service weapon, into the band of his jeans before covering it with his shirt. Konstantin checked the man for knives or secondary weapons but he was otherwise unarmed. The driving licence in his wallet named him as Patrick Cattigan. The picture wasn't flattering but it was definitely the man in the gutter. There was money in the wallet, and credit cards. Konstantin checked the name on the other cards. Patrick Cattigan. He dropped the wallet beside the body. He was already thinking of it as a body. And without medical attention that was all it was ever going to be. He found a small radio transceiver in the lining of the man's jacket pocket. It was an unsophisticated device that fed into a mic hidden in the sleeve cuff.

Konstantin sat down in the street beside his victim and pulled at his wrist to unravel the mic's wire, and with his back against the iron railings called out to anyone who was listening: "If one green bottle should accidently fall… it might just crack its skull and lie bleeding to death in Marylebone Lane."

A moment later a voice crackled back, "Who is this?"

"You tell me," Konstantin said. "After all, you are the ones following me."

"Khavin?" There was a pause, and then the obvious question, "What have you done to him?"

"Come and see for yourself. We're not going anywhere."

"Don't do anything stupid, Khavin."

"Do you need directions?" Konstantin said, but tossed the wire aside before the voice could answer. He scanned the buildings, looking for a place to hide. The doorway trick wouldn't work twice. He thought about burying himself in the s rubbish bags and exploding out of them but the chance of getting tangled up in the refuse and losing that precious second surprise would buy him was too great to make it a viable alternative. There were two rusty old fire escapes but neither looked capable of bearing his weight. Plus the bottom rungs were too high for him to reach. He mapped out a climb; from the railings to the first window ledge, from the window, using the huge keystone lintel above the door to haul himself up and across, like a monkey swinging from branch to branch, and with a little luck he might just be able to snag the bottom rung and drag the fire escape down low enough for him to climb it.

But again he was presented with the problem of what came next. He would have to climb high enough not to catch in their peripheral vision, and that meant climbing too high to simply drop on them from above.

He could, of course, just stand in the middle of the lane and meet them head-on.

They would walk into the narrow lane expecting an ambush. What they wouldn't expect was to see Konstantin standing in the middle of the road, smiling at them. Anything that went against expectations was good. It would unbalance them, which, in the long run could be every bit as effective as the split-second advantage surprise offered. More so.

Konstantin stepped over the body and walked into the middle of Marylebone Lane, cradling his right fist in his left hand as though in quiet contemplation or prayer. He lowered his head, letting his other senses take over. Away from the main thoroughfare of Oxford Street the city was quiet, but far from silent. He could hear all manner of cars and the constant babble of background noise made up of espresso machines and beer pumps and dragged chairs and drunken revelry, of doors and escalator gears, busses and subway trains, of gas mains and water, the hum of electricity and the fans of computers, sirens, alarms, shuffling feet and the constant chatter of conversation, all of it coming together to form the longest single note that was the sound of the city. He let the sound swallow him whole, allowing it to fill him up and sooth his soul, slowing his heart and calm his nerves. He centred himself, finding a Zen-like core of tranquility in the madness of the city. He stayed that way for a full nine minutes, breathing deeply, savouring the moment's respite. But it had to end.

He looked up as they entered the lane. There were four of them. They were taking no chances. Three men and a woman. He recognized two of them from Oxford Street. Two of the men were big, but it was slow muscle built up from too many hours in the gym, and for all their strength he discounted their threat. The other was smaller, wiry with a sportsman's physique – the powerful muscles of a sprinter not the leanness of a long-distance runner. He was the dangerous one of the three. The woman on the other hand looked glamorous enough to have stepped out of the pages of a magazine. There was a coldness to her face when she looked at her fallen comrade that reminded him a little of Orla Nyrén. This was her operation. The men were waiting for her word.

Konstantin ignored them and said, "Do your worst," to her.

"Teach Mr Khavin some manners, boys."

The three men spread out as best as they could in the narrow lane, and came towards him. Konstantin had chosen his ground well. On a wider street they could have made things very difficult for him but as it was the cramped conditions forced them a step closer together than they would have liked – and that step meant that Konstantin could face two at once. Not comfortably, but it was possible.

Konstantin said nothing.

The two muscle-bound brutes were to the left and middle, with the body of their point man on the ground by their feet. The wiry athlete stood to the right of the group, a few more inches away from the middle man than his counterpart. Konstantin factored in those extra inches as he choreographed the next few seconds in his mind's eye.

"Don't make this more difficult than it has to be," the man in the middle said, cracking his knuckles in some crude bullyboy attempt at intimidation. Konstantin stared at him. He was nervous. There was perspiration on his top lip and a nervous tick where he bit at the inside of his gum. He had pumped himself up, pushing his shoulders back like a peacock unfurling his plumage. Overcompensating. The words were just another part of that. People who talked were the weak link in any chain. The quiet man was always more dangerous.

After the first punch any plan went out of the window – then it came down animal instinct and survival. Action and re-action. Konstantin had no intention of being reduced to the role of reactor.

He waited until they were two steps beyond the reach of his swinging fist, and launched himself forward in an explosive burst of speed, driving himself into the gap between the middle man and the smaller athlete. He dropped his left shoulder as though ready to launch a punishing right cross towards the brute's face, but instead of a punch drove off his back foot and rammed his forehead into the wiry guy's face. It was a huge risk. The momentum of it threw Konstantin completely off balance, and if he misjudged it he had no hope of recovery before they closed on him and beat him down to a bloody pulp.

He didn't misjudge it.

The man had been braced for a punch. The forehead was the hardest part of any skull, but the frontal boss of Konstantin's was like the dolomitic rock of the mountains of his homeland. The athlete's head snapped back, but it didn't help. Konstantin felt the guy's nose rupture beneath the crushing impact. He staggered away, his face a bloody mess. He went down as Konstantin stepped back. The Russian had already discounted him. He wasn't important. He had no part to play in the rest of the fight.

The outcome of the next two seconds depended on the muscle-bound brute being predictable.

Pivoting on his heel, Konstantin whipped his entire body around and hammered his left elbow back, letting the brute's forward momentum do all the damage. It was basic physics. The height differential meant Konstantin's thundering elbow slammed into the man's throat, leaving him choking on the ground, clawing at his mouth unable to draw a decent breath. He was in trouble. There was no guarantee he'd manage another breath, and if he didn't it was an agonizing way to go. Konstantin looked down at the man. Nothing short of a miracle was going to save him.

"Call your dog off if you don't want him put down," Konstantin said, "Otherwise," he began to hum the tune of *Ten Green Bottles* as he faced up with the last man. His smile didn't reach his eyes. For all his muscle, the man looked genuinely terrified as he squared up to the Russian, meaning he had already lost the fight in his head.

"You're bloody psychotic," the woman said. She had an accent, almost Russian but not. Ukrainian, Konstantin decided. Well that made things interesting.

Konstantin saw the gun she aimed at his heart. It was a Sig Sauer P226. Standard military issue. Her hand was trembling. Only slightly, which was a testimony to her training, but even that little was enough, and unsurprising given that two of her men were out and the other was left with a face only his mother could love. She was every bit as likely to miss as to hit if she squeezed the trigger.

"Without question. Now that we've established that, answer me three easy questions and I might let you walk away from here," Konstantin said, ignoring the insult. He'd been called worse. "One, who are you? Two, who do you work for? And three, why are you following me? Answer any of these incorrectly and you die. I won't ask twice. Understood?"

She shook her head. "No, Khavin. On your knees." She jerked the barrel of the Sig Sauer down. "Now. Do it. Get down."

Konstantin pursed his lips and shook his head. He reached around with his right hand and drew the service piece. He centred it squarely on the woman's face. She really was quite beautiful, he thought, a little warmth creeping into his smile. Under different circumstances he might have said she was pretty. Holding a gun on him she was purely sexual. "I don't think so. Now, believe me when I say I will put a bullet in your pretty little face if you don't start talking. And then I'll put one into your dogs and I'll leave you here for the bin man to sweep up. So, what's it to be?"

Beside her, the last man standing pulled his own gun and aimed it at Konstantin, turning the showdown into a bizarre Mexican stand-off in the middle of a quiet London street. It didn't last more than a few seconds before Konstantin's patience for the game ran out.

"Disappointing. I had hoped we could be reasonable adults about this. It really would be a shame to have to kill you," Konstantin said. He swiveled and put a single shot into the man's kneecap, blowing it out from beneath him. "I don't enjoy violence."

The big man went down screaming and slumped against the railings like a drunk. He dropped his own gun. The blood pulsed between his fingers. He could barely stem the flow. The colour left his face, bleeding out over the paving slabs.

The woman didn't move.

The gunshot still echoed through the old Victorian stonework of the lane. It was the kind of sound that split a city in two. There was no other sound like it. People would be drawn to it like rats to the shit of humanity.

The woman said, "I'm going to reach into my pocket for my phone, then I am going to make two calls. Try not to shoot me, okay?"

Konstantin nodded. His eyes never left her face.

She reached into the hip pocket of her trousers and teased out a white iPhone. She handled herself well, given the circumstances. She was still shaking, but it was barely perceptible. She seemed – outwardly at least – calm. She was a cool customer. She used her thumb to dial for the emergency services. It was a nice move. Konstantin appreciated it. In her position he would have done the same thing. She could just as easily have used the radio transceiver to reach her people, call in the fiasco, but the phone humanized her. A radio made her seem more martial, less feminine. A phone, a rose gold iPhone at that, made her look more like a shopaholic than a mercenary.

"We've got a situation," she said. Her gaze flicked momentarily toward the two men on the floor. It was impossible to tell if they were dead or alive just by looking at them. She waited. He knew she wasn't listening to the Emergency Services operator. She'd called in her bosses. She enunciated very clearly so there could be no mistaking the gravity of her call, "I need a cleanup crew to Jason's Court, Marylebone Village. Four men are down. One has been shot. He'll need plasma for an on-site transfusion. Two others are unconscious, I can't give a clear indication of their injuries without getting my hands dirty but you should prepare for the worst," she paused for a beat, nodding to herself. "Severe head trauma. The fourth man has facial injuries." She reamed off their list of injuries every bit as clinically as her alter ego would the Shipping Forecast: Forties, Cromarty, Forth, Tyne, Dogger and Fisher.

She ended the call.

He studied her face.

She had chocolate brown eyes, the wonderfully rich colour of eighty per cent cocoa, and sharp Slavic features that meant she wasn't soft enough to be pretty. She had angles, not curves, and with each angle it was as though she wore a different face. The one she showed him now was ruthlessly efficient. Her hair was cut short, just brushing her shoulders. It was the sort of ragged cut they used to call feathery, and no doubt cost hundreds of pounds at the top stylists in the city.

She wasn't shaking anymore, he realised. Obviously fear brought out the best in her.

"They will be here in a few minutes, and we both know that wasn't a 999 call. The response team will be scrambling as we speak. So this whole mess is going to end one of two ways. The question is how do you want it to end, .Mr Khavin? I'd estimate we have no more than two or three minutes to come up with a mutually acceptable solution, hence the call I am about to make. Do you trust me?"

"Not in the slightest," Konstantin said, but he made no move to run. "I make it a habit never to trust a woman who pulls a gun on me." By his reckoning he had closer to ten than five minutes before any armed response unit could navigate the congestion, but he wasn't about to correct her.

"Perhaps you should make an exception, just this once. Contrary to what you might think, right now I am the only friend you've got. Put bluntly, I am the difference between freedom and a lifetime spent at Her Majesty's Displeasure."

"You talk too much." Konstantin said, "But you say nothing of any importance. All of these words but none of them answer any of my questions." He lowered the muzzle of the gun, aiming at the woman's left knee. "In other words, I would say you were a typical duplicitous woman."

"We agreed two calls," she said, dialling the first digits of the second number with her thumb.

"No, I agreed not to shoot you when you reached into your pocket. All things considered I am beginning to regret the decision. But it is not too late to change my mind. I think I will shoot you now."

She ignored him and finished dialling the last few digits. He could have pulled the trigger then if he had wanted to. He didn't. His curiosity was piqued. He'd asked those questions because he genuinely wanted an answer. He wanted to know who she was working for, and why they wanted her to follow him. In the land of the blind the one eyed man was king. It all came down to knowledge – being one step ahead of the enemy. As long as he didn't have the answers he was looking for he would always be one step behind. He wasn't a follower. It didn't come naturally to him. In another time and another place he would have simply knocked the phone out of her hand and beaten what he wanted out of her. But back then he had been a different man. Not better, not worse, just different. But that difference was all that stopped him from finishing what he had started here and being done with it. Let them – whoever they were – send more men for him. They'd meet the same iron-fisted fate.

She pressed the phone to her ear and started speaking almost immediately. "Talk to your thug, Charles… I'm afraid he's made rather a mess of things… Yes, you did warn me… Yes, I am sure it must be gratifying to be right all of the time. If only we were all blessed with your foresight. Some of us mortals have to suffice with hindsight… Yes. I appreciate that, Charles, but from where I am standing he isn't an asset to be managed, he's a rabid dog to be put down… Just talk to him before he does something I won't live to regret." She thrust the iPhone toward Konstantin. "Talk to the organ grinder. And be quick about it. I really don't want to have to explain this unholy mess to London's finest unless I really have to. And if the cleanup team arrives before we're out of here there's a good chance they'll shoot first and ask questions later. Frankly, putting a bullet through your face now is preferable to risking getting caught in the crossfire. Just so we understand each other."

He closed the gap between them, quite prepared to end this game here and now with a single bullet to her brain and walk away if she was playing games. It all depended on who was on the other end of the line. But, he had at least another minute before he needed to think about that, cars could only move so quickly through London, regardless of who was driving them. He took the proffered phone and put it to his ear.

"Khavin," he said. "Talk."

"Listen to me carefully, Konstantin." It was Sir Charles Wyndham's voice, or a very good impersonation. "The woman who gave you the telephone is Stacia Kanic. She's with the Secret Intelligence Service out of Vauxhall Cross. Put very simply our days of autonomy are effectively over, my friend. Orders from on high. I can't pretend I am happy with the situation, but now we need to make the best of a bad lot. All you need to know right now is that she is one of us. We will get to the formal introductions later, but I want you to come in with her. Try not to kill her unless you really have to. It'd be a devil to explain away. Plus, I think that lot rather like her."

"Understood." Konstantin killed the call. He looked at the woman and shook his head as he stuffed the gun back into the waist of his jeans. "I hope you are happy with yourself, boss. All you had to do was come up and introduce yourself. You could have saved these men a lot of pain."

"It wasn't me who decided to play at being Rambo."

"I don't play."

She had no answer for that. Instead, she turned on her heel and walked away, leaving Konstantin to deal with the mess he had made of her team. He couldn't do anything about the man whose knee he had blown out. He'd almost certainly never walk again – at least without crutches. So he turned his attention to the wiry athlete. Blood streamed from his newly broken nose. Konstantin held out his hand, offering to help the man back to his feet. "It seems we'll be working together once you are up and about again," he said. "Where are my manners? Konstantin Khavin. Pleased to meet you."

The man didn't take his hand.

SIX
AND I RAN, I RAN SO FAR AWAY

She couldn't hide forever. She was done with it. She didn't want to hide. She wanted to sleep, but sleep wasn't coming. Not today. Not tomorrow. That led to its own set of problems. For the last couple of days it seemed as though the old man had wanted to do nothing more than wrap her up in cotton wool like she was some sort of china doll; a broken one, ruined by a single imperfection that ran the length of her glazed face. None of them were exactly in the right frame of mind to save the world, though. They were all broken, just in different ways.

What they weren't, especially now, was a team.

Noah had been out of touch since the funeral. He'd gone to ground. She knew him well enough to know why; he was taking what had happened in Rome personally. Bearing the weight of *their* failure on his shoulders. That was Noah Larkin in one inglorious whole. It didn't matter if he couldn't fix it, or that it wasn't remotely his fault, he'd do the good Catholic boy thing and shoulder guilt enough for everyone. In his head it no doubt came down to 'but for a few seconds' scenario. It was a pointless way of thinking. Frost had gone for a bike ride, Lethe hadn't left his basement since they buried Max, and Koni was a law unto himself.

The old halls of Nonesuch carried voices, but not well enough for her to hear exactly where Frost told the Old Man he was going. And now there were other voices downstairs. She lay there for a full five minutes listening to them. They were raised in argument, but not to the kind of volume where she could make out what they were arguing about.

Orla sank back into the pillow.

It wasn't as though she could just pull the bedclothes up over her head and make like the world didn't exist. She was angry. Frustrated. She knew that she was angry with herself more than anything. It was basic psyche 101. She'd made a stupid mistake, and despite everything that had happened to her, she'd got lucky. And luck wasn't something she appreciated having to rely upon because next time... Orla shook her head. Next time didn't bear thinking about. So no, like it or not, hiding was a pointless exercise. The one thing she couldn't hide from was herself. She would always be there under the covers no matter how high she pulled them up, and her thoughts would always be there with her, keeping her company. Tormenting her.

Memories.

They were dangerous beasts. More than once over the last few nights Orla Nyrén had found herself lying in her borrowed bed thinking how nice it would be to simply cease to be. It was a seductive way of thinking, imagining there could be an end to it, to remembering, and all the pain that went with it once and for all. She wasn't an idiot. That was part of her problem. She was ferociously intelligent but all the intelligence in the world couldn't save you from yourself if you didn't want saving.

It was a self-destructive spiral.

But recognizing that was a long way from conquering it.

She'd kept the darkness at bay all the way from Israel, but the moment she set foot on British soil it came crashing in. And once she let it in there was no stopping it. It was overwhelming. She stopped being the woman who had escaped, naked, from Hell, and became the victim who had been stupid enough to be dragged there in the first place. It was debilitating. Crippling. Her first instinct was to simply curl up as the nrealisation of just how stupid she had been in switching hotel room, how careless and unprofessional she'd been letting Uzzi Sokol into her room when she was so vulnerable, sank in. It was the sort of mistake that could and should have gotten her killed. She wouldn't have expected that kind of carelessness from a rookie.

But for the Grace of God, she started to think, but killed the thought. She was in no mood to attribute her salvation to any divine being. She was here because she'd got lucky, but down there in that dark place she'd made every ounce of that luck herself.

Cracked, broken, it didn't matter, Orla Nyrén was a survivor.

It was her one defining trait.

She closed her eyes, wanting it to all just go away, but her mind went back to the basement beneath the Tel Aviv supermarket; to Sokol's fingers pushing up inside her; to his vile breath on her face. She could recall with horrific clarity the sheer excitement she aroused in him. That sick lust lingered now to haunt her. She couldn't scrub her mind clean of it. The tactile memory of his filthy fingers on her was too real to sleep through, so she finally relented, climbing out of bed.

She dressed, pulling on jeans and a faded tee-shirt, closing the bedroom door behind her and went, barefoot, downstairs.

The stone of the grand staircase was cold beneath her feet, but the fact that she wasn't wearing shoes meant she moved silently.

The foyer had been scrubbed top to bottom after the break-in. She could smell the astringent sting of Brasso and beeswax. There wasn't so much as the ghost of a stain to betray what had happened to Maxwell. At least not on the parquet floor. The varnished wood had been scoured. There were plenty of other ghosts about the place. Some considerably more high-tech than the others.

Orla saw the last of the day's light reflect off a recessed lens where Jude had hidden another one of his cameras. The boy had a serious Peeping Tom complex going on.

As she shifted vantage point she saw two figures, a man and a woman, towered over the old man in his wheelchair. They were making absolutely no effort to mask their anger as they delivered a tag-teamed dressing-down. They were like psychic twins picking up the train of thought left dangling by the other. It would have been amusing if not for the calm clarity to their anger and the precise, clipped nature of their tone. Their voices spiralled up toward the vaulted ceiling. Not once in the minute she eavesdropped did either of them give in to shouting which made the whole scene chilling to behold.

No one talked to the Old Man like that. But Sir Charles just took it. He didn't challenge them. He refused to rise to their baiting. He remained curiously calm. Detached. Finally, the one thing he said in his defence was, "I did warn you. That you chose to ignore my warning, where anyone with passing knowledge of my man would have been able to tell you it was a *fait accompli*, means that you have to live with the consequences." Orla had to strain to hear him but there was no doubting the steel in the Old Man's voice.

"I know what it means." For a split-second she thought the man was about to backhand Sir Charles as his fury threatened to bubble over. He mastered his temper. Barely. "But I am not sure you do. You've been left alone too long. There are rules. Consequences. Your man is finished. He killed one man and has left another crippled. He can't walk away from that. He has to be held accountable. The dead man had a family. A wife. She deserves justice." He began to pace, walking in tight circles around the Old Man's wheelchair. His footsteps echoed up hollowly toward the ceiling above her hiding place.

It took Orla a moment to realise that Konstantin was the 'my man' responsible for their anger, and a moment more for the extent of the trouble he was in to sink in. They'd misjudged the Russian, sending a team out to bring him in, and he'd reacted badly. That's what the Old Man had meant by *fait accompli*. One of them was dead when the cleanup team arrived on the scene. It wasn't the first person Konstantin had killed by any means, but this one was a member of Her Majesty's Secret Service. It was only going to play out one way. The Old Man only had so much influence, and Konstantin was always going to be the fall guy after the debacle of Koblenz. The big Russian was in trouble. Trouble was only one step removed from being an embarrassment. And embarrassments were what got swept under the carpet. They couldn't exactly cart him away to the Tower, but that didn't mean they couldn't make the Russian disappear in any number of other ways.

Orla crouched, one hand on the wooden balustrade, and peered down between the iron railings to better see without being seen.

Her first estimate was wrong, there were five more people in the foyer – from her new vantage point she could make out their feet, shins, and lower thighs of well-tailored legs – seven of them in total. They were waiting in force for Konstantin. After what had happened in the city they weren't taking any chances. It was a set-up and the old man was in on it – unwillingly, but he hadn't warned Koni to stay away, and as far as she was concerned silence was only a whisper away from complicity.

She studied the two Six operatives. The woman was Hispanic, with a Gaudi-like beauty that was all spikes and rough edges. She wore what Orla thought of as Six's standard issue uniform: a designer suit, Italian no doubt, cut to flatter her toned curves. The man's suit had the look of bespoke tailoring, Savile Row perhaps. Frost would probably have been able to name the tailor just by looking at the way it was cut. As though they could sense her eyes on them, they turned as one to look in her direction. Mercifully, they didn't look up.

Orla ducked back. She'd heard enough. She padded quietly back up to the landing and slipped into her room, closing the door silently behind her. Her mobile phone was on the nightstand. Konstantin's number was pre-programmed into it. She hit the speed dial, willing him to answer.

He did.

"Khavin."

"Koni, don't say anything, just listen to me," she barely risked a whisper, not trusting that the old place wouldn't betray her. Voices had a way of traveling through the old walls. She could hear the background noise of the city streets through the phone. The vibrant hum of traffic and voices. It clashed with the subdued silence of Nonesuch. He was walking through a river of people. She had no way of knowing whether he was alone or not so it was safest to assume he wasn't. "You can't come back here. It's not safe. They've got seven men downstairs with the Old Man, waiting to bring you in. They're claiming you murdered a Six operative, whether you did or didn't is irrelevant, I don't need to know, but it's pretty bloody obvious they intend to hang you out to dry."

"I understand," the Russian said.

"Give it an hour or so and street camera surveillance footage will be leaked to the news and you'll be public enemy number one for all to see. Someone will say they bumped into you in the street and you had murder in your eyes. They'll brand you a terrorist. Someone will make the link to Germany and you'll be the guy who killed the Pope only you're coming after our boys now… They'll blame you for anything they can, say you're suspected of a plot to assassinate Her Majesty or something, and you won't be able to fart never mind walk down the street." She wanted to say 'and you were dumb enough to give them this' but she didn't. Instead Orla said, "That's the only way it's going to play. Trust me. I know these people. I know how they work. You've got no choice, you're going to have to run, Koni. You can't come in. Do you understand what I am saying?"

One word from Konstantin. "Yes."

"When you hang up destroy your phone. You can't have anything with you that broadcasts a signal. Nothing they can use to trace your whereabouts. I'm going to get to Lethe before they do. They'll want him to find you. You know as well as I do what he's capable of. The kid's frightening but he's our wunderkind, not theirs. I'll get him to stall. Lead them on a merry dance for a while. Who knows how long he can buy you, just use that time, Koni. Go somewhere they won't think of looking. Somewhere only you know. Somewhere far, far away. And don't tell me. What I don't know I can't tell."

"Thank you," he said, and hung up. There was no sentimentality, no extra words, no goodbyes.

He was on his own now.

The spy going out into the cold.

Orla dropped the phone on the bed and walked over to the window. It wasn't night out there, not yet, but it wasn't far away. She could see the cars, a hideous display of wealth and arrogance, parked in the driveway. A Lamborghini Diablo, a flame red E-Type Jaguar, a Bugatti Veyron, her own canary yellow Lotus Elan, and Sir Charles' Daimler. They weren't the only cars down in the courtyard. Half a dozen soulless black government-issue Lexus's with huge grilles like Nicholson's 'Here's Johnny' grins were parked across the classic cars, penning them in. She dug her nails into the wainscoting of the old windowsill. Overhead she heard rather than saw the whump-whump-whump of a helicopter's rotor blades churning. They weren't taking any chances.

She didn't say, "Oh, Koni what have you done?" She wasn't an 'oh anyone' sort of woman. She watched them for a minute, realizing that there were at least six more men hidden around the grounds. The situation had the potential to turn ugly, fast.

Orla left her ivory tower and went downstairs. She didn't take the main staircase. She slipped along the corridor to one of the small panelled doors which looked just like any other room but in fact opened onto a small stair down to the mezzanine level, and in turn led to a second stairway down to Jude Lethe's lair in The Nest.

Jude was more than just a pack rat. He had built himself a warren deep in the belly of Nonesuch. He was a hoarder. An obsessive-compulsive gatherer of things. Anything that might be useful. Nothing was thrown away. But unlike the poor unfortunates who lived in the filth of their obsession buried beneath stacks of newspapers and magazines and food cartons and everything else, Jude was fastidiously neat, all of his amassed papers gathered into piles for scanning, digitizing, indexing and transfer to DAGDA, the new computer hive he'd spent the last week installing. It was an acronym of some description, but she couldn't be bothered with remembering what clever little word games Jude was playing to amuse himself, because that's what it all came down to, boys and their toys. As far as she was concerned a computer was a computer and it was childish to imagine some sort of personification simply because you gave it a name, like people who named their cars and assumed they had feelings and needed sweet talking to start on cold mornings. People, as the song playing in the other room suggested, were indeed strange.

She opened the door.

"What's occurring, pretty lady?" Lethe said, without turning. He didn't quite have eyes in the back of his head; it was far more obvious and technologically driven than that. Orla saw herself on one of his screens. The sense of dislocation was unnerving, but not as much as the fact he had every corner of Nonesuch under surveillance. Three of the monitors were split-screened to show four smaller images, twelve in total, which cycled through every camera he had installed around Nonesuch, showing the old manor house from every angle imaginable. It was like *Rear Window* for the ADHD generation.

Jude Lethe sat at his desk surrounded by screens and a mountain of Coke cans. On another screen she saw the photograph of the Masada dig, zoomed in on the false Akim Caspi. Solomon. Beside it, some sort of crawler was rapidly searching through facial recognition routines across social media profiles looking for a match. It was an impossible task. Likewise, another channel was open giving Lethe access to what looked like the Israeli Defence Force's network and was doing a similar search there. They needed a name. A real name. He couldn't just be false Akim Caspi forever and calling him Solomon gave him what he wanted. Whatever else he was, he wasn't the Messiah.

"Any closer to finding him?"

Lethe shook his head. "The guy's a ghost. There's nothing. I can't link him to Mabus, the Herald," Gavrel Schnur, the Toad. "I can't find a single order in military circles with his face on it, despite his posing as a lieutenant general in Tzahal, the Israeli Defence Force. I can't find anything in crowd photos of religious gatherings or manifestations of grief after terror attacks over the last few years. I'm running out of places to look. He's just not there. He doesn't exist."

"Immaculate conception?"

"Not funny. He has to be *someone*. We need a name. Names are power. Name the beast you're halfway to killing the beast." And that was something she could very much agree with, having slain her own beast.

"You'll find him," she said, and she believed it. There was nothing he couldn't do, eventually. If there was a digital footprint he'd find it. Simple as that.

She realised he was working on something else.

Papers were scattered across every surface. Surveillance camera shots from shops, she realised, ringed with red ink marking dates and times and number sequences she didn't understand. There was a map of London marked with quite literally hundreds of thumb tacks with different coloured heads and some sort of key beside it, explaining what each colour signified. He was clearly investigating something that had taken his fancy. She wasn't about to ask what. Some things you were just better off not knowing.

"Anyway, that's not why I came down here. We've got a problem." She tapped the screen as it cycled through the angles to reveal the delegation from Six clustered around the Old Man. "They're here for Konstantin. I need you to make sure they don't find him."

"Tell me what you need me to do," Lethe said. And like that he was a changed man, alert, energized, ready to use his powers for good or evil without question. He ran a short command through the console and suddenly they could hear every word being said upstairs.

Orla said, "I need you to lay down a false trail, something their nerds will find and think is real."

"Easy enough. It's all about the electronic paper trail. People are idiots now they rely upon computers. They've stopped thinking for themselves. Makes my life so much easier. Of course it helps that I've got the key to the world." Orla resisted the temptation to ask just what that key might entail. It was almost certainly something only a person well versed in nerd-speak would understand anyway. "We'll keep it nice and simple at first. I'll set up some credit card transactions, make it look like our boy's been on a shopping spree, chuck in an ATM withdrawal somewhere off the beaten track, maybe a couple of nights in seedy motels just reputable enough to take our flexible friend, then check him into a couple of flights out from opposite ends of the country. Amsterdam's nice this time of year, I hear. Then again maybe he wants somewhere hot. Thailand? Brazil... somewhere that doesn't have an extradition treaty. Make it look like he's really running. Then just for giggles I'll make sure he's booked onto the ferry down at Felixstowe. Actually," he said, clearly warming to the task. "It wouldn't be too difficult to doctor security footage to make it look as though Konstantin's in all those places at once. Give me twenty minutes and they won't know if they're coming or going. Or, more importantly, if Konstantin is."

"So, I can leave it with you?"

"I'm the ghost in the machine, babe. I think I can have some fun with this."

"I think I love you," Orla said, placing her hands on either side of his neck as though about to give Lethe a sensual massage or strangle him. "Even if you did just call me babe. It's not exactly a term of endearment in the grown-up world, kiddo."

"How about *schweethart*?" Lethe said, doing a really poor Bogart impression.

"Let's just stick with Orla, shall we?"

With that Orla went back upstairs, first to call Frost and tell him to come home, and then to meet the new boss, knowing, despite the wisdom of the song, they weren't going to be anything like the old boss.

SEVEN
MEET THE NEW BOSS, SAME AS THE OLD BOSS

Ronan Frost had been taking care of business.

There had been a lot of that recently, even if it felt more like pastoral care than soldiering. Mopping up other people's mess. And his own mess, of course. He wasn't exactly innocent in their failure. The factory had affected him. Stuff like that was meant to wash off him. He kept on telling himself he was a soldier at heart, no matter what uniform he chose to wear. But that place had been different. The women and children rounded up like lambs ripe for the slaughter.

He looked up and down the street. It was empty.

Stuff like that wasn't supposed to happen in the civilized world, never mind Middle England. It made him wonder what was going on behind all of those drawn curtains. He couldn't just trust that life was good anymore. Devere and his cronies had seen to that. Of course the newspaper headlines about Miles Devere's brutal murder in his own home the other day had gone some small way to redressing the balance. Coupled with the fact that Ronan had got the women and children out of that place before the signal came down to kill them, it felt like one little victory. But that wasn't what was gnawing away at him. It was the '*what if?*' of it all. What if he hadn't been there? What if he hadn't been able to ride in like the Lone fucking Ranger? What if Jude hadn't found the link in time? There were thousands of these 'what ifs?' and none of them bore thinking about. Thinking was weakness. He missed the grunt mentality of the soldier in the combat zone where thinking was not only frowned up it exponentially increased your chances of winding up dead. *Ours is not to reason why* and all that.

He kick-started the engine, gunning the throttle, and the Ducati Monster roared to life.

He had spent the afternoon with a woman, Connie, and her two-year-old son. She was one of the warehouse survivors. He'd been listening to her story and admiring her eye for detail and impressive recall. She'd recounted little details, like the swish-swish-swish of the guard who brought them their food, a big guy whose trouser legs rubbed together as he walked. Frost listened with rapt attention, trying to piece together the parts of the puzzle he didn't know—how Mabus's goons had found them, and the kind of threats they'd used to ensure their partners, husbands and fathers would willingly burn themselves alive thinking that their sacrifice would keep them safe. But then he'd never been in love, not like that, not utterly to the point of the death of self and the birth of us. So, how could he say what he would have done in their place? But it kept coming back to the same nagging question: all that death just to deliver a message? It didn't bear thinking about, but of course it was all he could think about. Because it wasn't over. Far from it, the herald had promised forty days and forty nights of fear. *This is the day all of your gods die…* Not just the figureheads of the Catholic Church. That would have been too easy, and would have fed into all of the crackpot theories that this was actually about religion, the promised coming of the antichrist and whatever other nonsense people wanted to believe to mean they didn't have to accept it for what it was, a simple and brutal act of terror.

Solomon was anything but simple, Frost knew. To think of the enemy as anything but your equal was to give him the upper hand in every encounter. All of your gods meant exactly that. The next attack was coming, and it wouldn't be a Catholic church. It could be a mosque, a Buddhist shrine, a Bahá'í temple, or a flaming indoor shopping centre for that matter. People worshipped the gods of Gucci and Prada, Yves Saint Laurent and Vivienne Westwood every bit as sincerely as they worshipped Jesus and Mohammed these days. Indeed, the last video testimony of Osama bin Laden had been to urge the young men to rise up against the paper tiger of the American economy, telling them to strike at the nodes of economy as that would hurt the West where it was truly vulnerable, in the pocket. It was easy to posture about being British and trudging in to work the day after the London 7/7 bombings, or about being a New Yorker and having a set piece in a *Spiderman* movie boasting proudly how 'You mess with one of us, you mess with all of us'. The reality was if you took away their satellite TV and their internet and robbed them of their sweat-shop manufactured creature comforts and had them distrusting something as simple as money you'd be halfway to winning the war before it had even started. That was why the Nazi's had instigated Operation Bernhard, bringing in one hundred and forty two counterfeiters from various concentration camps to begin work making printing plates, rag paper, ink and serial numbers to flood the British economy with fake money in World War Two. As his old CO back in Belfast liked to say, there were more ways to skin a cat, and sometimes the obvious one was not obvious at all.

Ronan stretched, working tired muscles. After one last look around he pulled the visor down on the helmet and tore away from the curb. The sheer power of the bike beneath him was invigorating. There were times when he only ever felt alive when he sat on the Monster, experiencing the sheer exhilaration of speed. It was transformative.

He covered the hundred and eighty nine miles between the outskirts of Manchester and Nonesuch in a little over an hour and a half, tearing through the night. During one stretch of motorway he was going so fast he didn't show up on the speed cameras, beating their shutters. He roared through the gates, tearing up the gravel drive, and skidded to a stop in front of the big house. The courtyard was filled with anonymous black sedans with tinted windows, as well as his team's own vehicles. Ronan killed the engine, and dismounted. He walked up to the main doors, helmet in hand, not sure what to expect on the other side. He didn't like the look of the cars. They screamed government. Orla's message had been vague. She'd said two things, neither of which sounded good: Konstantin was in trouble and the Old Man had lost control. Clearly the new management had arrived.

"Hi, honey, I'm home," he called, closing the heavy wooden door behind him, and was greeted by silence.

The first thing he noticed was that a couple of pieces on the old man's chessboard had been moved. Both the white king and the black were in check and the black bishop lay on its side. The old man was obsessive when it came to the game. There was no way in hell he'd leave the board looking like that, even if he'd become frustrated trying to work through one of his own puzzles. It was a message.

Not that Ronan Frost knew enough about chess to interpret it any more precisely than the house had been taken.

He walked slowly through the downstairs, deliberately leaving the command room until last. He swept the kitchens, the atrium, the old man's study, moving through them all one at a time, turning up nothing.

He didn't knock on the command room door.

They were all inside. Orla, Sir Charles, even Jude. The only notable absentees were Noah and the Russian. There were two immaculately tailored strangers with them at the table. Five more suits had taken up position around the walls and appeared to be going for some particularly stoic square-jawed intimidation. They might have been playing statues for all the reaction they offered as Ronan closed the door behind him.

If they'd hoped to bully the Old Man with a show of strength they obviously didn't have a clue who they were dealing with. Six could send in all the big guns they wanted to make their point, the Old Man would do his own thing, regardless. That was his charm. It was also why Quentin Carruthers had granted him autonomy from Vauxhall in the first place. It wasn't just because they liked to play spies in Hyde Park. On the most basic level it was practical. The Old Man was more use to the Government off the books than he was on. He trained his team up and sent them into places they weren't officially allowed to go—places where a British military presence might have been seen as an act of aggression if not an outright declaration of war. They had several cover IDs, including his own personal efavourite, specialist relic hunters, which was very *Indiana Jones*. Having a team that could go in, get their hands dirty without being a threat was expedient. It suited the Crown every bit as much as it suited the Old Man. On the books he was just a thorn in the arse. And a spiky one at that.

At least that was how it had been up until about an hour ago. The times, as Dylan sang, were a changing.

"I feel like a naughty boy who's just been summoned into the head master's office," Frost said, closing the door behind him. "Anyone want to bring me up to speed?"

It was the woman who spoke. "Would you be so kind as to put your gun on the table, Mister Frost? Don't take offence, it isn't that we don't trust you, but we've already had one regrettable incident today, and all things considered, another would be careless."

Frost pulled his Browning from the underarm holster and put it on the table. He looked at the woman. He couldn't make up his mind if she was attractive or not. There was something hard about her face that didn't mate with the usual Hispanic colouration. Her nose was sharp, her jawline sharper. The sunlight streaming in through the windows cast half of her face in deep shadow.

"Do you want my badge, too?"

"Metaphorically speaking," the woman said.

Frost took off his jacket, slung it over the back of the only free chair at the table, and sat. At times like these he envied Noah's *bollocks-to-the-lot-of-you* attitude. In his place, Noah would probably kicked back and put his feet up on the table, but Ronan wasn't Noah. "Now I really feel like the naughty boy. What's going on here?"

"Perhaps it's better we wait for Mr Larkin to arrive so we don't have to repeat ourselves?"

"I wouldn't bank on Noah showing up for a while yet," Frost said.

"Something we should be made aware of?" the woman asked.

"I doubt it very much. Noah's Noah and he's having a bad time right now. He needs to work through some stuff in his own time, and if you knew him you'd realise the worst thing we could do was try to hold his hand. He's not a hearts and flowers kind of guy."

"More like whores and whisky," Orla said, the words harsh but the tone belying them.

Frost smiled wryly, glad of the support. He felt very much alone in the room, surrounded by goons. It was like one of the Old Man's chess games. He needed a strategy, to work out what was worth sacrificing, what he should be protecting and what was already lost. But it was difficult without any real understanding of what pieces were in play. "So let's just assume he's not coming in. Now, let's get down to brass tacks instead of pussy footing around, shall we? I'd really like to know what the Hell is going on here, because it may have escaped your notice, but the shit has pretty much hit the fan out there," he gestured toward the window, "and sitting around here talking about who's got the biggest swinging dick isn't exactly helping things."

The woman planted her elbows on the table and leaned forward. She looked from Frost to the Old Man. No one else in the room mattered as far as she was concerned. This was where the power of the team lay, in the leadership. Frost sensed that she wanted him on side, but she wasn't giving much away.

"Which is why we are here, Ronan. May I call you Ronan?"

"It's my name."

"Well, Ronan," she said, belabouring it, "as I was explaining to the other members of your team before you decided to grace us with your presence, your days of autonomy are over. It's a nice set-up you've had here, but it hasn't worked for us. You may think you're being hard done by, but let's just consider the rather spectacular nature of your team's failures of the last few days, shall we? First with Khavin causing something of a diplomatic incident in Berlin, then in becoming prime suspect in the assassination of the most famous man in the world, I'd say it's rather fortunate you're only being officially brought back into the fold. Take into account Larkin's spectacular failure in Rome and Ms Nyrén's brief sojourn in Jerusalem and it's a miracle never mind fortunate. And that's just the stuff we can prove. Miles Devere has been a person of interest to the security services for quite some time. For him to turn up brutally murdered after a run-in with Khavin could just be an unfortunate coincidence, but I'm not a great believer in coincidences these days. Then again I'm not great fan of conspiracy theories either, so perhaps Khavin isn't the root of all evil. What this means in terms of your day-to-day operations is you report to me, and only me."

He looked across the table at the old man.

"Sir Charles has been persuaded to take his pension and will of course be allowed to remain here, it is his home, after all, but the day-to-day operations are now my responsibility. In time we'll be moving operations back to Vauxhall. I'm here to oversee the transition. But in the meantime, it's business very much not as usual."

Frost gave it a minute for the full implications of what the woman had said to sink in. At least now he had an idea of what the board looked like. It was time to make his opening gambit. "Let me make sure I've got this straight, this is just one big pissing contest between Whitehall and the Old Man?"

"I don't think that's the case at all."

"You don't? Let's look at the facts for a moment instead of the fall out. Koni got so close to the assassin he got mistaken for him, where were your people? Noah's off on a bender because he was no more than seconds from saving a lot of lives, and I ask again, where were you? Orla put her life on the line, got into the bastard's lair and out again, neutralizing the man we all thought was behind the city attacks, and for the third time of asking, where were you? Because you sure as hell weren't there and all of the finger-pointing in the world won't disguise the fact that we were. We were on the ground getting our hands dirty. We saved lives. There were some we couldn't save, that's the nature of conflict, there are going to be casualties. But any way you slice it, the women and children in Devere's warehouse would be dead if it wasn't for us. That's the sort of facts we should be talking about. Now like it or not, we're closest anyone's got to Solomon, we've got the inside track, and rather than let us finish what we've started you want to pull us off and lock us up in an office and you still don't think it's a pissing contest? What's your name, love? It's nothing personal, you understand, but I want to know who I'm going to hate…"

*

Her name was Constance Mendes. She led the briefing, filling them in on Six's thoughts in relation to the links between Flight VS300 into Delhi, BA0486 into

Barcelona, the Norwegian Air flight to Oslo and the other 'corpse planes' that had taken off from Heathrow, putting up a photograph of a man in a wheelchair. They had security footage from the terminal with Lael Kelly Logan smiling and hugging people and rattling his bucket for them to make the donations. They had footage of him starting to sweat. They had footage of him getting sick. They had footage of the paramedics wheeling him out of Terminal Five.

And last, they had still photographs of Lael Kelly Logan lying dead in Hillingdon Hospital.

"He's the link," Constance said. There was no room for doubt. "Lael Kelly Logan. Not what you'd think of as typical terrorist material on the surface of it, but there's no telling what a dying man will do. We've had a team in his house. They've recovered evidence that he willingly contaminated his body with a pathogen; an ampule and syringe. Both contain trace elements of the same pathogen that took out the corpse planes."

"Patient Zero," the man beside her said. Michael Knight. He'd fended off the obvious jokes about self-driving cars and turbo boosts as he'd introduced himself, even though the Irishman didn't have a clue what he was going on about. "My name is Michael Knight." Again, he was visited by the ghost of Noah; this time his friend was grinning as he shook the Six man's hand "One man can make a difference, eh?"

"Where did the pathogen come from?"

"It's very similar to an artificial weaponized virus developed by the Israeli military in the early 2000s and later abandoned," Constance said. "The labs that made this stuff were all shut down over a decade ago, so either someone has been sitting on this strain waiting for the right moment to unleash it on the world, or one of those labs has been restarted."

"That's my jam," Orla said. "Jude, I'll be needing tickets on the next flight out, and a full rundown on the locations of these labs." Frost glanced at the Old Man, waiting for him to nix the decision. Last time Orla had insisted on going to Israel there'd been a massive fall out between the two of them. This time Sir Charles didn't say a word. He just sat there in his chair listening without contributing.

"Easier said than done," Lethe said. Frost noticed his not-so subtle glance toward the Old Man for confirmation. "Most airlines are grounded right now."

Constance picked up the thread. "We aren't sure how, yet, but Logan is linked to Gavrel Schnur, the man you hunted as Mabus, and in turn, to the puppet master, Solomon. Whatever that link is, we will find it." She looked at Frost then, considering her next words and whether she wanted to say them. "I don't suppose you have anything that might shed light on the matter, Ronan? As you said, your team were so close to them." It wasn't a compliment. The verbal sparring wasn't particularly dexterous, but he was in absolutely no doubt that Constance Mendes was more than capable of punching her weight. You didn't amass as much power within Six without some serious moves. No, these were just a few exploratory jabs, testing his limits.

"You show me yours," Frost said. "It's only fair given you're running the show."

"Very well. This is what I think. There's a risk of jumping at shadows and blaming every bad thing in the world on Solomon and turning him into some sort of bogeyman."

"Reasonable," Frost agreed. "Sometimes shit just happens."

"Indeed it does. He isn't the antichrist, let's disabuse ourselves of that particular fantasy right up front. The thing is it's convenient for him to pretend to be." She turned to Lethe. "Jude, I believe now would be a good time for your little show-and-tell, if you'd be so kind?"

Lethe triggered something on the touchscreen surface of the table, and the huge screen behind the woman woke from sleep. All heads turned toward the face of the man on the screen. "This turned up on a bunch of fundamentalist channels." His glance moved instinctively toward Orla. She knew what else they'd found on those channels. She didn't say a word. "Supposedly we're looking at Solomon delivering his gospel. It's pretty standard kill 'em all, kill 'em all, mass grave stuff."

He pressed play, and Solomon began to talk:

"These are the last days. The good souls are gone. Only the corrupt survive. Men and women who have traveled so far from the path of right they have lost their way. Like Icarus we have flown too close to the sun. We have fallen in amongst the liars, cheats and thieves. We live in a world that worships money and machines over people. The mark of the beast is not something we are born with, but a branding we willingly accept and carry in our wallets. It is the mark of greed and corruption. There is no place for the spiritual in our lives, only the fiscal, the financial. But what happens when we cannot trust our money? What happens when our machines fail us? What then? Who do we turn to? What other false gods do we look for in our Time of Tribulations? Do we turn to the Holy See, filled with its own host of sinners and corrupt souls? Do we take guidance from those tortured priests who struggle with their own afflictions and perversions?"

The assembled group listened in silence to the words of their enemy. Frost couldn't decide if the message was being delivered by a madman or a charlatan, but assumed it was both. At last, Solomon's speech drew to a close with his final words:

"Now is the time we must rise up and strike these false gods down. We must purge the mark of the beast from our flesh. Melech Israel."

Lethe stopped the video. "Now, bearing in mind what you just heard, including the caution that sometimes a coincidence is just a coincidence, I want to show you something else before we talk about this. With your permission, boss?" He looked to Constance, who nodded, but didn't seem overly enamored with things. Frost didn't like how comfortable Lethe was with calling someone else boss in their own house.

Lethe triggered a series of images of Oxford Street: the flagship Debenhams shop, John Lewis, Selfridges, the clothes shops at the Circus: in other words, shoppers' paradise.

"Within an hour of Solomon's video going live, Oxford Street suffered a chip-and-pin attack."

"And slowly, for the Luddites amongst us?" Frost said.

"Chip and pin is the basic security credit card companies use to protect point of sales transactions. It's supposed to be the safest way of doing things, you need the card and the pin number, and each transaction is signed *verified by pin*. It was supposed to make it difficult to skim cards, having much more sophisticated security, but this, this was clever. Even I was impressed, put it that way, because they didn't steal anything."

"Okay," Frost said, skeptical. "I'm not really seeing the link." But just because he didn't see it didn't mean it wasn't there. He needed it spelled out for him. "Idiot's Guide time, Jude, because it sounds like one of those bloody riddles. When is a door not a door? And I really don't like riddles. So, how do you steal something without stealing anything?"

"They rerouted every single transaction for an hour, and just for an hour, mind. They could have left it in place until the security guys shut it down, so really this was all about proving that they *could* do it. What happened, very basically, is that wires were crossed. Let's say someone went in to Waterstones to pick up a book at the same time as someone else was in Currys buying a TV, when the transactions were sent down to central clearing they were scrambled, the guy buying the TV was charged for the collected works of Shakespeare, while the guy in Waterstones paid for a flat screen. Now, that doesn't sound so bad if you're the guy buying the TV," Lethe grinned, "but if you're the guy buying Shakespeare, that's one bloody expensive book, and there aren't even any pictures.

"Now, think about it for a minute. It's all about scale. That's one transaction, but we're talking about three hundred shops on Oxford Street alone, and between them thousands of point-of-sales terminals doing business constantly. There's always someone buying something. To put it into perspective, it's not unreasonable for a million shoppers to go through those terminals in a day if the sales are on. We're talking a street that has done two hundred and fifty million pounds of business in a day. That's a bucket-load of money that could potentially be highjacked. Like I said, it's not theft, what it is is chaos unleashed. You go to buy your little black dress for the party but your card's declined because you don't have the cash to buy a flat screen LCD TV in the account, or you're all lined up to buy a can of Coke and a newspaper and you're humiliated because the machine bounces your card because you've been billed for some Gucci handbag in Selfridges." He shook his head.

109

Frost was beginning to get the picture, and it really wasn't a very pretty one.

"And it's hot out there," Orla said, running the thought to its natural conclusion. He knew exactly what she was driving at: hot weather, frayed tempers. He could see the old bulldog mentality kicking in far too eagerly. All it needed was for the wrong guy's card to get bounced and it would turn ugly.

"So, the link?"

"Solomon's talking about a world that worships money and machines, and this happens? It *could* be a coincidence. I *could* just be jumping at shadows. But does anyone here remember Bin Laden's last message? It was all about Financial Armageddon. He was spitting and frothing about the faithful rising up and attacking the nodes of economy. He called the US a paper tiger on the verge of collapse, likening it to the old USSR, and said the power lay with Islam to topple it over the edge through a war on money. This isn't a million miles from that. Different religious nutter, same message if you ask me."

"I disagree," Knight said. "Terror groups have a tradition of going for a certain kind of target. If we stay with the al-Qaeda theme, in '95, Abd al-Rahman was convicted of the first World Trade rCentre attack, but he was also found guilty of planning to bomb the United Nations, the FBI building, the Holland and Lincoln Tunnels. What have all of these things got in common? Let me tell you, they're all landmarks. It was a 'holy war' of terror against the United States. It was big. It was visual. And that's what the Mabus Plot is." Ronan had never heard it called that. It sounded like the title of a bad potboiler. *The Mabus Plot. The Solomon Contingency. The Judas Initiative.* "It shares the same commonality, the suicides were all in symbolic locations, the hearts of their cities. Then it escalated, following the standard pattern. Stage two, hit the transport sites and communication lines, cut off people, isolate them: the Berlin underground, Trafalgar Square, places where a mass of humanity passes through. These things fit the pattern. Dodgy credit card scams don't."

"With all due respect," which meant none whatsoever, "Oxford Street's a landmark," Lethe said, defending his theory. He looked to Orla and then Frost for support before turning to Sir Charles. Frost could buy it. It was smart. The Third World War was never going to be fought on the battlefields, it was going to play out in cyberspace, buying elections, toppling governments, the whole nine yards.

The Old Man hadn't said a single word since Frost had entered the room. That was not only out of character, it was worrying. He needed to talk to the Old Man, but there was no way he'd be able to get him alone with all of these spooks loitering around Nonesuch.

Knight was still far from convinced. "Sure, but it is not a bomb, is it? It's not causing chaos. Not proper chaos. There's no blood. No spectacle. No fear. People aren't running down the streets screaming. They aren't jumping out of high buildings to their death because they know staying up there's worse. This is a thirty-second soundbite in the middle of the nine o'clock news: computer glitch causes shoppers to get the hump."

Lethe shook his head. Frost could see his frustration. Again, he looked to the Old Man for some sort of intervention, but Sir Charles wasn't there in anything but body. "I strenuously recommend we follow up on it. I think it's dangerous to focus on the religious aspect of the 'Religious Nutter'—"

"They murdered the Pope in broad daylight," Knight cut across him. "And then they gassed the Cardinals as they gathered to vote on his successor. I'd say religion was relatively high on their list of priorities, notably the Catholic Church. He talks about being the Messiah—"

"No he doesn't," Orla said. She leaned forward, taking the glass of water from the table in front of her and sipping at it before continuing. "He specifically says he isn't the messiah. Don't put words in his mouth. He calls himself the Voice. He's talking to the Chassid, the faithful, and his terminology is Judaic. I say Jew, you think money, don't you? The two go hand in hand in the modern vernacular, no matter how bigoted that may sound. He specifically mentions money and machines as things we worship and then right at the end urges the faithful to rise up and strike down these false gods. So, it might not fight your 9/11 version of terrorism, but Jude isn't an idiot."

Knight shook his head, but stopped short of rolling his eyes. "This is what he wants. He's got you running around chasing your tail instead of his."

Orla stared him down. "I'm sure you have a very valid point, Michael," the words were quite reasonable, but something about them chilled Frost to the bone. It was like listening to a serial killer talking about his next kill. "The psychology of terror follows patterns. We know there's an assassin out there still. We know that Solomon promised forty days and forty nights of fear, and that means it's not over. It can't be, because as horrible as the last week's been, it's a very obvious failure if it doesn't continue. And we know that the threat was: and then all of your gods die. All of your gods, not the Catholic interpretation of God. That means Islamic God of the Quran, the wrathful God of Genesis, the many Gods of Hinduism, but it could equally mean Jahweh, the God of Judaism, the Shinto Gods of the Japanese, or it could take in the arbitrary distinction between the old gods of mythology, the Sumerian gods, all two thousand and something of them, the Roman and Greek and Norse gods, the Celtic gods, and the new gods of money and machines and the whole cult of celebrity and every false god we elevate to the rank of divine. Hell, Hindu the entire living universe is merely a unique manifestation of Ishvara. This leads to the fact that there are something like three hundred and thirty million 'gods or goddesses'. Or maybe man's entire temporal existence is just an aspect of God, meaning they could be promising to wipe out every last damn one of us if you want to interpret it that way. Now that fits in with your paradigm of fear – make a threat to everyone. No one is safe."

"A comforting thought," Frost said. In so many ways Orla was the best of them. Certainly the smartest. Lethe was a genius, but it was a very focussed genius. Orla was just more.

"And it fits the theory of escalation," Orla said. "But shy of a nice game of Global Thermonuclear War how do you do that?"

"Like this," Lethe said, warming to his subject. "Systematic undermining of things we rely upon. Things we take for granted and trust. I haven't got the proof to link this stuff, yet, but yet's a powerful word. It means *I will*. I've been gathering data over the last five days. There have been Denial of Service attacks on three of the High Street bank's websites in the UK. BNP Paribas had security breaches in Belgium, France and London. You might not recognize the name, but BNP Paribas holds assets of about three point one trillion dollars and after the takeover of Fortis became the largest single deposit holder in the Eurozone. We're talking the very definition of Big Banking. It's all corporate and investment banking. Their customers are Big Business. And to pre-empt your next question," Lethe said, holding up a hand, "BNP's primary markets are France, Italy, Belgium and Luxembourg, but they're heavily involved in investment banking in London and New York as well as the emerging markets. Now… we've had attacks in London, in Paris, in Rome, which could be a coincidence, but I'm not so sure. They're active in every single territory that has been targetted. I'd say that makes BNP a credible target if Solomon's intent on bringing down the false gods of money and machinery, wouldn't you?

"And let's face it, BNP don't have a squeaky clean image: they make lots of their money from nuclear investment and were slammed to the tune of 384 million Euros for collusion to defraud customers by charging unjustified fees. They're basically everything John Q Public hates about banking manifested in a single company. About the only thing they didn't do was go cap in hand to their respective governments for bailouts during the credit crisis. They came out of the whole thing stronger, recording profits of about three billion when everyone else was close to slitting their wrists.

"They are also in bed with Devere Holdings to the tune of a couple of billion, which is just one of the little tidbits I turned up.

"So, like our Lords and Masters keep insisting, this could all be coincidence, but these Denial of Service attacks and security breaches are all part of a systematic global assault. It might not be *glamorous*," he looked at Knight then, "and there might not be any children running through the streets with blood streaming down their faces, but it's every bit as effective, just on an entirely different level."

Frost listened, absorbing it all.

He didn't understand the technical aspects, when Lethe got excited about something he tended to delve too deeply into the geek-ratio for a normal guy to follow, but Frost heard all he needed to: Devere, money, Rome, London. Links. Orla was right, they did fit the paradigm of fear in a very understandable way. But was Knight right, too? Was this all just one deep rabbit hole for them to dive into?

It might well be circumstantial, but on a gut level he trusted Lethe when it came to this sort of stuff. The kid could do things with a computer that didn't bear thinking about. More often than not it felt like voodoo. If there were links between these security breaches and Solomon's promised wave of terror he'd find them.

One image struck Frost: London without credit cards. It didn't take much imagination to come up with violence from that basic premise, the wrong man being told his card had been refused when he wanted his not-so-skinny latte, knuckles flexed instead of dragged, and it'd all kick off. The culture of the city had changed over the last few years. There was a loss of civility and a rise of rudeness among normal people. He still remembered all too vividly the first time he'd heard an overweight skinhead yelling at a girl to go home ignorant of the fact she was born less than an hour from where he was doing the shouting. The racists were coming out of the woodwork, enabled by a normalization of their hatred across the media with newspapers calling judges the enemy of the people and demanding isolation from the world and a return to Empire. Not so long ago all of the ills of society had been laid at the door of his people, with the Irish

115

being blamed for everything wrong, but now it was the Muslims, the blacks, the Poles, and basically anyone who wasn't Anglo Saxon, meaning white. "Can you trace the source of these service attacks?"

"Does the Pope shit in the woods? Well, not anymore, obviously, given he's dead—" he broke off there. He knew he was running off at the mouth, a sure sign that he was getting excited. "They're clever. They bounce the signal through a dozen nodes across the world, each one adding a layer of anonymity like an onion, so it's harder and harder to trace them, especially as a lot of these countries are deliberately trying to obscure data traffic just to spite Big Brother, going against treaties of disclosure and basically deliberately being a pain in the arse, but they've got a digital signature, so if you know what you're looking for, and you're persistent enough, and good enough, you can."

"And you're good enough?"

"Does that question really need asking, Frosty?"

"Then you know what you've got to do. Prove it. Find the links." A thought occurred to Frost. "Can you tell where that video was uploaded from?"

"Already one step ahead of you," Lethe said with a slightly condescending smile. "Get this: it originated in the Israeli Embassy in Vienna."

"That's twice," Ronan said, thinking aloud. First the diplomatic car that had followed Konstantin in Berlin, now this. That marked the beginnings of a pattern. "They used the Israeli Ambassador's car in Berlin, and now we've got a video originating from the Israeli Embassy in Vienna." Frost's mind was racing. How many Israeli Embassies and consulates were there? Did each one suddenly become a possible staging point for a fresh strike? They had to start thinking that way. "Could the assassin have returned to Rome? Could he be hiding in the Israeli Embassy there?" Even as he said it, he pictured the map in his head. "Yes," he said, answering his own question. "So what have we got? We've got an assassin out there, possibly in Rome, we've got Solomon in the wild, pulling the strings. We've got Lael Kelly Logan and planes full of dead people killed by some novichok-style virus, and nothing to positively link them," he looked at Lethe, "*yet*. We've got the threat of *all* your gods will die, meaning not just the Catholic God. So… what iconic things are there? What treasures of faith are out there? Where are they? What would Solomon take and use to break the faith of the people and keep up his guise of a religious fanatic? Give me a list. Anything holy, any religion. Doesn't matter. You're both right," he looked at Knight and Lethe. "He's not going to change his methods. Not now. Not when they're working so well for him. What's the most contentious thing he could blow up? What's the most devastating icon he could destroy? And let's assume that's his plan and has been all along. Hitting the different faiths one by one."

And with that he went to call Noah in from the cold. He could sulk and drink himself into a stupour later. Right now, they needed him.

EIGHT
BREAKDOWN

Konstantin was in trouble.

After the Old Man told him to come in, he'd allowed them to bundle him into the backseat of a 4x4, putting him between the blown-out knee and the wiry athlete. Stacia Kanic sat up front with the driver. She watched him intently through the rearview mirror. Every so often her eyes flicked back to the road. The woman obviously had trust issues.

Of course, she was right not to trust him.

"I need you to understand," Konstantin told her. "I didn't kill the Pope. I saw the man who did. He was one of the Swiss Guard, or at least posing as one. I nearly stopped him. Instead I got the blame."

"And Miles Devere?" Stacia said.

He didn't answer that one. Silence wasn't a denial or an admission of guilt, but it was fairly obvious which of the two was right in this case.

Orla had told Konstantin to run. He was surprised Stacia let him take the call. Though for now he wasn't a prisoner, Orla had made it pretty clear that if he placed one foot inside Nonesuch he soon would be. It wasn't that he was ignoring her. He could hardly make a break for it from the backseat of a cramped car, wedged in between the hired muscle, unless…

Konstantin leaned forward slightly in his seat, looking out of the side window at the grassy embankment as it rushed by. It was almost impossible to judge their speed, but given that they were on the M25 and for once traffic was free-flowing, they were pushing seventy miles an hour. Jumping was suicide, no matter how thick his frontal bone was.

He needed to slow the car down.

The easiest way to do that was disable the driver.

It wouldn't take much: the heel of the hand driven into his temple would daze him, a reach-around to choke the air out of him with the forearm would instinctively bring his foot up off the accelerator, inertia would do the rest. There were always ways. But given the fact they were moving over a mile a minute taking the driver out was last resort thinking.

He needed noise. An explosion of it. It had to be shocking.

Making sure his own seatbelt was secure, he asked the others, "Is everyone wearing their seatbelts?" and as the woman's head turned, instinctively anticipating trouble, Konstantin leaned forward in his seat and grabbed the busted knee of the man beside him with his right hand. He dug his fingers in deep and wrenched the bone of the kneecap sideways.

The guy screamed, seemed to choke on it, gagging, and then stopped screaming abruptly as Konstantin dug his thumb and forefinger even deeper.

It only took a second.

The man's eyes rolled up into his skull and he slumped back in his seat, his entire nervous system shutting down beneath the sheer unexpected agony of Konstantin's move.

It had the desired effect: instinctively the driver slammed his foot down on the brake, causing them to slew sideways across two lanes of traffic. He felt the wheels losing their traction as the driver battled the skid, and then the car started to roll. The fact that it was a sport-utility vehicle with higher ground clearance and centre of gravity against its relatively narrow track width necessary for off-roading meant it was going tip once it entered the sideways skid.

He didn't have time to think.

The wiry athlete went for him even as the woman went for her gun, but in close quarters he was always going to win that fight – it was all about sheer power. Konstantin brought his left elbow up. He couldn't get much force behind it but he didn't have to. The athlete's face was already a mess, and Konstantin's elbow didn't have to hit hard to cause excruciating pain. Before the athlete could bring his hands up to defend himself from a second blow, the 4x4 rolled and the glass of the windshield exploded inward showering them in a spray of shards as the roof buckled from the impact.

The woman, Stacia, wasn't belted in.

She hit the cushioned roof hard, her back cannoning off the headrest as her head and shoulder crunched into the roof. The gun flew from her hand, spinning out through the shattered window as the car spun.

Driver and passenger-side airbags deployed, ballooning to fill the front of the car, and for a moment the 4x4 reeked of fireworks.

The tortured screams of metal filled Koni's ears as the 4x4 skidded across the asphalt.

The world spun around them, upside down and downside up, and then it was flipping over again, bouncing on still driving wheels that kicked the 4x4 higher into the air on the second bounce.

And now he needed a miracle.

The vehicle came down on its roof again, rolling three more times until it was caught by the safety barrier between lanes, and came to rest, still upside down.

Dazed, Konstantin popped the buckle on his belt and braced himself for the fall. Every bone hurt. Every muscle had a fire deep inside it, smoldering from successive impacts. He felt the fire rising. It threatened to overwhelm him. But he couldn't stay there. He had to move. He had to get out of the car. He was bleeding. It ran down his forehead and into his eyes, filming his vision red. Konstantin shook his head, blinking back the blood, and regretted it instantly. His guts heaved. He forced himself not to vomit, swallowing back the gag reflex. He could smell petrol. The fumes were inside the car, cloying their way down his throat. Breathing hard, he lowered himself to the roof, and crawled beneath the unconscious athlete out of the wreckage.

He could have run then.

He should have.

But the acrid stench of petrol was sharp in his lungs. The engine block on the 4x4 was a ticking time bomb primed to explode.

Konstantin grabbed at the door handle, but the roll had buckled the frame. It would take the jaws of life to pry it open.

Someone was beside him, kicking in the *rear window* so he could get at the 4x4's passengers. A Good Samaritan. Konstantin looked around. He wasn't alone. Three men from other cars were running towards the wreckage, their vehicles abandoned a safe distance away. He didn't say anything. He leaned into the cabin and wrestled with straps of the athlete's seatbelt, trying to get at the buckle, but the man's weight put so much strain on it he couldn't get to the buckle to release.

121

The stench of petrol grew thicker by the moment.

Konstantin wiped away the blood.

His eyes stung.

His body ached. But he wasn't about to leave the guy to die when the car went up in flames. It wasn't personal; he was only doing his job. He was a foot soldier. A grunt. Just like Konstantin, in other words. Rolls reversed he knew the athlete would go back for him. So he crawled into the cab, working the strap from the man's shoulder, and when the only thing trapping him was the waistband of the seatbelt, wrapped his arms beneath the unconscious man's armpits and heaved him clear of the harness.

He dragged him clear of the car and carried him over to the embankment.

He would live, and as far as any of the Good Samaritans were concerned his busted nose was just another injury inflicted by the crash. He braced himself, hands on knees, trying to catch his breath and clear his head.

There were four men swarming around the wrecked car.

Two at the front passenger side, trying to get the woman free, one at the back with busted knee while the last Samaritan stood helplessly beside the driver's side door. It was shock. The hero reflex could drive an ordinary man to great things, but could just as easily leave him paralyzed. He wasn't moving. He stood rooted to the spot, staring into the 4x4. Konstantin couldn't see what he was staring at from where he was, but guessing didn't tax the imagination. It was a wreck. There were going to be injuries, airbag or no airbag.

Konstantin jogged back over to him

The windshield had rained down wickedly sharp shards of glass. The driver's face looked as though he was halfway through death by a thousand cuts, but he hadn't given up the ghost. He was clinging desperately to life and just as desperately to the spar of metal from the steering column the impacts had thrust into his stomach.

There was nothing he could do to help the man. "Have you got a phone?" he asked the Samaritan. He shook his head no, but reached into his pocket and pulled out a Sony. Konstantin took it from him and dialled 999.

"What service do you require?" the dispatch operator asked.

"Ambulance." He looked for a point of reference. He knew they were on the M25 but there were no obvious landmarks. He saw the number on the lamppost, 2112. There was a click as his call moved through the switchboard to the relevant service. He didn't wait for the woman to ask how she could help. He told her exactly what she needed to do. "There's been an accident. We're on the M25, the driver's hurt badly. He's got a piece of metal in his stomach, like a spear. We're at lamppost 2112. I don't know exactly where that is, but it'll give you a point of reference. Three people are badly hurt. They need immediate medical attention." He hung up before she could ask his name.

In the distance, halfway between him and the line of Samaritans' abandoned cars, he saw Stacia Kanic's Sig Sauer P226 lying in the middle of the road. He gave the man his phone back and went to claim it. He checked the magazine. It was full. The Russian pocketed the gun and carried on walking until he reached the cars.

No one was watching him as he moved from one to the next, checking the doors until he found one with the keys still in the ignition. A blue Volvo S60.

As non-descript a car as he could have hoped for. He clambered into the driver's seat, turned the ignition over and gunned the engine. Putting his foot flat to the floor he peeled away from the hard shoulder, hitting sixty before he drew level with the wrecked 4x4, and eighty, then ninety as the empty motorway stretched out in front of him. The needle on the speedometer topped one hundred and kept climbing.

Why run when he could drive?

He'd get rid of the car later, right now it was all about putting distance between himself and the accident.

NINE
SCENES FROM AN ITALIAN RESTAURANT

It had been a good morning so far.

Now Dominico Neri sat in the shadow of Giordano Bruno in the *Campo dé Fiori*. The market square was in that transition between lives when the stallholders were tearing down their scaffolding and the restaurateurs were dragging more chairs out to snare the hungry tourists. It was different in the summer. More desperate. The summer menu cost almost treble the winter fare. Today a decent three course antipasto, prima and second piatti would set him back a little over ten Euros. In the summer he'd be lucky to see change from thirty, but the view was better.

Not that he ever ate in the square. The detective came here because they served good cappuccino and he liked to watch the people go by while he dragged on his cigarillo and contemplated the mysteries of the world.

There were balconies and rooftop terrace gardens overlooking the square, but he couldn't think of a single time he'd actually seen someone out on one of them. Today was no different in that he was watching well-worn sad-eyed men wrestling with the steel tubing and the craggy faced women leaning in the doorways of the few shops leading into the square from Via Capo di Ferro, but he had a lot on his mind. And it wasn't just the fact that his people didn't age well. There were the usual array of stunning young women and too pretty boys, the time bomb of their mid-thirties ticking over their heads. He'd come here because of Bruno, another burned man. Burned men figured high in his list of torments these days. The Englishman, Larkin, had gone. He couldn't say he missed him, that was the wrong word: the man was like a black hole for trouble, drawing it in with his gravitational pull. He made life interesting in the same way that the old Chinese curse wanted people to live in interesting times.

Neri could happily live out his days in very dull, very drab, hours and minutes.

A tramp lay curled up in the shadow, his tiny feet bulked up by a dozen pairs of holey socks. He had a cigarette between his lips, pointing straight up at the sky. It quivered with the tramp's snoring. The man looked to be at least ninety but was probably only in his fifties. Living was hard for some people.

Only in Rome, Neri thought, drawing on his liquorice-paper smoke and savouring the nicotine as he took it into his lungs. In a few hours the tramp would be replaced by girls tap-dancing for tips and buskers torturing *Volare* with an array of piano accordions and battered acoustic guitars. His favourite was the old drunk who set up a tape recorder and mimed along to Frankie Valli and Sinatra. The old guy was as weatherworn as Leonard Cohen and looked as though city grime was the only thing holding him together. But, like a vampire, he didn't come out until night.

Neri looked up at the sinister statue in the rcentre of the square. Giordano Bruno. The philosopher had been burned alive in 1600 by the zealots of the

Holy See who thought his ideas were dangerous to the world—those ideas included, among other things, believing that the earth revolved around a stationary sun. A lot of good men, forward thinkers, died during that dark time, branded with crimes of heresy, sorcery, immorality, witchcraft, blasphemy and Judaizing. Given what was happening around Europe that last one bit particularly sharply. Neri wasn't a religious man, unless football counted. He didn't care if someone though the world was flat or followed the Mosaic Laws or the Seven Laws of Noah or Sharia Law or any other kind of law handed down from On High. He took people as he found them. And given his line of work that was most often in a state of decomposition.

Burning had been on his mind a lot these last two weeks.

It had all started with Nick Simmonds, the curious Englishman who had worked on the Pre-Lateran and Lateran Hebrew Codices in the Vatican Library before burning himself alive in Saint Peter's Square, including the Testimony of Menahem ben Jair, grandson of Judas Iscariot.

So much about Simmonds' death bothered the Roman, not least the fact that his garret down by Circus Maximus had been disinfected—not just cleaned—to erase all trace of the man before his self-immolation, or the fact that he had so easily infiltrated the sacred library of the Holy See and succeeded in stealing such a valuable and potentially contentious text—itself the kind of thing wars had been fought over in the past—but that he had done it as a virtual ghost and somehow coordinated his actions with twelve others across Europe's capitals

That bothered him.

That bothered him a lot.

He didn't like when he couldn't see both ends of the thread. He was an intensely logical man. This was a mess. Nick Simmonds was only one of thirteen dead people. For everyone else just a name on a list, but for Dominico Neri he was so much more than that. He was part of a tangled web that had been woven around the Swiss Guard, the Pope himself, and the dead Cardinals. He didn't have to be religious or God-fearing to mourn the deaths of a lot of good men, or feel the burden of responsibility, as irrational as it was. Blame was part of the Roman culture, too. And in that regard Neri was a good Roman.

He sucked on his cigarillo again, enjoying the smoke as it rafted up in front of his face. It looked, for a moment, as though the statue was remembering the flames of four hundred years ago.

His mobile phone vibrated inside his pocket. Neri checked it. The number was blocked. He wasn't in the habit of answering blocked numbers. As far as he was concerned the phone was for his convenience, not theirs.

Behind the high buildings of the market square, out on the *Corso Vittorio Emanuele II*, he heard the familiar shrill siren of one of the organ transport cars. As far as Neri was concerned it was by far the worst sound the city had to offer. He didn't care that it was saving lives. It just grated on his nerves.

His mobile phone vibrated again. He let it ring off without answering it and called the waitress over and held up his cup for a refill. He was a regular fixture in the café. He didn't need to ask for a second cup. They knew he was just as addicted to his caffeine as the rest of the population.

When his phone vibrated a third time before the second cup of coffee arrived he started to think he might have to take the call.

He really didn't want to answer.

Yesterday a plane had touched down at Fiumicino. There was nothing unusual about that. Thirty planes an hour went through the airport. But this was a corpse plane. Unlike a lot of the others he'd been hearing about, not everyone on-board flight BA556 was dead when the plane came to a standstill. They were, however, dying and nothing could be done to save them. Reports had already come in from Spain about the doomed BA0486. The emergency services were prepared, fatalistically so. The few surviving passengers lived through six hours of quarantine on the hard stand before the last of them died. Only then were the vacuum seals broken and the doors opened. Rome didn't deserve what was happening to it. It might have been a city of dubious morals run by liars and thieves, but it was hardly Sodom and Gomorrah.

When his phone rang a fourth time he knew he had no choice but to let the real world back in. "Neri," he said.

There was a static crackle on the line, then, "Neri, it's me, Noah." It took the Roman a moment to process the switch in languages and then link the name to the voice.

"Noah. I assume you aren't calling to claim that couch already, my friend?"

"I think we just caught a break."

"Talk to me," Neri said, resting his cigarillo on the ashtray's rim.

"It's thin, but I need you to check any video surveillance around the Israeli embassy, Israeli banks, any building or institute with strong ties to Israel.

We've got two instances our end of official Israeli involvement—a diplomatic car in Berlin and a video feed that originated in the Israel Embassy in Vienna. That's two. Now, if we suddenly find out that our assassin fled to the embassy in Rome, then that makes three. And three's not a coincidence. Three's a pattern that proves Akim Caspi, Solomon, or whatever he's calling himself today, is working from inside the protection of his government."

"And that makes him untouchable," Neri said, already striking a match to light up another cigarillo. "Why is it you never call with good news, my friend?"

"Oh no, no, no, my fatalistic friend. It is good news. It means we've got him. Maybe not today, maybe not tomorrow—"

"But some day," Neri said, sucking in another lungful of black tar smoke and savouring it.

"It's a start. More than that, it's the closest thing we've got to being ahead of the game."

"I'll look into it, but you should know that Rome isn't like London, there are only five thousand four hundred cameras across all of Rome. You have one and a half million in London. It's a fishing expedition."

"Yeah, but this is Rome we're talking about. Everyone's watching, just not officially. And if they aren't watching, they're listening. Information is power. So I'm asking you to trade in some favours, my friend. Someone knows something. That kid had help."

"You're starting to think like a Roman, Noah," Neri said. He didn't mean it as a compliment. Noah was right though, it went deeper than the dead monsignor, Gianni Abandonato, Gianni the Forsaken, deeper than the assassin who'd driven the knife home. Neri had stopped thinking of him as Swiss Guard. He wasn't. They'd found a naked body in front of the *Largo di*

Torre Argentina staked out like some sacrifice to the old gods in front of the *Torre del Papitto*. There was an irony in the choice of location, not merely because of the four ruined temples that made up the square, or the fact that it was only a few feet from the curia of the Theatre of Pompey where Caesar himself had been cut down, but that *Torre del Papitto* meant, quite literally, The Little Pope's Tower.

The cats had already started feeding on the dead man's arms.

His teeth had been smashed in, a few tombstone stumps remaining, and his fingertips sliced off. At that point he had just been another body. No ID. Nothing to link him to the Holy See or the Papal visit to Koblenz. Nothing to betray the fact that someone had brutally murdered the young man and like some doppelgänger stolen his life just long enough to drive home the fatal blow.

But it was all beginning to come clear now. Clear didn't mean they had any more answers than a week ago. Video surveillance of the square had proved all but useless. The assassin had come in over the railings, carrying the body on his shoulder, and worked fast. And without doubt he knew where every one of the security cameras were and their angle of coverage, because it took them two days for someone to note the passing similarity between the man and his victim. It took another two days for Neri to see that photograph himself, and realise it was the face of the man from the photo Noah Larkin had sent him of the assassination itself, pulling all the threads together. Of course, he had already passed the photograph on to the Vatican Police, meaning they had all the pieces of the puzzle long before he did, but the trading of information was proving to be its usual nightmarish combination of secrecy, bureaucracy, obfuscation and, when it came right down to it, outright lies.

The *Corpo della Gendarmeria* were responsible for border security, criminal investigation, traffic, security and other general police duties for Vatican City. Unfortunately for them, Papa had been murdered off their sovereign soil, meaning other law enforcement bodies were involved and they couldn't simply shut up shop and go into denial. Of course, the 'spirit of co-operation' didn't actually make them any more helpful than usual, hence it was taking them more than a week to admit the body in *Largo di Torre Argentina* was theirs.

But at least the dead man had a name now: Alessio Bisch.

His body was found twenty-nine hours before the Pope's assassination. Twenty-nine hours in which co-operation might have saved Peter the Roman's life. It wasn't worth thinking like that, of course. That way lay madness.

And, of course, it only begged more questions. Somehow the assassin had killed one of the inner circle, and for a while taken his place. They weren't twins though, so no matter how much the man kept to himself someone must have known he wasn't Alessio Bisch. And yet they hadn't stopped him. That bothered Neri. That bothered him a lot. It presented glaring flaws in every rationale he devised. He had wanted to drag the five remaining men of the inner circle in for questioning, but the Inspector General himself had denied his request, claiming it was a matter for internal policing. And that only served to bother him more, because all of these little things together were beginning to turn him into a conspiracy theorist and he didn't like that.

Neri drew on his cigarillo, tapping the ash off into

a chipped ashtray.

"I understand what you are asking, Noah, but you have understand it is a lot."

"I know. But if anyone's going to get this, it's you. You were there. You saw what I saw." He didn't say you failed like I failed, but that was the inference. "I haven't slept for a week. I keep seeing him. He was there, at the Conclave. I haven't told anyone this… I don't even know if it's true… or if my mind's playing tricks on me… But I saw him right after I killed the priest. At least I think I did. That's the thing, one clown starts to look a lot like another after a while, in the heat of the moment, so focussed on Abandonato… I don't know… The uniform makes them all anonymous. There was something about this guy, though. He came right up to me and told me no one had entered the chapel. And now I can't help but think it was him, standing right in front of me. And I missed him. Not once, but twice."

"Is this your confession, my friend? Because I'm not qualified to take it."

"I don't know," Noah said down the long distance line. "I really don't know… Maybe it *wasn't* him. Like I said, maybe I'm just torturing myself. But if he was there, then maybe, just maybe, he was finishing the job."

"Making sure no one got into the Conclave before the fires were lit," Neri said, processing the implications of the idea, and how it changed everything they thought they knew about Gianni Abandonato. "And that's why you want me to check surveillance footage around the Israeli Embassy? To see if, job done, he fled the Vatican in the chaos that followed?"

"He had to be hiding out somewhere. Someone

had to be helping him. Someone high enough up to make him disappear. I'd love photos of him and the priest conspiring, but I don't think we're going to find anything like that. If I'm honest, I'm not even sure the priest was a *willing* conspirator. The more I think about it, the more I think something's not right."

"Lots of things are not right," Neri observed, wryly.

"Amen. I'll be honest, I don't for a minute doubt Abandonato was behind the sarin gas in the Sistine chapel. The weight of evidence stacks up. He had the means and the opportunity. No one would have suspected him. But his last word to me was 'fire'. I thought he was goading me to shoot him. To pull the trigger and end his miserable existence… But what if he was trying to warn me? What if right at the last he'd had a change of heart and was trying to tell me to stop them lighting the fire?"

"Then he had his change of heart too late to make a damned bit of difference and he deserves to burn just the same," Neri said without a hint of compassion. He tapped more ash off the end of his cigarillo. He was beginning to wish he hadn't answered the phone. Life was a lot simpler a few minutes ago.

Noah didn't argue with him.

"If we can tie this guy in with the embassy, then we've got our unholy trinity," he said after a moment. "And three's no coincidence. It means we're on the right track."

"It also means we can't trust any of the Papal Guards. Have you thought about that?"

"I haven't stopped thinking about it. Everyone has their pressure points. We've already seen Solomon isn't afraid to use them. He's taken families before, held them hostage to force people to do things they'd never usually do, all in the name of protecting loved ones, even if it means burning themselves alive to do so. It's not unreasonable to think something similar was done to the guards. Could be worth some digging, check on their folks, see if anything's off. But right now I'm thinking the motto is trust no one. That's the safest way."

"You know, until about five minutes ago I was rather looking forward to the next time our paths would cross, thinking it would mean an excess of wine, women and a whole lot of bullshit about the relative merits of Serie A against the Premier League. You know, like men, not surrounded by death."

"We'll have that drink one day, mate," Noah told him. Neri wasn't sure he believed the man. They weren't the kind of people who ever came out from beneath the shadow of death. It wasn't in their nature.

"I will call in all the favours I have left. I hope you are wrong because I don't know what it means if you are right."

"I half-hope I am wrong, too. I would kill for a decent night's sleep. But I don't think that's going to happen for a while."

"I'll be in touch." Neri hung up.

A tiny blue Fiat blared its horn to move one of the market men. He was leaning on a precarious stack of fruit boxes and flirting in that cocky arrogant way of the good-looking. The object of his affection was a pale-skinned blond tourist. Her accent betrayed her Australian heritage. The Fiat driver hit the horn again, then pulled out, manoeuvring around the pair of them. He rolled the window down and spat out a stream of invective that would have had his dear old mum washing his mouth out with soap not so long ago. The market trader was unmoved and the Australian girl only had eyes for her Prince Charming. Neri wanted to go over and warn her, say, *"Look around the square, see all the pretty young Italianos, now look again, do you see any pretty old Italianos? Look at me. I looked like him twenty years ago. This is what's hiding beneath the oh so attractive mask. Not so pretty is it?"* But he didn't.

Market traders lined up at the fountain, filling their buckets to sluice down the cobbles and wash away any last traces of the fruit and vegetables and wilting flowers. The transformation took less than twenty minutes and then every last trace of the market was gone. There was fresh graffiti on one of the walls. Some street corner philosopher had sprayed GOD IS NOWHERE on the lemon façade of one of the restaurants, only because of the uneven spacing of the letters he had unintentionally sprayed GOD IS NOW HERE. Neri rather liked the duality of the message. The same letters in the same order, but offering completely different takes on faith. Sighing heavily as he pushed himself to his feet, the Roman had the distinct feeling that nowhere was a more accurate interpretation of the world these days. The other graffiti was less thought-provoking, offering the usual array of tags and the occasional one-liner like: *God must love stupid people, he created so many!* And *Is there life before death?* amid the proclamations of love for Roma and Lazio.

And it had started out as such a good day.

Maybe tomorrow would be better.

Somehow, he doubted it.

TEN
THE WAY IT IS

Sir Charles Wyndham didn't put up any outward fight, but that didn't mean he was resigned to the invasion of Nonesuch.

He'd let Constance and Knight have their day, let them go barking up the wrong tree.

They were so fixated on the notion that this was monotheistic, and as a result so wrapped up in the preconceptions that went along with their Christian interpretations. They didn't see the arrogance or ignorance of putting one god ahead of all others. That in itself was painfully ironic, but more so, it meant they were missing the obvious—there were three things according to Judaic teaching that defined a messiah, and for Solomon's seeming fundamentalism to ring true with the devout and feed his most zealous followers, these were things he had to adhere to. They were the 'grain of truth'.

If Solomon wanted people to see him as their messiah he was going to have appear to be their messiah, and that meant following certain pre-defined paths as dictated by the Torah. Whatever else he was, he was no fool. To make these claims, even in the way he did in that video, Solomon knew he was committing himself to a chain of action and event which, by very strict definition would mark him as a messiah: bring about the political and spiritual redemption of the Jewish people by bringing them back to Israel and restoring Jerusalem, establish a government in Israel that would be the centre of all world government, rebuild the Temple and re-establish its worship, restore the religious court system of Israel and establish Jewish law as the law of the land.

The Hebrew word for messiah, *mashiach*, wasn't a part of the early Judaism, had nothing to do with Jesus Christ, and wasn't explicitly mentioned anywhere in the Torah. In fact it was almost certainly added during the Age of the Prophets and related to the End of Days. The word translated literally to 'the anointed one' and what that itself referred to was the ancient practice of anointing kings with oil when they claimed the throne, meaning quite literally the *mashiach* would be the Anointed King as the world entered the *acharit ha-yamim*. The End of Days.

Popular culture was sure the signs that announced the End of Days were in place.

It was the perfect time for a madman to play messiah. People wanted to believe in something, whether it was a god, salvation, money, freedom of thought, information, or whatever other freedom they could conjure and claim worthy. The answers they were looking for were all there. All they needed to do was open their eyes to see them.

Nowhere in these teachings did messiah mean saviour.

Nowhere did it equate to divinity or the semi-divine.

The notion of the messiah returning to save man from his sins was a fundamentally Christian one, but the deep-seated familiarity of the Christian concept of a divine saviour meant that for the vast majority simply hearing the word messiah immediately brought to mind all of those divine, Godly, conceits.

It was a mistake to equate *mashiach* to the Hebrew term *moshiah*, which was the closest in terms of meaning to the notion of a saviour. The two words originated from very different etymological roots, with *mashiach* having its origins in *Mem-Shin-Chet*, which meant, literally to paint, smear, or anoint, while *moshiah*, which sounded so close to the English word, had its roots in the word *Yod-Shin-Ayin*, which meant to help or save, hence the mistake. Shin, the only commonality they shared, was the most frequently used letter in the Hebrew alphabet.

Ignorance of a culture was a dangerous thing, especially given the situation they were facing. Sir Charles could not abide ignorance. Understanding just what Solomon was talking about when he bandied about the term messiah was vital because it identified his eventual target. To build a temple he must first destroy a mosque. The Dome of the Rock. The Islamic Mosque on Temple Mount, built on the remains of the Second Temple, destroyed during the siege of Jerusalem. The First Temple had been built on Temple Mount, then known as Mount Zion, by Solomon and destroyed by the Babylonian King, Nebuchadnezzar II, having stood for over four hundred years. Dedicated to Yahweh, it had housed the Ark of the Covenant.

The Dome of the Rock was said to be the site where Mohammed made the Night Journey and ascended to heaven with Gabriel, making it the most holy site in the Islamic faith for centuries, while the Foundation Stone, the Rock the Dome was built on, is the single most holy site in Judaism, the Holy of Holies, the very first part of the Earth to come into existence, the world expanding around it. As Muslims prayed to Mecca, Jews all over the world prayed to the Foundation Stone.

You want to hurt two faiths, you bring down the Dome.

You want to be a messiah, you build a temple on its ruins.

There was a symmetry to this terrorist choosing to call himself Solomon, meaning he was aware… he knew his religious histories, which only reinforced the notion that the Dome was his eventual target. What the old man didn't know was if it was his next one.

He hated the idea of Orla returning to Israel, but she had proven herself time and again. It was time to let go. They weren't children, and they were no longer his to direct. For now. What he needed Orla to know was that although her target was the supplier of the virus used on the corpse planes, she should keep her eyes open for a potential attack on the Temple Mount. Sir Charles knew Orla Nyrén, which is why he knew he didn't need to tell her. She knew her comparative religions better than he did. If he'd made the link, she most assuredly had, too.

Better to stay quiet. Let Mendes and Knight take the fall. He just hoped his team wouldn't get hurt in the process. But if they did… well, as callous as it sounded, it was what they signed up for.

Sir Charles watched Constance Mendes now. She was deep in conversation on her phone to someone, he didn't know who. It was probably Quentin. The old bastard had known Wyndham far too long to expect him to sit back and let his cronies take over the team, which was precisely why he was doing exactly that. Let them see what it's really like outside the considerable reach and protection of Her Majesty's government.

Mendes hung up her phone and stood.

The pair were alone in the command room.

Frost was on his way back to Manchester on a mission he'd wisely kept to himself. Orla was headed to the airport, en route. Meanwhile Noah was God knew where, and Konstantin… Well hopefully Konstantin was somewhere *nobody*, not even the divine, knew where. If there was one man who could hide from his maker, it was the Russian.

Jude Lethe was the last member of the team left in the old manor house. He was in the Nest as usual, but now he had an unwelcome visitor.

Sir Charles had died a little inside when the moron, Knight, had followed the young genius down into his lair.

He knew they didn't trust him, or his people, and it was obvious they intended to monitor the entire team from the Nest, keeping tabs on Lethe's activities. He could only trust that Ogmios's most potent weapon had taken the necessary measures to lock down the more critical parts of his unfathomable network before he came up for the briefing.

"I know your game, Charles," Mendes said, dropping the sir. "You want me to fall flat on my face and make a spectacular mess. That's fine. It's natural, but don't forget that if I do, your team will be permanently disbanded. Is my embarrassment worth that much to you?"

"Ah, dear lady," Sir Charles replied with the faintest smile. "I am just an observer now. You hold all the cards. I have no intention of interfering. I am an asset at your disposal, as are the rest of my people."

"Where is Khavin?"

Sir Charles shrugged. "I have absolutely no idea. You need to understand how we operate. If I knew where he was, I would not be a leader, I would be a manager. My function here has never been to babysit the team. I provide them with the tools and information they need to do get the job done. Sometimes we succeed, but nobody pins medals on our chests. If we fall short Control demands we justify our existence and our methods. This is familiar territory, Constance. I have been here before. So believe me when I say I don't know where .Mr Khavin is. And before you ask, I have no idea where Mr Larkin is, either. This is how they operate. I make it my business not to get in their way."

She shook her head. "You think they're trying to *help*?"

"What else would they be doing?"

"How can you be so naïve, Charles? Khavin is a fugitive, he killed his own people, and Larkin, well frankly he's probably lying pissed in a gutter somewhere."

"Perhaps he is. Noah has never tried to hide his demons. And despite your best attempts to ensnare Konstantin, what I can guarantee you is that they are out there doing what they do best."

"Wreaking havoc and destruction?"

Sir Charles smiled.

ELEVEN
ONE DAY LIKE THIS

Being back here chilled Frost to the core.

The warehouse was quiet, seemingly abandoned.

The police had finished combing the place days ago, sealing it off with crime scene tape.

That was when the rats returned.

At first, he assumed it was police, but it was an inactive crime scene, after hours. The guards walking the perimeter weren't law enforcement. Which meant that when he'd brought the women and children out he'd left the job unfinished.

Two guards patrolled the perimeter. He watched them. They showed no signs of nervous tension. They weren't expecting company. The last time he'd been here, Frost had been forced to scale the chainlink fence to get inside the grounds. This time the gate wasn't locked. The ruined padlock still lay on the ground nearby. Nobody had bothered to replace it. Another indication that as far as the police were concerned this was a dead site.

But it wasn't, was it?

Connie was smart. She grasped the importance of attention to detail. The guards proved it, there was still something going on here. Frost was determined to put a stop to it once and for all. No need to scale the fire escape this time. The main door was wide open; Ronan himself had opened it to let the captives out.

He moved in, the Browning in his hand.

The inside of the warehouse was eerily quiet.

He wasn't taking any chances.

The metal shipping containers were still there, offering plenty of cover for anyone who might have heard him arrive.

It took Frost five minutes, but he covered the entire floor of the warehouse, backrooms, and the office on the gantry upstairs. The place was deserted. Which didn't make sense. Why guard an abandoned warehouse?

Bullet holes in the walls and blood on the grimy floor were the only indications that Frost had been here before.

He stopped in the middle of the warehouse floor and listened.

Connie remembered hearing the grinding of machinery coming from below where the captives were sleeping. She'd spent enough time in here to know every sigh and sound the building made, and fear had attuned her senses to the secrets of the old building. She was right. It was easy to miss it over the sound of his own footsteps, it was so faint, but if he listened carefully – there *was* something.

At first, he thought it might be a boiler, grinding away in the depths of the structure.

But the more he focussed on it, the surer he became that it wasn't a boiler; the faint clanging and thumping was too irregular.

In his preliminary search Frost hadn't found an entrance down to a sub-level, but that didn't mean there wasn't one.

He searched again, this time checking for any signs of disturbed dust or scuff marks on the floor of the building, thinking there must be a hidden trap door, or panel obscuring the stairs down. After a few minutes of fruitless searching, an alternative occurred to him. It was obvious, but clever just the same. One by one, he worked his way along the shipping containers, opening the doors to shine his torch inside.

The rusted hinges groaned loudly in the otherwise silent warehouse, testimony to their years of neglect, but he wasn't worried about being heard. If the machinery below was so muffled up here, then likewise any noise he made would be drowned out down there.

The second-to-last container offered up the prize.

There was a large hole cut in the floor. It looked like an arc welder had been used to do the cutting, given the blackened metal around the edges. It was comfortably six-foot by six-foot, and allowed access to the warehouse floor, where he could see the metal trap door.

He killed the torch.

Frost crouched and lifted the trapdoor, the Browning ready to take out anyone who unlucky enough to be standing guard below.

Immediately the sound of machinery intensified.

Light streamed into the shipping container, rising to fill it.

Ronan descended the metal stairs as quietly as he could. He paused to replace the hatch above his head, covering his tracks, and without a sound, moved down into the basement.

He found cover behind a storage shelf packed high with metal plates.

There were three obvious targets, two men and a woman.

All armed, weapons were holstered.

Their focus was on the machines making an unholy racket.

There were a dozen identical machines down on the floor, more than half running. They were old school printing machines. One was in the process of having its plates changed by the workers, another needed a fresh supply of the various coloured inks. Frost guessed the other machines were used for mixing the inks to the precise colours, or producing the fabrics, paper and plastics needed for the finished counterfeit currency.

It wasn't exactly the Royal Mint, but it was a pretty slick operation.

The rear of the basement was filled with forged bank notes, stacks and stacks of them piled high.

The machines printed more, churning out thousands of pounds worth of fake notes every single minute.

Frost moved closer.

He took cover behind one of the machines. He saw the fruits of its labour. Euros. If he hadn't seen the machine making them he would have thought they were genuine. They were decent forgeries, good enough certainly to fool most people. He had no idea if they'd get past a bank's security checks, but the average Joe taking them out of an ATM would have no idea his wallet was stuffed with forgeries.

To his right, he saw the familiar greenbacks of stacks of US dollars lined up against the wall. Beside them, Malaysian Ringgits. There were enough piles to suggest a lot of global currencies were being copied here. It was an obvious comparison to the Nazis World War 2 scheme to flood the British market with fake money. And Lethe was right, coupled with the chip-and-pin attacks undermining public confidence in credit cards, introducing a vast amount of fake currency into circulation would put the kind of uncertainty into people that would have them despairing soon enough. Cash was supposed to be king. When that failed, what then?

One of the two men approached his position, checking the nearest machine.

Frost ducked down behind a mountain of fake Canadian fifties.

As the man passed, he seized his chance.

Stealth wasn't necessary. The noise from the machines drowned out any warning of his attack. Frost rose fast and drove his elbow into the man's chin as he half-turned, dropping him like a stone. He crouched over him and hammered his fist into the man's face twice to make sure he wasn't getting up again, then ducked in behind the next machine, watching the two others.

The remaining male was big, huge in fact.

He didn't look like he knew what he was doing with the machines. Frost marked him as the grunt. She was the boss. She pointed to a large stack of bills and the big man began loading them onto a trolley. She half-turned, glancing his way.

Frost dropped back out of sight. He had no way of knowing if she'd seen him.

"Gustav," she called out above the racket. "What are you doing?"

Ronan took a risk.

"Be right there," he yelled back, putting on a lousy Russian accent. Koni would have taken the piss for weeks, but partially drowned out by the rattle of the presses she seemed to buy it.

She had her back to him now. Ronan waited until the big guy had moved out of view, then he broke from cover and walked casually towards the woman.

Assuming he was Gustav, she paid him no mind.

He was close enough for them to be lovers before she looked up.

The shock on her face was priceless.

Frost had no problems hitting a woman in a situation like this; he slammed his knee into her stomach before she could open her mouth. She doubled over, struggling to breath as he delivered a powerful two-handed jab to the back of her neck.

This time she went down and didn't move.

Frost heard something.

He looked up in time to see the big guy's fist heading for his face.

He barely managed to duck out of the way, feeling the rush of displaced air against his cheek as the ham hock sized hand missed its mark.

Momentum unbalanced the big man.

Taking advantage of it, Frost roared and propelled himself forward. He twisted as he collided with the grunt. Wrong-footed, the big man toppled over, colliding with one of the machines.

A hail of sparks and the deep groan of mechanical protest answered his fall, but he wasn't down for long.

As the grunt tried to stand, Frost kicked out, imagining himself at Wembley, last seconds of the final, one on one with the keeper, and drove his foot into the man's throat. This time he hit the machine with such force it toppled, pieces of it shattering as they hit the floor. Some chemical inside leaked out of the damaged guts, and in a couple of seconds Frost was standing in the middle of a small fire.

The grunt lay within the wreckage of the press.

Shielding his face from the fire, which had already spread to an electrical cable and was racing quickly towards the walls of money, Frost backed away.

He was happy to let this place burn.

The whole fucking lot could go up in flames.

There had been enough horror here to last the lifetimes of those women and their children… the execution of young boys in front of their mothers… it was a suitable fate for the condemned building.

Something hit Frost in the back of the head.

Hard.

He staggered, dropping to his knees.

Instinct told him a second blow was coming.

He threw himself to the side.

The red of the fire extinguisher came at him a second time, cannoning off his shoulder. It would have split his skull open. Frost rolled, seeing the woman back on her feet and determined to take him out before she used the extinguisher for its intended purpose.

His consciousness swimming, the back of his skull on fire, Frost struggled to stand and felt his legs collapse under him. Fuck. Shit. That was really fucking stupid of him. He should never have ended her. Amateur hour.

She swung the canister again, this time barely missing his knee as he tried to scramble away. He needed to take control of this quickly or he was going to be suffering a world of hurt.

He rolled again, scrambling beneath another savage swing, but couldn't go anywhere. Fire blocked his escape. Four of the presses were engulfed in rising fire, all looped in to the condemned building's power grid. He saw the first lick of flame reach the junction box in the corner. The heat coming off the banknotes was brutal. Everything in the basement was being consumed with frightening hunger.

The woman was caught in a moment of indecision, trapped between watching the counterfeit currency going up in flames and the consequences of her operation's destruction.

He knew the look in her eyes.

It as the realisation she was a dead woman, even if he didn't kill.

Frost stole that second.

He kicked out hard, his heel catching her just below the kneecap.

It wasn't the cleanest strike – and wouldn't do any lasting damage, but it was enough to pitch her backward as she tried to recover and removed the immediate threat of a counter.

Her face twisted in rage.

Frost didn't waste the valuable seconds he'd bought with the kick.

He drew the Browning and fired twice, putting one in her chest, one in her face.

The fire extinguisher hit the concrete. She stared at him not knowing that she was dead, then fell back into the flames.

Dizzy, the blood pounding through his skull and his lungs filling with smoke, Frost struggled to stand but couldn't stay upright for long. He managed one step before dropping to his knees again.

He needed to get out of there.

Biting back on the pain, he dragged himself toward the stairs, willing his mind to clear and his balance to return as he crawled on. It quickly became impossible to see through the dense smoke. The heat was incredible. The fire had spread to the ceiling. If he didn't move fast, it would engulf the stairs, cutting his exit off, and leaving him down there to burn.

He had no intention of dying. Not now. Not ever.

He couldn't give a shit that it was undignified, he was desperate.

Browning still in hand, he began to roll towards the stairs.

The manoeuvre was cumbersome and clumsy but kept him effective and close to the floor where there was still some air. He moved faster than he would have done by crawling. The smoke stung his eyes. Frost started coughing as a mouthful of smoke bit deep in his lungs, choking on it.

The edges of consciousness began to bleed into the concrete.

He was in trouble.

He clung to the mantra: *I will not die here.*

And rolled again and again, the Browning held out in both hands as he barrel-rolled across the floor.

He misjudged the distance to the foot of the stairs, hitting the guide rail where it met the bottom step.

He took the impact on his arm, hard, the Browning slipping between his fingers. It hit the concrete near his face. He grabbed it even as the sudden movement sent a shiver of pain the length of his arm. He wasn't about to leave it behind. The gun was part of him. He focussed on the fresh pain in his arm, trying to ignore his heaving lungs and dizziness. The sheer scouring heat of the flames against his skin was astonishing.

Hand over hand, Frost pulled himself up the stairs, one rail at a time.

I will not die here. He clung stubbornly to the thought as it turned to a prayer and from that to wishful thinking.

He wasn't going to make it.

The fire would engulf the trap door any second.

He forced himself to draw on reserves of strength that only existed by sheer force of will and climbed for his life. Each new step had him coughing lungs up onto the next one, but he wasn't stopping.

The fire ceased to exist.

The world reduced to Ronan Frost and half a dozen steps on a makeshift ladder. He centred himself, calming his breathing as best he could as he climbed. His vision swam and eyes wept blinding tears, but he pushed himself up.

Without realizing he'd come so far, Frost felt the trap door against his head.

He twisted his body, and with one final colossal effort heaved on it, forcing it upward. It wasn't especially heavy, but weakened as he was, it felt like the weight of the entire warehouse had collapsed on top of it. The surface was searing hot against his hands.

Frost gave it everything he had.

The trap door moved an inch.

Two, five, letting in a wave of cold air that felt like the elixir of life in his lungs as he pulled himself up into the shipping container, rolled onto his side and slammed the door down again, sealing away the fire.

He lay on his back, feeling the heat through the floor, for a full two minutes, trying to hack the crap up out of his lungs.

The door wouldn't hold the fire for long.

The metal floor of the shipping container warmed with the rising heat.

It wasn't done.

He had to move or was still going to die in this fucking warehouse, and that wasn't going to be how he went out. It just wasn't happening. He'd made it this far. He was walking out of this place.

Frost holstered the Browning. He needed the walls of the container to steady himself as he hauled himself up to his feet, and even then stumbled back against the inside of the open doors before he lurched out into the precious air of the warehouse, facing the huge cargo bay doors that opened onto the night. He swallowed lungful after lungful of precious oxygen.

He could see the outside world.

He could feel draught cooling his skin.

It called to him.

All he had to do was put one foot in front of another and stay upright.

Outside, he kept on going.

Frost put twenty feet between himself and the huge warehouse doors.

Through them, the floor was already ablaze, smoke spilling up through the cracks and fissures of the collapsing floor. It wouldn't be long before it engulfed the walls and spread out across the struts and scaffold of the ceiling and the whole thing collapsed in flame.

He walked away from it, happy for the building to die.

It deserved it as much as any four walls had ever deserved to come crashing down.

Finally, halfway to the gate and the waiting Monster, he allowed himself to sink to his knees and pitch forward, hands digging into the dirt as he focussed on just breathing.

He wasn't going any further.

Not for a while.

The warehouse burned behind him.

He could still feel the heat despite the distance.

He didn't care. He could breathe.

He tapped his earbud.

"Lethe, are you there?"

"Always, mate. Always. What's up?"

"I need an ambulance. Warehouse by the Canning Docks, you remember it?"

"Of course I do. What the hell are you doing back there?"

"Just make the call."

"Already done. Why didn't you call me earlier?"

"You couldn't have helped earlier," Frost said. He was out of words. He gave in to a brutal coughing fit, then collapsed onto his back and waited for the paramedics.

TWELVE
SOMEWHERE UNDER WONDERLAND

Noah charged out of Fiumicino Airport like a caged animal finally freed.

He was a changed man. Not exactly energized, but revitalized, his takedown of Jordan Walker had his blood pumping. He was ready to inflict the same kind of pain on Solomon and all of the shitheads who followed him.

He greeted Neri with a brief handshake.

The Italian didn't look pleased to see him. That in itself raised a smile.

"You look like a man who has been reborn," Neri said. "I am afraid to ask what you have done, my friend."

"Like I'm going confess my sins to a policeman," Noah said, grin widening.

"Unshared confessions weigh on the soul, my friend. But if you're looking to atone, you've come to the right city."

"I'm good," Noah promised him as they walked to Neri's car.

Noah kept the conversation general, falling back on old standbys like football, until they had pulled out of the car park and onto the A91 to the city.

As the road opened up before them the conversation turned to business.

"So, what have you heard?"

"Not much, just bits and pieces, but I did call in a favour at the Israeli embassy."

"Tell me you got something."

"They were definitely harboring someone, though my contact didn't have a name. But when I showed him the picture of the Swiss Guard our assassin replaced, he did admit there was a passing resemblance to Alessio Bisch."

"Is he still there?"

"No. He was smuggled out to the airport forty-eight hours ago."

"We missed the bastard." Noah smacked his hand against the blank dashboard. Neri looked like he was worried the airbag would deploy. He muttered an apology. Neri, wisely, said nothing.

"Please tell me there's some good news in this?"

"Rome is an international hub. He could be anywhere in the world—"

"That's not my idea of good news."

"But…"

"Don't make me beat it out of you."

Neri smiled a wry smile of his own. "I pulled in *another* favour. This time from an ex at air traffic control. You have no idea how much it cost me to call a woman who hates me as much as she does … but I said I was related to the corpse planes and convinced her it was her duty to help me. There was a flight to the UK that was delayed for the boarding of a final passenger who wasn't on the original manifest, despite the fact the pilot had already reported boarding was complete. It fits in terms of the timeline for smuggling the fake Bisch out of the embassy."

"It's thin."

"It's all we've got."

"I'll get word to Lethe. Maybe he can verify your suspicions." He thought about it for a moment, the lights of Rome passing by. "If our assassin is in England, then I came here for nothing."

"Ah, not for nothing," Neri corrected him. "I need your help."

"Neri, my friend, you know I'd love to help you, but I've kinda got an assassin to find."

"Let me be blunt, your friends in England can find him. I need you here."

"After what happened last time I was here, I'd have thought I was persona non grata in Rome."

"There are places I cannot go, and where lies and deceit are so commonplace they are spoken at every turn. None of our officers can investigate. That is why I need you. You can."

"I know I'm going to regret this, but investigate what?"

"I have… how can I put this diplomatically… heard that someone is planning a burglary tonight."

"Inside Vatican City?"

Neri chuckled. "Where else?"

"The Carabinieri seem unconvinced, or at worst, complicit. From where I am it is hard to tell, either way. But something *will* be stolen from the vault tonight."

"And you want me to stop it?"

"It can't be me."

"Neri, look mate, we've been through a lot. Hell, I almost consider you a friend, and believe me, I don't have many of those. But I'm not the kind of guy who goes out of my way to help his friends. I'm a selfish fucker, which, frankly is why I don't have many friends. My priority is finding the assassin and putting an end to him after I've forced him to spill his boss's whereabouts so that I can put an end to him too, and the circle is complete. I'm not here to police the Vatican."

"Oh, come now, Noah. You aren't an idiot. And it doesn't smell like you've been drinking, so use your brain for a moment. A planned break in at the Vatican Archives, coming so soon after the death of the Cardinals? The Holy See is in chaos. It is the perfect opportunity for someone to steal from the secret vaults."

"Sure, any opportunist could be looking capitalize on the mess."

"Or it could be connected. I know where I'd put my money, and I am a gambling man."

Noah stretched in his seat.

He wasn't going to get any sleep tonight anyway, so why not break into a vault in the depths of the Vatican to prevent another break in?

Actually, it sounded like fun. But he wasn't about to admit that to Neri.

THIRTEEN
WE'RE ON A ROAD TO NOWHERE

Stacia Kanic wanted her gun back. Losing it to Khavin was humiliating.

She didn't do humiliation.

The Russian was proving to be the bane of her existence.

She wasn't used to failing.

It wasn't just that Khavin had bloodied her nose or made her look stupid; he had cost her some of her best men. And those men were her men. She was invested in them.

But beyond that, the bastard had taken her gun.

You didn't do that to a fellow operative.

It wasn't a special gun. The Sig Sauer P226 was standard issue. Along with the Browning, it was favoured by a lot of Six. But for Stacia, this weapon had a personal connection that went beyond the anodized aluminum alloy.

She had used it to shoot her own mother.

Her mother, sworn to protect Ukraine, her motherland, had turned traitor to her country when she aligned herself with Russia. The shame still burned bright in Stacia. Her mother had begged her to let her go, but she couldn't, not knowing what she knew. The risk of betrayal to the FSB was too great. So she carried out the kill order.

Killing people changed you forever. Killing your own mother, went deeper. It didn't just change you, it transformed you. After that bullet, you became the phoenix reborn.

If she could face her mother, look her in the eye, and pull the trigger, she could handle anything Konstantin Khavin threw at her. She hated Russians at the best of times, traitors more so.

She had commandeered a Ford Focus.

She put a call through to Nonesuch.

"Should I know you?" A voice asked. Jude Lethe, the technical support for Sir Charles's motley crew. She didn't have the patience for games.

"Tell Knight that Stacia needs to speak to him."

"Don't touch that," Lethe said, not to her.

Another voice came on the line.

"Knight."

"Khavin got away. Wrecked my car and my team. I'm in pursuit. I need more resources to bring him in."

A heavy sigh answered her. "Are you up to the job?"

"I'll bring Khavin in or I'll take him down. One or the other."

"Good. Rendezvous at Checkpoint 3. I'll have a car, team and equipment waiting for you. I shall let your number one fan know what's going on."

With that, Knight killed the call. Typical Knight, always with the snide digs before he hung up. Stacia had worked for Mendes for considerably longer than Knight had and had her trust. Michael Knight was the kid on the block, and as far both of them were concerned, an unwelcome addition. Knight was a career spook. He wanted Mendes's job, plain and simple, and everything he did was a means to that end.

Whether it was personal or just deep-rooted misogyny she couldn't say. But if Knight was running the show, she was out. That much she knew. So, failure wasn't an option.

She made the blue Volvo heading off the M25 exit ramp onto the A2, heading east.

The Russian was following the speed limit now he was on the smaller road, which meant pursuit wasn't challenging. She had no idea if he knew he had a tail.

Checkpoint 3 was north of London and she was headed in the wrong direction.

She knew she should break off pursuit, follow Knight's orders and report in to Checkpoint 3 immediately. But doing that meant losing eyes on, and losing eyes on meant losing him. This guy had got out of Russia once, and walked away from assassinating the Pope in plain sight.

She really wanted her gun back.

Judging by his route, she figured the Russian was heading for the Dover docks.

It was the smart play.

Leave the country.

Air wasn't an option, not with the corpse planes grounding so many planes and the remaining flights and airports so empty at the moment. Six had eyes everywhere. The Tunnel wasn't a good move. Too confined, too much risk of being trapped on the train or in the tunnels themselves. A ferry crossing was harder to track, and once in France he could drive anywhere in continental Europe without once having to show identification. He could drive all the way to the Eastern Bloc and make himself a new life if that was what he wanted to do. Once a traitor, always a traitor.

Stacia knew she ought to call it in. Six could have operatives dockside before he arrived. But the nagging suspicion that Lethe was still operational, and almost certainly working to help the Russian evade capture wouldn't leave her, which meant any attempt to communicate with Knight, or even directly to Six, would find its way to the Russian.

They needed their own man in the Nest to neutralize Lethe.

Then she'd call for backup.

Not before.

The whole team needed to be retired alongside Sir Charles, at least until they'd learned to work within the rules. They had talents, there was no denying that, and Six was nothing if not practical when it came to the protection of the realm. They wouldn't waste those skills, but they'd want to reeducate them before letting someone like Lethe loose. The man was a living, breathing security nightmare.

As they passed Faversham, the motorway dead-ended. Stacia followed Khavin back onto the secondary road again, taking the Canterbury turn. Traffic was a little heavier as they passed the town, but picked up again as the road continued on toward way to Dover.

She saw that Khavin was taking more risks now.

He was going faster, weaving in and out of traffic on the dual carriageway as he

looked to make up some of the time he'd lost in the crawl.

Stacia matched him mile for mile, careful to vary her pattern of pursuit.

If he was as good as she'd been told, he'd know she was back here. There was no getting around that, but that didn't mean she had to make it easy for him.

She knew where he was going. That gave her the ace. She could hang back, knowing if she lost him he'd still have to get onto the ferry, and that meant plenty of opportunity to pick him up again.

The game of cat and mouse continued for a while, without Khavin trying to shake her.

Up ahead, Khavin slowed. She knew why. He'd made her. He was slowing to see if she'd overtake. The problem was, if she did he'd see her in the driver's seat, and if she didn't it was about to go from a simple tail to a chase.

She cursed herself.

She dropped into position behind a tractor trailer.

Khavin saw and adapted his flight. The Volvo accelerated hard, tearing away as fast as its engine could in a shriek of engine and rubber. Abandoning any pretentions of stealth, Stacia Kanic manoeuvred out from behind the rlorry and floored the accelerator.

The Focus was faster than the older Volvo. In under two minutes she was riding his bumper.

She could see his eyes in his rearview mirror.

He knew she was there.

It was time to take him down.

Stacia yanked the wheel hard and stood on the accelerator, her only thought to plant the Ford's front wing into the rear side of Khavin's trunk and force him into a spin.

The Russian anticipated the move, following her swerve. He kept his rear rbumper in line with the Ford's front.

They careened back and forth across the wide road, Stacia trying to force the Ford's hood ahead of the Volvo's rear tire.

He shut her down every time.

Suddenly he was pulling to the left, into a new lane that split from the road.

Khavin was taking an exit ramp she'd missed.

Hot on his tail, Stacia reached out to the SatNav and switched it on.

She didn't need it to negotiate motorways, but out here was unknown territory. She wanted a SatNav record of the dance he was leading her on.

Khavin didn't slow down as he powered up the off ramp. She matched him.

Two lanes of traffic, at least for now.

Khavin took full advantage of the width of the road to swerve around a truck heading in the same direction.

They surged through the crossroads, ignoring the give way sign.

Khavin braked so hard Stacia nearly crawled up his arse.

He yanked the wheel and turned right, surging out into the crossroads not caring what might be coming the other way.

She saw another Ford slam on its brakes and slew sideways as its driver struggled to avoid a collision.

Stacia followed the Russian, allowing her back wheels to drift as she tailed him under a flyover spray painted with not-so inventive graffiti. The Dover Road. She had no idea where the Russian was leading her.

After the bridge Khavin took an immediate left, following a loop around and doubling back on himself. It was a single two-way road, pinched very narrow by hedgerows and trees encroaching on the asphalt. Stacia had no choice but to ride his arse as Khavin took increasingly reckless risks, overtaking like he was playing an increasingly suicidal game of chicken.

Khavin swerved back into the left lane cutting up a small truck. The move left Stacia exposed in the right lane, facing down a panel van, horn blaring, only feet between them as she wrenched the wheel to the left, barely avoiding collisions both head on and sideswiped. Heart hammering, she mounted the grassy bank on the side of the road even as Khavin surged ahead. The traction-control shuddered as the rear wheels carved deep trenches into the grass. She wrestled the wheel, shifting into first gear. The wheels dug deeper into the grass bank but didn't slip, and with a full rotation of the steering wheel, Stacia was back in pursuit.

Both cars overshot a right turn – Stacia didn't have time to take in what the signposts were telling her. She was on a road to nowhere. The greenery on either side was broken up by high hedgerows.

She had one thing uppermost in her thoughts: the singular desire to bring Khavin in alive.

The SatNav announced Bonny Bush Hill, a relatively straight road blessed with precious few white-knuckle moments. Khavin overtook cars in their lane, forcing oncoming traffic to concede the road.

Another right turn neared, fast.

Another car came the other way.

Khavin didn't hesitate.

With the slightest flare of the brake lights, he cut across the other lane, hurtling into the side road with inches to spare from impact.

Stacia had no choice but to slam on her brakes. She couldn't risk mimicking the move for fear of killing herself and the other driver in the process.

The car hammered by in a blare of angry horns.

Stacia took a second longer, then turned the wheel and floored the accelerator, laying down twin black lines of rubber as her tires tried to do the impossible.

Khavin had three hundred yards on her, driving far too fast on what had narrowed into a single lane through a tiny village.

He was driving like a man who wanted to die.

Committed, she had no choice but to match his speed. She blew through a crossroads, praying no kids were going to step out, and pushed the Ford up to 65mph on a road that made 65 feel like 120mph. Occasional houses lined one side of the road. Anyone pulling out of their drive, or coming the other way, and they were dead. Or maybe she'd get lucky and they'd hit Khavin first.

She thought she'd lost him, then caught the flare of brake lights as he doubled down for a switchback in the road. She chased him onto an even narrower lane, hearing the rush of trailing branches scrape along the side of the Ford as she negotiated another bend.

Stone cottages disappeared in a blur of leaves.

She reached a dead end, two choices presenting themselves, left or right, no clue two which way the Russian had chosen.

Left or right? Left or right? She wound down the window, idling the engine, to listen and caught the distant sound of his engine. Right. She screeched off in pursuit, having lost more precious seconds.

Another narrow single lane country road. Straight at least. With the village behind her, the landscape gradually shifted into fields of wheat and barley. The SatNav told her she was on Covet Lane heading southwest.

She could go faster now.

But so could Khavin.

Covet Lane seemed to go on forever.

Khavin disappeared into darkness of the hedgerows in the distance. The trees stretched over the road to form tunnels of leaves.

She forced more out of the Ford, closing the gap as Khavin led her onto a rougher track that was barely a road. A strip of green ran down the in the middle where grass had reclaimed the land.

The road snaked in a series of s-bends and sudden turns.

Still Khavin ploughed on, no retreat, no surrender. It was almost admirable, even if it was suicidal.

The Volvo lurched as it hit a deep pothole, followed by another jolt as the back wheel followed the front.

She saw roots pushing up through the track and slowed to negotiate them.

There was no gap between the car and wild growth that marked the sides of the lane.

And then Khavin's luck ran out.

An oncoming panel van loomed out of a leafy tunnel into the light.

It had been invisible seconds before.

The Volvo slewed to a halt, kicking up mud.

She had to react fast not to rear end him.

Both cars stopped.

The lane was so narrow, thick hedgerow on either side, there was nowhere to go, and no way to force a path around the van.

The truck's air horn sounded, but Khavin couldn't reverse with her blocking him in.

He had the gun. She didn't.

Cornered, he was more than just dangerous. She'd already seen that first hand.

She opened her car door.

The truck's air horn sounded again.

Khavin shifted into reverse and floored it, hurtling backwards into the Ford's hood. The impact shivered through the Ford. Stacia grabbed for the door, wrenching the shift into reverse and put her foot down, trying to save herself from being bullied off the road.

Suddenly she was hurtling backwards, wrestling for control of her own vehicle.

The engine screamed as it begged for another gear.

She kept her foot down, putting a few feet between them.

Her eyes locked with Khavin's.

His face was a mask of concentration.

His stare burned into her with singular focus. He wasn't giving an inch.

She had no choice but to break eye contact, twisting round to watch the road as she reversed desperately away from him.

When she looked back less than half a minute later Khavin had gone.

It made no sense.

Cars didn't disappear.

She slammed on the brakes, shifted into first and surged forward again, looking for the Russian. As she came back around the corner, she saw Khavin. He was on the other side of the van, having realised there was a passing place at the cost of his wing mirror. She was stuck on the wrong side.

She couldn't follow him.

She had to reverse to the next possible passing place, losing precious minutes.

She checked the SatNav. All roads eventually led back to the main Dover road.

Fuck.

He'd played her.

She slammed her fist on the steering wheel.

She had no choice to head for the docks and pray to a god she didn't believe in that he'd get held up at customs while she chased her tail.

*

Konstantin Khavin pulled into a layby. The entrance of the docks was two hundred yards down the road. He saw a student waiting alone at the bus stop. He was maybe eighteen, and hauling a backpack twice as big and heavy as he was.

Konstantin got out and extended his hand to the kid, with the car keys hanging from his fingers.

"Hey kid," he said.

Seeing the big Russian walk towards him, the boy took his ear buds out and looked up at Konstantin with obvious worry.

"You know how to drive?"

He spread his hands. "I ain't got no money," he said. "I can barely afford the bus. Go rob someone else."

"I'm not robbing you, I asked you a question is all."

The boy stared at the keys with suspicion.

"Let me try a different one. How'd you like my car, my phone and a couple of hundred quid? You've just got to do me a favour."

He laughed. Now his expression was confusion. "I'm not sucking you off, old man."

"Again, you're not my type. There's a ferry ticket on the phone. What I want you to do is drive my car onto that ferry and take it to France. After that, you can do whatever you want. That's it."

"Is it stolen?"

"Do you care?"

"Not really."

Tentatively, the student reached out and took the keys, then held them at arm's length. Konstantin opened his wallet and unfolded a small wad of twenties counting them out into the kid's other hand.

He stuffed it in his pocket and then took Koni's phone.

"If you drop the phone before you get on the ferry, I'll know. Keep it on you until you drive onto the ferry. It's got the ticket on it. Code is 3-5-3-5-3-5. Stay in the car as long as possible. When you're in the channel, toss the phone over the side or keep it. It's a good phone. You can do what you want with the car and the money."

The student didn't say thanks.

He just got into the driver's seat, tossing his bag onto the passenger side.

Konstantin watched him close the door and turn over the engine.

Less than a minute later he drove away.

Koni watched him turn into the ferry dock.

Time to disappear.

FOURTEEN
LOSING CONTROL BY THE HOUR

Jude Lethe was sulking.

He knew it wasn't very mature.

He knew he should do better.

But the fact was he didn't want to. Plain and simple. He wanted to be a pain in Knight's arse. He wanted to make it as difficult as he possibly could. The Nest was his place, not Knight's. Nonesuch was his home. The Old Man was as close as he'd had to a functional relationship in his life.

So, fuck Knight and the horse he rode in on.

He didn't belong here.

Lethe was used to autonomy – or at least the illusion of it. The Old Man trusted him. He pretty much never came down here. Admittedly it wasn't exactly wheelchair friendly what with cables all over the floor and the racks of servers. He was used to playing pick-a-path through their maze-like arrangement.

What really fundamentally fucked him off was the fact Knight had ordered him to kill the '80s playlist.

The guy liked to work in silence.

That was Hannibal Lector creepy.

Lethe hated silence.

But none of that compared with the current rage festering inside Lethe.

The twins had made space for themselves on opposite sides of the room, and cleaned off desks he never used, connecting to DAGDA, the Nest's main computer system with their own laptops. He wanted to punch them square in the face, and he wasn't a violent guy. The intrusion was physical and virtual. It rattled him. This was his world. He didn't like sharing.

Abshir and Shamshi.

Twins. One male, one female, though looking at them it was obvious they shared the same genetic code, their features were so unerringly similar even through the veil of masculinity and femininity that they were essentially the same faces that looked back at him.

Shamshi was the woman. She was quiet and focussed. She had rectangles of computer screen afterglow reflected in her eyes. Her hair was scraped up away from her face so when she leaned forward over the keyboard her bangs didn't fall into her eyes. First impression, she was a yes woman, content to take the commands of Knight, no matter how banal, as the word of god. The few times they were forced to exchange actual words she was polite, aware they were invading his space. More often than not any need to actually talk was replaced by an instant message popping up on his screen. She didn't use emoticons which was a mark in her favour, at least.

Abshir, conversely, acted as though Lethe didn't exist. He questioned everything Knight asked him, pushing for a rationalization of why his way was best, but ultimately did what he was told to do. Sharp-witted and sharper-featured, the painfully thin Abshir was all angles and elbows as he attacked a keyboard, hammering the keys like he was losing a game of Whack-a-Mole.

Both twins were ferociously intelligent, that much was obvious, and so young they made Lethe feel ancient. But that was his world. The most dangerous black hats and white hats were barely out of their teens.

At least Knight was there to remind him his pension was a long way off yet.

The twins messaged each other constantly, the flurry of shared intel and ideas streaming between their terminals constantly. He needed to believe they weren't as good as he was – though whether that was frail ego or truth without a face-off they'd never know – but they good. And he could respect that. DAGDA was easily the most complex system either of them would have encountered, no matter how good they were, but they were adapting to its idiosyncrasies with impressive ease given it was a custom-built interface.

Not that he feared for his job.

He didn't need it.

He did what he did because he enjoyed it.

He could walk into any industry in the world, commanding top dollar.

It wasn't about that.

It was about this place. His home. Interfaces and GUIs didn't matter. It was his family they were not-so slowly trying to cut out of his life, and that wasn't happening. Supporting Orla, Koni, Frost and Noah in the field, being their eyes and ears, accessing crucial field intel in seconds and acting on it was more important than opening doors for them, both real or virtual.

And one truth he wasn't big on sharing just yet was the fact that two brains were not always better than one.

Lethe was at least a step and a half ahead.

As soon as the Old Man got wind of new management incoming, Lethe had invoked the partial lockdown initiative.

The protocol was intended for the worst-case scenario of Nonesuch being compromised with enemy combatants demanding control of DAGDA.

Lethe had developed a subnet within the system which would look and feel like it was the whole network to anyone coming into it who didn't know better, but it was basically a container where he could dump a user demanding access. A closed cage. From inside it would *appear* to have access to everything, internal and external, allowing full utilization of nearly all of DAGDA's abilities, from instantaneous backdoor access into every banking network on Earth, to hacking the Prime Minister's webcam on her family's iPad. It was all there to fuel the illusion that Lethe was cooperating.

But they weren't in control.

Through a series of failsafes Lethe could countermand or outright shut down anything they tried to do before they did it.

The twins were working away happily inside their cage.

He hadn't meddled with any of their shit yet.

Yet.

That word.

He couldn't remember who it was who had first told him it was the most powerful word in the English language—the Old Man probably—but they were right. It came freighted with the expectation that it was only a matter of time.

Lethe continued to follow his hunch, investigating the Oxford Street credit card attack from within the cage. He knew they were logging every keystroke, or thought they were, so he needed to keep the illusion up, but there were two root terminals open on his screen that were outside the cage, allowing access to the full system.

And that was where his real work was being done.

In one he ran an active chat with Noah via text message. He cleared every message as it came in in case of prying eyes. The Pope's assassin, the man who had replaced Alessio Bisch, was no longer in Rome, most likely en route to the UK. In the second terminal Lethe had sent a series of messages to Koni's phone. He hadn't had a reply from the Russian in too long. He tried not to worry, but it was hard not to.

Lethe used the reflection in one of the many screens to check on Knight. The Six man stared at something on Abshir's monitor.

"What am I looking at?" Knight asked.

"I'm running one of my own routines," Abshir replied in a thick Manchester accent.

"Yours? I coded that," Shamshi said, shaking her head.

"I wrote the base code," her brother argued.

"The fuck you did."

"I don't care who wrote it," Knight cut across them. "What does it do?"

"Okay, so Khavin is supposed to be on one of two ferries, that's the operating theory, right?"

"Right. One to Calais, the other to Dunkirk."

"And Kanic doesn't know which one he boarded?"

"Correct. She's only just arriving on site now."

"We know Khavin was driving a blue Volvo stolen from the scene of the crash he caused. This program is checking the social media posts of everyone in the vicinity of the nearest cell towers."

"Looking for the blue Volvo?"

"Yup. If any traveler caught it, even partially, in a photo or video on their mobile phone, it'll get flagged. I'll have access to all their images and with luck will be able to work out which boat the car is on."

"Right now I'm checking the security feeds at the boarding gates," Shamshi added. "I've got reports that our people stopped someone in a blue Volvo but it wasn't our guy."

"Bring up the guy's face."

"Give me a sec."

Shamshi flicked through the various cameras monitoring the vehicle deck of the Calais ferry. One of them was on the fritz.

"Faulty camera?"

"Impossible to tell."

Lethe said nothing. His subtle sabotage of the camera showing the Volvo was long gone from his screen. No matter how good the twins were, they weren't tracing the interference back to him.

He assumed Konstantin had already found alternative wheels and was long gone.

Jude didn't look for him.

Everything he'd set up relied upon the people in this room assuming the big Russian was heading for the continent.

A flashing window popped up on Jude's screen.

Ronan Frost's status had changed.

He was out of critical care and had been admitted to one of the wards.

Knight noticed the alert.

"What is that?"

"It's Frost. He's out of immediate danger. I'm going to go see him."

"I don't think so. I need you here."

"No, you don't. You've got Tweedle Not So Dum and Tweedle Maybe A Little Dumber here." Abshir and Shamshi looked up from their terminals and both flashed Jude identical mock grins. It was creepy.

Knight considered it.

"Nyrén is landing in two hours. She's going to need support. We're busy trying to find Khavin."

"I've managed to support all five operatives and kept a multiplayer game of Call of Duty going at the same time. I'm sure you'll be fine."

Knight's face remained blank, but it was obvious he was trying to master rising anger.

"Fine," he said at last.

"I'll take him some flowers and put your name on the card."

"You do that."

FIFTEEN
WEIRD SCIENCE

Orla's return to Ben Gurion airport was very different from the last time she was there.

Then she'd been met from her private plane by a Uzzi Sokol, who had ushered her through to the arrivals hall as though customs and security didn't exist. Sokol was dead now. She'd killed him. Just like she'd killed his boss, Gavrel Schnur, the erstwhile Mabus. Now she was coming for his boss, Solomon. The problem was both men had more mundane bosses, too: the IDF. Like every other security agency in the world, the Israeli Defence Force took a dim view of those who murdered their own.

Orla had fled immediately afterwards, not facing any of their many questions. No one in their right mind would come back to the scene of the crime so soon. And not on an El Al flight, but at least she hadn't walked through customs on her own passport, flagging every alert imaginable to every conceivable agency. With luck they wouldn't know she was here for a while. But the Israeli's were good when it came to this kind of stuff. It wouldn't be long before they realised she was here.

The flight had been surprisingly good, though after the Corpse Plane incidents few people were flying unless they absolutely had no alternative. Fliers stood out these days, even if the contagion had seemingly died out with no fresh cases being recorded since the initial first wave of deaths.

The arrival hall was unsurprisingly quiet with the airport operating at a fraction of its capacity. She had no checked baggage.

She planned to stay a couple of days. No more.

She made her way toward the bank of lockers in the east wing of the airport. She took a key that she hadn't used for a long time from her pocket and along with the memorized code, opened locker 136C.

A go-bag was stuffed inside.

She grabbed it and re-locked the door.

The taxi took her to the Best Western opposite the US Embassy.

It wasn't exactly The Ritz Carlton, but it was a regular low-key tourist hotel, and that was how she wanted to play it.

Informing the IDF that she was coming last time hadn't worked out too well.

This time she'd approach them, under an alias, when she was ready.

First, she wanted to do some reconnaissance.

She was careful.

She wore a headscarf, showing as little as possible of her face.

At the front desk she gave the same name as on her passport, Julia Lethe –wishful thinking on the part of Jude – and had gone straight up to her room. She politely refused any help with her bags.

Once in room she took the go bag to the bed and opened it.

Inside were all the things she hadn't wanted, or hadn't been able, to carry into the country: spare clothes, a burner phone, security cards to various institutions under assumed names, another passport under yet another name, and, most importantly, a gun.

It wasn't her preferred Sig Sauer P228, but she would never have got that through security.

The Jericho 941 was standard issue for Israeli security services and had been easy to obtain back when Orla lived in the city.

She'd set the bag up before she left the first time. Before the Toad. Before the Beast.

She popped a magazine – there were several in the bag – and sighted the Baby Eagle, refamiliarizing herself with its weight in her hand. It was a good gun. She could see why it was popular. The go bag also contained an underarm holster. When she changed into more practical clothes she slid the holster on under the cropped jacket.

She checked herself in the mirror, looking for lines. She didn't want the weapon being obviously visible. Satisfied, she removed the holster and weapon and put them in the hotel safe. For now she would have to leave it behind.

Orla took a moment to call up the map of central Tel Aviv and to orient herself. She traced out the route to the location of the lab Lethe had pegged as most likely responsible for making the weaponized virus. He'd checked all four lab locations known to be involved in production over a decade ago. Two had been shut down and refitted as apartment blocks and another was derelict. Only one lab appeared to be up and running, business as normal.

The location was about 2 miles away, near Olchilov Hospital.

Orla wasn't averse to walking, two miles was comfortable, but people on foot stood out. A car would be less conspicuous.

She opened the GetTaxi app and called a cab.

It dropped her on the corner of Weizmann and Berkowitz, just down from the hospital. It was near noon and Orla was hungry. The half-circle benches around the trees on the wide pedestrianized corner of the intersection were full of people feasting on food that might have been foul but smelled ridiculously delicious to her complaining stomach.

She saw a guy peel open a sabich in a pita and thought about offering him fifty bucks for it, it smelled that good.

Instead she headed out along Berkowitz, away from the hospital.

The exterior of the building was innocuous. A large sign labelled it the suitably vague: The Tel Aviv Research Trust. How many people who walked by this place every day had any idea what went on in there? Not many or they'd be running and screaming in panic.

Orla pressed a finger to the bud in her ear.

"You there, Jude?"

"In transit actually. Off to see Ronan. He's… absolutely fine. Nothing for you to worry about."

A thousand images of Ronan's potential fate flashed through Orla's mind, but she dismissed them. The Irishman could look after himself.

"Good. We all set up?"

"Yup, the divine Ms Lethe's appointment is in fifteen minutes."

"Thanks."

"No problem."

"Oh, and Jude."

"Si?"

"Tell Ronan he's an idiot for me."

Then she hung up. She stepped forward and opened the door to the building. She strode up to the reception desk like she owned the place. A young, pretty, corporate face looked up and smiled as she approached.

"Good morning," she said. "Do you have an appointment?"

"I'm here to see Dr Lavi. We're working on a project together."

"And your name?"

"Julia Lethe."

"Let me see if I have you here. Here we are. You can go on up to floor four. There's a waiting room there near the lift. You can't miss it. Someone will call you when he's ready."

"Thank you," Orla headed to the bank of elevators.

She had to pass through airport-like body scanners, but since she's left the Jericho back in the hotel that wasn't a problem.

Once inside the lift, she took a name badge and pinned it to her lapel, and a security badge, which she clipped to her belt, all courtesy of Jude.

On the fourth floor Orla bypassed the waiting room and walked purposefully along the corridor to the research labs.

A security guard stepped forward from his post, clearly not recognizing her.

"Pass please." His name tag identified him as Stefan. He was all attitude. Give a petty man a little authority and you created Cerberus. He towered over Orla, nearly twice as broad at the shoulders. Orla stopped, making a show of looking surprised but continuing to smile sweetly.

"Here you go," she said, unclipping the pass from her belt and handing it to him.

The one-headed dog on the door stared, trying to unmask the lie it represented by sheer force of will.

"I don't know you." It wasn't a question.

"And I don't know you. I work on the third floor. Dr Wang asked me to come collect some files from Dr Lavi."

"I'm going to call this in," he said. He reached for the walkie attached to his shoulder.

Orla sighed. "I was really hoping you weren't going to do that."

He reached for the call button on his radio and was doubled up in pain before his hand could close around it. The body blow had his lunch heaving up as he gagged. A second punch to the temple turned the lights out as he sprawled out on the luxury carpet.

He didn't move.

Orla stepped over him, ignoring the smell of vomit. She wasn't that hungry anymore.

A second guard stepped out from his office as Orla passed, investigating the noise.

He barely had time to register his fallen colleague before Orla put him down. She jumped up, placing a foot squarely on the door frame that she used to launch her elbow into his face. The guard's head slammed into the opposite side of the frame with so much force it splintered the wood.

An arc of blood sprayed across the wall behind him.

She stopped only long enough to relieve the guard of his Jericho sidearm.

There were no other guards in the office. That didn't mean there weren't more on the floor.

They hadn't had the chance to call in reinforcements. If Jude Lethe had done his job the cameras on this floor were sending false images to the front desk and the security offices.

There were no alarms.

Orla checked her borrowed gun to ensure it was loaded with a bullet in the chamber.

She held it out in front of her as she advanced down the corridor.

The sunny smile was gone.

Lavi's laboratory was the third door on the left according to the name plates.

Orla pushed the door open.

The room was surprisingly large and full of equipment.

In the near corner she saw a room within the room, a smaller windowed office. There was no sign of Lavi. Benches of equipment obscured her view of the main area. There were vats of chemicals stacked on shelves along the wall opposite the windows, as well as the bank of glass-fronted freezer cabinets at the back of the room. Did they contain the deadly pathogen used to infect Lael Kelly Logan and, subsequently, thousands of airline passengers?

Lethe had better be right about this place.

Already a person of interest in the deaths of two IDF agents, now she'd broken into a medical facility and assaulted two security guards. It didn't look good in terms of innocence.

"Doctor Lavi!" she called, ducking her head to the side to try to see around a bank of equipment. "Uriah Lavi?"

A toilet flushed from somewhere to her left, beyond the chemicals.

Orla advanced rapidly, gun level, eyes fixed on the source of the noise.

A small man emerged from a side room, wiping his hands on his trousers. He was middle-aged, balding and slightly overweight. He saw Orla and demanded, "Who the fuck are you?" in a surprisingly deep voice for such a small man. And then, "Oh God, she sent you! You've come to kill me! I've given you all I have. There isn't any more. Please. I've done everything you asked."

"Talk," Orla waved the Jericho in the direction of a nearby chair beside one of the workbenches. Lavi shuffled over to it, sinking down.

"Just get it over with. Kill me. I can't take any more of this."

"You engineered a virus to kill thousands of people."

He shook his head. "How was I supposed to know?"

Orla stared at him. "Because that was what you designed it to do."

"No. Not innocent people. It was a weapon of war. To be used on the Palestinians. You have to understand that…"

And there it was. The truth of the matter. When you rationalized things, decided the other side were terrorists, then all bets were off, never mind how many innocents were caught in the crossfire.

Orla felt rage rising inside. She had to bite down on it.

She wasn't here to preach to the brainwashed.

"Talk to me about the virus. Why did you kill the program originally?"

"You're not with her, are you?"

"Not with who?"

"Ezra."

"First name?"

"Leah, Leah Ezra. She took my last two vials."

"I thought everything was ordered destroyed."

"The military decided it was too risky to infect terrorists and send them back to their nests to infect others of their kind. As soon as they realised what we were doing to their released prisoners, they'd just send patient zero into a populated Israeli settlement and use the weapon on us. I was supposed to develop an antidote, but I could never get it to work. So I was ordered to destroy all of it."

"And Ezra knew you didn't follow orders?"

"She convinced me to modify one of the vials. That was tricky, since I haven't worked on it for years and I'm not exactly equipped to handle deadly pathogens anymore."

"Modify it how?"

"The virus was intended to live and spread for 24 hours after it is released to the air. In that time it can multiply and infect hundreds of people, but it isn't self-replicating. It won't simply keep on spreading. We didn't want an uncontrollable outbreak. There needed to be a limit to the death. International agencies monitor these lands, you understand?"

She did. All too well. Orla felt her finger tightening on the gun's trigger. Just a fraction. Not enough to fire the first round. But the temptation was there. She did not like this man. He was willing to slaughter of thousands of people like they weren't even human, and had the balls to worry how it would make his country look.

"The modification to one of the vials was intended to lengthen the contagion period?"

He nodded. "It wasn't easy, but it's amazing what you can achieve with a gun to your head. You have to believe me when I say this, but I *begged* her not to make me do it. Unleashed, a pathogen like this could wipe out life on this planet. I am not a monster. After I developed the pathogen I worked for years to develop an antidote. Or tried to. I do not want to be remembered for manufacturing an extinction event."

"You are a despicable human being, Doctor Lavi."

"I am a modern-day Oppenheimer," he said. "I saw what my creation was capable of, but I could not put it back in the box once I had set it free. All I wanted was peace. I have a family. I wanted nothing more than for them to be safe." He squinted at her name badge. "Do you have kids, Miss Lethe?"

"No."

"I was told that if I didn't modify the pathogen they would tie me to a chair in front of a sealed glass cage and make me watch the virus at work on my wife and children. What would you have done?"

She didn't even have to think about the answer. "I wouldn't have created the virus in the first place. I'm going to leave now. I assume your family is still alive?" He nodded. "Good, let's keep it that way." The threat was obvious, talk and they got hurt.

"I won't say anything," Lavi promised. "I want you to stop her. Ezra *used* the virus in an *airport*. I never thought she would actually use it."

"The virus attack, the sarin gas in Berlin, the poisoned water in Rome, they're all connected. The same madman is behind all of it. He calls himself Solomon. Leah Ezra is one of his pawns. So are you."

She saw the pain in his eyes as he raised his head to look at her.

"I am... a terrorist?"

Orla didn't answer.

She placed the gun on the desk in front of him and left him alone with his conscience.

Orla heard the single muted shot through the lift doors as she descended. She tapped the ear bud.

"Leah Ezra," she told Lethe. "Find her."

SIXTEEN
GIVE ME THE GOOD NEWS FIRST

Ronan Frost coughed again.

His lungs were shredded. Smoke damage. It felt like someone had gone at them with a cheese grater. Even so, he was done lying around in a hospital bed. He pulled the drip feed out of his arm and dragged himself out of bed.

Every movement hurt.

He gritted his teeth against a fresh wave of pain as he pushed his left hand down on the bedframe to climb out. His hand was bandaged. He saw a white grease leaking out beneath the bandages. Frost stood unsteadily. He was one lucky bastard. Thirty seconds longer getting up through that trap door and he'd be covered in second and third-degree burns. As it was he was bruised and battered, but otherwise relatively unscathed.

A nurse approached. He knew the look on her face. She was not a happy bunny.

"What do you think you're doing?"

"Leaving," Frost said. He sidestepped her.

"I don't think so."

"Where are my clothes?"

That raised a wry smile. "They were burned. We threw them out. So, unless you intend to walk through

Manchester city centre looking like you escaped the funny farm, you're not going anywhere."

Irrefutable logic.

Ronan couldn't track Solomon with his arse hanging out the back of a hospital gown.

"Well, then… I suppose I should thank you for your excellent care, and ask for directions to a department store." He burst into a fresh bout of coughing. "Obviously I'm fine now, as you can tell. I'll be checking myself out."

"I don't think so. Don't make me call security, Mister Frost."

"Honestly, I would love to stay. You seem like a delightful woman," Frost said, offering a charming smile, "But I really must be going."

He ducked and moved around her, seeing a guard at the end of the ward.

"Do as you're told, sir," the guard told him.

"I know you're just doing your job," more coughing. "But believe me when I say I really don't want to hurt you. If you would be so kind as to let me through."

"Sorry mate, nurse says you're not well enough to leave. And she's the boss. Why don't you just climb back into bed and watch the Test Match?"

Frost sighed. "I'm guessing you wouldn't fight a sick patient."

The guard answered with a sigh of his own. "This is silly. Get back into bed."

"You can't actually keep me in here, you know. It's against the law. So why don't you just run along and get me a wheelchair so you can escort me to the door?"

"You're a real pain in the arse, mate, you know that?"

"I have been told that before, yes."

He saw Jude Lethe behind the man. He walked up to the guard. "I've got him," he said. And to Frost. "Okay, you're discharged into my care, now don't be a dick about it. Thank everyone and we'll get you out of here."

"My stuff?"

Jude waved a plastic carrier bag at him. "Shall we go then?"

"Thank you, Dr Lethe," Frost muttered.

"You're welcome. Come on. There's a lot to catch you up on."

The pair shuffle-walked through the waiting area. Ronan stopped once to heave up a gut coughing, but eventually they made it to the outside world.

"Clothes?"

"In the car."

"You could have brought them inside."

"I figured people would be fed up of you by now."

Frost nodded.

He was looking for the Monster. It wasn't anywhere to be seen.

"I have to sort something for Orla, then we'll be on our way."

"Where's my bike?"

"Still at the warehouse. We'll pick it up on the way."

They reached the car.

"What?" he said, looking at the expression on Frost's face. The rest of the team were all flash and bang with their motors. He was much more practical.

"I like to travel inconspicuously," he said, patting the Honda's roof.

"You mean the Old Man won't let you drive any of his toys."

"This suits me just fine. Get in."

While he settled himself into the passenger seat, Lethe took a few minutes on his phone. Frost knew better than to ask what he was up to. There as a water bottle in the cupholder, so he helped himself.

"Orla got a name from the lab, Leah Ezra. Ezra stole the virus from the Israeli research facility and arranged for it to be smuggled it into England, where it was given to Lael Kelly Logan, who in turn took a trip to Heathrow and acted as patient zero."

Frost nodded, following the chain of custody.

"I'm sending Orla Ezra's last known location, in Jerusalem."

He drove slowly from the hospital tcar park out onto the main road.

The morning rush was over. They drove in a silence punctuated by Ronan's coughing fits.

"So, what have we got on Solomon? The bastard's playing us, his message to Noah makes that abundantly clear." Frost took another swig of water.

"I didn't want to say anything until I've confirmed it, but I'm working on the theory Solomon is in England."

Ronan swallowed his water with difficulty.

"That would make things easier."

"The assassin, came back here too. I told Koni. He's going after the guy. My thinking is he can lead you to the snake's head."

"You are a legend."

"I know."

"So, what makes you think Solomon's here?"

"Chatter. I think it was between the assassin and someone at Humanity Capital. It hinted strongly that it's Solomon who wants the assassin to come home so that they can work together to enter the next phase."

"Which doesn't sound good."

"It sounds fucking scary."

"And Koni's still here?"

"Yep. Stacia Kanic thinks he's on the Continent. I've been feeding clues to the cuckoos in my Nest to make sure it stays that way, too."

"Mendes and Knight?"

"In the dark."

"Keep it that way. I don't trust either of them."

"Me neither."

"So how do I find Solomon?"

Jude checked his mirrors. Frost had already done the same thing five times. He was so used to being followed.

"We've got a one shot deal. I know where one of his operatives is going to be, and when they're going to be there. Catch them. Do your thing. Make them talk."

"Go on."

"It's complicated, but I ran a pattern match over the victims of all the attacks so far, looking for any correlation between them. They look like random victims, people who happen to be in the wrong place at the wrong time. Thing is they're not."

"No?"

"Some aren't, anyway."

"They're targetted?"

"I think so. In each of the Berlin and Rome attacks, and on one of the corpse planes, I've identified three people who have something important in common."

"Which is?"

"They hold Keys to the Internet."

"They hold the what?"

"Keys. Look, I know you're a Luddite so I don't expect you to understand, but trust me. Basically we're talking about a bunch of people from all over the world who meet once every three months to jointly build a master key to the internet, which allows everyone to access sites by using a URL—"

"Like google.com?"

"—Exactly. It's like a big phone directory."

"Okay, but honestly, so what?"

"If the key doesn't get built the networks start to throw errors, people won't be able to access the sites they want to, and it doesn't take much for crooks to start redirecting users to their own sites. Set up a bunch of fake sites that mirror the banks' front pages, redirect domain names to point to them and you're looking at financial chaos. Bank details, the works, giving the thieves access to the real accounts. Just think about the scale of it. There's no way it's not related to the chip and pin attacks."

"The warehouse was a counterfeit operation. They had every currency imaginable in there. That's how the fire spread so quickly."

"Undermine virtual currency, undermine actual paper money. It makes sense. I'm telling you this is Solomon's endgame. I don't know exactly what Solomon intends to do with all of this, but it's too much of a coincidence that keyholders are dying in these attacks. There are only seven keyholders in the world. Seven. It's not like you are likely to bump into them in the street. Now two other keyholders in Europe have been murdered in the last week. With everything happening with the Pope and the Cardinals, nobody's seeing the big picture. But just because no one is reporting it doesn't change the fact that Solomon is taking out the keyholders with his mass murder attacks."

"You're going to lead me to the next victim, aren't you?"

"That's why I love you, Frosty. You're not an idiot. Ralph Henning. He lives in Brighton. He's Solomon's next victim. With the assassin already in the country we're up against a ticking clock."

"So, I find Henning, take out Solomon's assassin, break him, and find out all there is to know about his boss."

"Which may be nothing given the way terror cells work, but yeah, that's the theory. At the least, you need to get his tech. Mobile phone. Anything he might use to communication with Solomon. I'll find the connection from there."

"Leave it with me."

Lethe nodded. "I've sent you Henning's details. There's a recent photograph in there, too."

They drove in silence.

Eventually Frost asked, "So where will you go? Back to Nonesuch?"

"Christ no," Lethe said vehemently. "I don't want that prick Knight staring over my shoulder all the time. I'm heading into the thick of it. Oxford Street. That's where the chip and pin attack started. I'm hunting big game."

"And beating the Christmas rush."

SEVENTEEN
YOU MAKE MY DREAMS COME TRUE

"I'm terribly sorry to interrupt your day," Sir Charles said, turning his head so the young lady pushing his chair through the park could see his cheerful smile.

"It's no problem," Shamshi replied. "If I'm being honest it's rather nice to get out of that dungeon."

"Oh yes. It's… not my idea of home, but .Mr Lethe seems quite happy down there."

"Hence the tan," Shamshi chuckled at her own joke.

Sir Charles's smile was genuine.

It did feel good to be out in the open air. The company did not hurt, either. Shamshi was young, yes, but unlike Lethe seemed worldlier. Her vitality was refreshing. In many ways it reminded the old man of his younger days.

"Since Maxwell's passing, my goodness it feels like such a long time ago now, I have felt like a prisoner in my own home. I miss him. He was a good friend. But selfishly, I miss what his loss means for my life. I will miss my friend, and I will miss this, these walks. We spent a lot of time in this park."

She nodded. "I prefer to be outside. My brother thinks his love of man caves makes him a better hacker than I am. He's wrong. Look around you. If I bring my laptop here and sit under that tree over there," she pointed, "I can route through a 4G network, bounce the signal around the world, and enjoy the beautiful day doing whatever I want to do. Who's going to be stop me, even if they trace me here? A basement has one exit, nowhere to run when they come for you. I like to see them coming. I like to disappear in plain sight. I'll sacrifice some of the speed of a superfast connection for the freedom to live my life the way I want to."

"And a very refreshing attitude that is, my dear," Sir Charles said. He motioned toward a bench by the water, positioned next to an old tree that appeared to be growing upside down. "Over there I think."

Shamshi left him sitting there reading the morning newspaper.

A few minutes later, a dapper man joined him on the bench and offered a weary sigh as though the weight of the world weighed him down.

Quentin Carruthers took one of his customary sandwiches from the brown paper bag and tore off a small piece to throw to the ducks.

"Grace Weller's killer is dead," Sir Charles said, without any preamble or greeting.

"I know. Which is why I rescued your man from Berlin's clutches. This is not news, Charles."

"And I appreciate that."

"If you'll forgive the bluntness, things are not going so well for you, old boy."

"We've seen worse."

Quentin sucked in his breath as if to say, *I doubt that*. "To be brutally honest, I have never seen such a mess. The Pope and all the Cardinals in Rome are dead. On your watch. Your men were in the middle of it." He shook his head. "You are lucky I haven't sent your entire team to the Tower. You need to understand the reality of the situation. Being off the books, old boy, does not mean you are free from recriminations. I still have to answer to the powers that be for the atrocious mess you've made. And I am not happy."

"I have already been read the riot act by your flunky, Constance. What I want to know is where were your people? We fed you reliable intel. You left us swinging in the wind."

"Oh, no no no, you do not get to throw this back at me. You fucked up, Charles. After Berlin, I had to show real change or your operation would have been entirely shut down, the Directive revoked. And frankly that's what should have happened. They should draw a line under it. Call it a failed experiment. I've lost good people around this whole mess. But I stuck my neck out for you, Charles. Do you know what would have happened to your people if I hadn't? They would be at River House being debriefed for hours to determine the extent of their involvement. And their treachery."

"We were making progress."

"You humiliated me."

Discretion was always the better part of valour. Sir Charles kept his silence.

Quentin tossed a complete sandwich at one of the gathering ducks, hitting it on the side of its head. The bird unfurled its wings in a quack of outrage, but very quickly adjusted in an attempt to devour the sandwich despite its size.

"Look, I'm doing you a favour. It's over," he continued, seemingly oblivious to the duck's battle. "We both know it is. But I'm letting you go out on your own terms. That makes you lucky, because, roles reversed, I'm not sure you'd afford me the same honour. But listen to me when I say this, you don't have many friends left. Not in Six. Not out in the real world. There are people I can't protect you from, and they want you gone. Six have put people in place, orders are for your team to stand down. And you, old man, if you'll take my advice, it is time for you to retire."

"It doesn't have to be that way," Sir Charles said, knowing he was wasting his breath. "You have it in your power to stop that from happening."

"But, my dear boy I do not want to stop it from happening. I have had enough of the trouble you always bring to my door. The truth is I am just an old queen who should have given up this nonsense a long time ago. I am too old to fight my own battles, never mind yours. You're not the only relic here. There are people looking to claim my scalp. Factions. I am done. You are done. We are the past. That's the way it has to be."

Quentin Carruthers stood up. He made an exaggerated show of stretching his back, working a knot in the muscles at the base of his spine, and complaining about how much his bones ached.

"One last thing. Have you spoken to your boy, the Russian?"

"Should I have?"

"Yes. He has a piece of a puzzle. I think you'll find it most enlightening. I know you like a problem. Put the pieces together. Work out what they mean. There's a message to you in there."

"And you're not going to tell me?"

"Even this beautiful garden has ears, dear boy. So no."

And with that rather enigmatic farewell, he walked away. The Old Man wasn't fooled. The old queen's gait was as spry as ever. Sir Charles didn't trust him as far as he could throw him, but Quentin was right about one thing, he was too old for these games.

He shook his head and watched the determined duck trying to tackle the feast without its fellow birds getting their beaks on its prize.

He looked up to see Shamshi, listening to music beneath a weeping willow a hundred yards away. He raised his hand.

It was time to return to Nonesuch.

EIGHTEEN
DEATH ON TWO LEGS

Konstantin fished the key from his pocket and opened the apartment door.

The stolen Sig Sauer aimed the way – he wasn't stupid. No unnecessary risks.

The apartment belonged to the Old Man. When he bought it he'd paid a measly few thousand. Now it was comfortably worth north of two million. Location, location, location. Close to the Edgware Road Underground things didn't get more central.

It was ripe for developers and profit.

Konstantin was surprised the place hadn't been gutted and renovated. But no, it was the same place as Sir Charles had bought in the '60s, with nothing fancier than a lick of paint and new carpets. The building was well maintained, and the apartment itself was comfortingly bland, like a thousand other apartments across the streets of England. The safe house wasn't listed on any official paperwork. No one outside the team knew of its existence. They each had a key.

But that didn't mean Konstantin was going to take a chance.

He moved through the place room by room, making sure it was clear.

He moved quickly through the small entrance hall, advancing into the combined living room and kitchen area, gun steady in front of him, his eyes scanning the place for any trace of disturbance. Anything out of place. That meant the absence of the what should be there as much as the presence of what shouldn't.

The mug on the desk in the corner was a dead giveaway.

Steam still wreathed from the liquid.

He listened without moving.

Whoever it was, they had to still be there.

Assassins didn't make coffee.

Enemy agents didn't put their feet up and watch the cartoons.

"It's Konstantin," he said, loudly enough for his voice to carry through the apartment. He put his gun away and moved to the window, monitoring the street below. No suspicious cars or people on the street seven stories down.

"Oh, thank fuck it's you."

Konstantin saw Jude Lethe's reflection in the glass as he straightened up. Lethe carried a laptop in one hand and a gun in the other.

"Are you even trying, Lethe?" He shook his head. "Leaving a coffee mug out on the table? It's amateur hour."

Lethe put the laptop down beside to the mug. "Can I get you one?"

"No. I'm here for a shower, a change of clothes and to re-arm." He tossed the Sig Sauer onto the sofa. "I do not like this gun."

Jude stared at it for a moment. "What happened to yours?"

"One of Six's people have it. Kanic. I have hers."

Jude moved to the wall mounted TV and swung it out of the way. He pressed his palm to the wall behind, eliciting a soft click from a hidden panel. A second later, the entire wall section slid downwards to reveal a small but impressive arsenal.

"Help yourself,"

"You know why I'm here," the Russian said as he scanned the racks and found what he was looking for. He took the Glock 19 and loaded a magazine, then sighted it on an invisible target beyond the windows, feeling the familiar weight. "Why are *you* here?"

"Six's goons are running Nonesuch. The Old Man's given up the ghost. I tell you, he's moving about the place like a ghost. I think losing Max has hit him hard."

"Never underestimate the old bastard," the Russian said.

Lethe shrugged. "I want to believe you, mate. But," another shrug. "But even so, there's no way can I go back. I wouldn't be able to help you, for a start."

The Russian said nothing.

He helped himself to a couple of spare magazines, a couple of grenades and a silencer. He noticed the tranquilizer gun and a case of darts. "How effective are these?"

"They won't put a Rhino down, but don't use it on a kid or they won't wake up."

Konstantin holstered the dart gun and pocketed the case of darts.

Lethe sat at the desk with his laptop while the Russian replaced the panel and the TV, then joined him.

"The assassin is back in this country?"

"Yes. Noah believes he was smuggled out of Italy by the Israeli Embassy. We are working on the assumption he is being hidden in the London embassy.

You shouldn't have come back here. It's too risky. There are cameras are everywhere. They can find you."

"You can make me invisible."

Lethe shook his head, exasperated. "You people will be the death of me." Something on the screen caught his eye. "Orla's back online."

"Where is she?"

"Tel Aviv. She's tracking the woman behind the Corpse Planes. Leah Ezra."

The Russian nodded. "I'm going to bug out. You do your thing."

"Sure. Hey, just FYI, I found Kanic."

The Russian waited.

Lethe filled him in. "She's about to dock in Dunkirk."

"Then she is a fool. Lead her a merry dance, Lethe."

"That, my taciturn friend, would be my pleasure."

NINETEEN
VOICES CARRY

Noah was used to waiting.

The man had the patience of a sniper. That meant he was more than capable of sitting in a foxhole for twenty-four—even thirty-six—hours, not moving, just waiting for the shot. He didn't have a rifle this time. His Heckler and Koch USP 9mm was holstered at his side. He was dressed head-to-toe in black.

He hadn't planned on a stakeout.

His entire plan was considerably simpler than that: break a head or two if necessary, other than that, head down, wait, opportunity would arise. It always did.

One in the morning was approaching.

Any sounds from outside the building had long since faded.

This wasn't part of Rome's more excitable nightlife. No one would ever call The Holy See Party Central.

The Vatican Secret Archives weren't the most glamorous of hidden vaults. The floor was concrete, the ceilings low, the lighting basic, and currently switched off. It wasn't like they made it out to be in the movies. It reminded him more of an underground car park than a secret air-sealed lab.

Rows and rows of shelves with their contents protected by metal cages stretched out further than he could see in the gloom.

The ones he could see contained nothing more impressive or valuable than books, documents and binders.

Noah wasn't a great one for research, but he knew it had its place. There were plenty of people out there who would look at this stuff and think bucket list. There was material in the archive that no historian or scholar could see, though what shocking truth it could hold he could only imagine.

Neri smuggled him in during the shift change with the help of a friend of the Roman's, a cleaner in Saint Peter's Basilica.

Neri had called in more than one favour to get Noah here.

He needed to make it count.

The Italian had mumbled something about probably not being executed if he was caught. The word probably wasn't particularly reassuring. He had images of the Swiss Guard imprisoning him for life and arranging for his soul to fuck off to the Bad Place in the process, given their special connections. Not being caught felt like the best option.

The shadow in the gloom was almost imperceptible.

Noah came alive immediately.

He rose from his position and moved up after the shadow shape as it passed by.

His body protested at the sudden movement; it was a side-effect of too much crap in his system for too many years. It was only going to get worse, but he wasn't going to dwell on it. That shit was enough to drive you out of you mind if you let it get into your head.

Noah's gun was out and held ready as he followed the figure.

The shadow was hard to track, moving silently between the endless shelves, but Noah was good.

He concentrated with intense focus, maintaining line of sight on the intruder without giving his position away.

Noah moved like a ghost.

The intruder was good. Better than him. He moved fast, but with precision, knowing each twist and turn of the racks as well as if he walked them every day.

Noah battled his body's insistence it needed more air to compensate for the exertion. He forced his breathing to remain slow and steady in the deathly silence.

The shelves came to an end.

The intruder was hooded, he realised, catching a better glimpse in a flickering light as he stopped before the steel door set into the furthest wall.

Noah hung back, watching the darker darkness that betrayed his presence.

The intruder reached out to a panel beside the door and keyed in a code – the beep of each keypress echoed through the archive with electronic disregard for the silence.

Noah heard a series of locks disengage.

He ducked back as light flooded out from the chamber beyond as the vault door opened.

The door swung into the wall. The noise reverberated around the giant underground room, causing an echo to hum through the endless iron cages in answer.

The room beyond was well lit, enough to illuminate the reveal the face of the intruder, who Noah saw wasn't a he at all. The woman pulled back her hood as she crossed the threshold.

Before he could follow, the door automatically swung shut behind her, plunging Noah back into darkness. It took his eyes too long to adjust. It seemed even darker in here now.

He remained in place, allowing his breathing to regulate before he hurried to the door. The keypad was backlit so he could see the numbers, but no way of knowing what the code was. Neri had said this was all a closed system, which meant it was pointless calling in to Lethe.

Noah had patience to spare.

At some point, the thief was going to come back this way.

He melted back into the shadows, being careful to position himself beyond the reach of the light would that would spill out of the vault when she opened the door.

He didn't have to wait long.

Under five minutes.

The door swung open again, spilling light into the archive.

The woman clutched her prize in one hand.

He couldn't see what it was.

She closed the door and turned.

Her would need a few seconds to readjust to the darkness.

Now was his chance.

He launched himself from the shadows.

His gun stayed holstered – his belief was simple, you didn't draw unless you intended to kill, and he had no desire to kill her.

He needed to know who she was, who she worked for, and what she'd came here to steal. A why wouldn't hurt, either.

She recovered from the surprise of his attack far too quickly.

She crouched low, sweeping out a leg to take Noah's out from under him. He went down hard, slamming his shoulder into one of the racks. A shockwave of agony shivered through his bones. She was already off, moving even faster.

Noah pushed himself to his feet and set off after her.

The problem was he was chasing her through a maze that she knew the way through. He didn't. But he was one stubborn bastard.

He refused to fail again.

She was a lead.

A breadcrumb.

Where that trail led, to others or even Solomon himself, he didn't know. But maybe if he was lucky it would put him face to face with person who'd murdered the Cardinals and give him a shot at redemption.

He gritted his teeth and forced his legs to move. He didn't give a shit about noise or breathing now, he just wanted to catch her.

The thief ran on, just on the edge of his vision.

He couldn't let her extend her lead otherwise she'd melt into the darkness of the vault and he'd lose her for good.

One option was putting a bullet in the base of her spine.

That would slow her down, and maybe not kill her.

But in this light, at this speed, he was just as likely to hit her in the base of the skull as spine. He didn't want her bleeding out before she told him what he needed to know.

Which meant running.

But fuck, she was fast.

Noah wasn't exactly slow, but she moved like the wind.

What didn't make sense, and was struggling to register in his mind, was that despite the frantic nature of her escape, she still wasn't making any noise. You could only be so quiet, even with padded soles. If she got beyond his field of vision, he'd be deaf as well as blind.

Noah reached a crossroads.

He hesitated for a second, then cursed himself for losing that precious second.

He tore onwards, ignoring protests from his lungs and his legs.

The moment's pause was enough to allow her to slip away.

He ran on, heading in what he thought was the direction of the only exit.

A fist slammed into his jaw, coming out of the dark. It was like a hammer to the side of the face. His head snapped back. The impact shifted his momentum and sent him crashing into the nearest rack of caged shelves. He couldn't brace himself or cry out as he sprawled blindly across the floor, only instinct saving his head from splitting open on the concrete. His right arm took the brunt of the blow all along the forearm. He felt something happen inside that sent shockwaves of pain through him.

Something hit him. Hard.

He was so dazed he didn't see whatever it was.

A kick this time drove into his gut, leaving him gasping and doubled up in pain as he struggled to breath. Another kick lifted him bodily and slammed him back into the metal cage.

He caught the next kick as it looked to punt his face into tomorrow with both hands, then he twisted.

Hard. He wrenched down on the bones, torturing the ligaments.

She howled, but spun somehow, keeping her balance on her standing foot, but he wasn't about to let go.

Noah sent her hurtling into the cage opposite.

The woman crashed into the metal, her arms up to protect her face.

He was on his feet.

No thought of anything but putting her down now, he kicked out, connecting with the back of her knee as she tried to stand.

She went down hard but didn't stop fighting.

Her foot swept out again, but this time Noah was ready. He jumped the sweeping limb like a kid playing skip rope.

She was on her feet in an instant.

Noah found himself ducking and weaving to avoid a flurry of wickedly sharp punches and kicks. He wasn't elegant, but he was good at not getting hurt. He need her to tire. There was only so much a body could do before it weakened, even if you were strong. She was lean and fast, but she was already breathing hard. More blows rained down on him, but Noah wasn't giving ground now. He was beginning to enjoy himself.

She moved in too close.

It was her first mistake.

He might not have been as fast, but he was fast enough to grab onto her forearm, pulling her off balance as he stepped in. He twisted her arm savagely, forcing the woman to move with him or have her arm broken. When her back was to him Noah forced her arm up her spine.

She had an answer to that, too.

She walked up the wall of the cage, and once high enough she used his own force to fuel her flip as she went backwards over his head.

He tried to turn, but a boot struck him in the small of the back and slammed him into the wire mesh. He hit the cage and staggered back. She was on him instantly, raining punches into his face with blistering ferocity. Noah managed to block a few, but more connected. His face exploded in pain as his vision swim. He could hear the blood in his skull. With sheer brute force he managed to throw her off, ignoring every punch as she tried to unmake his face.

He spat blood, dropping into an atavistic crouch, his fists like clubs, ready to do pain.

She still held her prize. He didn't know how she'd managed to hold onto it in the fight. It was too misshapen to be a knife, but there was a wickedly sharp end aimed at his stomach. He had no intention of getting stabbed, even with some ancient relic retrieved from the Vatican's inner vaults. It didn't matter what killed you if you were dead.

He didn't waste time speculating.

She came at him again, but he quickly realised she had no intention of using the weapon, she was protecting it from him, as if afraid of damaging it.

He blocked a blow against his forearm and ducked low to avoid a roundhouse kick aimed at taking his head from his shoulders.

Roaring with exertion he powered forwards, crashing into her and slamming her to the ground. It wasn't elegant but it was effective. Brute force against style. He drove his elbow into her jaw. Her head cracked off the stone floor, but she still kicked out and clawed at his face until he put another blow into the centre of her face, rupturing her nose.

She stopped fighting back.

But Noah wasn't about to be fooled twice.

He held his position, watching her in case she wasn't out.

She didn't make any attempt to move.

Because of the darkness he couldn't tell if her eyes were open. He placed a finger against her neck to feel for a pulse. She was still alive. He released her and pushed himself away, still on the floor. With his back against the shelves he sat there gasping for breath. So many conflicting pain signals fired off in his brain.

He didn't think anything was broken, but he was going to be a mess of pain for days.

The lights flickered on.

The power came on in a cascade, starting from the direction of the exits and sweeping towards Noah like a tidal wave of dim illumination.

He did not want to get caught down here.

His plan had been to get the thief outside, but that had gone out of the window.

Noah pushed himself to his feet, ignoring the protests from his battered frame. He stooped again to grab the weapon from the woman's limp fingers and disappeared deeper into the vault.

Let the Swiss Guard find her, and hope they thought she was alone.

It wasn't much of a plan, but he was improvising.

He had no idea how many were down here or what had tipped them off. Sensors maybe? A silent alarm triggered when the vault was opened? Infrared cameras picking up their heat sources? Pure blind luck? A phone call from Neri…

He discounted the last. The Roman stood to gain nothing from betrayal. It was too easy to imagine enemies at every corner. Neri was one of the good guys.

They had found her.

Their voices carried. Noah heard them speaking in German to each other. The problem with his plan was obvious: their first questions all wondered who had beaten seven shades of shit out of her.

Meaning they knew someone else was down here.

Noah crept through a gap between shelves into the next aisle.

He worked his way towards the exit, willing his footsteps to be silent.

The lighting was deliberately kept low so as not to damage the fragile documents stored down here. It helped Noah. Shadows were plentiful. But all it took was one guard to walk across the aisle and look up and he was fucked. Nowhere to hide. Another gap between shelves allowed him to cut through to the next aisle.

He ducked into it just as a guard stepped into sight.

Noah froze, holding his breath as the man's torch beam roved across the aisle.

Satisfied, the guard moved on.

Releasing his breath, Noah crept back into the aisle and kept moving as fast as he dared.

He was nearly at the exit when two guards came into view.

Cursing his luck, he ducked down beside one of the wire cages. This one contained a chest which offered some cover, but barely enough to hide him.

Noah made himself as small as possible, relying upon the gloom to mask his bulk.

It took him a moment to realise the guards were dragging the woman between them. Her feet trailing on the ground as they carried her outside. He wasn't going to get to interrogate her now. He'd have to make do with the artifact she'd come here to steal and work back from that.

Noah gave the guards time to climb the stairs before he followed them out of the vault.

*

It took him more than an hour to escape the confines of Vatican City and make the rendezvous point with Neri. The late-night café on nearby Borgo Pio was empty save for the Roman who sat with his familiar coffee and licorice paper cigarillo burning away to itself in the ashtray beside him.

Neri regarded him with a mixture of sympathy and disdain.

"You look like shit, my friend," he said as Noah slumped down into the seat opposite him.

"I feel worse."

"I assume things got out of hand?"

"Well, I got the shit kicked out of me by a woman, so you could say that."

Neri waved to the lone server busily wiping down the counter. She nodded and moved to the espresso machine.

"The thief?"

"Yep. Didn't get a chance to question her. The guards dragged her off."

"What was she after?"

By way of an answer, Noah reached into his pocket and withdrew the artifact. Making sure the server was busy, he placed it on the table between them. In the low lighting of the café he could see it was a metal spearhead, worn and faded, chipped and cracked.

It seemed utterly unremarkable, like something an archeologist might get excited about before ending up in a museum for generations of bored schoolkids to peer at through glass on day trips.

Neri, on the other hand, reacted quite differently.

"Merda Santa!" he breathed, hurriedly grabbing the artifact and concealing it beneath the table. "I do not believe it. It cannot be."

"I assume it's more than a lump of metal then?"

"Signore Larkin, in one evening you have just become the most wanted man in Italy. More so than the man who murdered the Pope and all of the Cardinals. You have stolen the holiest of artefacts, the spear that bled Christ."

"The Spear of Destiny?" He shook his head. "Not possible. The Holy Lance is kept in Saint Peter's Basilica."

"A legend to throw would-be thieves off the scent. Look at the age. The design. The place it was stored. The fact that our thief went to the secret archive to get it, rather than the basilica."

Noah was trying to keep up. "Why steal this one? I mean even if it is the real one… Isn't the spear tip in Vienna more widely recognized? Steal that, people understand what has been stolen."

The server brought them both espressos.

Neri thanked her.

As soon as she had moved away he continued.

"I have no idea."

"What do we do? Take it back?"

"I don't know," admitted Neri. "We could return it to the Camerlengo, perhaps?"

"Or perhaps we should keep it until we find out who sent the thief and can know for sure they won't be back. We need to know what she intended to do with it. There's too much going on here, Neri. Dead Popes, the coins of Judas, the Spear of Destiny. None of it is random."

Neri took a sip of his coffee. "Whatever we do with it, one thing is for sure, keeping ahold of it is dangerous."

"I don't want to keep it. I just want to make sure I'm giving it back to the right person."

"I don't know. We need to get this back to the Vatican as soon as possible. And we need to make sure you are not implicated in the theft." Neri looked like Noah had just handed him a grenade with the pin removed. His eyes kept shifting downwards to where the spearhead lay.

TWENTY
ANTICHRIST SUPERSTAR

"There is no justice here. It is not fair, and it is not *right*. They pray whenever they want, we are not permitted."

The crowd murmured their agreement at this affront.

A few clapped and cheered.

They were easy words. They stirred the disgruntled.

"How many of you have spoken prayers into your phone or knelt in worship while pretending to tie a shoelace? I tell you now, hiding your faith, and the need to hide your faith because of bigots and fools emboldened by this normalized racism, is ridiculous! What are these people so afraid of? Am I different because of the colour of my skin? Does my God offend thee? We need to show them that we are unafraid, that they cannot intimidate us, and they need to be shown we have every right to pray at the Temple Mount. Individually we are vulnerable, we are likely to be dragged off and beaten by mobs or Waqf. But together, side by side, all of us walking to our place of prayer, they cannot touch us."

These words were met with more emboldened cheering.

A chant was taken up.

They called her name as they rose to their feet.

The woman at the dais waved a hand for silence.

The gathering of two-hundred or so, some visibly identifying as Jewish, others not, hung on her every word.

The hall behind the Jerusalem synagogue was only intended to seat one hundred or so. It was standing room only. Orla stood at the back, listening to Leah Ezra.

She was surprisingly young, perhaps still in her twenties though she had the kind of ageless face that could easily conceal an older woman. She wasn't tall, neither did she exude an aura of physical power, but there was something to her, a quality that was rare. Orla studied her. If this was the woman in possession of the mutated Heathrow virus, it was hard to fathom why she had chosen to preach in a tiny hall to a crowd about Jewish prayer rights at the Dome of the Rock. But people were deceptive. That much Orla knew first hand.

"Things are changing," she went on, the crowd with her. They adored this woman, that much was obvious. "More Jews visit the Temple Mount every year. That is a fact. All across the city the call to prayer before dawn is being curtailed. Believe me when I tell you it won't be long before we rid Jerusalem of the Arab menace altogether. This is our chance, my friends, this is when we need to stand up and make the world listen. Today."

More shouts and cheers.

Orla didn't join in.

"There will be risk, of course. The mobs will try to stop us. The police will look to intervene. The Waqf will not be gentle. But they cannot take all of us. By the time the sun sets tonight the shockwaves of our actions will ripple out across the world. Together we will take a

219

giant leap towards taking back what rightfully belongs to Israel!"

This final line was met with jubilation and fists in the air.

Orla knew fanaticism when she saw it.

It came draped in every faith and every flag, but it was always the same.

And she knew full well the dangers posed by organized protest in this city. The risk of escalating violence could result in thousands dead on both sides. But one thing was painfully clear, Leah Ezra didn't care. And neither did her faithful. They'd been spun a line, wound up so tightly they were ready to go off, no concern for their own safety or the safety of any others. There were no children at least.

"Between noon and one we will head for the Mughrabi Bridge. It is important we do not move in groups. Don't bring any religious artifacts and make sure you are dressed appropriately. We do not wish to bring unwanted attention to our movement, which means we must look like regular tourists. For those of you who are Jewish, that means not wearing anything or saying anything that identifies you as such.

"We enter separately.

"We do not acknowledge each other.

"If you have problems getting in, do not fight, just go home. That is just as important, as fighting risks undoing everything we have planned. Retreat is not surrender, it allows for the greater victory.

"The rest of us head for the Dome of the Rock, and we assemble there on the hour at two to pray.

"I encourage those of you who do not follow the Jewish faith to take a printed sheet at the end of this session and ask you to familiarize yourself with the words written on it. Do not bring the paper to the site. Don't make it obvious you intend to start praying. Don't all start at once. This is not a flash mob. It is not performance art. It is prayer. We need this to go as smoothly as possible, and without raising suspicions. It is only the beginning. We don't want the police or the Waqf or any mobs following us. We'll be watched, of course, but we are just tourists come to see the sights. They have no reason to stop us as we have not come to pray. We have no desire to cause trouble. Do you all understand?"

A cry of, "yes" went up.

Orla joined in.

She needed to be part of this protest.

There was more to this than making a statement about prayer rights.

The option to bring local law enforcement in was there, but there was no way of bringing them in without revealing the lethal nature of the pathogen the woman had stolen. Was Ezra intending to unleash the virus today? Was that the next inflicted pain of Solomon's promised forty days and forty nights?

Perhaps.

Or perhaps the woman really did care about this cause.

She needed to know a lot more about Leah Ezra and who, in turn, she worked for.

Orla had to wait in line for almost an hour before she could shake hands and speak personally with Ezra at the end of her sermon.

When she finally reached the front she introduced herself with her best Israeli accent.

"Tamar Mizrah." She shook Ezra's hand warmly. "I'm a new convert to your cause. The article you wrote about metal detectors at the gates to the Temple Mount – it resonated with me. I went back and read

221

more of your work," she said. "It's been enlightening."

"I'm glad to hear it," Ezra said with a practised smile. "I only wish I had a book for sale today. I feel like I should be signing something."

Orla made a show of laughing along at the woman's ice-breaker. It wasn't much of a joke, but it was practised, and it clearly wasn't the first time she'd said the same thing today.

"Will you be at the protest this afternoon?"

Orla nodded. "Wild horses couldn't drag me away. I myself have been thrown off the Temple Mount three times for praying at the Dome. It is ridiculous. We do no harm, we simply wish to commune with the Lord. They accuse us of intolerance, but isn't a ban on public prayer the most intolerant of actions?"

Ezra smiled warmly. "We are on the same page of the prayer book. I look forward to seeing you there."

"I was going to ask," Orla continued, delaying Ezra's obvious attempt to move the line along.

"Yes?"

"It's just that, well, I'm on my own and I don't have anyone to go with. I intended to just show up this afternoon, but I haven't done this kind of manifestation before… I was hoping to find a partner."

Leah Ezra smiled regretfully. "I'm sorry, I'd love to partner with you, but my face is known to the Waqf. I must walk alone. I am sure you understand. And, if I'm ejected, at least they will not throw you out with me. Believe me, going alone is for the best. You can follow me if you like, but you should keep your distance."

Orla nodded.

"See you there."

"I wouldn't miss it for the world."

TWENTY-ONE
THIS IS THE SEA

Brighton seafront was as rundown and windswept as ever.

Frost rode the Ducati Monster past the rapidly disappearing remains of the West Pier. He gazed out across the English Channel, watching crazy people brave the cold as they dipped in the sea. God love the Brits and their temporary insanity.

There were always a few willing to pretend they were on a beautiful sandy beach in the Caribbean.

Frost wasn't here to enjoy trudging his way across the pebbly shoreline while seagulls tried to crap in his chips.

He was here to save a life. That kind of mission brought clarity. He tried not to think about the likelihood that he was already too late.

He steered the Monster in between two parked cars, ignoring the fact it wasn't a designated parking space, killed the engine and dismounted.

He scanned the windows of the apartment building. The peeling paintwork on the façade exposed the damage caused by decades of coastal weather. The entranceway captured the typical faded regality of England with its once impressive columns looking like the were held up by the gum stuck to them.

Frost used one of the cracked call buttons at random.

A few seconds later an equally cracked voice burst over an ancient intercom, "Whatever it is you're selling, I don't want it."

Frost did his best to smooth the edges off his Irish accent, "It's Bill in 301. I forgot my keys, can you just buzz me in?"

There was a moment's pause followed by a buzz and the click of a lock disengaging. It never failed to amaze and depress him just how many people didn't know their neighbours. People lived in a world of isolation that only ever came together once every four years for the grand disappointment of the World Cup when everyone could smile and say, "Well, maybe next time."

Frost pushed open the door and ducked inside. He crossed the oversized hallway and climbed the staircase, taking care not rip the holes in the worn carpet as he did. Henning's apartment was on the fourth floor. Frost drew the Browning as he rounded the final landing. Staying close to the stairwell, he scanned the landing in front of him. Five doors surrounded the narrow space, two on each side and one dead ahead. Looking at the gold numbers, that was Henning's.

He tried the door.

Locked.

Maybe he wasn't too late?

Instead of ringing the bell, a couple of seconds with a bump key had the door open.

Frost crept inside.

The place reeked of stale cigarette smoke. It was painfully obvious it hadn't been cleaned in a long time.

Frost closed the door behind him and relocked it.

Alone with the stench the place reminded him of

being back in Dublin growing up, except back then you went inside to escape the clouds of cigarette smoke. Stacks of papers were everywhere. For a moment he stood by the door, perfectly still, listening for any signs of life within the apartment. You knew when there was life in a place. This one was empty. Even so, he raised his gun ready and moved deeper inside.

The kitchen was a disaster area. There were piles of plates and pans in and around the sink, and grease thick on every appliance as well as flecks up on the walls where it had splattered. The dishes had been there for more than a week, judging by the mold festering in them. Either Henning was a slob, dead somewhere else, or he'd run, abandoning the place.

The sound of a key turning in the lock discounted a couple of his options.

Maybe the guy had no problem living in squalour?

Ronan ducked back into the kitchen entrance, taking up position behind the dividing wall, ready to make a move as the newcomer came in.

Keys landed in a ceramic dish.

Someone let out a deep sigh.

Assassins didn't sigh.

Frost stepped out of the kitchen, Browning levelled on a wiry middle-aged man with John Lennon glasses and Boris Johnson hair. The man fell back in fear at the sight of the gun, face ashen. The photograph was good. This was the guy. "Ralph Henning?"

"Yes. Please don't kill me."

Frost jammed the Browning down the waistband of his trousers. "I'm not with the bad guys. They're behind me. I need to get you someplace safe. Right now."

"Why should I believe you?"

"You hold a key to the internet?"

Henning gave a nervous little laugh. "Well, that's a very fantastical way –"

"Yes or no."

"Yes."

"There were seven of you, right?"

"Were?"

"Two have been murdered in the past few days. You're next on their list."

If it were possible, Henning turned paler still.

A noise surprised both men, coming from the corridor outside.

It could be a neighbour, but Frost wasn't taking any chances.

He grabbed Henning and shoved him towards the kitchen, holding a finger to his lips as he drew the Browning again. He motioned with the weapon to keep down.

Henning obeyed without question.

Frost trained the Browning on the still closed door, ready to unload a full clip into it if he had to.

He waited.

He listened.

He suppressed the strong urge to cough.

A key scraped into the lock.

It turned.

The door pushed open.

Ronan glanced down at the dish beside the door.

In it sat a handful of loose change.

He'd been played.

He spun around as the assassin barrelled into him.

The Browning spun out of reach as the man's momentum took him down and sent him sprawling across the hall carpet. Glasses gone, the wiry assassin was on top of him, one hand gripping Frost's throat with vice-like strength, choking the air out of his lungs.

He gripped a knife in his free hand. Frost struggled to neutralize the knife's threat, needing both hands tight around the assassin's wrist to prevent it plunging into his face.

The real Ralph Henning stood in the doorway, caught in the horror of the scene playing out in his hallway.

"Ralph," Ronan gasped. "Run. Get the fuck out of here. And keep on running. Go!"

Henning snapped out of it.

He ran. He didn't care about his keys or anything else. He charged down the stairs. Frost could only hope there wasn't a second man down there waiting to clean up.

The assassin abandoned attempts to strangle the Irishman. He gripped the knife with both hands, trying to force the blade down into Frost's face. Frost struggled to match his strength. It was easier to push down with the leverage of bodyweight behind you than it was to push up and stave off the blade.

The two remained locked like that for what seemed an age, grunting and straining, sweat streaming from trembling muscles, the muscles burning from the desperate effort. And Frost was losing. Weight, momentum, leverage, even his reduced lung capacity made it harder for him, and he was tiring fast.

He couldn't win.

Not like this.

Not in a fair fight.

Frost stopped pushing back and instead directed all his strength to redirecting the blade, which arced down towards his face as he whipped his head sideways at the last moment.

The tip nicked his ear before it slammed into the wooden boards beneath the carpet. It jammed there for a precious second.

Off balance, the assassin failed to adjust quickly enough, giving Frost one shot to dislodge him. The Irishman bucked him. He rose to his feet, fast, even as the assassin scrambled to his. The other man came at him as Frost backed into the lounge, hurling himself into the attack. Frost rode with it, ducking under the first swing and trading proper teeth-slamming-back-into-jaws blows. He took punishment in returned, the assassin's fist crunching into his ribs, then an upper cut twisting him away. He nearly fell. The man came at Frost again, but this time he was ready. Using his momentum against him, Frost threw the assassin into the TV stand. The impact knocked over the flat screen, and as the man tried to save himself, Frost was on him again, gripping his shirt to heave and drop him crashing down through the glass table top.

Frost stood over him, gasping for breath.

He'd lost sight of the Browning.

The assassin struggled to stand, blood dripping from a jagged cut on the side of his face. His palms were slick with blood where he'd pressed them down into the shards of glass to help himself stand.

He still held the knife.

Frost had no extra breath for one liners.

He stood his ground and waited for the assassin to make his move.

He needed the man to make a mistake.

He didn't expect to get lucky.

The assassin had to know Henning was long gone. And now he knew he was a target, running.

Frost could see the calculations running behind the man's eyes.

He needed to finish this, fast, or he was toast.

Frost ran.

The assassin was a split second slower in reacting, and that bought the Irishman a precious second.

Frost tore through the open door, crossed the landing in three strides and threw himself down the stairs, taking them four and five steps at a time with no care for how he might land. It was all about speed. He needed to hit the street first. In here he was alone. Outside there were a lot of potential witnesses. And his backup weapon on the Monster.

Two floors from the door, he changed his mind.

Instead, where the stairs turned, he ducked the other way, flattening himself against a door, banking on it being marginally out of line of sight as his pursuer came charging down after him.

The assassin reached the landing seconds later, knife in hand.

He didn't stop.

He rushed down the next flight of stairs.

Frost launched himself from the doorway, using his weight and momentum to pitch the man down the stairs face first.

He barely managed to avoid going down after him.

The wiry assassin reached out, trying to brace for impact as he fell, hitting the wall at the base of the stairway as they turned back on themselves for the final descent.

The knife spun from his hand, clattering away down more steps.

Frost was already moving.

Three steps from the bottom he launched himself at his enemy, just as the man was beginning to stand. Frost's knee rammed brutally into the base of the man's spine, bending his back like a bow. The impact threw him forward, arms outstretched, as Frost came down on top of him. Still falling, Frost used his momentum to grab the assassin's head and with a single twist snap his neck even as he hit the floor.

Ronan landed awkwardly, stumbling several steps before the wall stopped him from going over.

Heaving air into his lungs, he leaned against the banister on the first floor.

The assassin wasn't getting up this time.

Frost checked him for ID, but there was nothing to identify him.

Frost wasn't sticking around. He heaved himself down to the last set of stairs and descended.

A man stood in his way.

For one heart-stopping moment, Frost assumed it was the second assassin come to finish the job.

The man held out his hands as though trying to catch Frost from falling and asked, "Are you okay, mate? What happened up there?"

"I'm fine. My friend fell. Call for an ambulance. I think he's…" He didn't say dead because a normal person wouldn't.

"God. Right. Yes. Sure," said the man, turning to go back to his apartment. The door still open. Frost watched him go inside, then disappeared out into the street.

Henning was nowhere to be seen.

He scanned the street in both directions for any sign of the intended victim.

Plenty of people. No Henning.

He needed to think.

The police would be here any minute. It was time to leave.

Frost mounted the Monster, put on his helmet and gunned the engine. He pushed the bike back into the roadway with his feet, and with a twist of his wrist launched into traffic.

He tore along the seafront, weaving between cars, bicycles and a couple of scooters as he put distance between himself and the dead man.

He didn't stop until he was on the outskirts of town, then he parked the Monster up and took off his helmet.

He was about to tap the earbud he always wore, but thought better of it at the last moment and instead used his mobile phone to call Lethe.

"Frosty?"

"Fuck, Jude, I don't know what you're playing at, but you sent me a picture of the assassin?"

"The assassin?"

"It was his picture, not Henning. You nearly got me fucking killed."

"Woah, slow the fuck down, Frosty. I sent you Henning's picture."

"Check your messages, Jude. You did not send me Ralph Henning's photo. I'm getting a little bit pissed off with nearly dying."

"No, no, no," Jude's voice said on the other end of the line. "That's not possible. This is not the picture I sent you."

"And yet it is."

"No, it isn't."

"The pictures don't lie."

"I don't know what happened. Maybe I did fuck up."

"You need to get your shit together, Jude, or one of is going to wind up dead. And that someone is me. Am I clear?"

"Yes."

"Good. Now find me the real fucking Henning. He ran out of there like his arse was on fire. I need to find him before anyone else does. Can you at least not fuck that up?"

"Listen to me, Ronan. I didn't fuck up. Someone is fucking around inside my system. They did that to you. I don't even have the assassin's picture on my phone. Someone switched it."

"I thought you had control of the tech?"

"Not the entire network. Somewhere between my phone and yours that picture got switched out."

"Is that even possible?"

"Anything's possible. Look. I'll track down Henning. But the chances are they'll know I'm doing it if they're looking for it. I'll call you back."

Frost killed the call.

This was bad.

Before he could begin to grasp how bad a voice asked directly into his ear, "Frost, where the hell are you?"

"Brighton. Now, if you don't mind telling me who the fuck I'm talking to?"

"Michael Knight. Your turn. What are you doing in Brighton?"

"My job."

"Well, that's over. I need you to come in. Now."

"No can do. There's an assassin's potential vic who needs saving and I'm the cavalry."

"You are no such thing."

"I think you'll find you are wrong, given I'm here with the wind in my hair and all that."

"No, Agent Frost. I am not wrong. You are to return to Nonesuch immediately. Do not pass go, do not collect two hundred pounds. Got it?"

The connection went dead before Frost could tell him to go fuck himself.

He kickstarted the Monster and headed back into traffic.

TWENTY-TWO
SWEET SANITY

Konstantin Khavin walked past the gates to Kensington Palace Gardens, his face turned away from the security guard and cameras at the gate house.

The gates were open and anyone was allowed through, but as he approached the Israeli Embassy he knew he'd fall under increasing scrutiny.

He wasn't about to get too close. Yet.

He made the man wearing the kippa. He sat reading under a tree in the gardens opposite the embassy. Ninety nine times out of a hundred he was as innocent as anyone else enjoying the grounds or shopping along the high street. This, the Russian was sure, was the hundredth.

He sat down next to the man.

"I have a gun," he said. "I don't want to hurt you, but I need information. Do you work at the embassy?"

The man lowered his book and stared straight ahead. "Yes, but I'm nobody. I have no access. I don't know anything. You are wasting your time."

"I am a desperate man. Do you understand what that means for you?" The other man nodded.

"There are security guards everywhere. If you hurt me, you won't get away."

"But what if I don't have a choice?"

233

"I don't want to get hurt."

"And I don't want to hurt you."

"What do you want?"

"Two men arrived at the embassy recently. They came in from Rome."

The man pretended to read his book. He turned the page.

"I can't tell you that."

"Listen to me carefully. I can kill you here and now without anyone noticing. I am not bragging, it is just a fact."

"They arrived two days ago. I don't know where they are now. The basement, maybe. That's where the safe room is."

"I need your ID card."

"That's a bad idea. If you try and enter you'll be shot on sight."

"I've had worse ideas and lived to tell the tale, believe me. You're going to stay here while I'm gone." It wasn't a question.

"Am I?"

"You are feeling sleepy."

"No, I'm not."

Konstantin delivered the sedative with a pinch to the neck. It was over as quickly as that.

"What did you just do to me?"

"You'll be fine. The needle's clean. It's just a mild sedative. You'll wake up with a bit of a headache, but no real damage done."

He was talking to himself. The man's head lolled back against the tree as his breathing changed. Konstantin waited for a moment to ensure he hadn't overdosed him, and then reached over and snagged his security card. He looked nothing like the embassy worker, but he wasn't about to let anyone close enough to see the photograph on the card so it didn't matter.

Konstantin walked away, passing through the trees, crossing the narrow roadway and along the long iron fence. Before he crossed onto embassy grounds he took out his mobile phone and dialled through to Lethe.

"I'm here."

"Cameras please."

"Working on it. I came up with a good distraction for you. I think you'll appreciate it. Give me a minute."

Konstantin took the tranquilizer gun from its holster and loaded a dart in the chamber.

Seconds later he was rewarded by a muffled explosion from somewhere inside the Embassy. He glanced over the fence to see smoke pouring from a basement window.

"Do I want to know?"

"Overloaded an electrical circuit. It's a big bang and a small fire. It should keep them occupied for a bit. Go do your thing."

Konstantin was already on the move.

One of the two guards at the gatehouse left his post, running towards the source of the smoke. His partner called for help on the radio, not watching the road. It was that easy. Konstantin walked up to him, and as the man moved to silence the interruption and wave him away, punched him out. One punch. Side of the face. The man went down like he'd been poleaxed. The Russian shot the embassy man in the chest with the tranquilizer dart.

The drug would only take a few seconds to disseminate through his system. The punch would make sure he didn't get up again before it took effect.

Konstantin moved on.

He reloaded the tranq gun with a fresh dart.

More guards were on the move. They only had eyes for the fire.

Smoke billowed out onto the driveway.

Konstantin was the only man walking away from it.

With a swipe of his stolen security pass, he was inside.

On the other side of the door the place was a furious tide of motion as embassy workers rushed towards the basement entrance, some carrying fire extinguishers, others following protocol and heading to the assembly point in the yard outside as the fire alarm cycled.

Konstantin had to move fast to beat the tide of workers going the other way.

He jumped over the security guard's desk. Sidestepping the metal detector, he took out the guard as she stood to block his way. The woman went down hard, cracking her head on the scanning screen as the conveyor belt rolled on x-raying abandoned bags and briefcases.

He darted her and loaded another as a burly guard ran at him, drawing his weapon as he shouted for Konstantin to drop his.

The Russian had already felled him before he could get off a single shot, the dart protruding from his throat like a feathered tongue.

Konstantin surged across the distance between them, grabbing the man and pulling him out of sight. He covered his mouth with a huge meaty hand so he couldn't scream until he stopped struggling.

Konstantin let him go and moved on.

He passed a staircase and kept going, covering the tranq gun as several doors to offices and function rooms opened and dozens of workers filed out, heading for the exits.

It was all about looking like he belonged, so occasionally he'd point the way and say, "Go, go."

He found the basement entrance, but before he could open it a guard threw open the door. Two armed men came through first, both carrying semi-automatics.

That changed things.

They weren't local security.

The uniforms weren't IDF, either. Konstantin didn't recognize them.

Konstantin stashed the dart gun, switching it for his Glock.

He had no qualms about ending their lives.

He held back for a moment, ducking out of sight.

He needed to get down there. That was where they had the assassin locked up, thinking he was nice and safe. Konstantin was going to enjoy rocking his world.

The armed men shepherded a herd of workers out of the way, then waved to someone back in the shadows through the doorway.

Konstantin gripped the Glock.

He recognized the man instantly.

Those features were burned into his brain.

The man who had pretended to be Bisch.

The Pope's killer.

Lethe had quite literally smoked him out. But before he could take the shot he saw a second, even bigger target following him.

Konstantin recognized Solomon from his videos of doom and prophecy.

Both of them in the same place, both a bullet away from their makers.

He could do it.

He could finish this right now.

It wasn't a hard shot. It depended upon how good the guards were, but he was good enough to put a bullet between both the assassin and Solomon's eyes before most men could react.

But then he'd be dead.

He held back. There would be a better opportunity, one he stood a hope in hell of surviving.

The would-be Messiah was on his emobile phone, talking to someone.

Issuing instructions.

"Your only concern is to thread the needle, understand? That is the extent of your role. Thread the needle." Solomon took the phone from his ear and addressed one of the guards. "Shut that damned thing off, I can't hear myself think." The guard nodded and moved away, speaking into his sleeve.

"We shouldn't stay here," the assassin said. "We are exposed. We need to get you to the safe room."

Solomon nodded and motioned for the remaining guard to lead them onwards.

He put the phone back to his ear.

"You let me worry about Bonn. It is all in hand. Herr Franks purchased the well and will attack tonight. I don't want to hear from you again until you have the gold."

Solomon killed the call.

The guard ushered the two men into an empty office and closed the door.

The alarm finally silenced.

They'd soon see just how safe their safe room really was, Konstantin thought, enjoying the practicality of killing the pair of them in the one room they stupidly thought would protect them from the Russian's revenge. They had fucked with his life so badly he couldn't go back to his own home. He wasn't the forgiving type.

Konstantin saw the second guard approaching his position. He stepped out and put a bullet in the man's head. Even with the suppressor on the shot was loud. So was the sound of the dead man falling.

There was still enough general chaos to mask it, though.

Konstantin moved to the door, going through it in his mind, burst in firing, take out the semi-automatics, don't give them a chance to return fire.

Konstantin rushed the door, driving his foot into the lock plate and splintering the wood around the hasp. The door slammed open. The first guard had no time to react before a bullet to his neck opened the artery. He went down, bullets raking up the wall as his nerves fired off the magazine in his death throes.

Konstantin stood still, an island of calm amid walls of blood.

Solomon and the assassin faced him.

There was nowhere they could hide.

Neither man betrayed any fear looking down the barrel of his gun. He could respect that. There was dignity in knowing you were dead and simply accepting it as your due.

He levelled the Glock on Solomon, squeezing the trigger as he put three in the man's chest and two in his head.

Solomon didn't fall.

The acoustics in the safe room were all wrong; even with the suppressor the sound was devastating. There was an echo to each shot. A ricochet.

He fired again.

This time the bullet appeared to hang in the air, caught.

It took Konstantin a second to notice the thin spiderweb of cracks that seemed to have formed in the air around the compressed bullet, and by the time he realised what he was seeing, his enemy man had stepped up to the bulletproof glass partition that sealed off the other side of the embassy's safe room. Smiling coldly at the Russian, Solomon made a gun out of his fingers and put them to his temple, the threat obvious as Konstantin stood there impotently.

The absolute contempt in Solomon's eyes burned into Konstantin.

Something snapped inside the Russian.

He threw himself at the glass, hammering the hilt of the Glock off the toughened plate relentlessly, over and over again. The spiderweb of cracks slowly spread, but the damage was superficial. They ran through some sort of protective film and didn't touch the core material at all. He could have hammered at it for an hour and it still wouldn't have shattered.

And Solomon knew that.

Konstantin needed to find another way into the safe room, but it was obvious there wasn't one. And he couldn't just stand there and wait for the glass barrier to come down. It was about the fine margin of seconds. He needed to get a message to Lethe and admit how close he'd been to ending it all here and now, and how badly he'd fucked up. They still had a chance, but every second he stood there staring at the two men was dead time, lost to them forever.

"You are a dead man," the assassin mouthed at him.

The Russian said nothing.

He didn't waste energy on idle threats.

He committed their faces to memory. Every crease, every line. Every mark made by life so brutally lived.

He would not forget.

Solomon had the brass balls to turn his back on the Russian and walk across the room to sit on the corner of the table and watch him, smirking, like he had all the time and patience in the world. It was enough to drive

Konstantin out of his mind. He raged inside, his grip on his temper barely in check. But he knew what the other man was doing. He was keeping him there. He was giving his own people a chance to come cut off his exits and turn this into the inevitable last stand.

The Russian wasn't dying like this, not with a sheet of bulletproof glass between him and these cowards.

He needed to get out of there.

He could hear more guards coming now the alarm had been silenced.

He couldn't go the way he came; not out the main door. They'd have the place on lock-down.

He needed an alternative. This was where Lethe normally came in, a friendly word in his ear saying this passageway, that stairwell, the other unarmed doorway. But he was on his own down here, blind.

He moved to the window. It was closed but unlocked. He pulled the window open, looked back over his shoulder at the watching Solomon, and jumped out onto a gravel verge beside the paved courtyard.

Every second was precious.

He needed to think.

And he needed to get the fuck out of there.

So close. Touching distance from both men.

No point crying about it.

He moved swiftly, leaving the courtyard via a narrow passageway of trees. It led him to a pathway running along the side of the building. He didn't look back once.

He could see the perimeter wall.

It was climbable.

He holstered the Glock as he ran.

He heard boots on the gravel behind him.

There was nobody between him and the wall.

He didn't slow down.

He hurled himself up and over the top, throwing his body into the bushes on the other side of the wall. He came down hard, shredding his hands on the thorny branches as he pushed himself back up to his feet and burst clear of the foliage.

He headed north, running hard.

And didn't stop running.

Something about Solomon's words stuck in his mind, like he was talking about two separate attacks. One was a heist. Thread the needle. Threadneedle. The centre of banking in London. Threadneedle Street. Money not mass murder. He could live with that. But Bonn? Solomon had described that as an attack. That was his word. And it would happen whether Solomon was alive or dead. Tonight. He reached for his phone to keep Lethe in the loop. He kept the message short and sweet: Attack planned in Bonn. A well. Franks in charge.

The phone rang in his hand a second later. The number was Lethe's, but it wasn't Jude who said his name.

The man on the other end of the line had a thick Mancunian accent.

Konstantin killed the connection.

The first nrubbish bin he passed, he tossed the phone inside.

Lethe's phone was being monitored. Someone from Six had intercepted the call.

He was alone now.

In the cold.

And there was no way he could go to Germany now. That left the second strike, whatever it was, unchallenged.

Threading the needle.

TWENTY-THREE
LIVING IN A BOX

Jude Lethe was frustrated.

His phone wasn't connecting. It had taken him a couple of minutes to work out that someone had put an intercept on it in the provider's database. It was either blocked or cloned. Whichever, it was a pain in the arse. He'd have to hack it back later, but what it meant was that right now he couldn't contact any of the team.

But he was prepared to put money on any call he made to Nonesuch going straight through to Knight, no problem.

They were fucking with him.

Never had he been so glad he'd sandboxed the twins in the Nest, only giving them limited access to DAGDA.

He looked at the text Koni had sent through. Franks in charge. An attack in Bonn. A well. It wasn't much. And it felt odd that Solomon would repeat what had already worked so well in Rome. Repetition actually tended to diminish the fear, normalizing the event. Hitting the water twice felt wrong. It didn't keep people guessing.

He had stuff he needed to do before he could think about that, and he was on a deadline. It wouldn't take long for someone to realise that the Scotland Yard credentials he'd forged were, well not to put to finer point on it, fake.

The manager of the clothes e shop stood behind Lethe, wringing his hands nervously as he watched him. Jude wasn't an expert in body language like the others, but even he could tell a man with something to hide. He assumed the manager was skimming the cash register. Not a sophisticated crime, but for a minimum wage slave it was better than going hungry as living costs spiralled through austerity. Lethe didn't care. He wasn't going to judge the man. The only thing he cared about was the chip-and-pin attack that happened here.

Randomly switching transactions around on the busiest shopping street in the country was designed to cause chaos, perhaps even incite violence.

Lethe was worried for two reasons.

One, the level of expertise involved in tampering with transactions at the point-of-sale level, regardless of the multiple retailers involved, the various methods of payment used and the supplier of the hardware and software that handled the transactions of each different shop. There was no reason to believe this couldn't easy transcend one street, spreading like a virus across all of London, and then moving out city by city. Chaos was the only word for it, and chaos was only the start.

The second was far more sinister.

What if it was all just a distraction? In this day and age so much of the world seemed to be a case of pointing one way, yelling look, over there, what in the world can that be, while in the other direction someone is fucking you. If the magician promised him there was nothing up his sleeves and wanted him looking there, then Lethe was just the kind of man to keep his eyes on anything but the magician's cuffs.

And when he went digging in the system kernel, he found exactly what he'd feared he would.

Malware planted by the attackers, which effectively allowed them access to critical systems in the entire company's operations.

Scrambling payment transactions was just the tip of the iceberg in terms of what they could do to retail companies. They could cut off payments to staff, redirect payments to untraceable offshore accounts, mess with supply chains to create shortages in shops and induce panic buying. Change it from fancy shoes to basic food staples. The possibilities were limitless with this kind of access.

And who was to say the plans stopped with retail?

What was next?

The credit card companies?

Airlines and air traffic control?

International banking systems?

The sophistication of this attack was breathtaking, and with limitless possibilities.

If Solomon was really behind this, he had it in his hands to cripple half the planet.

Lethe copied the malware code onto a thumb drive and stood up from the computer.

"Thank you," he told the shifty manager. "You've been incredibly helpful."

"Is that it then?"

"I've got what I need."

"Will you be coming back?"

"I don't think so."

"Do you know if the company will press charges?"

Jude frowned.

"I'll give you a grand right now if you destroy the evidence."

Lethe said nothing. It was what Koni would have done. Give the man enough rope to hang himself.

"Two grand."

"I have to go."

"Please. I'll give you five thousand pounds. It's all I've got."

Jude snapped closed his laptop and stowed it in his messenger bag. "What happens next is between you and your conscience," he said, leaving it at that.

The man nodded. "I'll quit. I'll go now."

"If you think that is the right thing to do," Lethe said.

He left the manager alone with his conscience.

The man wasn't part of the cyberattacks, and certainly hadn't planted the sophisticated malware in the kernel of the main network, so he was irrelevant.

Lethe desperately wanted to call up the Old Man and report in his findings, but that wasn't an option, even if Nonesuch was the only number he could connect with right now. He had never felt more isolated, which was ironic given that he was fighting his way through Oxford Street's hordes of shoppers.

The flat was empty.

He made himself a pot of coffee, fired up the laptop and got down to work.

His pathway to the Nest and the full power of DAGDA was still live, and as far as he could tell uncompromised – though it was too early to tip his hand. He took a second to scan through Abshir's keystroke logs. Surprise, surprise, the man had access to his mobile provider's phone logs, and he could see several unsuccessful attempts to listen in to his conversations. He shook his head. He'd expected more subtlety from the man, but when these had failed,

Abshir had used brute force to manually block Jude's access to all but one number.

It took him a matter of seconds to undo everything Abshir had done.

So much for being on the same side.

Lethe opened another sandbox on the Nest's servers and inserted the malware.

The sandbox was a quarantined area, controlled to allow the malware to do its thing without allowing it to spread beyond the boundaries of the sandbox. Sometimes you needed to study a virus to really understand it, like a rare animal in captivity.

The code didn't disappoint.

Lethe simulated a computer owned by the creators of the malware, trying to gain access. The code executed a clever reverse IP lookup to determine if it would allow the access, and rejected his poking and prodding. But in so doing, under observation, he was able to capture exactly which IPs *would* be allowed to access the malware infected system. It didn't take long from there to find the perpetrators.

They were based in London.

He reached for the phone but thought better of it.

He wasn't calling it in to Nonesuch. He could message the others, but they had enough to worry about. He had a gun. He had the location. These were coders, not assassins.

Before he shut down the laptop, he executed a search for a Franks with connections to Bonn, and turned up hundreds of thousands of hits on such a common name, but only one that fit the profile of a well-established businessman with the wherewithal to purchase a town's water supply.

Dieter Franks ran the Bessere Welt Company based in Hamburg, with satellite offices in Berlin, Cologne, Munich and Bonn.

It didn't take Lethe much in the way of digging to establish links with Humanity Capital, and the Deveres.

And there it was, on the website of General-Anzeiger: BSC had recently purchased a disused waste water well, used to dispose of contaminated water from the fracking process. Since Germany had put all fracking on indefinite hold, all of these facilities had ceased operation.

It made sense to sell the land.

Jude didn't have time to go down this particular rabbit hole, but it was all beginning to come together in his head. If Koni was right and an attack was coming, someone needed to look into it, though. Whatever Solomon had planned was almost certainly meant to kill thousands of people. That was the scale the man operated on with his forty days and forty nights of fear. They needed someone on the ground to investigate.

But who?

Noah was in Rome, making him the closest. But he had his hands full.

Konstantin and Frosty were up to their necks in the shit here.

Orla was half a world away chasing a deadly pathogen set to wipe them all out.

He wasn't about to fly to Germany himself, so that left just one option.

Lethe used his master-control override for the Nest and began planting leads in Abshir's alerts, playing Pied Piper. The breadcrumbs all pointed the same way; a Russian suspect in the assassination of the Pope heading to Bonn, according to intelligence reports gathered across continental Europe. In one he dangled a supposed meeting between Koni and a certain Herr Franks. No details. Too blatant with the breadcrumbs and they'd know they were being manipulated. Right now he needed Six to do their job, and more specifically their agent on the Continent currently charged with tracking down Konstantin Khavin to do hers.

It was time to see how good Stacia Kanic really was.

TWENTY-FOUR
SABBATH BLOODY SABBATH

The priest's corpse lay sprawled on the flagstones of Saint Peter's Square.

Blood pooled in the channels between the stones.

It ran in a crimson river away from the flesh, following the slight incline away from the basilica.

He clutched a weapon in his hand.

Noah recognized it as soon as he saw it.

He had handed that very same weapon to the Camerlengo that morning.

He hadn't wanted to.

He'd protested that it was the absolute wrong thing to do.

But this was Rome, and he'd bowed to Neri's wishes.

But it irked him that almost got himself killed keeping the Spear of Destiny out of the thief's hands only for it to end up in the same place ready to be stolen again. It was a weird kind of defeat and frankly Noah was fucked off with losing. But Neri was right, it belonged to them. It was up to them to protect it.

Not him.

He couldn't save the world.

Christ, he could barely save himself.

They hadn't told the Camerlengo *how* the ancient weapon come to be in their possession. Let the priests worry about that. He wasn't about to own up to having breached the vault last night. Neri concocted some half-arsed story about someone trying to sell the artefact in a Carabinieri sting. The Camerlengo clearly didn't believe what they were selling, but graciously accepted the priceless relic.

Noah took a risk.

He dropped a fake rumour, saying that the seller had tried to lie his way out of it, offering up some woman who had supposedly broken into the Vatican vaults with a partner who had escaped. It was close enough to the truth that it was an easy lie to sell. Noah asked if the Camerlengo knew where the thief was now, which earned a muttered line about her being outside of Roman jurisdiction. He didn't ask once about the so-called partner.

And now here they were, standing amid a crowd of tourists watching the dead priest through their camera phones. It wasn't random, however it might look. But how had it come to this, a corpse in Saint Peter's Square, with the most holy relic on the planet in his blood-soaked hand?

Neri talked in rapid-fire Italian with a bystander.

He broke off and returned to the body.

"Anything?" Noah asked.

"Lots of eye witnesses," Neri replied grimly. "This man had a video. The priest started shouting that the Messiah has returned in multiple languages. Then he cut himself open with the Spear of Destiny."

As suicides went, it made a statement.

It was up there with burning yourself alive in Trafalgar Square.

"Solomon," Noah said.

"If you say so, my friend."

"Do these people have any idea of the significance of the spear tip?"

"None. But this world is divided between here and out there," he waved a hand and Noah wondered what he meant. "People online are already claiming it is a conspiracy, and that the Spear of Destiny has been used to bleed the way for the antichrist. They claim it is an omen that more death is coming."

"Which it is," Noah said. "And whatever you think, I'm not keen on giving it to back to the Camerlengo if it means we're painting a target on his back."

As though summoned by the mention of his title, the Camerlengo came bustling down the steps of the basilica, flanked by a number of dignitaries, other priests and Swiss Guard. He ignored the corpse, bearing down on the police with a mixture of outrage and disgust on his face.

"What are you doing here?" he demanded of Neri.

"There's a body," Neri nodded toward the dead priest. "I am a cop. The two go hand in hand."

"You are on Vatican ground. You are not police here. You have no authority."

Noah was about to give the priest an earful, but Neri was more than capable of handling himself. "As you say," the Roman said, smoothly. "Think of it as civic duty. The last thing we need is somebody else being hurt or disturbing the crime scene."

"You need not have troubled yourself, officer. This is not a crime scene. It is a suicide."

"Did you see it happen?" Noah asked.

The Camerlengo ignored him.

One of the guards retrieved the spear tip from the dead man's hand.

He wasn't wearing gloves and took no care to protect the evidence. He just picked it up with his fingers and pocketed it.

"We will of course hand the scene over to you to do as you see fit."

"You have no choice in the matter, do not act like you are doing us some great service, Neri."

Noah had to ask, "What I don't get is how we gave you the Spear back a few hours ago and you assured us it would be returned to the sanctity of the vault. So how did this man get hold of it?"

"I gave the Holy Relic to Father Francesco to put back in the vault. It appears he had other plans for it."

And with that, the Camerlengo turned on his heel and headed back up the steps to the basilica, his priests following in his wake.

The Swiss Guard covered the body.

Neri and Noah walked away from the square.

The crowd showed no sign of dissipating.

"How can you let him talk to you like that?" Noah asked as they crossed the road. "I felt like breaking his nose and he wasn't even talking to me." He shook his head.

"This is just how it works, my friend. This is their turf. They do things their own way. We have no choice but to play their games. The Holy See is another country."

"It's another world, if you ask me."

"The rules are bigger than both of us."

"You believed him?"

Neri chuckled. "Of course not, I am not a fool. Every word out of that snake's mouth is a lie."

"So, what now?"

"Right now, I smoke," Neri said, taking a thin-skinned licorice cigarette from the silver case in his pocket and putting it between his lips.

"The Pope is dead. The Cardinals are dead. What happens now? Who's the boss?"

"The Camerlengo." Neri lit the cigarette and took a long drag.

"So, he's the Designated Survivor?"

"To an extent. There is no precedent for this. Popes have been murdered, but never have the Cardinals too. News channels have been discussing it every day since the conclave. Word is that the Camerlengo will become the next pope until all the Cardinals have been replaced and they can hold a new vote."

"That might be years."

"I believe so."

"Are you thinking what I'm thinking?"

"Noah, my friend, nobody is ever thinking what you are thinking."

Noah ignored the comment. "What if the Cardinals weren't murdered just to make a statement? What if it wasn't only an act of terror?"

"You are suggesting, what? That the Camerlengo is in league with your mysterious Solomon."

Noah didn't say anything.

"You think Solomon intends to control the Papacy?"

"All your gods are dead," Noah offered.

"I like you, Noah Larkin. Your imagination is rivalled only by your ability to piss people off."

"I am a man of many talents."

TWENTY-FIVE
THE SOUND OF SILENCE

Orla already knew this wasn't merely some form of peaceful protest, but all of her worst fears were confirmed when Leah Ezra passed through security before the bridge to Mughrabi Gate, the non-Muslim entrance to the Temple Mount.

There were no metal detectors, but Israeli police searched the bags of everyone who entered and confiscated anything that might resemble a Jewish religious relic or artifact, as well as turning away women who wore clothes they considered to be inappropriate.

She stood in line two people behind Ezra, patiently waiting for her turn. She watched the group leader. She recognized a lot of the faces from the meeting hall. None of the other protesters talked with each other. Orla was the only one even looking at Ezra.

The woman's backpack seemed light.

When the officer checking it opened it she saw him lift out a couple of books.

No bomb.

No virus.

Orla kept watching. Moments later, just as Ezra was about to take her bag and move away, the guard casually switched it for an identical one hidden beneath the table. This new bag was heavier and bulkier. It was a blink-and-you-miss-it move.

Nobody except Orla noticed.

She wished she had her gun with her, but there was no way she was getting it through the checkpoint.

Orla made it past security. Together with her fellow protestors, she began the walk across the long wooden bridge towards the gateway to the Temple Mount. Shielded from the harsh sun, it was still uncomfortably hot. She saw the crowds of people gathering at the Western Wall. She walked passed a number of riot shields stacked against one wall.

At the end of the bridge, the group passed through the Mughrabi Gate.

As instructed, the group split up and headed in different directions.

Some moved directly towards the Dome of the Rock.

Others headed for the Al-Aqsa Mosque.

Ezra set off in a direction between the two and of course, nobody followed her.

Orla glanced back toward the gate. She saw others she recognized from this morning's gathering, moving mainly in pairs now. They each followed different paths, as per instructions. In fact, Ezra's followers took their marching orders to extremes. Not once did Orla notice one of the faithful even glance in Ezra's direction.

Orla bucked the trend and followed Ezra's path, now with some distance between them. The glare on her sunglasses meant she could watch the other woman without anyone noticing.

Orla followed Ezra, keeping her distance.

She scoped out the area as she walked, pretending to take in the sights. It didn't take her long to identify the location of every Waqf guard on patrol, and extrapolate from that every potential mob of Muslim men keeping a watchful eye on the Jews passing by.

Leah Ezra paused at a stone pillar and glanced around to see who was watching her.

Their eyes met for a moment.

Orla removed her sunglasses temporarily, nodding just very slightly to acknowledge the leader of the group.

She walked on, passing Ezra, and resisted the temptation to look back.

She pretended to read an inscription carved into the wall.

Finally, she looked back.

Ezra had eased herself out of sight behind the pillar, all the while taking photos on her phone. The backpack was on the ground between her feet.

Orla moved quickly but casually, positioning herself so she could watch the woman.

Ezra took a thin glass tube from inside her jacket.

She reached down to her bag. It was hard to tell exactly what she was doing, as the contents of the bag were hidden from view, but she heard the faintest snap as the vial clicked into place in whatever was in there. A couple of seconds later, she took a second vial from her pocket and repeated the action.

Thinking on her feet, it was likely the vials contained the pathogen responsible for the corpse planes, and the bag contained a dispersal device.

Or a dirty bomb.

Either way, if she did what she intended it was going to get ugly.

Orla was willing to bet her life on it being a bomb, albeit a small one.

A high yield wasn't necessary. All that was needed was enough to spread the deadly payload a decent distance. The air would do the rest.

It was a smart move.

The alternative was Ezra smashing the vials herself to release the virus. The infection rate would be limited and the police would know immediately a potential contagion had been released. Ezra would seal her own fate, dying a slow painful death and the entire area would be quarantined while the pathogen was contained. Set off a bomb, that changed everything, even if it was no more sophisticated than a few fireworks. The immediate aftermath would be sheer confusion.

Some would die in the blast, but most would run, and running, take the infection with them.

Add to the hell of that, police and paramedics arriving on the scene to help would be infected, too.

And the site itself would remain a hot zone with nobody realizing it until people started dying all across the city.

By then, half of Jerusalem could be contaminated.

If they were looking at the mutated pathogen with no single-infection lifespan it could be far worse.

Orla had no idea how long the virus would remain infectious.

Weeks?

Detonating the bomb under the Dome wouldn't cause any significant damage to the structure itself, with the shape of the building serving to keep the virus contained for a considerable time, infecting anyone who ventured inside.

Plus, a bomb would kill Ezra instantly – which was a better way to martyr yourself than the virus.

Orla weighed her options.

No gun meant no showdown with Ezra, no one shot recovery of the pathogen. Hand-to-hand? If she ran at Ezra the Waqf would take her down before she got close.

Option three was to hang tight.

She had to force herself to stop staring at Ezra. She didn't want someone noticing her obsession. This wasn't like anywhere else in the world; someone would notice because they were always on the lookout for potential threats. All Orla could do was turn away and walk deliberately in the opposite direction, not looking back.

She glanced at her watch.

It had taken longer than she'd expected to clear security. The time set for them to gather drew near, meaning she was running out of time.

Two Waqf dressed in blue shirts and trousers rode past on a golf cart.

Orla ignored them. They did the same to her.

They stopped beside a man and woman further along the line. She couldn't see what it was about the couple that bothered the Jordanian men, but it was obvious they weren't happy. They argued for a couple of minutes. Orla kept her distance. She couldn't be sure, but she thought she'd seen one of them at the synagogue that morning.

Time to go.

She mounted the steps up to the platform where the Dome of the Rock towered over the countryside. It was truly a magnificent building. The two-tone walls, white on the lower half and blue on the upper were adorned with an intricate mosaic of green and yellow tiling and, running the circumference of the structure, scripture from the Koran. Above, one of the most recognizable cupolas in the world. The golden structure dazzled in the sunlight, reflecting the majesty of the heavens here on Earth.

It was every bit as breathtaking now as it had been the first time she had stood outside it, years ago. She had never stepped inside. It was forbidden for non-Muslims to enter. But Orla had no intention of obeying the laws if Ezra broke them first.

As she approached the entrance of the building, one of the Waqf stepped forward.

"Too many people at the Dome," he said, meaning non-Muslims.

She nodded.

From her vantage point she could see dozens of people standing and more walking around the building. She recognized almost every one of them as part of Ezra's demonstration. Ezra must have known so many people approaching the building at once would unnerve the Waqf.

Leah Ezra was on the platform now, approaching the Dome of the Rock. She paused once to take a photograph. Orla might even have believed the pretense. Her followers kept their distance. It was fascinating to watch her move; they parted around her like the Red Sea as she moved between them. It was anything but natural.

As the Waqf in front of Orla sidestepped to wave away an approaching couple, Orla ducked around him and fell into step a short distance behind Ezra.

At least a hundred of her followers had assembled.

Orla could sense the tension amid the Waqf.

They spoke into radios and struggled to convince people to keep their distance until the size of the crowd could be reduced. It was escalating too quickly for their comfort, but the last thing anyone wanted to do was defile such a holy place with weapons or threats of violence, no matter how implicit.

Ezra ignored them all and pressed on, only one target in mind.

Orla followed.

Something changed in the atmosphere around her. It took Orla a second to realise that the police were moving in. They weren't carrying their riot shields, but they were deep in conversation with the Waqf. The men studied the crowd. It was a powder keg.

Ezra stopped to take another photograph, this one close to the entrance.

She signalled the nearest small group of her followers and they began to chant, closing their eyes and lifting their arms in worship.

The effect was immediate.

Police descended.

They weren't gentle.

Two men were led away by their collars, kicking and fighting.

Another was beaten down and pushed face first into the ground, then dragged by the feet across the flagstones. He cried out in pain as his back was cut up by the rough terrain.

But there were too many people praying for the police to easily brush them aside. The Waqf waded in, backed by groups of Muslim men and women howling, "Allahu Akbar" at the devout deep in their prayers. It was exactly what Ezra must have hoped it would be. And more, as one of the men howling hurled a rock at one of worshipping women. The edge of the stone struck her in the head and she went down at the feet of her fellow praying protestors. The sounds of prayer rose defiantly. Another stone was thrown. And another.

The police ignored the man stoning the women and instead stepped up their attempts to drive Ezra's followers from the Dome.

Orla ducked as something whistled inches away from her head. Another rock. She hadn't opened her mouth to pray. Her only crime right now was being a woman on the Rock, which was crime enough for some.

She matched the woman's movements.

Ezra reached the entrance to the Dome.

She put a praying woman between her and the police, forcing the cops to deal with the woman first. She lost her balance and ended up on her knees.

Chaos erupted all around Orla, but she only had eyes for Leah Ezra.

The yelling and the stones was matched by the pushing and shoving of the protestors. The press of people, the rising stink of sweat and musk and the threat of violence heady within it provoked a flight response in Orla, but she fought it down. She could do this. There was no Toad here. No Beast. This was about more than just banishing those demons. More was at stake than that. It went beyond her.

She saw other protestors standing in astonishment, unsure of how to react as the barrage of abuse turned physical. They had come to pray, not fight. They were that naïve.

The truth they seemed ignorant to was that there were Muslim men and women in the crowd who had been paid by anti-Israeli groups to stir up hatred on the Temple Mount. This was always going to happen. But the anger and rage were palpable.

A surge of people pushed forward, breaking the police line.

They piled on top of the kneeling woman.

Her screams were desperate.

Ezra stepped across the threshold, entering the Dome.

Orla was torn between wanting to help the fallen woman, but if she didn't stop Ezra thousands could die. One woman's suffering to save the many. It wasn't a choice.

She followed Leah Ezra inside.

Inside the Dome of the Rock was serene – at least for now.

There were a few dozen people inside, most in silent prayer before the centrepiece of the building, the large outcrop of bedrock. The pilgrims believed that the rock was where the Prophet Mohammed ascended to heaven. There was a strange aura to it, something magnetic.

Orla stood behind Ezra, unnoticed.

For a moment the other woman paused, simply standing there, seeming to drink in the great stone around which the building had been constructed, and the stunning interior's reds and golds and greens – every surface, every inch covered with intricate designs, patterns and texts.

The constant drone of large fans mounted high on pillars topped with gold was all Orla heard for that brief moment as she stood quite still.

The first cries went up.

Ezra was already moving.

She pushed her way from the outer ring into the inner circle, walking across prayer mats and shoving kneeling and prone people aside.

Orla didn't hesitate. She ran after the woman, avoiding the clumsy attempt by one man to stop her. She couldn't be precious, couldn't be careful. She lashed out at the face of another man who tried to grab her arm, catching him in the forehead with her heel of her hand and sending him sprawling to the prayer mat.

She ducked under the swing of the next man, the confines of the Dome echoing with outrage, and came up hard with her elbow, ramming the point under his chin. His head snapped back with a sickening crunch. Blood exploded from the man's mouth as he went down.

The last sixty seconds had gone to shit. Spilling blood under the Dome was the last thing she needed. She was already up to her neck in it.

Ezra was doing the same, kicking and punching at everyone foolish enough to try and bring her down. She was as determined as Orla, and nearly as skilled. She fought her way to the wooden fence keeping them from the holy rock itself.

Ezra slung her backpack over the fence and then pulled herself up, feet kicking at the face of man as he tried to drag her back down.

More people swarmed into the Dome; Orla saw them in her peripheral vision.

She knew what she was about to do violated even more sacred laws than her presence or the spilled blood, but it was that or thousands of corpses on her hands.

Even if it meant she died here.

She didn't have a choice.

It was a path she'd chosen a long time ago.

A man stepped towards her, rage contorting his face. He looked to be possessed by all the demons and devils of his faith, so twisted were his features, so hate-filled his eyes. Orla rocked back on her heels and kicked out, her kick landing square in the centre of his chest.

As he fell back her other foot connected with his shoulder as she used him to brace herself and push off, the man staggering back as Orla vaulted over the fence.

She landed hard on the sacred rock on the other side.

Deafening screams of horror and outrage drowned out the whirr of the fans.

Leah Ezra stared at her. The bomb mechanism was out of the bag. Ezra primed the device, not taking her eyes from Orla.

Orla roared, rising. She threw herself at the other woman.

Ezra swung the bomb like a baseball bat, hitting Orla full in the face as she charged.

Orla didn't bother trying to duck it. She took the punishing blow and went down hard. She scrambled to the side as the first of the Waqf reached the fence. They weren't armed but, unlike their fellow Muslims who were here to pray, they had no compunctions about stepping upon the bedrock, or spilling blood in this place.

They climbed the fence.

They wouldn't reach Ezra in time.

It was up to her.

Her vision blurred, her head pounding with pain, Orla swept a leg out at Ezra, catching her in the back of her right knee. The nerves fired and Ezra collapsed. She fumbled the bomb as she went down.

Orla threw herself forward, eyes locked on the mechanism, and caught the bomb in one hand, inches above the sacred rock.

Ezra was already up and on the move.

She took down two Waqf as they tried to grab her, and scrambled over the fence. She fled the Dome.

Orla lay with her back to the rock, her arms wrapped around the terrible device and its deadly payload.

She was dimly aware of hands dragging her up, pulling at her, tearing at her clothes, handling her roughly, leaving bruises.

Still she kept hold of the bomb.

It was different this time.

They may tear her apart, but nobody else would die here on the Temple Mount today.

She had won.

But what price victory?

TWENTY-SIX
TAKE ME TO THE RIVER

If Stacia Kanic had wanted to carry out kill orders on Russian agents she would have stayed in Ukraine.

Khavin wasn't in Bonn.

She was good at finding people, and the big Russian wasn't here.

Knight didn't take the news well. He ranted about tearing the city apart to find the bastard. He insisted Khavin was here for a man Franks, a German-born business mogul heavily invested in energy.

The twins' intelligence had tracked him here, to a Portakabin on the outskirt of the city, in a muddy field near a fracking site. There were concrete barriers around the waste water well. She had no idea why she was here, or whether Khavin would be, but Knight was adamant.

She followed orders.

Stacia knocked on the door.

A voice invited her to enter.

Inside, two men stood talking by a whiteboard. She saw a decent sketch of layers of rock with a pipeline running down the middle.

"Can we help you?" A man in a suit asked. Balding, overweight and sweaty, he seemed irritated at the interruption. There were no smiles. His companion, dressed in jeans and wearing a hard hat, said nothing.

"Dieter Franks?" Stacia said.

"That's me," said the man in the suit.

"Excellent," Stacia held out her hand and Franks shook it tentatively, trying to read the situation. "My name is Stacia Kanic. I work for the European Water Safety Commission."

Franks rolled his eyes. "I'm fed up of talking to you people. Look, when I purchased this facility I cleared it with your office. I have the documentation. There's nothing to see here."

"Of course," Stacia said, improvising. "I've read the documents. Everything's in order. It's standard practice for the EU to send a representative to all new waste water facilities for inspection before they commence operation."

"This isn't a new facility," the man in jeans pointed out. "It was up and running until the government shut down fracking operations. Then the site was suspended."

"Absolutely, but you understand how it is, suits in my office consider the repurposing to be a new operation. It's just rubberstamping stuff, really. A couple questions and then I'll be on my way."

Franks sighed deeply. "Very well, Ms Kanic. Ask your questions."

"Has anyone from either German or Russian agencies visited the site recently? In particular, this man." She held up her phone, the image zoomed in on Konstantin Khavin's face.

"Never seen him in my life" Franks said, eyeing the image.

She nodded. "I have to ask, with fracking operations currently suspended in Germany pending further environmental assessment, why have you bought this waste water disposal facility?"

Franks sighed. "It's all in the documentation. Fracking isn't the only industry that produces waste water. We intend to service other industries in Germany, Belgium and The Netherlands."

"I see. And how much waste water do you plan to process?"

"No more than twenty-five thousand gallons a month. This will be a much smaller disposal operation than was required when fracking was permitted."

She nodded again, like it all made sense to her. "I think that's just about it. Thank you so much for your time."

"You are welcome, Ms Kanic."

She paused on the threshold, ready to head back outside, then turned to ask, "I assume it will be okay to call you if I have follow up questions?"

"Of course." Franks took a card from his breast pocket and handed it to her. "My direct line. Easier than trying to track me down through various office switchboards."

"Thank you. Good day."

Stacia let herself out of the makeshift office.

So Khavin hadn't been here, so either she was ahead of him, or Knight was wrong. She knew where her money was. She walked back to her rental car and gazed past the well to the queue of tankers parked in the mud. More were arriving, and site workers were talking with their drivers and allowing them access. Judging by their capacity there was at least twenty-five thousand gallons of water already on site, which meant Franks was lying. Why risk such an obviously disprovable lie?

She got in the car and dialled through to Knight.

"Have you found him?"

"Khavin isn't here," she told him. "I don't think he was ever here."

"The twins have photographs of him in Bonn and solid intel that he came out to talk to Franks."

"Something odd is going on here. Franks lied to my face when he had absolutely no need to. I read the documents Franks submitted. This operation isn't scheduled to start up for another two weeks, but there are already a bunch of tankers lining up with waste water."

"Not important, Kanic. This is about Khavin. I want you to return to Bonn. I'll have the twins scare up fresh leads. He's not getting away from us."

"Respectfully, Michael, what if Khavin wanted to talk to Franks because he believes something big is going down? What if this is connected to a planned attack here in Europe?"

"You are not there to save the world."

That was an odd thing to say. She didn't say anything in return.

The silence stretched a few more seconds before Michael Knight said, "Control has issued a kill order. You are to terminate Khavin. Understood?"

"Terminate?" The order didn't sit well with her. She wasn't an assassin any more. This wasn't how they operated.

"That's what I said."

"And Franks and the well?"

"Irrelevant. Return to Bonn and await further instructions."

"Very good."

She killed the connection.

She watched as Franks and his site foreman talked with the workers while they connected the first of the tankers up to the well.

Franks looked her way and offered a slight wave. She started the car and drove towards the perimeter. Instead of leaving, Stacia Kanic waited until the tankers were in between herself and the well, and then stopped the car again.

She didn't care what Knight said, something was off here, and if Khavin was involved she wanted to know what. A quick look couldn't hurt. She got out of the car and walked over to the nearest tanker.

A driver sat in the cab, reading a newspaper.

"Good afternoon," she said to him, in German.

He seemed surprised. He straightened in his seat and adjusted his collar as though wearing a tie.

"Can I help you?"

"Yes, please." Stacia held up her ID. "European Water Safety Commission. I need to take a sample of the water in your tank. Do you mind?"

"Need to clear that with the foreman."

"I already have."

"Then please, go ahead."

She walked around the side of the tanker and climbed the narrow metal ladder to the top. She kept low as she moved towards the hatch, not wanting Franks to make her as she unscrewed the access port and lifted the cap clear. She expected to be assailed by the rank odour of industrial runoff laden with chemicals and pollutants. Instead, she smelled brine. She dipped a finger into the water, brought it out and put it to her tongue. Salt water. Waste water from fracking could usually be expected to have a high salt content, but would have other astringent ingredients strong enough to burn her nose and throat.

Why bring seawater to a waste disposal well?

Why not dump it in the sea? The shoreline of The Netherlands wasn't so far away.

More to the point, who was disposing of seawater?

She climbed down the ladder to ground level and thanked the driver.

She got in her car and drove away, intending to return to Bonn as Knight had ordered. She needed to find Khavin, though she doubted very much he had ever been in Germany.

TWENTY-SEVEN
RUNNING ON EMPTY

The plan was to confront the Camerlengo and grill him on Noah's theory about his path to power.

It was up there with Stanley Kubrick's moon landing in terms of conspiracy theories, but after everything that had happened, Neri wasn't willing to rule anything out.

The idea that the Camerlengo of the Holy Roman Church could be even tangentially responsible for the deaths of the Cardinals was insane.

But Noah had been right about Abandonato, so maybe he was right to suspect the Camerlengo?

His head was spinning.

He sucked on the cigarillo, then tossed the butt away.

He hated this place.

Vatican City.

They found the holy man sitting cross-legged on the grass, to the side of Saint Peter's Basilica. He was surrounded by a couple of dozen young people, seemingly giving a sermon. Neri glanced at Noah, half expecting him to say something deliberately contentious in an attempt to force the holy man to bristle.

But Noah was fascinated by the group.

They were divided equally between men and women and represented all the major ethnic groups.

Their teacher was speaking slowly and clearly in English, suggesting they hailed from a multitude of nations.

They stared at the Camerlengo, eyes almost vacant as they hung on every word.

It was eerie.

"Pain is a price we must all pay to live in God's world and accept his grace," the holy man explained.

Nobody reacted.

They merely stared at him.

Neri had never seen anything like it outside of a cult.

Stranger still, not a single one of these youngsters had a smart phone in their hand.

One of them glanced toward Noah.

She was slightly older than the rest; mid-twenties perhaps? Caucasian, angular features, powerful but slender build, athletic. Maybe a runner or a swimmer? Her red hair was tied back in a ponytail. He realised he was profiling her. Of the gathering, she was the only one who wasn't under the Camerlengo's spell. Her eyes kept flicking towards Noah, almost in recognition.

Neri didn't recognize her, but that didn't mean Noah didn't. There seemed to be some sort of connection there.

It wasn't sexual attraction, the old cop realised. It was something else.

"For those we've lost, we shed a tear. Some of them were dear friends to many of you here. Know that their actions are rewarded in Heaven, and their sacrifices have brought glory to their memories."

One of the students started sobbing at this: a Japanese girl, with her hair in pigtails, wearing knee-length socks and a short schoolgirl skirt.

Now it was Neri's turn to feel a spark of recognition.

There was something familiar about her. Not her face – he hadn't seen her before – but seeing her dress and hair – the combination was hardly unique. Still, it itched at his mind.

Their selfless sacrifice.

What did that mean?

Whose sacrifice?

What was he referring to?

"We have to go," Noah said suddenly, tugging on Neri's arm.

"Something I should know?"

"Something's not right. I need to check something. It may be nothing, but I can't shake the feeling that someone just walked over my grave."

Neri didn't understand the phrase, but Noah's need to be anywhere but there was obvious.

The Camerlengo noticed them now, and a look of fury crossed his face as he recognized them.

They turned away, leaving him to tend to his flock.

*

"Her," Noah said simply, stabbing a finger at the screen.

Neri peered at the security footage of a young woman who sat down next to a backpacker on the station platform.

It wasn't the highest quality image, but the woman was dressed like a Japanese schoolgirl.

He watched again as the girl took out a thermos flask and, moments later, the backpacker beside her exhibited the first symptoms of poisoning. After that, everyone started dying. It was harrowing enough the first time he had seen it. Watching it again was ghoulish.

"The Japanese girl. She released the sarin gas at Berlin's Potsdamer Platz station."

"What is your point?"

"She reminds me of the girl at the *Kum ba yah* meeting."

"There are a million girls who dress that way. "

"And how many of those millions are being told their friend's sacrifice brings them glory from God?"

"Oh, Jesus. Sometimes following your train of thought is like chasing a goose with a fishing net."

Noah wasn't listening.

He had his phone out and was dialling a number.

Seconds later, a voice answered.

"Noah? I'm a little tied up right now."

"Two seconds is all I need. The gas attacks in Berlin. Have the suicide attackers been identified?"

"Sure. I can pull up names if you want."

"No. I'm looking for patterns."

"Well they were all young, between the ages of eighteen and twenty."

"Anything else?"

It sounded like Jude was checking something. "Hmmm. Let me see. No links in terms of nationality. Multiple countries of birth. All students, but no two attended the same institution in the same country."

"Backpackers?"

"Yep. The usual places. I see passport control logs them all over Europe. All the capitals. Paris, London, Madrid."

"Rome?"

"They don't check passports when you move around in Europe these days, only points of entry, so interrail can be a real pain in the arse to track. I'm using credit card transactions and emobile phone records. Okay, here we go. Yep, plenty of hits for Rome."

"How many?"

"All of them. I'm seeing cellular and credit card activity in Rome prior to Berlin. Just a few days before. Do I want to know why you're asking?"

"Where in Rome?"

"I can't be that specific. They moved all over."

"Try."

"Fucking hell, Noah, I have my own shit to deal with."

"I said try," and the way he said it silenced Lethe.

"Okay, no this is weird. All of their mobile signals converge in one area for days, in some cases weeks."

"Where?"

"Vatican City."

"Thanks."

"There's something else."

"Hit me."

"I've got this program I wrote. It searches pairs or groups of people for common online behaviour, like if they all bought underwear off Amazon, or if they all read the same news site."

"And?"

"They all have a forum in common."

"A forum?"

"A chatroom. It's on the dark web so they would need to have been invited. Activity suggests they used it to communicate for months. Law enforcement didn't find this stuff of course. Takes a special algorithm to make the connections."

"What were they talking about it?"

"Oh man… This shit is fucked up. It's all prophetic destiny. You should read some of this. God gave us this life to make an impact. We bring glory to his name

277

by our deeds, and our deeds should be bold and have great impact."

"How many people are we talking? Five? Fifty?"

"Could be hundreds."

"Any mention of Vatican City?"

"There's a user called GodsProphet who keeps inviting folks to come and meet likeminded individuals and learn more about God's plan, but doesn't mention a location. Most of the time I assume they're talking in private messages. Getting into those will take more digging."

Noah nodded. "So, he's brainwashing these kids for months online and then luring them to his cult?" It fit the pattern they'd seen out there on the grass, but that didn't mean Noah wasn't just constructing a bogeyman that made sense where there was no sense to be made.

"Possible."

"Get me everything you can on these kids. Not the ones we know were involved in the Berlin attacks. The others."

"Sure, I'll send them along. It'll take a while. I'm kinda between a rock and a hard place right now, but I've got your back."

"Good man."

"You're welcome. Now, listen –"

But Noah had already killed the call.

Neri stared. "So?"

"New wild and crazy theory for you," Noah said, putting his phone away. "Our friendly Camerlengo is recruiting willing victims for suicide attacks across Europe. He's indoctrinating them. Maybe he's a fucking hypnotist. I don't know. But vulnerable kids, lonely or just plain inquisitive kids get invites to his chatroom on the dark web and wind up in his cult."

"The Japanese school girl, I assume?"

Noah nodded.

Neri shook his head. "You have quite the imagination."

"Why do you find this so hard to believe? After what happened to the water in Rome, you still doubt that something like this could happen?"

"It's not that I disbelieve, my friend, it is that I need *evidence*. This is all speculation."

"Evidence is a luxury. Sometimes you have to go with your gut. The Camerlengo is up to no fucking good, Neri. And we're bringing him down."

"Even if what you say is true, you do understand that we cannot simply march into Vatican City and arrest him."

"I have no intention of arresting him."

"Do I want to know what you are going to do? Or will I have to arrest you?"

Noah shook his head. "I don't know. But we have to do *something*. You get that, don't you? Those kids we saw today, they're the next batch. He's grooming them. The difference is this time we're seeing the pattern before it turns deadly. Forty days and forty nights of fear. That's what Solomon promised. He isn't done making statements and causing terror, but for once we are ahead of him."

Neri shook his head. "You blame yourself for this… I understand that. But it is too much of a burden for one man to bear."

"That's why I've got you. So there's plenty of blame to go around." He smiled when he said it, but Neri could tell he was deadly serious.

Noah's phone buzzed. Then it buzzed again.

Lethe had sent a series of images.

Noah scrolled through them even as more arrived on his phone. He didn't recognize any of the first batch of faces, but stared at a picture of a Japanese teenager, smiling in a Facebook profile picture. He showed it to Neri.

"Recognize her?"

"Yes, okay. She was there today. This is a real connection. This is actual evidence. We can work with this."

"Too fucking right. If the last batch of suicide attackers attended the Camerlengo's Suicide School, it's a good bet that the next batch are being prepared for another attack."

Another image came through. This one Neri recognized as the young woman who had been so fascinated by Noah.

"Catalina Sosa. Originally from Argentina, she's been living in Vatican City for at least a year. Lethe says she's a forum administrator. That means neck deep in this. And that's why she knew me."

"God damn you all the way to hell, Noah, I am starting to believe you."

"About time."

Something about the woman, Sosa, had been bugging Noah. Finally, he placed her. It was a guess, but he knew he was right. "We've met before. In the vault. She's the thief." It was hard to explain how he knew, given he'd only ever seen the thief in the dark, but it was in how she'd held herself. Shape and size, athletic build. And she'd know the place inside out. It made sense, and explained her reaction to him, too. But why would the Camerlengo's right-hand woman try to steal a relic the holy man already had access to?

Neri interrupted his thoughts. "So, what do we do?"

"We find God."

"I'm not following," Neri admitted.

"We crash one of their gatherings."

TWENTY-EIGHT
THE CLOSEST THING TO HEAVEN

It was dark when Lethe pulled up beside the wrought iron gate. Like the wings of dying angel, one side of the hinges had broken where the rust had eaten through them leaving the gate itself hanging half open. He killed the Civic's engine, taking with it the lights.

He abandoned his car at the side of the road.

Side-stepping through the gate he walked down the driveway that led to the old house.

It was the polar opposite of Nonesuch. If the manor ever fell into this kind of disrepair the Old Man would have been cursing bloody murder even as he turned in his grave—meaning never in his lifetime, at least. Even in the semi-darkness there was no hiding the desolation. Even major repairs wouldn't save parts of the place. The roof on the east wing had collapsed, taking down part of the wall and leaving a few straight lines where windows had been. On the central and west wing, he saw lights burning inside. More broken windows and damaged brick walls.

Lethe kept to the shadows.

The shrubs and bushes provided ample cover, running wild.

The lights meant someone was in there. The fact they flickered erratically suggested candles, which meant no electricity, which was in keeping with the disrepair.

He half-expected to see a Most Haunted van parked up outside the orangery, promising ghost hunters instead of the terrorists he believed were inside.

It had taken more skill and persistence than he'd expected to pull off the reverse IP lookup, bouncing through three VPNs to mask their server as the signal went around the world and back to a service station on the northern leg of the M25.

A Little Chef restaurant and service centre was hardly a main terrorist hub.

He had poked around a bit, earning plenty of odd looks from the attendant, but had located a box jacked into the petrol station's LAN and power supply. It was essentially an LTE transmitter, like the ones phone companies used on cell towers. On top of a tall mast, that kind of transmitter could service mobile phones up to ten miles away. Down at ground level the range was significantly less, but with enough juice it could handle a couple of private connections up to maybe half a mile away.

Which meant scouring the countryside for possibilities.

He didn't fancy driving around playing Hide and Seek. Instead, he disconnected the power, leaving the cables loose so that it appeared as though someone had caught the cables accidentally, then got into his car to wait. It could easily take all night until someone needed to make a call and couldn't, but he wasn't going anywhere.

Five minutes later, Noah called.

He spent fifteen minutes searching for stuff about the Berlin gas attacks and the known suspect pool.

Cars came and went as he worked.

Lethe kept one eye on them, looking for anything out of the ordinary about their behaviour.

Thirty minutes later a car pulled up behind him.

Two men got out.

One headed for the little shop to distract the attendant, buying cigarettes and coffee, while the other crossed directly to the box he'd disconnected.

With them distracted, Lethe scrambled out of the Civic and put a small SatNav tracker under front right wheel arch. Done, he walked back to the small shop and loaded up on Kit Kats and Coke.

He stood behind the distraction guy as he paid for his cigarettes and coffee with his card and left.

On the forecourt outside he was joined by his companion. They crossed the dark lot to their car. A few seconds later they pulled out, leaving the service area.

Lethe took his time. He browsed the magazine rack before he went back to his car. If he'd had access to his full set-up it would have been easy enough to skim the name from the register's last transaction, but he was hamstrung out here on the run. He gave the men plenty of time to get to where they were going before he followed. It wasn't like they could lose him.

Ten minutes later he pulled up outside the gate to what could easily pass for the set of the latest Hammer Horror film.

Approaching the house, he muted his phone and took out his gun.

He still didn't feel comfortable carrying it, even after Peru, but Frost had spent some time teaching him how to shoot. And like the Irishman, he favoured the Browning 9mm. He didn't have Orla's accuracy, Konstantin's hand-to-hand bone-crushing effectiveness or Noah's raw brutality, but Frost had taught him how not to get himself killed. Theoretically. He'd learned the lessons of Peru the hard way. You didn't come out the other side of something like that without being changed. Even so, he preferred being behind a screen.

He passed by a couple of vehicles, one of which he recognized from the car park.

He crouched down behind the trunk of the sedan and pulled a bullet-proof vest over his head and put on infrared goggles.

Raising his head over the back of the car, Lethe surveyed the decaying building.

There were no heat signatures on the west side.

Towards the centre he saw two hot spots. Guards. Two wasn't so bad. Two he could handle. Maybe.

The bulk of the heat signatures were on the east side. He marked at least half a dozen individual hot spots in a single room. They were stunted, so he assumed the terrorists were deep in conversation around a table.

It would be good to know what they were talking about.

They hadn't secured the building. The front door was off its hinges, but there was no way to get past it without making a shit ton of noise. Instead, Lethe snuck in through a broken window on the west wing, intending to creep through the ruined interior.

He stayed low, moving slowly along the walls, watching constantly for movement. The first room was empty. No heat signatures immediately beyond it. He could hear vague sounds of conversation but no actual words.

He gravitated towards them.

Lethe put his back to the wall by the nearest door, remembering Frost's advice.

He saw a ripple of heat move beyond the doorway,

nearing. He didn't dare move. He didn't dare breathe. Not so much as a whisper of air could slip between his lips. The guard stopped, less than a yard from where he stood, the wall between them.

Lethe shrank back from the door, Browning aimed squarely at the centre of mass as the heat signature moved closer.

He tried to control the slight tremble in his arms.

This was cool.

He could do this.

Focus.

Stay calm.

Wait for the guy to come to him.

Pistol whip to the side of the head, brutal but better than the alternative.

He didn't want to shoot. There'd be no hiding then.

A flicker of movement caught his eye. He'd been so focussed on the man on the other side of the wall he'd missed the second heat signature. Stupid. The blaze of colour filled his eyes as the world exploded into agonizing brightness. He recoiled from the flare, even as it was thrown at him, losing the gun in his panic. A moment later, he felt himself lifted off the ground and slammed into the wall. The impact drove the held breath from his lungs.

The goggles were ripped from his eyes.

The sour stench of the man's breath was overwhelming.

"We've been expecting you, Mister Lethe."

Lethe felt a sharp pain in his neck, a stabbing sensation, and the world started to swim.

In that moment he lost…

*

... consciousness.

He woke in a cage.

Nothing metaphorical about this one. Metal bars, heavy padlock on the door, the works.

Lethe's face pressed up against the bars. He lay slumped in the corner. The cage was no more than six feet square. It stood in the centre of a dank room. He assumed he was still in the nightmare house.

Memories of those final seconds flooded back as he struggled to his feet.

They were expecting him?

Shit.

He needed to think.

Had they been watching the service station and made him?

Pulled his plates to get his name?

That didn't make sense.

He'd been careful.

A guard sat on the far side of the room, staring at a game on his mobile phone.

Lethe's own mobile, gun and infrared goggles lay on a table next to him. Meaning they didn't consider him a threat. Given he was in a cage, that was a reasonable working hypothesis.

"Excuse me?" He called.

No reaction.

He rattled the cage bars and tried again, louder this time.

"Fuck stain, I'm talking to you."

This got a reaction.

The guard looked up from his game. He didn't look best pleased at being summoned. To be honest, he looked at Lethe like a dog that had just taken a shit on his favourite rug.

"Water? Please?"

The man stalked across the room, coming too close.

"You want chocolate fucking biscuits, too?"

"The water's fine."

The guard pushed his face towards the bars.

The move was the first Frost had taught him.

The secret was in the speed of the attack, not the force. It didn't matter that the guy was fifty pounds heavier, and the difference in relative strength was irrelevant. Lethe's hand snaked out, grabbing the guy's wrist and yanking his arm into the cage. Then, before the guy could pull back, he twisted, hard, his back to the guard as he bent the man's arm back until the bone broke, using his entire bodyweight to pull down.

The sound of the man's screams was one of the most satisfying things he'd ever heard.

Almost as good as the unmistakable bone crack.

That had been sweet.

He didn't stop twisting, either, grinding the ends of the bone against each other until the guard blacked out from the pain, just as Frosty had promised.

The padlock key was on his belt.

It took less than fifteen seconds to get out of there, gather up his phone, gun and goggles and bug out.

Fuck the Intel, he just needed to get out of here.

He tried to think. What did he know? No windows meant this room was on the interior. He moved out. Through the door, closing it behind him. He was in a corridor. Choice of three doors. Browning levelled, he picked one, stayed low and left the area.

His phone buzzed.

He wasn't about to check it. Not until he was out of there.

It buzzed again.

It could wait.

He put the goggles on and scanned all around him for the tell-tale signs of life.

There were no heat traces, no ripples of movement, meaning he was alone.

He pushed them up onto the top of his head, preferring to see what was in front of him. The second door led to a bigger room. He felt the draught before he saw the broken window. There was a hole large enough for him to scramble out through. He pulled his shirt off and wrapped it around one of his hands, knocking out the rest of the glass, before he clambered through and dropped down into the bushes beside the house.

He waited, listening.

Nothing. Silence supreme.

He needed to get some distance between himself and the house.

The phone vibrated in his pocket again. Three in sharp succession. There was an undeniable urgency about it. He pulled the goggles down again, scanning the driveway and grounds beyond to be sure no one was lurking around out there, then pulled out his phone.

Orla.

The first read:

In jail, Jerusalem.

In deep shit.

Life threatening shit.

The second:

Need info on a Benny Ginzburg, IDF.

And the third:

Desperate.

He needed to fuck off and keep on fucking off until he'd fucked off so far out of there no fucker was going to see him for all the offs he'd fucked.

But he didn't.

Two seconds, he promised himself, remotely accessing DAGDA. The connection demanded his credentials. A couple of seconds later he'd got into Benny Ginzberg's file and sent the details on to Orla. He had no idea who Ginzberg was or why Orla needed the info. He could find that out later.

A breach alert went off.

His flesh went cold.

He realised what they'd done, even has he was kicked out of the Nest.

The bastards had installed a key logger remotely on his phone.

It had already recorded the password he'd entered and everything else he'd sent before that.

"Well fuck you very much." Ignoring the keylogger he tapped out a text to Orla telling her that a cuckoo had taken over the Nest and he was out.

He stopped a second before sending it.

The keylogger hadn't been on the phone before. He wasn't stupid. The phone was a burner. It hadn't been out of his possession since he'd sorted the handset and number. So, it had to have been installed while he was out cold in the cage.

And that meant they wanted him out, didn't it?

They wanted him to escape, recover the phone and access the network.

His heart stopped.

They knew his name.

They'd been expecting him.

It took him two seconds to see that the number associated with Orla's text wasn't hers. They'd switched out the number in his Contacts.

"Well double fuck you."

He had handed over the keys to the kingdom and locked himself out.

He selected the number of the fake text and dialled it.

"Abshir," came the response.

"Well played, you prick," Lethe said. "Fucking Six."

"They told me you'd be more of a challenge."

The line went dead.

Lethe selected Frost's number – double checking it hadn't been switched – but didn't get as far as dialling.

Three words. The voice gruff. The breath foul.

"On your feet."

He didn't repeat himself.

Lethe looked up into the muzzle of a Glock.

He did as he was told, trying to hold up his hands and stand at the same time.

They took the phone from him again.

He recognized the cigarette buyer from the service station.

A second man relieved him of the Browning and the goggles.

"My, my, my, haven't you been a naughty boy. Back to the cage for you."

TWENTY-NINE
HOME ON THE STRANGE

Ronan was in no mood for stupid questions.

There was no good reason he'd been called back to Nonesuch.

None.

The debrief was intended to waste his time.

"Mister Frost, I appreciate that you are eager to return to the field." Constance Mendes was the picture of patience as she sat across the table from the Irishman. He wasn't giving an inch, but if his intransigence rankled her, she didn't let it show. "The reality is you are going nowhere until you answer my questions, so we might as well get this over with. It would be better for both of us."

"We could have gone through this charade over the phone, but oh no, I've got to come in, and lose the best lead we've had. Forgive me if I'm just a little pissed."

Michael Knight sat on the corner of the Old Man's desk. Sir Charles was nowhere to be seen.

"Ah, but here's the thing, it's easier for you to lie on the phone, Frost, and frankly put, I don't trust you so I want to see your face when you try and lie," Knight said. If Mendes was the picture of serenity, Knight was jacked up on caffeine. He wrung his hands, offering weird facial ticks as he spoke, and seemed to be keeping himself perched on the edge f the desk through sheer force of will.

Frost wasn't feeling the love.

"Now, tell me, where is Khavin?" Knight demanded.

"Truthfully? No idea," Frost replied. It was the first honest answer he'd given them. The only thing he knew was that the Russian was still in the country, beyond that he could be anywhere.

"Unsurprisingly, we've not heard from Larkin or Nyrén, either," Mendes said. "Needless to say, that makes us a trifle concerned. This operation is sensitive to say the least."

"Like the song, that's just the way it is. We can go for days off the grid," Frost explained, like he was talking to a child. "Given the line of work, it ought to be obvious you're not always in the position to make calls home. We don't need babysitting. We're good at what we do."

"Well, you might not call home, but you call each other. We know Larkin has been in contact with Lethe," Knight cut in.

Mendes stared at him, like he'd shared too much.

"So?" Frost smiled. "Are we done here? Dressing down delivered? Can I get back to work?"

"Who is this man?" Knight took a photograph of a bloody corpse from a manila folder on the desk beside him.

Ronan moved over to him and took the photo, anger and frustration sinking like a stone in his heart.

"Ralph Henning," he said, identifying the dead man. "If the name isn't familiar to you, let me be more blunt. He's the man I was trying to protect before you called me in here for this shit show."

"We received the image quarter of an hour before you arrived," Knight said. "My next question is, who told you his life needed protecting?"

Ronan Frost returned to his chair.

"Lethe did. And the odds are he'd still be alive if you hadn't called me in."

"You didn't clear this with us," Mendes said.

"I tried, you called me off, that's a fact. You fucked up and now he's dead. I should have ignored you."

"Or briefed us properly on your situation. We could have sent backup. You aren't alone anymore. We have safe houses. We have agents equipped to deal with the threat."

"I briefed Knight properly. I explicitly told him there is a potential vic out there and I was the cavalry. He wanted me home. It's on your head. Knight fucked up. That's a fact. And now Henning is dead and we've lost our route to Solomon."

Mendes let out a sigh that conveyed disappointment. She walked over to Frost and sat in the chair opposite. She leaned forward and said, "We're on the same side here. You need to accept that. Knight, the twins, me, you. We all want the same thing: to put an end to the threat Solomon poses. We're here to keep people alive. I know you are upset, and I know you guys had a way of doing things here, but that needs to change. We need to be kept in the loop."

Frost wasn't listening to her salesman's patter. Something had been bothering him. Something Knight had said. They knew Noah and Lethe had been communicating. Then there was Mendes's reaction to his slip. They were being spied on. And that meant they'd cracked Jude's security protocols, giving them full access to the network. Nothing they said from here on out was private.

"Old habits are dying hard," he said, assuming that would satisfy her. "And since Henning's dead it's not like I need to return to Brighton now, I want to freshen up, shit, shower, shave, get some proper food from the kitchen, watch the world fall apart on the news."

"You do that," Mendes handed him the remote and left the room.

Knight followed her.

Alone in the Old Man's study, Frost allowed himself a wistful glance around the room. He missed the Old Man. It had been a few days since he'd shown his face. Frost assumed he was licking his wounds.

He turned his attention to the screen.

The bulletin was nearly done.

Frost red buttoned it, restarting the broadcast from the beginning.

The lead item grabbed his attention immediately.

An attempt in Jerusalem to bomb the Dome of the Rock.

He watched images of Orla being dragged away by police. Any fool knew Orla wasn't responsible, but reports marked her as the only agitator in custody. The bombing hadn't been successful, so she'd done her job.

She could handle herself. She was the last woman in the world who needed a white knight.

Next up was footage from Saint Peter's Square: a priest had committed suicide.

In the background of one shot, Frost noticed Noah.

There were precious few details, meaning the item was brief and focussed mainly on the investigations and periods of mourning after the death of the Pope, the Cardinals, and the aftermath of the terror attacks on Berlin and Rome. Of course, those reports were joined with stories of the corpse planes. It was a bad news week, he thought. So bad, that Henning's death didn't even register on the local news, neither did the warehouse fire at Canning Docks. Still, at least that meant his ugly mug wasn't pasted all across the evening news. He could live with that.

He felt like telling Mendes that if she was so worried about what the team was up to, she should just watch the news.

The final item caught his attention.

It was an advisory, telling commuters to steer clear of the area: Threadneedle Street was closed for road maintenance overnight.

He kept thinking about that long after the adverts began.

Threadneedle Street. Home of the Bank of England. And beneath it? A series of vaults containing a huge quantity of gold.

Something tweaked the edge of his memory: the discussion with Lethe following Solomon's message.

We live in a world that worships money and machines over people. The mark of the beast is not something we are born with, but a branding we willingly accept and carry in our wallets. It is the mark of greed and corruption. There is no place for the spiritual in our lives, only the fiscal, the financial. But what happens when we cannot trust our money?

Lethe talked about it like it was a war on Financial Institutions.

He didn't speak to Mendes or Knight before he left Nonesuch.

Whatever their motivations, the new management weren't on the same side as the five-strong team. So be it. They had survived before. They'd survive now. It would have been useful to have Lethe look into the street's closure, but with Henning dead, Lethe missing and no other leads to chase, this gave him something to do.

It was preferable to being in the same room as Michael Knight.

THIRTY
WELCOME TO THE JUNGLE

A basic grasp of Polish helped Konstantin.

He'd spent the last hour in the company of workers who had been standing around as evening became night, waiting for someone to give them instructions.

Threadneedle Street had been closed for nearly two hours now.

No one seemed to know what they were doing beyond digging up sections of the road to locate and repair a broken fibre optic cable.

They'd been told the road needed to be reopened at dawn. They were already behind the aggressive schedule.

"I vote we just start digging," Konstantin said, to much laughter.

"Maybe we'll strike gold!" another guy chimed in.

They weren't Solomon's people.

Police stood at either end of the street with their cruisers' lights flashing, turning away pedestrians who tried to walk this way. More officers stood outside the Bank of England. It was all very quiet, really. They took no notice of the workers, and while Konstantin was wearing a helmet and hi-vis jacket, they ignored him too.

He couldn't really blame them.

It's not like they expected the world's most wanted man, accused of the Pope's assassination, to be shooting the shit with a bunch of road workers in the middle of London.

Life was funny like that.

Konstantin heard it before anyone else.

The unmistakable whirr of approaching helicopters.

Two of them, both with twin-rotors.

He recognized the powerful engines, the immense reach of the blades slicing through the air.

He could feel the enormous downdraft from where he was.

He looked up.

Mi-26s. Two of them.

The largest and most powerful helicopters ever put into production.

Konstantin didn't need the visual confirmation. He recognized them from the engine sounds alone. He'd flown an Mi-26 back in Russia. Built by the Soviets in the 70s, these monster choppers were capable of lifting twenty metric tons of payload and were the largest helicopters ever to go beyond the prototype stage and see service.

Konstantin could see their lights now.

Solomon wasn't fucking about.

He returned his attention to the relatively serene street and its occupants: police and workers, trying to figure out how it was going to play out. Solomon, he assumed, wanted the gold held in vaults below the street. He'd expected a more conventional heist. Massive Soviet helicopters hadn't factored in to his assumptions.

More fool him.

Okay, so choppers to airlift the gold, but how did they expect to get it out of the vault?

The explosion was apocalyptic.

The tremor split the street down the middle, rupturing a gas line and sending jets of flame spewing into the sky.

The façade of the Bank collapsed in a river of rubble.

The windows of buildings on all sides exploded outward in a rain of lethal glass.

Police officers died immediately, their remains twisted by the flames and the incredible heat.

The workers stopped laughing. Some dropped to the ground in terror, others screamed and threw up their hands as though they could protect themselves from the incredible heat.

The fire lit up the sky, turning night to day for miles around.

The force of the blast sent burning vehicles twisting and spinning into shop fronts.

The inferno raged beneath the surface of London, spewing molten rock and shattered masonry like hot magma from an erupting volcano.

He had seen nothing like it. Not in any war zone. Not in any combat.

Konstantin Khavin kept his feet.

The big Russian shielded his eyes from the intense light.

His ears rang.

All around him people scrambled to get away from the devastation.

Konstantin started walking toward the centre of it.

He would have run, but the heat was still overwhelming.

He walked towards the giant crater in Threadneedle Street where the ruins of the Bank of England smoldered.

The choppers moved in lower.

Their massive rotors fanned the flames, whipping up the debris around him.

Konstantin took cover behind a burning car – so twisted by the blast it was impossible to tell the make or model.

He kept his distance as flames lashed out at him.

The tornado effect of the massive helicopters caused deadly vortices of fire to grow stronger and climb higher, burning bright against the night.

Lines dropped from the choppers, quickly followed by armed soldiers rappelling down them. They descended rapidly, dropping into the crater punched into London's skin. Konstantin realised that they were wearing protective clothing to shield them from the heat, meaning the could go deeper than he could. They had assault rifles slung over their shoulders. Next came the fire-resistant nets.

The big Russian risked breaking cover, approaching the crater's edge.

He peered in.

It was all but impossible to see through the smoke and flames. The heat made his skin feel like it was melting.

He could see the silhouettes of soldiers working.

They loaded bar after bar of gold into the nets.

Konstantin tried to climb down into the crater, but the heat drove him back.

All he could do was retreat back behind the burning car.

Two more soldiers descended to street level, their weapons ready.

They fired at anything they saw moving, including the wounded workers and the few policemen still alive, trying to crawl away from the flames. The crackle of gunfire was muted by Konstantin's temporary deafness and the persistent drumming of the giant helicopter rotors, but that didn't make the bullets any less lethal.

More victims of Solomon's reign of terror dropped to the shattered street, torn apart by the bullets.

He had to stop them.

Somehow.

He wasn't here to cower behind a car.

Konstantin's gun was in his hand.

He stepped out from behind the twisted wreckage and started firing.

One head exploded, one jaw mashed to blood and meat, as both soldiers died before they could fire another shot.

Konstantin felt no satisfaction in the killing.

The heat was too intense to linger. He needed to move. He thought about unloading everything he had into the hole, but the chances of hitting anyone was slim. He wasn't about to waste bullets. He retreated behind the wreck again. Second by second his hearing was adjusting, filtering the screams of the explosion and the mad tinnitus of everything that followed into more recognizable sounds. Sirens roared from every direction, audible over the *whomp* of the chopper's rotors, and the fires raging around him. He could hear the dying too, some burning others in agony from bullet wounds. The sounds of their pain didn't differentiate. They were just as dead, either way.

The chopper lifted away, pulling the net from the crater, laden with gold. The metal shimmered and danced in the firelight. Helplessly, Konstantin watched it go, soaring into the air, the enormous whine of the chopper's engines dragging the spoils of the heist higher.

He changed his mind about wasting bullets and emptied his magazine into the massive helicopter impotently.

This was on him.

These people were dead because he had underestimated Solomon's propensity for evil.

He had to put it right.

The second chopper descended as the first skimmed the high rises of London and disappeared into the darkness.

Another empty net lowered into the crater.

Sweat poured from him, running down his spine and stinging his eyes.

A fresh wave of police—the Armed Response Unit -- rushed into the street, followed by an army of paramedics.

Konstantin watched as more of Solomon's soldiers descended, their rifles firing on the newcomers indiscriminately.

Some of the ARU managed to take cover, others weren't so lucky.

A chunk of masonry gave up its attempt to cling to the building opposite the bank and crashed to the ground.

Konstantin slammed a new magazine into his weapon, broke cover and put a bullet in the nearest terrorist.

The man went limp, hanging from his dropline.

The Russian didn't hesitate. He rushed forward, holstering the Glock and grabbing the line. He climbed upwards until he reached the dead man and used his corpse to anchor himself as he stripped the harness and transferred it over to himself. The corpse fell out of the sky. Securely attached to the line, Konstantin pulled out his gun again and took several shots at a soldier on the nearest dropline. Konstantin's third bullet punched through his skull and he spun on his line like a broken mannequin.

Konstantin was the only man in the air now.

The Armed Response guys on the ground took shots at him, but the smoke and downward air currents from the chopper threw off their aim.

Taking no chances he engaged the winch, using a remote control on his stolen harness, and ascended with painful sluggishness towards the belly of the helicopter.

The net was lifting beneath him, filled with bullion.

The helicopter itself lifted, too.

The ground troops were still down there, grunt work done their escape was down to their own devices. Konstantin didn't waste a second thinking about them.

The winch was too slow.

The net was lifting faster than he was.

He needed to adjust his thinking.

He deactivated the winch and unclipped himself from the line.

Gritting his teeth, Konstantin climbed hand over hand up the dropline as fast as his screaming muscles could lift his weight. London was a long way below. The net rushed up to meet him. Freezing winds tore at him, numbing his hands. All he could do was climb. He saw the winch outside the cargo hold doors.

The doors themselves were closed.

He glanced below at London. It felt as though half of the city was burning, but it was far less than that. Given her history, it should have been predictable. Solomon was playing games. A new great fire?

Emergency vehicles came from all over, converging on the scene. Their blue and red lights fused to form a purplish ring around the burning centre. The explosion had knocked out power and many of the surrounding streets were dark for the first time since the Blitz.

Konstantin would make them pay.

He pulled himself up, hand over hand, the dropline passing through his legs, which he used to stop himself from falling backward.

The wind grabbed at his shirt. The cold buffeted and bullied him, but he wasn't about to fall. He reached the winch, and used it to stand, one foot in the huge hook, and peer in through one of the windows. He made three men inside, talking. Two armed. One, in a suit, looked hauntingly familiar.

For a heartbeat he thought it was a ghost, and all he could think was, haven't I killed you before? But then he saw the subtle differences of age. The family resemblance was uncanny. He was looking at Devere Senior. The man behind Humanity Capital.

He wrenched open the door.

His first shot took one of the armed men in the head.

He fired at the other, but he was better.

The armed man threw himself behind a packing crate.

Devere himself ducked but with nowhere to run, turned instead to face down the Russian. The movement drew Konstantin's eye away from the far end of the lengthy cabin. He almost missed the two women who were on their feet, rifles ready.

Konstantin threw himself to the deck, the bullets missing by inches to bury themselves in the metal shell.

"Stop firing, you morons!" Devere yelled.

He stood taller now, recognizing that this had become a negotiation.

Konstantin climbed back to his feet. He watched the assault rifles, measuring the women behind them.

The second armed man broke cover from behind the crates and aimed a pistol squarely at the Russian's head.

"Drop your weapon," Devere told him.

He had no real choice but to do what he was told.

It took a moment, but finally Devere said, "I know you, don't I?"

The man moved closer, but not so close that the Russian could turn it into a hostage situation.

He waited for Devere to say: You killed my son.

"It's Khavin, right? The infamous papal assassin." His voice belied his age more than his physique did. He was in pretty good shape for a man at least in his early sixties.

"What are you trying to do here?" Konstantin asked.

"Do? Isn't it obvious?"

"Talk me through it."

"Why would I possibly want to do that?"

"You won't be able to introduce this much gold into the marketplace, it's useless, even if you melt it down."

Devere laughed at this. "Such a keen grasp of economics. I shall take your advice under advisement. Restrain him."

They grabbed an arm each and cuffed him, then forced the Russian to sit on one of the benches along the inside wall of the chopper. The women stood either side of him, both rifles aimed at his head.

"Much as I'd love to see if you could learn to fly, I'd like to know why you decided to play hero. I do not like coincidences. Especially not at this stage of the game. Why are you here?"

"That's easy," Konstantin replied. "I am here to stop you."

Devere laughed again. "You are quite delightful, I'm sure. You can live, for now."

THIRTY-ONE
YOU SHOOK ME ALL NIGHT LONG

Stacia Kanic wasn't going anywhere.

"Khavin has been spotted in Stuttgart," Knight told her over the phone. "You're to leave immediately."

"But—" she began.

"I don't care what you are about to say, Kanic. Stuttgart. Your mission is to kill Konstantin Khavin, not to go chasing magical water."

"With respect, I really think—"

"Get out of there now, or you are out, period. Notice expected on my desk before morning."

"A few hours, that's all I need."

The line went dead.

That was weird.

The words he'd chosen — *Get out of there now* — you didn't use those words if you wanted someone to go somewhere, you used them if you wanted them to leave somewhere in a hurry. It wasn't just semantics. Knight was precise. Why did he want her out of Bonn? Why the urgency? Why not wait until morning? It wasn't as though it would make a realistic difference in the hunt for Khavin.

So, what did he think was coming? What was he afraid of?

Even as she packed her stuff, Stacia couldn't get those tankers and their saltwater out of her mind.

Why would anyone dispose of sea water?

Google had given her one possible solution, but that seemed ludicrous. She'd found research to suggest saltwater could be deliberately used to induce earthquakes.

The other thing she'd found digging around to learn more about earthquakes was that US States like Oklahoma had experienced a massive increase in the frequency and strength of quakes in the years since fracking operations began there. Indeed, the risk of tremors was one of the reasons cited for Germany halting the fracking program altogether.

Stacia made up her mind.

She would stay, and first thing in the morning she would return to the well and find out for sure what was going on.

*

She didn't make it to morning.

There was a moment of disorientation. She didn't know what had woken her, only that she'd lurched up and was staring at 3AM lights on the room's alarm clock.

A bad dream?

No.

The rattle of the windows dismissed that notion.

She sat up in bed feeling the mattress move beneath her.

The window frames trembled.

The stuff she'd left on the nightstand, her gun, badge, jewelry and loose change danced across the surface.

A few seconds later, the rumbling stopped.

The night returned to silence and stillness.

Stacia pushed herself out of bed and crossed the small room to switch on the light. The flex still swung gently making the light cast weird moving shadows across the room.

She dressed in a hurry, put on her boots, grabbed her gun, coins and her car keys and left the room.

Whatever was going on couldn't wait until morning.

Franks had started already.

She remembered the tankers, and their over-capacity, and thought about the conspiracy theories about deliberate earthquakes and realised he could have been pumping waste water underground for hours, if not days, round the clock, and only now generated enough buildup of pressure to cause that tremor.

What the fuck was going on here?

And why was the Russian bothered about it?

How did an earthquake tie into the assassination of the Holy Father?

Honest answer? Fucked if she knew.

She was halfway down the stairs when the next tremor hit.

She saw the hotel walls ripple, pictures falling from their hooks. The steps undulated away from her. The second strike seemed to be considerably more intense than the first. Was that normal?

She needed to get out of there.

She gripped the handrails and pushed on, reaching the bottom as the quake kicked up a gear.

Stacia Kanic raced through the lobby, a deep fissure in the ceiling chasing her.

Chaos erupted around her, but there was nothing she could do about that. They practised for this, they ran drills, they knew how to marshal guests out of the building and were best prepped to keep people safe.

A receptionist stood in the middle of the foyer, waving people toward the emergency exit.

Behind closed doors, people woke to a nightmare.

The lights went out and another loud crack tore through the masonry, this time from the direction of the stairs.

Stacia didn't stop, didn't look back. She raced across the foyer, around the receptionist, avoiding the other guests as disorder and panic took hold and crashed out into the street.

A crescendo of car alarms greeted her.

The road beneath her feet buckled beneath the strain, the blacktop cracking alarmingly.

The ground heaved.

Buildings trembled.

Everywhere she looked chunks of masonry and broken glass rained down.

A car screeched to a halt nearby.

Stacia didn't have time to find her own in the tcar park. Instead she ran to the vehicle in the street.

She pulled her gun and screamed at the driver to get out.

He was so terrified, so lost, he obeyed.

Stacia backed up so as not to hit him, as fresh tremors pitched him onto his hands and knees, then slammed the car into gear, tires squealing. She swerved to avoid a rupture in the street – a huge sinkhole opening up and swallowing several parked cars in a mindless cacophony of terror. It was like nothing she'd experienced. It defied understanding. Bonn was being torn apart. Turned inside out. It was a war zone where even the ground couldn't be trusted.

She mounted the pavement to skirt it, smashing into a signpost and a rubbish bin before swerving back onto the road. She stuck to the centre, ignoring the white lines.

The horror continued to unfold around her.

Buildings along the road were stripped of windows and lost their decorative façades as older buildings collapsed, tearing away their structural integrity. Smoke and flames rose up from ruptured mains.

Stacia had to breathe hard and steer fast to avoid being crushed by falling chunks of masonry as the city came apart.

More cars were on the road now, frantic residents trying to escape.

Still the ground shook, the tremors worsening.

At one point the road began to tilt alarmingly.

Stacia stepped on the accelerator, resisting the natural urge to brake.

She slammed into a man trying to avoid a rain of brickwork, knocking him to the ground where a rupture in the tarmac swallowed him up.

She couldn't afford to give him a second glance.

She couldn't think about him.

The road levelled out again as she passed the rupture, but as she approached the impressive Bonner Münster church, she was confronted by the sight of the huge central tower twisting and buckling, seconds from crashing down. They were all helpless, and nothing rammed that message home more brutally than the tower ripping through the roof of the ancient church.

The roads around the Münsterplatz were wide and open, allowing her space around the devastation.

The ground did not stop shaking.

The tremors came up through the wheels. She felt them through the steering column.

Taller structures lost their fight with gravity.

And it showed no sign of ending.

The power was out all over the area. Dust and debris clouded everything.

Huge piles of stone and debris blocked several roads out of the city.

She surged through the streets, driving like the devil was on her tail, and out onto the Am Hauptbahnhof, her headlights revealed the damage to the central railway station itself. The road led out of the old town and in the direction of Dieter Franks's well.

Most other cars on the road had been abandoned or had collided with collapsed structures or each other in the process of trying to avoid the city coming down around them. Stacia's focus was on keeping moving, regardless of what horrors she saw around her. She wasn't emergency services. The dust and darkness provided cover for her flight.

Thousands of people had to be dead, many more injured.

Knight knew.

He had to know.

Get out of there.

He knew.

How far would the shockwaves spread?

How many more innocent people were at risk because she hadn't trusted her gut back at the well?

The guilt fuelled her.

Approaching the well site, she didn't bother with stealth.

Her headlights picked out people running from the area.

This was ground zero; if Bonn had been tortured she couldn't imagine what it had been like here.

It didn't matter. These people were irrelevant. They were the grunts. She had only one target.

The stolen car churned deep grooves in the mud as she spun to a stop by the Portakabin that served as site office.

She threw open the car door and was out, gun up, and hit the door. The hasp exploded in splinters as the door buckled inward. She put a bullet in the first man she saw. No questions. No recriminations. No excuses. He didn't get up again. She saw the jeans and hardhat. It was Franks's foreman. Ex-foreman.

Dieter Franks pushed himself to his feet.

He reached under his arm for a gun.

"Don't you fucking *dare*," Stacia spat.

He froze.

"Ms… Kanic, was it? I believe you just murdered my friend."

"Whatever you are doing, stop it. Drain the fucking well. Reverse pumps. Do it now!"

"Won't help."

Stacia put a bullet in Franks' shoulder.

He gasped in shock, sinking back into his seat. Ignoring the gun, he clutched at the rapidly spreading blood red rose blossoming on his jacket.

"I said drain the fucking well!"

Franks gritted his teeth. "It won't but Bonn back together. It's done. You saw the devastation out there. This region isn't prepared for huge tectonic shifts. This quake might just have been the most devastating in the country's history."

"Say another fucking thing that isn't 'stop the pumps' and I'll put a bullet in your face."

"It's pointless."

As last words went they were hardly memorable.

Stacia shot him in the head.

She left the cabin and hurried over to where one of the tankers was being drained into the well's intake valve. A man stood nearby, watching a gauge that told him how much was left in the tanker.

She could hear machinery pumping liquid from the intake valve.

"You," Stacia yelled, pointing her gun at his head. "I want you to pump that fucking well dry or I'll shoot you like I shot your boss."

He didn't argue.

He pressed a button and the machinery stopped.

He pressed it again and it roared back to life, only this time with a different tone to the pump.

Stacia put two bullets in him and then collapsed to the grass.

One tanker was never going to be enough.

They'd pumped dozens upon dozens down into the well.

She felt utterly helpless.

But it wouldn't get any worse.

That had to be worth something, didn't it?

Ten minutes later she was still there, adrenalin still coursing through her. What else she could do?

The gauge the man had been holding dangled at the side of the cab. It registered full. A deep rumbling started from the metal skin of the tanker as the pressure built up.

It would blow if she didn't kill it.

Which was what she wanted.

She wanted the tank to rupture but the pumps to keep drawing saltwater from the ground.

Stacia took cover behind the bulk of her stolen car as the integrity of the tanker's shell gave way, and a jet of water fountained from the gash in the steel, building in height and width as it sprayed saltwater. Another plate in the metal wall ruptured under the pressure, spewing seawater all over the ground. More and more spilled, turning the muddy ground into a quagmire.

And still more saltwater pumped up out of the earth.

She needed to get out of there before she couldn't, the mud was already threatening to make this stretch of the service road unpassable.

Stacia got into the stolen car and, with some slipping and sliding, pulled away.

She couldn't go back to Bonn.

Aftershocks were inevitable, but they would diminish in scope and severity as the water pressure settled.

She could only pray no one else would get hurt.

Her thoughts returned to the conviction Knight knew. And if he knew, she couldn't trust him. It was as simple as that.

She already knew Konstantin Khavin was nowhere near Bonn, and never had been.

So, who had led her here?

Not Knight. He wanted Khavin dead, that was the sum of his interest here. He didn't want her getting involved.

So, who?

She could only come up with one logical explanation, someone had planted a false trail for her to follow.

Driving out on the autobahn was sobering.

The motorway itself was damaged in several places, making it hard to negotiate without lights to guide her. The devastation on either side of the motorway was heartbreaking. Emergency vehicles tore past in either direction, the first responders gbarrelling into hell because they had no choice.

Franks was just a money man. A man on the ground. Stacia already knew who was behind the attack. The same man to blame for Berlin, for Rome, for the corpse planes, for the attempt to blow up the Dome of the Rock, for the Pope and the Cardinals.

Solomon.

It had to be.

And now more than ever she doubted the truth she'd been fed from Six about Khavin's guilt. These people were trying to stop the world going to hell and Stacia Kanic was on the wrong side of the fight.

THIRTY-TWO
REASONS TO BE FEARFUL

The images coming out of Germany were beyond devastating.

In all his very heavy years, and despite everything he had seen, Sir Charles Wyndham had never believed he was living in a time darker than this one.

Bonn had taken the brunt of the massive earthquake, a sustained 8.2 on the Richter scale, lasting an astonishing thirty-five minutes.

The Western World hadn't seen *anything* like this in years. Cologne reported widespread damage. Even as far away as Brussels the aftershocks were being felt, with reports of people running into the streets when the shaking began. The quake was felt, albeit in a much-reduced capacity, in Berlin and Paris, setting off car alarms and waking people from their slumber.

Images of the devastation in Bonn were harrowing. He wasn't a sentimental man, but the suffering of so many people reached him on a fundamental level. These were the innocents who had been caught up in Solomon's forty days and forty nights of biblical fear. These were the innocents who suffered because he had failed on so many levels.

On the screen, fleets of ambulances rushed towards the epicentre. Bonn's hospitals were damaged so badly they couldn't cope with the wounded. The ambulances were being forced to drive massive distances in search of help for the dying.

It was still too early to put a number to the death toll, but the anchorwoman promised somberly that the initial fears ran to the tens of thousands.

It would only get worse as the air ran out for those buried under rubble, the Old Man knew.

Added to that, there were perhaps one hundred thousand or so carrying injuries, and over a million people forced to evacuate their homes, and the scope of the devastation began to take shape.

And this lay at Solomon's door.

They could look at the plate tectonics and seismic reports and everything else, but this all came back to one man. Even cut off from the intelligence reports coming in to Control the Old Man knew what he was looking at: the most heinous terror attack in the history of ever-spiralling terror attacks.

He had no idea if any of his people were in Bonn. Mendes kept him out of the loop. All he knew was that Noah was on the continent, and the suspicion was that Konstantin was there, too. Either one of them could be buried under that rubble.

He dismissed such dark thoughts.

He had given up trying to reach Lethe. He was no longer at Nonesuch, that much was obvious, but where he had gone from there, and whether he was safe, was anyone's guess.

Shamshi brought food to his room.

He didn't try to question her; he knew she was under strict orders not to tell him anything.

The Old Man was becoming increasingly convinced that this was less forced retirement and more house arrest.

He glanced around the bare-walled room – not his own haven downstairs but rather an upstairs room chosen for him because there was a lock on the door. He missed his own room and his own bed.

The knock when it came was soft, as if the person on the other side of the door didn't want to wake anyone else up.

"Come in," he said.

He heard the door unlock, which rather negated any real control over whether his visitor should be allowed to enter or not.

The door opened part way.

"Did I wake you?" Shamshi asked.

"No, no. Please, come keep an old man company. It will be a grateful distraction from the harrowing news everywhere I look."

She stepped into the room and closed the door behind her, more softly than he might have expected, like she didn't want the soft *snick* to be overheard.

"I saw," Shamshi said, gesturing to the TV. "So horrible. I can't even imagine. You go to bed at night and that happens…" She shook her head.

"Is there something I can do for you, my dear?"

Shamshi seemed to wake from a daze.

She tore her eyes from the television.

"Oh yes. Well, no. I just wanted to make sure you're okay. I was going to get some sleep and I saw the light under the door."

"Well that was most kind of you, Shamshi. As you can see, I continue to exist. I cannot say much more than that sadly."

"I'll let you sleep."

Sir Charles wheeled himself a little closer to where she lingered by the door.

"Before you go, were any of our people near the quake?"

"Stacia Kanic, well she's with Six, not one of yours. But she was there."

"She's the one pursuing Khavin?"

"Yes. She was in Bonn, but Knight ordered her to leave hours before the quake."

The Old Man didn't question that, but he lived in a world were there was no such thing as coincidence, meaningful or otherwise. "She should be in Stuttgart now. She's safe."

"I'm glad to hear it."

"She was lucky. He got wind of a sighting of Khavin in Stuttgart. I assumed Abshir gave him that information because I didn't see it."

"And he called her right before the quake?"

"Like I said, really lucky."

"Indeed," the old man said. "Tell me, is Lethe still downstairs?"

"He left a while ago. Haven't seen him for hours."

"And Knight's not worried about that?"

"Should he be?"

"Lethe doesn't tend to leave his nest. He isn't one for the field."

"I know how he feels," Shamshi said, with a slightly lost smile.

"And Mendes?"

"She went to bed some time ago. Left Knight in charge."

Sir Charles smiled kindly at her. She was too young to be dragged into this. What he was about to do was cruel and she would feel the ramifications for the rest of her life. But it needed to be done. She truly believed she was on the side of the angels.

"Can I ask you to indulge an old man before you leave?"

She looked nervous, but she nodded.

"You don't have to answer me now. I want you to go away and think about something."

"Okay."

"Consider Mister Knight and how he reacted to the earthquake. Did he seem shocked? Why didn't he wake Mendes? This is a devastating event. Why did he send Stacia Kanic away from Bonn on evidence that might well not exist? Ask yourself a rather peculiar question, all things considered, but is it possible he knew the earthquake was coming? And if you find yourself thinking he did, ask yourself a tougher question. Ask yourself how that could be possible?"

Shamshi seemed conflicted.

"And then ask yourself something completely different. Because I wonder why Mister Knight isn't worried about Lethe. That boy is lethal with a computer, the most dangerous human being I know, and Knight knows he's loyal to me. In his place I'd want to know everything that boy was up to. All of it. So where is he, and why doesn't Knight care? Like I said, no need to answer me now. Take some time to consider things. There is a truth we aren't seeing, Shamshi. Goodnight, my dear."

"Goodnight," she said.

Shamshi left the room as quietly as she had entered it.

He heard the lock click.

There was going to come a time when she was going to have to pick a side. He hoped he'd said enough to plant a seed of doubt. Let her stew on it. With luck the seed would grow.

THIRTY-THREE
PARADISE CITY

He resisted the urge to draw his gun.

If someone stopped him, the whole lost tourist excuse went out the window with a Sig Saur in your hand.

Sneaking around Vatican City was getting to be a bad habit.

Noah felt like he was being typecast.

At least this time he wasn't looking for an intruder.

He had come to drop in on a meeting. Neri's people found out about the gathering. It felt like finally the Carabinieri were coming around to the idea that someone inside the Vatican was working with the terrorist who called himself Solomon. But any attempt to make contact with the Swiss Guard had been rebuffed. Unsurprisingly, really, considering the giant shitting on they'd taken in the eyes of the world. First the loss of the Pope, then the Cardinals, both very much on their watch. it was hardly a shining moment. No, they were looking for scapegoats, not the truth that the most senior surviving member of the Holy See was up to his neck in the killings.

He noted the increased security. According to the Neri's friend, the cleaner, it was usually pretty quiet at this time of night. Neri's old friend had been more than happy to smuggle Noah inside the Vatican's walls. He had noted the Camerlengo's mysterious late-night meetings with young students and immediately feared the worst—though his worst was another sex scandal, not the presence of a terrorist cell. Neri's explanation that some of those kids had been involved in the Berlin attacks was almost a relief.

And so Noah descended into the crypt of Saint Peter's Basilica.

He heard someone speaking in the distance.

Not a conversation, he realised. Someone preaching.

There were no guards down here.

He assumed they'd all been dismissed so they wouldn't overhear the bullshit the Camerlengo was filling these kids' minds with.

The same students Noah had seen on the green gathered around the holy man again. This time they sat in the front few pews of an underground chapel. The low ceiling and aisle ran down the side of the single column of benches. Their leader spoke in muted tones, and the long, narrow chamber made his voice sound rich and full of bass. The peculiar acoustics made it hard to make out exactly what he was saying.

Noah crouched down behind the last pew, out of sight.

Peering up, he saw the Camerlengo turn to the altar behind him and took his chance to move forward along the line of pews.

He was shielded in both directions by the wooden benches.

Noah repeated this manoeuvre until, with agonizing slowness, he reached the halfway point of the chapel's length.

An alcove at the wall-end of the pew held the tomb of some saint or other, Noah couldn't read the inscription, and to be honest, couldn't give a crap. He was the least religious man in the world.

As the Camerlengo spoke again, Noah took out his phone and started an audio recording.

"The task ahead will not be easy, my children," the holy man promised. "You should know that at the outset. Some will make the ultimate sacrifice. Others may end up prisoners of Unbelievers. But the glory that awaits us in the next life will be beyond anything any of us can imagine in this. We must be prepared and go willingly to earn that paradise."

That sounded like incitement to suicide to Noah.

"Our departed brothers and sisters have liberated so many souls in Germany, it's time we did the same."

Noah took out his gun and stood up.

"That's enough of the pseudo-cult bullshit, mate," he said, aiming the gun at the Camerlengo as he stepped out into the narrow aisle. "Time to pack up the hymn books and become familiar with the law. I can imagine what they'd do to your kind in the big house."

The assembled students turned around, and seeing him and the gun, gasped. The acoustics of the chapel amplified the sounds weirdly.

A few stood up, but as they were packed into the pews and the only exit was the single aisle with Noah in it, they couldn't exactly make a run for it.

The Camerlengo didn't move.

He didn't seem in the least bit bothered by the gun pointing at him.

"Children, this is Noah Larkin," he said, as though introducing a guest speaker. "Welcome to our gathering, Noah."

"I don't know what you're planning to use these kids for –"

Noah never finished the sentence.

Catalina Sosa launched herself at him from somewhere to Noah's left.

She moved so quickly he didn't have time to bring his gun around to fire.

The weapon skittered off under a pew as Sosa's vicious left palm cross almost broke his arm. She followed it with a dazzlingly fast strike from her right, taking him under the chin and driving his head back. Both blows connected before she landed in the aisle.

A third blow had his senses reeling.

It took everything Noah could muster to dodge the blows raining down on his face.

Sosa wasn't tall, she was skilled and fast. Faster than Noah. And way more disciplined.

There was no way he could keep fending her off in such an enclosed space.

He relied more on brute force than elegance.

She drove the heel of her right hand toward his temple, missing by half an inch.

It was the half an inch he needed.

Noah ignored the next combination of blows and moved in as fast as he could, grabbing the woman around the waist as she tried to batter him. His thinking was to try and twist her round and slam her into the crypt wall. Instead, as he turned her, Sosa read his intent, and planting her feet against the wall she ran upwards instead, breaking his hold.

The chapel was low enough that she managed to – for a moment – defy gravity and appeared to run onto the ceiling, using Noah as leverage.

Then her weight came down on his neck and she launched a brutal kick at his chest, connecting hard.

Noah went down awkwardly, his head cannoning off the end of the nearest pew.

He struggled to protect his face as she hurled kicks and punches at his body.

Each boot or fist connected with a detonation of pain that seemed to dim and dim and dim as they all blurred into one.

"That's enough, Catalina."

Immediately the battering ceased, but the pain didn't go away.

Noah lay bruised and dazed on the stone floor. Instinctively he reached for his gun but it had fallen somewhere he couldn't see.

His right eye already too puffed up to see through.

The woman moved like a dancer rather than a boxer. She looked eager to deliver more blows if called upon.

The Camerlengo leaned over Noah and tutted.

"That didn't go quite how you imagined it, now did it, Noah?"

Noah spat blood onto the white stone floor.

He grabbed the end of the pew in an attempt to haul himself up.

He made it to his knees, but that was it.

"Could have been worse," he said, looking up at the holy man.

"I'm sure. Well, I'm going to have you locked up now, for trespass. Or would you rather I let Miss Sosa play with you?"

"Locking up sounds like a fine idea," said Noah, despite how much it hurt to move his jaw. "Best idea I've heard in a long time. Surely you didn't come up with it all by yourself?"

"You aren't as funny as you think you are, you know?"

"It's okay. I'm saving the punchline 'til later."

"Oh yes, and what's that?"

"Next time I'll just shoot you," Noah promised.

"You'll need your gun back for that," Sosa said.

THIRTY-FOUR
MONKEY GONE TO HEAVEN

Ronan Frost stood in the devastation that was what remained of Threadneedle Street.

He was close to the edge in so many ways.

He stared down from the rim of the giant crater into a section of the vault.

There were stacks of bullion, literal piles of gold, exposed to the morning sun for the first time in perhaps centuries. The crude wealth was enough to buy several small countries and the loyalty of some not so small ones.

Police were everywhere.

His credentials cleared, giving him something close to authority on the scene as he fell under the umbrella of the Secret Services now.

Ambulances had long since ferried the wounded away, even so at regular intervals along the shattered street there were bodies covered in tarps and puddles of blood barely dry and still sticky on the tarmac. The burned-out shells of vehicles were everywhere. It reeked. Everything stank. His nostrils stung at the acrid tang. The smoke cloyed and clawed at his still sensitive lungs. More burning.

Sirens filled the air.

Officers and military personnel ran back and forth barking orders to each other, trying to help, to understand, and struggling to grasp what was happening around them. Some simply stood there, looking on, unable to actually help.

Beyond the smoke the air was ripe with the reek of blood and death.

A brisk morning breeze swept down the street, whipping up debris and the edges of the body coverings.

A squad of soldiers arrived, disembarking from the military truck. They fell into line on the road. Their commanding officer yelled instructions with precision and clarity, no room for doubt or misinterpretation. He knew what was demanded of his boys. The unit jogged towards the crater. Police moved aside to accommodate them as they took up position around the ragged circumference, hands on rifles, standing guard over the gold.

Because the gold could be guarded. Because that made sense where very little else did.

Such an audacious crime. Military helicopters to airlift bullion? And so much damage. Lethe was right, it wasn't about some petty religious bollocks, it was all about the money. It always was. The Irishman had grown up around enough pricks to know that the old adage about show me a cause and I'll show you someone getting rich off it had never been truer than it was today.

Short the currency. Hold the gold. There was a killing to be made there.

Frost kicked a chunk of rubble over the edge, then turned his back on the crater before it struck gold.

He stood before the shattered frontage of the Bank of England, the offices and lobbies and hallways exposed to the elements in ways even the most ambitious architect could never have imagined.

It was all too random, too hard to predict and too hard to stop. There didn't seem to be any method behind the madness. An earthquake in Germany? This. He didn't for a minute believe the quake was a natural event. Solomon had probably detonated a nuke down a mineshaft or something equally heinous. It was just a case of throw as much terror at the wall and see what sticks.

Without Lethe to join the dots it felt like an impossible task. How were they meant to anticipate where Solomon would strike next?

They were always on the back foot, reacting. Their impact was always after the event. And the new management weren't helping with their officious do it by the book BS.

"I need you to leave this area, sir," a grim-faced soldier held his rifle ready, not aimed at Frost, but it didn't need to be.

"It's okay, soldier, I've been cleared," Frost reached for his inside pocket.

"Do not move," the soldier barked.

"I'm about to show you my warrant card, soldier."

"I repeat. Do not move. Hands behind your head."

"I can't do both," Frost said, immediately regretting the flippancy to his tone. "We're on the same side."

"Keep your hands behind your head, turn around and start walking, sir."

It was just easier to do as he was told.

Besides, he'd learned all there was to learn here, at least until detailed forensics, cameras and other evidence could be examined, and that was above his pay grade. Which meant he needed to explore other options. Finding Lethe was a good place to start.

Frost walked away from the crater, keeping his pace slow and steady.

He heard the soldier walking behind him, no doubt aiming his assault rifle at the small of Frost's back in case he got any ideas. He escorted Frost some distance beyond the immediate blast zone. He felt the prod of the barrel, pushing him in the direction of a patrol car and a group of police men fresh on the scene.

"Seriously? You're going to have me arrested? Just let me show you my badge," Frost called back over his shoulder.

The soldier ignored him.

He walked on a couple of steps, not hearing the echo of the military man's boots on the rubble behind him.

He turned to half-glance back there. The man had stopped at a shop window. Frost turned back toward him, hands still on his head. The glass had been blown out and a lot of the display items were damaged beyond repair, but a single flat screen TV was still switched on and showed the image of a man talking. The volume was up, and with no glass in the window Ronan could hear clearly what the new king of terror was saying.

The soldier ignored him, eyes transfixed on the screen.

"These are the last days," Solomon echoed the first words to the world. "Civilization falters, the authorities are powerless, and you must choose. You must decide where to place your faith. In your corrupt leaders? Men and women who lie to your face daily, who proclaim fake news when you know the truth is being buried. Men and women who chase their own self-interest and damn you all to hell and austerity demanding sacrifice so that they can grow fat. Do you put your faith in your failed banks who took your bailouts to stay alive then awarded themselves billions in bonuses for their failures while you queue up at food banks just to survive until the end of the month? Do you turn to your holy leaders who are beset by scandals, taking advantage of the most vulnerable under their care? Tell me, who can you trust? Who can you believe?"

Frost's arms were by his sides now.

He stood shoulder to shoulder with his the military man and both watched the screen, listening to Solomon's snake-tongued sermon.

*

Stacia Kanic struggled to stay awake.

She sat in traffic waiting to enter Stuttgart.

Every road was jammed with refugees fleeing the quake.

With nowhere else to go they took whatever means of escape they could find, carrying everything they owned on their backs. They came looking for shelter with friends and relatives, and queued up on the doorsteps of every shelter, hostel and hotel, only to be turned away. Schools were being opened up to provide temporary beds. There were Good Samaritans posting on Twitter that they had spare rooms for the needy, first come first served, and a sense of community and coming together despite it all.

According to the booking app on her phone every single hotel room in a hundred-mile radius was booked up. There was nothing showing as available in Stuttgart. Still, she had the car.

As the sun rose over a shattered Germany, Stacia was still in stuck in traffic and the second reality of the problem facing her was making itself known. Her commandeered Audi was running out of petrol.

Vehicles sitting stranded on either side of the road stood as testament to this spreading problem. The petrol stations were dry. In panic everyone had rushed to fill up their tanks, leaving the people fleeing the epicentre to drive on fumes until they could drive no more.

The likelihood of being stranded was very high.

It wasn't as though she could requisition petrol through government sources, either.

She turned on the radio, tuning in to the State radio for the latest situation reports, hoping to hear that relief efforts were getting through and the situation was expected to return to normal within days. Instead, she heard a voice that immediately captured her attention. She gripped the steering wheel, suddenly wide awake in the middle of a recurring nightmare, listening to the words of a lunatic.

"Now is the hour, now we must free ourselves from the shackles of corporations, from the chains of religion and the dead weight of politicians. Look around you, now, look. The people of Germany were judged as sinners by God Almighty and paid the ultimate price. Like Sodom and Gomorrah their city lies in ruins. It will never recover. The Lord himself is leading us all towards a new day. Reject the lies of our false leaders. Do not risk judgment falling upon your home."

Stacia shivered. There was nothing worse than these fire and brimstone preachers and their mega churches. Why the world gave them air time was beyond her.

Judgement Day?

Well, she had science on her side, and science said there was nothing miraculous about the devastating quake.

She felt trapped and helpless.

And she felt manipulated, by Solomon and Franks, by Mendes and Knight, by the twins, and maybe just maybe by Jude Lethe too. No one was telling her the truth. They were all playing with her destiny, trying to get her killed or to kill someone.

It was time to break the pattern.

But she needed to get out of the traffic jam first.

*

Orla lifted her head from the desk.

She hadn't been asleep.

It was impossible to rest.

She had a splitting headache, part dehydration, part due to the fact she'd almost had her head split open. The cuffs securing her to the metal table clinked as she stirred.

A television was on behind her.

The chair was a deliberately uncomfortable plastic one.

One of the arresting officers rose to his feet. He stood watching the face of a man on the television, seemingly mesmerized by his words.

Orla had been there for hours. It was different in Israel; no food, no phone call.

She was content to simply sit there, let them try to sweat her. There were crimes to her name but in the big picture she'd done nothing wrong. They'd interview her in time, but never when she was in good shape. That wasn't the way you broke someone. You wanted their weaknesses at the centre.

She recognized his voice first.

She looked at the screen.

Behind Solomon she saw the familiar lines of the Temple Mount and the Dome of the Rock. And for a disconnected moment she thought he was here, in Jerusalem. Within touching distance. But of course he wasn't. It was just a super imposed image. Technology.

"Behind me," Solomon said, "lies the most holy site on earth. Yesterday, followers of the new way attempted to destroy the Dome and eradicate the sinners who defile the divine *Shekhinah*. Today the Dome of the Rock still stands, but tomorrow it will fall like all of the follies of mankind."

A female officer approached and sat down opposite her.

There was no kindness or understanding in her eyes.

She knew the sort.

Orla didn't bother trying to proclaim her innocence. The woman wasn't ready to listen.

"The lesson in our failure? That there are no limits to our reach. There is nowhere safe from our believers. Rise up, my friends, proclaim mankind to be corrupt. Follow a new path. Find a new hope. Should that be me? Perhaps. But, believe me, I do not claim to be a Messiah, whatever they try to convince you when they spin their lies around my beliefs. I swear to you this: the days of terror will continue. Your leaders will be brought to their knees."

His words chilled Orla.

She'd risked everything to take down Ezra and they were using their failure as proof of their strength? Kill one, another will take their place. Kill a dozen, a dozen more shall rise.

And with Leah Ezra still out there no one was safe.

She had to get out of here.

*

"Those in power know their days are numbered. This age of avarice is coming to an end."

Noah paced in his cell, listening to the voice of Solomon as the tinny little radio broadcast his words. They were the ramblings of a man trying very hard to convince the world he was fundamentally a mad man. He wasn't. Noah knew that. This whole thing was bullshit.

The Swiss Guard assigned to watch over him seemed equally unconvinced.

"The business men who bleed our world dry will lose their heads in the coming revolution."

"Do I really have to listen to this crap?" Noah cursed.

The guard said nothing.

"Those venal men who prey on the weak and poor, bleeding them dry like vampires, who even now look at injecting themselves with the blood of the young in an attempt to cheat their maker, they live to steal from every man, woman and child who does honest work. Those are the men we need to humble. And to humble a man like that what do you do? You make them poor. That alone is their greatest fear. You make them what they are terrified of when they see it in the faces of others. You make them normal."

He needed to get a message to Neri.

Not that the Roman had favours enough to call in to get him out of the Camerlengo's jail.

But he had to make the man understand that another attack was imminent.

And that his jailer was coordinating it for Solomon.

"Why, just yesterday, on the steps of the great basilica of St Paul, known as the Vatican to most of us, a young priest took his own life. He carried out this tragic act in full sight of hundreds of witnesses. You will have seen the video footage. But what they aren't telling you is the means of his suicide. This young priest, unable to bear the hypocrisy of his fathers, ended his own life with a relic as old as The Christ himself. The Spear of Destiny. Why do such a thing? Fear. He saw the End of Days were opening up before him and could not continue in his life of false piety. Like all within those twisted walls, he knew that man has put himself above God and was willing to pay his part of that price."

"Oh, for fuck's sake," Noah yelled at the guard. "Just turn this shit off. Seriously. If you don't I'm going to rip the fucking TV from the wall for a bit of peace."

How the Camerlengo had driven the priest to suicide, he didn't know. He didn't understand the minds of people who actually believed in the idea of something bigger. He was a practical man. He believed in what he could prove. And right now he couldn't prove the link between the Solomon and the Camerlengo and the dead Cardinals, but he would.

The question was could he do it before Solomon convinced ordinary people to abandon the tenets of their civilization and devolve into chaos?

He slammed his palm into the bars of his cell door.

He hoped to fuck Neri was working on getting him out of there, because he didn't believe God was.

*

Konstantin watched the grinning face of Seinfeld shift into a snowstorm and from that haze of white noise, saw Solomon appear.

The Russian recognized him from their encounter at the Israeli Embassy.

It was a face he would never forget.

The big man had no intention of living out his days at Devere's pleasure. He was getting out of the room Devere's goons had locked him in, but for now the most pressing problem was that the door was solid steel and the windows were barred. So he wasn't going anywhere.

"Judgment falls upon our heads. My friends, you *must* be ready," Solomon droned on. Konstantin had heard it all before. These were the same lies spouted by every craven and deadly politician he had ever listened to in his homeland. It was behind the eyes. This was no religious fanatic. It was a charade. An act. He was playing to the perceptions of the world to gain what he wanted. And if he had to posture like an unhinged bin Laden, then so be it. He could mouth the words of a deranged maniac.

One fundamental lesson a tyrant could learn from his people was that beyond their willingness to cause real terror they knew it was meaningless if you weren't prepared to play the role in public afterwards. You must feed the beast to become the beast. To become the beast, you must feed the beast. It was an ouroboros.

"Now is the time to make your choice. The path of tomorrow is opening up to you. One way lies a new dawn, the other lies more subjugation, more suffering, more humiliation at the hands of the one percent. The rich will take more and more from this earth, bleeding her dry, and ultimately leaving the rest of us with nothing. We break our backs to enrich the liars and false prophets. We buy private planes for the preachers in their mega churches who do not understand the concept of charity and need. They seek to gather wealth through your poverty. Where is the righteousness in that?"

Konstantin changed the channel.

The face of his enemy was there, too.

And on the next.

And the next.

Solomon was broadcasting on every channel.

"Last night in Threadneedle Street, London, my disciples executed the most audacious heist the world has ever seen."

Now he had Konstantin's full attention.

"I took this gold from the people who hoard their wealth and their power. And it is my intention to share that wealth with those who need it most."

Altruism?

The big Russian shook his head even though there was no one in the room to see it. No, that wasn't Solomon's MO. He wasn't buying the change of heart? You didn't promise forty days and forty nights of fear and deliver riches halfway through.

*

Jude Lethe sat in a cage.

He was angry with himself.

He'd opened up the Nest and DAGDA was no longer under his control. It was a stupid, stupid mistake. He was making a lot of mistakes these days. They all were. It was because they were reacting to the smoke and being dazzled by the mirrors. They needed to see beyond the showmanship and lies. Solomon wasn't a genius. He wasn't some terrorist savant. But right now, this moment in time, the team was no more. The Ogmios Directive was a meaningless piece of paper that would be lost now it was no longer convenient.

Lethe had no idea where his friends were – or if they were even alive.

And, to add insult to injury, the fool they'd assigned to watch him was staring at some stupid daytime horror show of humanity that existed purely to make you feel good that there were people out there so broken and weren't you lucky it wasn't you. It was poverty porn. He hated this shit. All of it. Hours of shows dedicated to showing bailiffs doing repossessions, and toothless people struggling to live on benefit street. It was vile. The television was an ancient CRT screen, eleven inches, complete with round antenna. A haze of snow crackled across the picture at regular intervals, and midway through another paternity battle and lie detector test, the white noise resolved into a face that Lethe knew.

He was, literally, a captive audience as Solomon delivered his sermon.

"I promise you, London, I am a man of my word, and I make this promise to you. As the chimes of Big Ben strike eleven this morning, I will redistribute the gold among the poor and hungry of London. All who gather in Trafalgar Square will feel my generosity. They will understand. Their lives will be touched in such a way that they will never be the same again. Come, my friends. It is time to share in their wealth. That is my promise to you."

Lethe knew a bullshit when someone peddled it.

Redistributing stolen gold?

He still remembered when that PR company had pulled that stunt blowing ten grand into Liverpool Street Station in five pound notes. The free-for-all had been damned near lethal, and grabbing a few hundred quid was a hell of a lot different to someone dropping gold bullion into your lap. It would be chaos.

And that was what it was all about, wasn't it? Not some benevolent sharing of the wealth. It was about causing chaos in the heart of London. Meaning he had something else planned for when the eyes of the world were all turned to the gold.

*

Sir Charles Wyndham struggled from the bed into his chair.

The television was on of course. He hated the damned thing, but he was going out of his mind under house arrest. He'd heard every single word Solomon said.

And the man loved to talk.

Millions around the world were waking up to the news that Bonn was in ruins and London had been victim of his latest attack.

But this gloating, this face of terror thing, was unseemly. It spoke of a new generation of fools obsessed with being seen. But that was hardly surprising in a world driven by Twitter and Facebook and Instagram and whatever other social connectivity the kids were addicted to these days. Solomon was positioning himself as the King of Fear.

The man wasn't deranged.

Everything about him and the face he showed the public was calculated for maximum effect. What they used to say about people like him was that there was method to their madness, but that mistakenly assumed madness was present at all.

Forty days and forty nights.

What was his endgame?

What was the next strike?

Because it didn't end here.

"It's a trap, you fools," Sir Charles murmured, directing his statement to all the people already halfway out of the door, dreaming of riches. This was a man who had poisoned their water, infected their planes with a lethal pathogen, gassed their subways and murdered their religious leaders. But they would flock to him because he was promising them gold.

"There are only two things you should put your faith in," Solomon continued. "God and Gold. Everything else will fall."

The Old Man heard movement outside his room.

He turned away from the television set, fed up with listening to the lies of Solomon. He was hungry. Perhaps it was Shamshi bringing him breakfast.

The key turned in the lock.

He released the brakes on his wheelchair and waited for the door to open.

It didn't.

It took him a moment to realise someone was offering him a chance to flee.

*

"And you didn't think it was important enough to wake me up? What the hell is wrong with you?"

Constance Mendes was incensed.

Knight stood before her in the heart of the Nest, his head bowed like a naughty schoolboy.

"Honestly? There was nothing you or any one of us could do. It had been a hard day. It wasn't going to get better. So, I made a judgment call."

"And you fucked up, Knight."

"Will you shut up? Please? I'm trying to listen," Abshir protested.

Solomon's face filled the largest screen above his desk.

"Recording?" Constance snapped.

"Of course," Abshir said.

"Good. Then shut the fuck up when the grownups are talking. We can watch it back later and study it to our heart's fucking content. Right now, I'm pissed, and I am making sure everyone knows just how fucking pissed I am. Got that?"

Knight nodded. "I apologize, Director Mendes. It won't happen again."

"You're right, it won't."

"I think he's wrapping up," Abshir said, pointing at Solomon on the screen.

"God's wrath is terrible and mighty." It was the usual brimstone and thunder stuff. "You should Fear Him. He will deliver unto us all more acts of terror. This land will suffer. But if you are truly Chassid, you will be spared. Only the wicked, corrupt and evil need be afraid."

Constance Mendes looked around the basement room.

"And just where the fucking fuck is the other one?" She demanded, meaning Shamshi.

*

"Melech Israel."

Solomon dismissed the cameraman. As was becoming tradition after he made one of these public addresses, he reached for his phone and called Frasier Devere.

The man answered as though he had been sitting with the phone in his hand, waiting. "I must commend you, Devere, your men did an excellent job at Threadneedle Street."

"Are you going to tell me who killed my son?"

Solomon smiled.

He liked driven men, dfocussed on one thing and willing to do literally anything to get it. With the right piece of information, they could be turned into the most effective tools.

"Not yet. I told you, after phase 2. Now reassure me, is everything ready?"

"We'll be at Trafalgar Square for eleven."

"Excellent. I am very much looking forward to seeing this redistribution of wealth in action."

"We took a prisoner."

"Did you now? Was that wise?"

"We didn't have a choice."

"Explain."

"He hitched a ride, so to speak."

"And your mysterious hitchhiker? Anyone of interest?"

He was already thinking in terms of bargaining chips and how best to exploit the inconvenience when Devere said, "Definitely of interest, given he's the prime suspect in the murder of Pope Peter II." Konstantin Khavin. That was almost too funny. "I was going to kill him."

"No, no, keep him alive for now. The man has meddled in our plans more than once. He has information I will need for the final conflict."

"You want me to interrogate him?"

"In time. But not now. Keep him safe."

Solomon ended the call.

All was going well. Almost too well, in truth. The only true threat came from a divided team, their key players neutralized. With all but the Irishman incarcerated, there wasn't much they could do to thwart him now.

Finally, Solomon was beginning to enjoy himself.

*

The broadcast was over.

Ronan Frost crossed the police blockade to his waiting Ducati Monster.

He had to get to Trafalgar Square.

Something was going to happen, and it wasn't going to be some benevolent handing out of cash like Robin Hood.

Even though he wasn't far away, the streets were already filling with people pouring out of office blocks and shops, hoping to strike it rich.

He had no idea what to expect when he got there.

With no Lethe in his ear to guide him, he was just going to have to improvise.

He hated improvising.

THIRTY-FIVE
OUR SPIRITS IN THE MATERIAL WORLD

The police chief was not happy.

She wasn't used to being ignored by her prisoners, but it was obvious that Solomon's broadcast had rattled Orla. There was more going on here than met the eye. More actors. A larger threat. The woman needed to understand that. But how could Orla explain that in a way that forced the police chief to understand?

"I hate to interrupt you," the chief said, not bothering to mask the sarcasm in her voice. Her name badge said her name was Tal Jabarin. "Perhaps you could spare me a minute?"

"I work for the British government, for a group known as Ogmios. We are part of MI-6," which wasn't lying now, technically. "And that man is very much on our terrorist watch list."

Jabarin sighed. "Is there anyone who can vouch for you?"

"You can reach out to Michael Knight, he is my direct superior. Or Constance Mendes, Director."

"I will, but for now," Chief Jabarin consulted her notes. "You were arrested on the Foundation Stone, inside the Dome of the Rock, carrying a backpack with a bomb in it."

"Appearances can be deceptive."

"We examined the contents of that device, and have determined the bomb was designed to disperse a deadly pathogen, similar to the one we believe caused the Corpse Planes across Europe last week. You can see how this doesn't look good for you."

"I can. But, I assume you gathered witness testimony? Did they tell you about Leah Ezra? Did you talk to any of the people taken from outside the Dome? The ones who assembled to pray in protest? Ezra organized the protest as cover. She intended to gain access to the building. You're not going to want to hear this, but someone at the checkpoint, one of your officers I believe, took her backpack with text books and switched it for the pack with the bomb in it. If I hadn't been following Ezra a lot of people would be dead or dying right now. That's what you realise when you look beyond the obvious. What I discovered only hours before the attack was that this version of the pathogen isn't like the one used on the Corpse Planes. That one was designed as a single shot virus, beyond the first contagion it would not replicate. This one had been mutated. It wouldn't have stopped spreading until half of Jerusalem's population were dead."

"I'm sorry," the chief said. "Can you just go back a second. I want you to clarify something I think you said, but my English could be wrong. Did you tell me one of my own officers was responsible for handing the woman the bomb?"

"Not the pathogen. She already had those. Just the dispersal mechanism, yes. The device was powerful enough to do structural damage to the Dome, perhaps even collapse it. But that was never the aim. It was about the worshippers on the Temple Mount carrying the virus down from the rubble."

"That's a quite fantastical tale."

"What can I say, we're living in fantastical times. You only have to look at what happened to Bonn."

That confused the woman for a moment. She inclined her head, eyes narrowing as she told Orla, "That was an earthquake."

"It was, but you are labouring under the misapprehension that a quake has to be natural in origin. North Korea has suffered seismic activity to the point of entire mountain ranges being on the verge of collapse and there was nothing natural about those quakes, either. Now, consider the attack on the Bank of England, the horror of the Corpse Planes landing themselves, the papal assassination, the list goes on and on."

"And your attack on the Dome fits into this pattern."

Orla matched the woman's stare. It was easy to forget she was just doing her job, and in her position she would have been equally doubtful, but just for once it would be nice to be believed.

"Okay, look, Devil's Advocate, so say I was the one planning to blow up the Dome, ask yourself this, I was in there, I was lying on my back clutching the bomb. I'd won. Why didn't I detonate it?"

"You fell. You hit your head," Chief Jabarin said. "It isn't a stretch to say you were dazed."

"Believe me, even dazed I could trip a switch. No. That's beyond credibility. That's trying to shape reality around the narrative you want it to be. That's a mistake. Ask the Waqf about the woman they failed to stop fleeing from the Dome. She is the key."

"The Waqf believe we are all terrorists."

"They still know what they saw. As do the hundreds of people gathered to pray. Question the faithful within the Dome itself. Question the demonstrators outside. Ask questions. Ask what Uriah Lavi was cooking up in his lab in Tel Aviv, how he was forced to modify its effect, and ask who he sold it to."

"Lavi died yesterday." The way she delivered the news had Orla immediately on the defensive.

"I didn't kill him."

"I never said you did."

"The implication was pretty fucking obvious."

"Well, you must know we have you on security camera infiltrating his laboratory. We have the testimony of the guards you encountered. And we know he was alive when you went into that room, alone with him. It's not an unreasonable thing to imply, is it?"

Orla sighed. "I told him what his virus would be used for. I told him the ramifications of his study. The death it had already wrought, and the suffering it would bring to Israel and Palestine. Instead of doing something about it he chose to take his own life. I am not his keeper. I don't waste my compassion on broken men who create terrible things."

"So, what do you devote your time to?"

"Saving the world," she said, three words channelling Noah's flippancy.

"You are a regular super hero," the woman said, unimpressed.

"Can I have a pen and paper?"

"You intend to write a confession?" Jabarin raised her hand, making a gesture for someone behind the two-way mirrors to oblige, and a moment later the door opened, and a fresh-faced officer entered with the pen and pad.

Orla scratched out a number and pushed the pad across to the woman.

"Call it."

Jabarin took the pad.

She took out her mobile and dialled the number.

A moment later, someone picked up.

"This is Chief Tal Jabarin of the Israel Police. Who am I speaking with? Abshir? I have Orla Nyrén here. Yes. Nyrén. You don't? Okay, well I'm sorry for disturbing you."

She dropped the call and turned back to Orla. "He says he's never heard of you. So what now?"

Orla shrugged. "He's lying."

The officer entered the room again, carrying a message for the chief.

They spoke in whispers.

Orla couldn't hear much beyond the shape of the sounds, no actual words.

Message delivered, he retreated and Jabarin turned back to her.

"Interestingly, despite their denials, it would seem that your story checks out. My officers conducted interviews with witnesses who confirm that there was another woman. Several of the statements confirm she was carrying the bag on entry and it was you who stopped her."

"Sense prevails. Thank you."

"Oh, I wouldn't be thanking me. None of the witnesses from inside the Dome were grateful to you. Indeed, they were incensed that two non-Muslim women entered the Dome and because of your violation of the sanctity of the Dome and defilement of the Foundation Stone they are demanding that you be held accountable."

"I saved their lives!"

"Which is why you are being deported rather than detained. There are already protests mounting on the West Bank. If action is not seen to be taken there will be violence. That is the nature of balance here. You must have known that."

Orla was on her feet, hunched because she was still chained through the metal loop on the desk. "But more people will die if we don't stop Ezra."

"Do you think we are idiots here? Her picture has already been circulated. She is known to us as an agitator. My men are searching the city for her. She cannot get far."

"And the viral canisters?"

"They are in evidence."

"They need to be destroyed."

"That will not happen, Miss Nyrén. We are fully aware how deadly this pathogen is. Measures have been taken. But we operate by a rule of law."

"I'm going to say this slowly. I'm going to ram the fucking point home until you get it. One of your officers handed over a bag with the bomb to Ezra. That same officer has access to your evidence storage. You have potentially just put a lethal pathogen back into his hands. Understand?"

The chief did. She barked orders at the glass.

A few seconds later a male voice came over the speaker. "Tayeb is guarding the pathogen."

"Tayeb was on entry duty at the Temple Mount yesterday," Jabarin said. "Go. Make sure that damned stuff is secure. I'm not about to let this turn into a shit show."

Less than a minute later the voice returned.

"Tayeb is missing. He never delivered the pathogen to evidence."

"This might be a good time to release me," Orla said.

THIRTY-SIX
ENTER SANDMAN

That last punch felt like it had cracked his eye socket.

The pain didn't bother Konstantin.

He wasn't concerned about his looks, either.

Brutality gave a face character.

At least that was what he chose to believe when he looked in the mirror.

Frasier Devere was enjoying himself. It was rare for a man so immaculately groomed, in bespoke tailoring, to inflict the violence himself. His kind left it to their thugs. But Devere wasn't normal in that regard, or many other regards.

The big Russian's hands were tied to a wooden frame, attached to the wall of his cell. The frame had been mounted specifically for the purpose of torture. Or sex games. He wasn't sure which, but the result was much the same. The bonds were strong. He wouldn't be able to force his way out of them. Hs legs were likewise restrained. Which meant there wasn't much he could do other than endure the fists.

After another punishing blow, he spat blood and looked up to ask Devere, "You won't break me, you do know that, don't you?"

"Every man has his threshold," Devere said. "Believe me." He drove his fist into the Russian's stomach. Konstantin doubled over as far as his bonds would allow. "But, luckily for you I am not interested in exploring yours, I am merely killing time."

Konstantin didn't ask. Silence had a way of making people like Devere talk. They looked to fill it, to show how smart they were, how in control, and conversely how helpless you were before them.

"All was told not to kill you. No one said I couldn't entertain myself while my people finish melting down the gold."

Devere was gearing up for another punch when the door opened.

He recognized the man from the helicopter.

"We're ready. Choppers are warming up."

Konstantin made a show of hanging from his restrained limbs in the agony of defeat. That last blow to the stomach had shifted the wooden rack on the wall, giving a tiny amount of play that could move the whole frame back and forth an inch. He wasn't going to let Devere see it. He hung there panting hard, using his weight to hold the rack in its usual position.

"Very good, pass the word. We're moving out."

"Understood." The man left the room.

"Well then, I guess this is where we say our goodbyes, Mister Khavin. It's been a blast." Devere worked his knuckles.

"My pleasure," Konstantin replied, offering a weak grin.

Devere left him.

The moment the door closed, leaving him in the dark, Konstantin set to work getting himself free.

He lunged forward then slammed himself backwards, repeating the violent back and forth again and again, working the damaged fixture until the wall plug had torn out and part of the frame hung free of the wall.

He kept an eye on the door. He was making more than enough noise to draw the unwanted attention of the guards, but they obviously didn't care that he was fighting to free himself. Maybe they assumed he simply couldn't? There was an arrogance to captors, a psychology, that convinced them they were just smarter, faster, and stronger.

Well, he had news for them, and he was really looking forward to breaking it in person.

A corner of the rack came away from the wall in a cloud of brick dust.

The wrenching sound should easily have been heard outside the cell.

It gave Konstantin more leverage on the remaining anchor points.

He worked the entire frame back and forth repeatedly. Each savage jerk on the joints forced them wider and weaker.

The Russian ignored the swelling around his eye socket, the burning pain in his ribs and the swelling along his jaw.

He tensed, gathering all of his considerable strength.

He counted off a silent three, two, one countdown and pulled forward with every ounce of strength he could muster.

With a shriek, the frame buckled but somehow held firm.

He fell back against the wall.

Closed his eyes.

Focussed.

Life and death.

Moments turn on a dime.

Destiny is shaped by single seconds. Things done. Things not done.

He wasn't dying here.

Konstantin threw himself forward, and this time the wooden structure splintered around the joints, needles of raw wood raining down on the concrete floor as the entire frame came apart.

Konstantin hurled the bulk of it away from him, still anchored to the two main stathes.

The noise, finally, drew the guards.

They surged into the room, nightsticks held ready. Two of them. He weighed the risks in his mind, identifying the obvious hesitation in the way they carried themselves. It was a weakness he was more than happy to exploit.

Konstantin lifted his arms, still tied to lengths of wood at the wrists, transforming his cage into a weapon.

The first guard lashed out, trying to drive his nightstick into the Russian's face. Konstantin blocked the lunge with crossed arms, the wooden brace on his arm absorbing all of the shock of impact from the nightstick. He pulled his arms apart, pushing the nightstick aside in an easy parry with one arm even as he jabbed the other into the guard's face. The jagged splinters sliced through skin and tendons, making a mess of the man's face. He'd never be called pretty again, but that didn't matter. Men weren't meant to be pretty. A second blow opened up a vein and launched a fountain of blood.

The guard dropped his weapon, desperately clawing at his face, trying to put it all back together again as he dropped to his knees, howling. Right now, it was more shock than pain. The agony would follow. If the Russian didn't kill him first.

The second guard backed up, learning the lesson his partner's beauty treatment had taught him first time of asking.

Konstantin stood over the kneeling man and decided to neutralize him. It only needed a single forearm smash across the back of his skull to leave him sprawled out on the floor like a whore.

The other man retreated further, moving warily, watching the Russian. He didn't take his eyes from Konstantin. He was content to bide his time. Let the man's nerve break. He would strike eventually. They always did. Patience was the Russian way. Endurance. Last to blink won every time.

Konstantin didn't blink.

The other man did, as he knew he would.

He came in low, swinging the nightstick up and across, trying to get through his guard and crack the side of his skull open. It was a massive, wild swing, with enough power behind it to shatter the bone plate.

The Russian took the entire impact along his left arm, half on the wooden brace, half on the meat and bone.

The pain that roared out behind it was a bastard, but he still didn't blink.

The guard tried to adjust, wanting to press what he thought was his advantage.

It was a fatal mistake.

Konstantin stepped into the man's charge, ramming both hands forward into his chest as though to push him away. He felt a moment's resistance as the makeshift stakes impaled the man, using his own weight and momentum against him. Eye to eye, winner, loser, the two men stared at each other.

Konstantin withdrew both stakes and the guard collapsed to the floor, dead.

The Russian took a moment to extricate himself from the remains of the frame, then relieved the dead guard of his nightstick and walked out of the makeshift cell.

It wasn't hard to find his way outside, despite the fact they'd brought him down here with a bag over his head.

The roar of the choppers reverberated around the building, leading the way.

No one tried to stop him.

He didn't see another living soul in the place.

He exited the main building through large double doors onto a wide patio.

He was immediately assaulted by intense heat.

It was enough to physically batter him back a step as he raised his hand to shield his eyes. Before him was a scene like no other he had witnessed in his life.

One of the Mi-26 helicopters thundered overhead, producing such incredible force with its downdraught vertices it was hard to stay on his feet.

Directly beneath it, on a heatproof plinth, rested the largest crucible Konstantin had ever seen. It was simply massive. An enormous industrial crucible.

Workers in protective clothing struggled to attach heat-resistant cables to the giant metal loops on lip of the huge container.

Konstantin watched as to one side the powerful crane that had been used to lift the crucible onto the heat-resistant pad was turned away, it's arm swinging toward the house. Behind the crane he saw a large A-framed building with an open roof. Steam billowed up from within in great clouds.

Devere had said they were smelting the gold down.

The walls of the crucible itself were glowing under the sheer heat it contained.

Suddenly, the cables snapped tight as the military chopper rose higher.

The workers struggled to steady the enormous bowl as it lifted inch by inch up from the ground. It started to swing alarmingly before it was even twenty feet up, caught in the cross winds. Some of the boiling contents slopped over the side, splashing on an unfortunate man below. His suit offered no protection from the molten metal.

His screams did not last long.

And still the chopper rose, gaining altitude quickly now.

The swinging cargo threatened to smash into the building as the chopper banked, such was the extent of its movement. The chopper soared higher, taking the huge chalice clear over the roof.

Konstantin watched Devere's workers return to the building.

Looking up, he realised both Mi-26 helicopters were airborne.

The first was some distance away, but even from his vantage point the Russian could make out another huge crucible suspended below it.

Two choppers, two vats of molten gold.

It didn't make sense.

Why transport the stolen gold before casting it?

Konstantin knew the answer of course. It was all about the message, all about the show. Stealing from the rich, giving to the poor – it was the easiest way to win over the masses, especially if those same people were terrified of who might be the terrorists' next target. The contradiction of your saviour also potentially being your killer was one Konstantin grew up with. It was positively Russian in its twisted nature. Solomon was playing with everyone's expectations, fears and emotions.

Konstantin needed a weapon and he needed transportation.

Both were easy enough to find.

355

THIRTY-SEVEN
DON'T FEAR THE REAPER

Sir Charles weighed his options.

He could leave the Manor, but in doing so would admit defeat.

Add to that, he wasn't sure what he'd do once he got out now that Maxwell was gone. His options once he reached the threshold were limited. He could make a few calls, but who would he reach out to? Not Quentin, that was for sure. There was no way Knight and Mendes had him on lockdown without that old bastard's say so.

Alternatively, he could return to his study.

He doubted anyone was in there. That would give him some freedom to at least be himself.

He could make his way down to the Nest, and perhaps confront his captors for what good that would do.

But, assuming they were human and had to sleep, he could at least try and find out where his people were, and if any of them were still alive.

It was a first step.

He had to help himself, but he couldn't do that without the help of the others. Which meant getting at least one of them back to the Manor to put an end to Knight's rule of terror. He was absolutely convinced the man was a traitor. It was the only thing that made sense. They had a cuckoo in the nest.

He pushed his chair across the wide landing. Stealth was impossible, but he took care to avoid the creakiest floorboards. Even so the old house groaned at his passage. The Old Man reached the top of the stairs. He glared accusingly at the stair lift. He hated the damned thing, but right now he had no choice.

Someone had deactivated it, of course, and his attempts to power up the wretched contraption were unsuccessful.

He felt a dark rage bubbling up within him.

They were playing with him.

Were they sat there in Lethe's little cave watching his lack of progress on the monitors and laughing to themselves?

He hated being laughed at.

Sir Charles put the flat of his hand to a concealed panel and pushed, causing the section of wooden wall to pop open. He reached into the recessed area behind it and flipped a switch. It was answered by the reassuring hum of power returning to the stair lift, and a corresponding green light on the chair's control panel.

He rolled his chair into position, locking down the wheels before he pressed the button to descend.

The lift made a horrible racket as it took him down so very, very slowly. The old mechanism ground against the gears, setting his teeth on edge. He'd forgotten how much he hated this thing. There was a reason he never visited the upper floor of the Manor; it was humiliating.

With no one rushing to intercept him, he could only assume they were in the basement.

After what felt like an eternity, he reached the bottom.

He took care to shut down the stair lift again, not wanting the green light to give his escape away, then wheeled himself into his own room.

Closing the door behind him the Old Man paused for a moment, listening to the silence of the house, then headed straight for his oxygen tank. Moments later, precious oxygen poured from the plastic mask into his lungs. He left the mask in place for two rejuvenating minutes, allowing the miracle gas to clear his lungs one breath at a time. It was as close to magic as anything ever could be in this world.

He removed the mask and shut off the valve, then went over to the bureau in the corner. Opening a drawer, he took out a gun and a box of bullets. He loaded the Walther P-38 in seconds, his hand motions rapid and precise. The was no sign of the frailty he felt in the practised movements. Loaded, he placed the gun on his lap and covered it with a blanket.

He left the room, heading for the drawing room, which in moments of melodrama he liked to refer to as the Crucible.

The conference room was empty.

He made his way over to the hidden lift that led down to the Nest.

When he reached the basement, there was no sign of Jude Lethe.

Instead, Shamshi's brother, Abshir, sat in Jude's place in front of the multiple screens, his fingers rattling out rapid fire commands from Lethe's keyboard. It irked Sir Charles greatly – would he be so quick to leap into Lethe's grave?

Constance Mendes and Michael Knight stood behind Abshir, their attention on the screens. Neither noticed him enter. The last time he had spoken with either of them, it had been very much a one-sided conversation with him remaining silent whilst they called the shots. He had gambled on Quentin Carruthers changing his mind and pulling these interlopers from his house. That hadn't worked out as planned.

"I think perhaps you people should leave my home now," he said with the full authority of a man used to being obeyed.

Mendes and Knight turned to him. Mendes didn't seem surprised to see him. Knight though looked quietly furious. It was her reaction that interested him.

"Ah, good morning, Sir Charles," said Mendes.

Knight forced a smile. "We didn't expect to see you down here."

"I'm sure you didn't," Sir Charles replied pointedly.

"Let me take you back upstairs."

"I don't think so. I'm done being locked up in my own house."

The two men stared at each other, neither one giving an inch.

Mendes turned back to the nearest monitor.

"I think it only good manners you update me on my team?"

"We don't have much," she replied, not taking her eyes from the screen. "Nyrén is still in Jerusalem. What we can tell you is she foiled an attack on the Dome of the Rock where a terrorist linked to Solomon intended to let loose a mutated version of the Corpse Plane pathogen."

"Good girl," the Old Man said.

"Frost was last seen near Threadneedle Street, caught on surveillance cameras near the blast zone."

"And Khavin?"

"In the wind, though we have reason to believe he may have been in the same area before the blast happened. A man matching his description was involved in the attack."

The old man shook his head. "Not involved. If he was there, he was trying to prevent it."

"We can only work with the evidence. Our operative in Germany has been instructed to bring him in, but as I am sure you can appreciate, communications in the country are a mess right now."

"You believe Konstantin was in London, but your agent tasked with bringing him in is in Germany? On top of things as ever," the Old Man said.

Knight ignored the jibe, continuing on behalf of Mendes. "As for Larkin, well, there's no missing him. He's making an arse of himself in Rome, as per…"

"And Lethe?"

"Jude left here yesterday, and I haven't seen him since," Knight said.

"And that doesn't worry you?"

"Should it?" Mendes asked.

"I'd be concerned, he is a homebody. I'd be more concerned if I had something to hide, because he is about the most dangerous human being you are likely to meet."

Knight rankled. Good.

But it was Mendes who answered him. "I've tried to be straight with you, Sir Charles."

"I appreciate that. Sincerely."

"Then why the constant jibes?"

He didn't answer, instead he offered a question of his own. He was careful how he couched it, not wanting to tip Knight off as he said, "Weren't there four of you?" He deliberately didn't mention Shamshi by name.

He got the rise he wanted, another barely perceptible stiffening.

"Shamshi was working late."

"Ah, very good. Well, now that everyone is accounted for, I think it bears repeating, this is my home, not the property of Her Majesty, and as such I think it's time all three of you should leave my house."

"We're not ready to transfer to Vauxhall yet."

"I really don't care what you are or are not ready to do."

"We're not going anywhere," Constance Mendes told him.

"Ah, dear lady, I didn't mean you, I have no problem with you." He pushed aside the blanket and lifted the Walther. "I meant him."

He levelled the gun on Knight.

Even a cripple like him wasn't missing from this distance, and they all knew it.

Abshir pushed his chair back and rose, quickly, on edge. "What the fuck are you doing, old man?"

"Everybody stay calm," Knight said. "Charles is obviously having a few problems. No need to panic. Why don't you put the gun down, old man?"

"We're on the same side," Mendes said, which he doubted very much.

And he said as much, eyes never leaving Knight. "Are we? Because I get the impression Mister Knight is not on our side."

"Michael has worked for me for the last five years," Mendes said, "I trust him with my life."

"I wouldn't if I were you. I assume you had no idea he had me under lock and key."

Mendes frowned. "So you said. I ordered the Manor's entrances to be locked down."

"Did you also order the door to my room to be locked?"

"For your own safety," Knight said defensively.

"Bullshit, young man. You know it and I know it. This is my house. What about the earthquake? I'm fascinated to hear how you knew it was coming."

Mendes turned back to Sir Charles. "Now you're just being paranoid."

"Put the gun down before you accidentally shoot someone," Knight said.

"Riddle me this, then: why did you tell Stacia to get out of Bonn a few hours before the earthquake hit?"

"Oh, Christ on a bike, because Khavin was seen in Stuttgart."

"Except he wasn't, was he? He was in London."

"It was the intelligence we were working with at that time. This is insane."

"That's enough, Sir Charles," Mendes said. "Knight was right the other day. You're jumping at shadows. Not everything that happens in the world is because of Solomon. Now give me the gun."

"No. Given me Lethe and I'll find you the truth. I'll find out how he did it."

Mendes hesitated. He could tell she was torn.

Knight was having none of it. "He's not all there, Constance. Dementia. I told you. I can't believe you're still listening to him."

Mendes came to a decision.

"Give me the gun, Sir Charles. I trust Knight and I barely know you. That is just the way it has to be. I don't know what game you're playing, but nobody in this room is going to die today."

Sir Charles sighed. He flipped the gun over so the trigger guard hung from his finger and held the weapon out to Mendes.

She took it and disarmed it.

Knight was on him immediately, ramming his head back with a hand under his chin. "Don't push me, old man. We're *all* having a bad fucking day and I'm quite happy to take it out on you."

"For Christ's sake, Michael, let go of him."

Knight offered him a final sneer before he did as he was told.

"Take him back to his room, his *own* room," Mendes said. "And don't go getting any ideas about locking him up again. We are still guests in his house."

Knight scowled. "Fine."

"And Knight," Mendes added. "If anything happens to him, so much as a nose bleed, you *will* answer to me."

Sir Charles had done what he could.

He'd planted a seed in Mendes's mind.

He could only hope she'd see that Knight was rotten to the core.

THIRTY-EIGHT
BITTER SWEET SYMPHONY

The morning sun's rays finally reached the bars of Lethe's cage.

He was tired, but he couldn't sleep.

He was starving and so thirsty he was going out of his mind, but no one was feeding him.

Even his guard had abandoned him.

They'd left one man behind to watch over him, but now even he was gone.

The house creaked and groaned like a bastard, conjuring ghosts for him to fear. He was a victim of his own overactive imagination as he heard the lost souls wander the ruin. He wasn't sleeping even if he was exhausted. It just wasn't happening.

He wished he could MacGyver his way out of this situation, but the truth was, without access to technology, he wasn't going to achieve very much. He just wasn't that kind of hands on hero.

He heard a key in the lock.

It was an unmistakable sound.

He was on his feet, at the bars, chest tightening as he waited for the newcomer to show themselves. He didn't want to imagine what they were going to do to him, so of course it was all he could imagine, and in every version of it the pain was too much.

Floorboards creaked, following the newcomer around the house.

There were no voices.

Did that mean they were alone?

Could he overpower a single person?

Finally, the door opened, groaning on rusted hinges.

Shamshi's smile was the brightest thing Lethe had seen all day.

He couldn't quite believe that she was here and that he wasn't hallucinating her as his saviour.

"There you are!" she said, hurrying over to the cage.

Jude held his hands out. She took them both in hers.

"What are you doing here?"

"I'll tell you, but before that, key?"

"Over there, on the table. By my phone."

She hurried over and grabbed the keys and started trying them in the padlock.

"I came to find you, obviously," she said. "I didn't like what Abshir did, it was dirty. And then luring you here and leaving you in a cage? I couldn't believe he would agree to that."

She flipped through the bunch of keys, trying each one in turn in the cage's lock.

"The men who were here, they were Six?"

"I don't know."

"Well, whoever they are, I think they are balls deep in this. They're in Solomon's pocket."

"I know. Sir Charles knows," Shamshi said, finally finding the correct key.

The lock *clicked*, and the cage door sprang open.

He was out of there in a second and swept her up into a hug that she didn't resist.

He checked his phone. The battery had been pulled. He checked his gun and knew it was light even before he saw the magazine was missing.

"I have a phone," Shamshi said, offering it to him.

He took it. It was useless. She had no carrier. "Looks like Knight's wised up. You've been cut off."

"Shit," said Shamshi.

"It's fine. We need to go to Trafalgar Square. Solomon plans to drop a bunch of money. It's a trap."

"What can we do?"

"I don't know. We're just going to have to make it up as we go along."

"Sounds like fun."

THIRTY-NINE
GOODBYE YELLOWBRICK ROAD

Noah blinked back the daylight.

"My hero."

"Shut the fuck up. Seriously. I've run out of favours," Neri said, taking a drag from his cigarette. "So now I'm making promises—and no you don't want to know."

"Well now I do," Noah said as they approached the Roman's car.

The roof of the car divided them as Noah stared into Neri's eyes.

"Mate, seriously, what the fuck *did* you promise them? I'm fresh out of kidneys to trade, and my liver is shot. So, what did you offer those bastards?"

Neri sighed and dropped his cigarette to the flagstones, grinding it out underfoot.

"We have a a long-term investigation into the Vatican's systematic cover-ups of child abuse. It's been going for years."

"You didn't promise to abandon it? I'm not being the reason those kids don't get justice."

"No. I didn't. But I intimated I could influence things. Stall the investigation."

"You would do that?"

"Christ, no. But they don't *know* that."

"You're learning, my friend. Anyone would think Romans had a natural flare for skullduggery and corruption."

He opened the passenger side door and got in, Neri following suit.

"You look like shit, by the way," Neri said, starting the engine.

Noah ignored him, just as he ignored the pain from his swollen eye, bruised jaw and cracked ribs. "So, what did I miss?"

"The big announcement. Our friend the Camerlengo is to be the new Pope, at least until all the Cardinals can be replaced and a new conclave held."

"Which is what we figured."

Neri backed out of the parking space and headed towards the car parkt's exit.

"Did you get your proof?"

"Sort of," Noah said. "The Camerlengo's minions are brainwashed. We're talking scary cult brainwashing. They've all drunk the Kool Aid. They'll do *anything* he tells them. He's in bed with Solomon, and they're planning another attack. And that's where I got hit by the brick wall that is Catalina Sosa. I didn't stand a chance." He touched his damaged face to emphasize the point.

"You're not kidding," Neri said.

He could have sworn the Roman chuckled.

They drove in silence for a couple of minutes before Neri admitted, "I have more bad news for you."

"Oh great. Do I want to know?"

"The assassin is no longer in the country. He hasn't been for some time."

"Not surprising. It's not like they were going to keep him under lock and key. And besides we've got more stuff to worry about like the coronation of the Camerlengo."

"They don't do coronations. He's not a king. He gets inaugurated in five days' time here at Saint Peter's."

"So, we have a little time."

"To do what?"

"Stop him," Noah said. "It's all part of the forty days and nights spectacle, so it's going to tie in with the bullshit Solomon's being peddling about the Messiah. That's what this whole thing has been about. Fulfilling some ancient prophecy to pave the way for the Antichrist."

"That's a leap."

"Well, he keeps saying he's not the Messiah, so what's the alternative? They're peddling End of Days shit. It's one versus the other."

"I am glad I do not live inside your head, my friend."

"It makes sense to me."

"Which is why I pity you as much as I like you," Neri said. He wasn't smiling. Neri moved the car through traffic, following the roads to the police station. "You do know he is already Pope in all but name?"

"Shit. Do you have his schedule for the next few days?"

"Yes," said Neri, pulling into his reserved parking space and turning off the engine. "He's heading to Barcelona today. He intends to give Mass tonight at the Sagrada Familia."

Noah looked across at his friend. "You're about to tell me we need to go to Spain, aren't you?"

*

Noah was wrong about the new Pope waiting to make his speech.

The broadcast came twenty minutes after Neri and Noah arrived at Rome's police headquarters. All the televisions in the station showed it. He would never get used to the Catholic nation's obsession with the figurehead, but there it was. He stood, transfixed with the fascination as he'd seen in others listening to Solomon's sermon, as his other predictions came true.

"Peoples of the world, I wish I stood before you during better times. The world around us grieves fresh tragedy, demanding more of us. It needs our strength. And here, now, I make this promise to you as your new Pope, I am strong enough to shoulder all of your burdens. I am brave enough to stand in these darkest of days and show you the way back to the light. We will not fall, because good people, people like you, will not fall. It does not matter that terrible plagues have rained down upon us, that the land itself has rebelled, that violence seems to be everywhere. The only thing that matters is that we find our way back to the light, for the light will always be our salvation. We must find our way back to God. And, my children, as I look out among you I am reminded that there is one who can do just that. There is one and only one Messiah, and I pledge my allegiance and that of the Holy Roman Catholic Church to him."

There was an audible gasp from someone behind him.

Noah assumed the gathered spectators didn't understand the implications of the new Pope choosing not to name Christ as their messiah. No one could possibly believe he could mean Solomon, a man who had wrought a reign of terror. Messiahs and Antichrists. The definitions, when it came right down to it, weren't all that different. It just depended upon the perspective from where you looked at the rebellions they wrought.

"My friend Petrus Romanus was brutally murdered, my colleagues, our Cardinals are all dead. I did not choose this office. I was not born to it. But I will do my duty. I will carry my burden and do all that I can to help you, the faithful, to the glory of Our Father. I will stand side by side with our Messiah. I will follow his path. I will not abandon your soul to oblivion. I will not shy away from the fight to come, for these are The Last Days. And it is time to choose sides."

The broadcast ended.

Noah stared at the screen.

It took a moment to realise that the message must have been pre-recorded, given where he'd chosen to make the address. He recognized the wall from the gardens where, as Camerlengo, the man had delivered his lessons to his suicide artists.

Neri approached. "Okay, my friend, get your passport. I've arranged us a helicopter to take us to Barcelona. With commercial flights still grounded we're going military style. A lot less comfortable, and no pretty hostesses for you to annoy, but it will get us there."

"Sounds good to me."

"I will have no jurisdiction there, you understand."

"Jurisdiction? We don't need no stinking jurisdiction," Noah said, doing a terrible Blazing Saddles riff.

Neri looked less than impressed, but then, he could imagine what Noah had in mind when he said that.

FORTY
FAKE PLASTIC TREES

The twelve-storey apartment block was the typical Jerusalem sandstone brown.

It stood west of the Old City and the Temple Mount, near the Downtown Triangle.

The alleyway leading to it and the parking area in front were full of police cars and officers waiting for orders.

Orla stood beside Chief Tal Jabarin. Both women gazed upwards, shielding their eyes to the sun so they could better see the balcony on the seventh floor.

A man in police uniform had taken up position on the balcony, and aimed an Uzi indiscriminately over the heads of the onlookers.

Jabarin lifted a bullhorn to her mouth.

"Tayeb, it doesn't have to end this way. We can help you. But I need you to put the gun down. Please. Just put the gun down. No one needs to get hurt here."

Orla remembered him from the Temple Mount.

He was skittish. He kept moving. Bringing the Uzi up, aiming it down toward someone in the crowd, lifting it again, shuffling. Unpredictable. "Nobody's leaving this building!" Tayeb yelled. "Anybody tries, I start firing!"

They had snipers in position. Orla heard one report in to Jabarin, "I have a clean shot."

Jabarin hesitated, looking to Orla.

Orla read the situation. A clean kill was always beneficial. But it was the unknown variables, in this case Leah Ezra, that always needed to be factored in. What would she do if Tayeb died? What was their relationship? Did she already have the pathogen? "Hold off," she said. "We take out Tayeb, Ezra releases the pathogen and we all lose. We need to find and neutralize her."

Jabarin nodded. She'd been following the same train of thought. She showed the flat of her hand to the sniper, indicating he should hold. Then she raised the bullhorn once more. This time her words were for any other residents still inside the tower block.

"If you can hear this, I'm asking you to remain inside your units. Close your windows and doors. Do not attempt to leave the building. You are in no danger. I repeat, you are in no danger. Please, just remain inside your homes and wait for the situation to resolve."

Orla knew this uneasy standoff couldn't last.

Someone would panic.

They always did.

Someone would develop some irrational desire to run, and the moment they burst out of the front door the shooting would start. And once one shot was fired half a thousand more bullets would tear into the buildings and people all around as panic turned everything into a target. And from there it would only get worse if Ezra was inside with the pathogen.

What worried Orla was that it was just too easy to track Tayeb here.

It felt like a set up.

Ezra wasn't a fool. She was meticulous.

Tayeb hadn't returned home or tried to flee the city, but rather had raced to this arranged rendezvous point, an apartment owned by friends who were currently out of the country. He'd made no effort to cover his tracks. Maybe it was just down to panic. Maybe he'd been careless.

Or maybe, just maybe, Leah Ezra had set this up and wanted to lure the police here.

It was the middle of the day, which meant a lot of people who would normally be at home were at work.

Orla tried to think it through, putting herself in Ezra's shoes: releasing the virus inside the building would keep it contained to an extent, but outside, with all of the police gathered, it would very likely turn them into patient zero in a larger outbreak, and there was something darkly poetic about having the people supposedly there to protect you damning each and every one of you. She could see Ezra thinking that way.

"Sidearm," she said to Jabarin.

The chief stared at her. She could see the cogs ticking over as the gears turned, weighing up the risks of enabling a women she'd been sure was a terrorist an hour ago.

Moving with care, not wanting to draw Tayeb's attention, Jabarin reached down to her hip and drew her handgun. It was a regulation piece. A Jericho. She handed it to Orla, keeping the weapon behind her back so it couldn't be seen from the seventh floor, and Orla stuffed it into her belt at the small of her back.

She didn't say anything else.

She put her hands in the air and moved away from the police cordon, staying in parallel with the building.

She headed toward the entrance but tried to make it look as though she was running away.

It was a risky move, but Tayeb was either distracted by something or he bought it. No bullets were fired.

As soon as Orla reached an angle where the shooter could no longer see her, she made her run for the entrance – a large stone arch filled with glass, with an extended awning that reaching out from the doors.

Confident she hadn't been made, she punched in the four-digit door code and entered the building.

Several residents had gathered in the lobby, too scared to leave for fear of being shot, but not willing to stay in their rooms in case a bomb went off and took half of the upper floors with it. So, they cowered here, waiting for the police to make their move.

Orla smiled at them reassuringly.

"Go out the door and turn left. Stay as close to the wall as you can, and in single file, run. He won't see you if you stay pressed up against the wall. Move out into the street and he will see you. Understand?"

Grateful residents nodded and one by one headed for the doors.

Orla set off in the opposite direction, towards the lifts.

One lone gunman was nothing to worry about; the sniper could take Tayeb out in a heartbeat. He was careless. The standoff would have been over before it began. But the pathogen changed things. Even if Ezra wasn't in the building, playing puppet master, if he had the glass test tubes on him and he fell, all hell would follow with him as he came down, a falling angel of death.

She took the lift to the sixth floor, one short.

Ezra might have had eyes on the seventh, though any kind of call signal would show movement in the lift.

It occurred to her that Ezra could quite easily have summoned dozens of her followers, too. Hopefully the wall-to-wall news coverage of the attempted bombing of the Dome would convince them to stay away from Ezra.

The lift doors opened with an uncomfortably loud chime on the otherwise silent floor.

Orla moved out, walking along the corridor.

She saw a mother and daughter cowering in the hallway.

Voice barely above a whisper, she demanded, "Why aren't you inside?"

"We don't know where's safe," the mother replied.

"Take the lift down. You can go through the main entrance, keep to the left wall, and stay as close to the building as you can until you're around the corner and clear."

The mother looked at Orla like she'd just given her daughter a future, gathered the girl into her arms and hurried toward the still open elevator.

Orla waited until they were safely inside and the door closed before she moved off.

She reached the stairwell's fire door.

Leading the way with the Jericho, Orla opened the fire door and stepped through into the concrete stairwell.

She checked both up and down before taking a second step, moving up with the assumption that anyone she encountered was a threat.

She climbed to the seventh, stopping by the door to listen.

Nothing.

Or at least nothing she could hear, which wasn't the same thing.

She opened the door and slipped through.

There was nobody here, but she had a problem.

Normally, Lethe was in her ear filling in the gaps. Even after the lab, she wasn't used to going it alone. She needed to get her bearings, making a mental map of the apartment building in her mind, and filling in the details from the landscape as she remembered it from outside, including a count of the windows, which relied upon her remembering correctly.

A heartbeat later she was on the move.

A guess on the number of windows would only get her so far, though. She needed accurate intel. And the only thing she could think to do was advance, listening at every door for tell tale signs of movement inside.

At the first door, she heard nothing.

The second, faint sobbing. She discounted it and moved on.

The third was silent.

She listened for longer than at either of the first two.

Still silent.

And then she heard Tayeb's voice.

"Oh no you fucking don't." The curse was followed by burst of gunfire and distant screams.

Orla closed her eyes, wanting to believe it was only impotent anger and that the people she'd sent out there hadn't stumbled into his sight line. Hopefully not that mother and daughter...

She needed to think.

Distract.

Do something.

She hammered at the door, crying, "Help me! Please! There's a guy with a gun. He's shooting people. Please let me in!"

She heard movement behind the door, the light of the spyhole going out for a moment before she heard the lock turn.

The door opened.

A man stood there, holding an Uzi in one hand and the open door in the other.

Orla didn't recognize him, but that was irrelevant.

Before he could open his mouth to bark at her, she grabbed him by the shirt and hauled him out into the corridor. She slammed him up against the wall as the door closed behind her. It wasn't pretty, but it was effective. Her forearm smashed the man across the Adam's apple as she drove him into the wallpapered concrete. There was no give in the wall. She'd ruptured his hyoid bone. He couldn't breathe. Killing him would be a mercy. She didn't feel merciful.

She kicked the Uzi away and stood over him.

She watched him fail to breathe.

And for a moment he was Uzzi Sokol, he was Gavrel Schnur, he was Youssef Saddiq, the Beast of Jenin. He was everyone who had ever hurt her.

And she wanted him to die slowly, in pain.

But he wasn't any of those people.

She knew what was going on inside her head. It wasn't healthy. But then she wasn't fixed, was she? She should never have come back here. Not that she had a choice. She was doing more than banishing ghosts, she was making them.

He was just the most recent one.

Orla stuck her gun back in her belt and relieved the dying man of his Uzi.

She moved into the apartment, ready to make more.

She heard Tayeb clearly, taunting the police on the ground as he waved his machine gun erratically. He fired two shots at them, trying to disperse the crowd. Either one, or both, might have hit someone.

Time to end this.

She crossed the entrance hallway into the kitchen, dropping into cover beside the fridge. She saw a serving hatch through to the living room, and through it, Tayeb.

She saw shadows move across the hatch.

He wasn't alone.

"We need to leave."

It was Leah Ezra.

Orla watched the woman move towards the windows, still out of sight of the officers below.

"Let me settle a couple of old scores, first," he said.

"Fine, just be quick about it. There's a timer on us. Once the mechanism drops we've got five minutes to get clear of the blast zone before dispersal starts. That isn't a long time."

"Tell me again why couldn't just evac by chopper?"

Ezra chuckled.

"Fine, window cleaner's rig it is."

"Where's Ruben?"

"No idea," Tayeb said, loosing off another couple of shots.

"I don't like it," Ezra said, moving toward the apartment door. She peered through the spy hole.

Orla rose.

As though instinctively aware, Ezra turned to smile her way.

There were no words. No recriminations or Scooby Doo decrials against her meddling. The entry wound from the Jericho's bullet was a small, precise circle, no more than the size of Orla's pinky finger. The exit wound took out the entire back plate of her skull, blood and brains everywhere as she fell. One shot.

Orla swung in Tayeb's direction, but he was already squeezing down on the Uzi's trigger, loosing a burst of fire at her.

She threw herself to the fake tiled floor, below the hatch, as chunks of wood, drywall and masonry spat out.

"Who the fuck are you?" Tayeb screamed, firing again. The shots tore into the wall, high and uncontrolled. He emptied the full magazine into the kitchen, a jagged line of pock marks tearing the wall before his bullets ran out.

Tayeb ejected the empty magazine.

He didn't have time to reach for the replacement.

From her crouch, Orla put two bullets in him, one in the head, one in the chest.

There was a moment of disbelief between dying and knowing he was dead, and then Tayeb pitched forward, crashing to the floor.

Orla moved fast.

She found the dispersal bomb in the main bedroom. She saw the built-in timer, armed but not active, and didn't hesitate. She pried open the mechanism to get access at the guts of it inside, grabbed a handful of wires and twisted them free of their couplings, and then removed the twin vials of the pathogen and placed them in the inside pocket of her jacket. The glass was thick enough it wouldn't accidentally crack or shatter simply because she jostled it.

Orla went out onto the balcony, offering no sudden moves, nothing that might cause an itchy trigger finger to pull, and raised a hand for Chief Jabarin and her officers to see.

"All clear," she called down to the woman, before she turned and slumped down, back against the balcony's half-wall. She rested her wrists on her knees, gun hanging between them, aimed at the concrete floor, breathing deeply as she struggled to centre herself. The cooling breeze gentled over her face.

The tension began to subside, but she was a long way from being at peace.

She would never feel that kind of harmony as long as she was in this place. Too many demons for that.

She didn't move for two full minutes, waiting for Jabarin's team to arrive and secure the scene, and even then she didn't look up until Jabarin herself arrived.

"You're quite an impressive individual," she said to Orla. "I half expected you to run away, if I am being honest. Did you recover the pathogen?"

"Yes."

"And the seals weren't compromised? They're still safe?"

"Yes."

"Then perhaps you would consider handing it over?"

"I don't think so, Chief. No disrespect, but the last time you had them in your possession they walked out of your evidence locker, and several people are dead now who didn't need to die. That's an undeniable fact. What is purely speculation on my part is that the death of one rotten officer doesn't mean there are no more rotten officers to accidentally fall. Even with Ezra dead. This is a cause. These are fundamentalists. It's all about the endgame. It doesn't matter dick to them how many fall along the way. So, can you guarantee me the vials won't disappear again?" Jabarin didn't answer. "Can you be sure the IDF won't sequester them, with the full intention of using them as weapons?" Again, no denial from the Chief. "So, then, that's where we are. I like you. I think you're good people. I don't think you want to risk this disease getting out, whoever is behind the leak."

"But I can't let you walk out of here with them."

"Then I guess we are at an impasse. Maybe you should make something up to arrest me for?" She set it with a smile, believing she'd got the woman's number. She wasn't the kind of cop to lie for the greater good. It was a gamble. "Or you can let me walk out of, get myself out of Jerusalem, I know someone in Tel Aviv who can neutralize the threat of the pathogen once and forever, and you can sleep soundly knowing millions of people aren't going to die because of the decisions we made here, today."

Jabarin considered her offer. They weren't alone in the apartment, but the first responders were busy securing the scene for the forensics units and ensuring that the dead really were dead. No one was listening to their conversation. She leaned in to Orla and whispered, "Go, you have my word you will not be stopped. Not here. Not at the border. I just pray I don't regret this."

She held out a hand for Orla to take and helped her up.

The two women nodded once, no more words necessary.

FORTY-ONE
RAINTOWN

Trafalgar Square was crammed with people.

There was barely an inch to breathe.

Ronan figured upwards of ten thousand were already gathered in the huge square, more stuck in the streets feeding into it, desperate to get their slice of the golden pie.

Ronan had been trying convince people to leave, but he was on a hiding to nothing.

These people thought Solomon was on their side.

Even after of all the terrible things he had done, with people too scared to drink the tap water, to fly on a plane, ride on the Underground, or even use their credit cards and a dozen other things they usually did every day, he was promising them the one thing that might be their salvation even as the world fell apart around them.

Gold.

As the hour neared, the people in the crowd began to chant, their voices coming together, while others sang. Some danced while others climbed onto the plinths of the Landseer lions, straddling the great beasts as those down below cheered and blew horns and most chillingly of all, laughed.

After all, everything Solomon had threatened in his forty days and forty nights of fear had come to pass, so why not this?

The Bank of England vaults had been breached.

Maybe he really was some modern day Robin Hood, and sharing out the gold would be his ultimate revenge on the one percent who battered the life out of the working men and women of the country? In that way they could almost justify the other attacks, as every revolution was born out of bloodshed, wasn't it? So, maybe Solomon was their leader. He couldn't be any worse than the ineffectual and venal power-hungry career politicians that had infested Whitehall. A man of the people. Behold the light.

There had been so little to celebrate of late that this felt like a release, all of that tension, all of that fear, bubbling up, needing to be free.

More splashed and kicked up water in the fountain.

The spirits were high.

All Frost could do was watch.

He took a swig from the bottle of water he'd bought from a newsagent on the walk to the Square. As he drank, the already warm water soothing his sore throat, he scanned the crowds, looking for any familiar faces, for anything out of the ordinary. It was as often the absence as it was the presence of something off that set alarm bells ringing.

He moved through the crush of people toward the steps leading to the National Gallery.

The first wave came from the police.

They marched in ranks, in full riot gear, and carrying batons which they beat against their transparent shields in a form of tribal intimidation.

They came from the west moving eastward across the Square.

Bullhorns called for people to clear the Square.

"Your lives are in danger. An attack is imminent. Please disperse."

The police pushed forward, but the people pushed back.

Some went down, trampled beneath the feet of others, but the line held strong. The defence thickened, pushing back. They weren't about to be easily broken.

There was a limit to the force the police could bring to bear.

They broke, and an almighty cheer went up as the crowd surged forward, a tidal wave of humanity smashing through the riot shields sweeping the officers away. The tide of resistance rose.

They weren't keeping people safe, not now. Now they were risking more injuries.

Frost was seized by a powerful urge for self-preservation. The only smart move was to get out of there before things went sour. In the back of his mind he knew there was a good chance no one would be able to leave later. And if they didn't want to be saved that wasn't his problem. A grim thought surfaced in the Irishman's mind: *Let them all die, it's their own fucking fault.*

He didn't like that line of thinking, but he wasn't a cop. His job wasn't to protect and serve at all costs. He let the anger swell within him. Maybe his rage would spark an idea.

He could pull his gun and try shooting into the air, but that kind of stunt would only result in a stampede.

A dull rumbling noise grew around him. In less than a minute it became louder than the crowds.

He tried to locate the source.

Whitehall.

Looking up, Frost spotted two massive helicopters in the distance. Huge machines, creating a louder and louder din. Beneath each chopper hung a massive bowl-shaped crucible.

Russian Mi-26 heavy lifters.

Monster-choppers, massive machines capable of lifting an incredible payload.

As they neared, he saw the crucibles in more detail. They belched smoke. His first impression was that they were on fire.

He didn't like this.

He backed up a couple of steps, making it to the terrace at the top, and gazing out over the heads of the gathering, as the two massive helicopters circled Nelson's Column. The excitement in the crowd was palpable. Their voices rose in cheers as the choppers circled, crying out, "Gold! Gold! Gold!"

The choppers separated, one to the north-east side of the Square, nearer St Martins in the Field, while the other drifted to the south-west and Admiralty Arch.

The crowds mirrored them, dividing into two distinct masses that surged beneath the downdraughts of the mighty rotors.

This had the peculiar effect of leaving the centre of the Square almost empty as everyone forced their way beneath the helicopters, wanting their share of the prize.

Not good.

Not good.

Not good.

It wasn't riches in those crucibles hanging over their heads.

Riches didn't smoke.

There was no acrid smell of burning in the air though.

Not smoke, then.

Steam?

Frost was caught in a moment's indecision; he could make a break for the cover of the National Gallery, it was only half a dozen steps to safety, or he could try to get down there and help people.

Around the fringes of the crowd he saw the police had been replaced. There were dozens of black clad men and women armed with assault rifles circling the perimeter of Trafalgar Square.

Few in the crowd noticed, so transfixed were they by the promise of the helicopters above.

Frost caught a movement on the fringes of the crowd; a policewoman going down. It was the arc of blood from the knife wound that drew his eye. He saw the man who had killed her stash his knife a second before he took the fallen officer's place.

He unshouldered an AR-15 and turned it in toward the crowd.

Ronan felt powerless. One man against the tide. It wasn't as though he could shove people out of harm's way.

There came a double-*clunk* noise as both helicopters released their payload at the same time.

The cheers of the crowd were gut wrenching in how quickly they changed, because it was gold that fell from the sky, just not the coins they had dreamed of. It poured like a liquid, orange-red colour, almost white, as it rained down in wave after molten gold wave, splashing and spitting, each drop so brutally hot it burned straight through flesh to bone. A single droplet to the skull burning through the bone plate to the brain beneath, searing through motor controls, language centres and imagination as though it wasn't there.

Some, taking the brunt of the golden rain were so badly burned their clothing and flesh seared and smoldered even as it incinerated.

But the gold cooled as it fell, and as people screamed and tried to run in the grip of sheer desperate panic, many more were engulfed in a stream of white-hot molten metal, one-thousand degrees Celsius of death.

It cut short their screams in an instant, turning them into twisted statues that momentarily glowed red even as their molds were burned away.

People tried to run.

They didn't get far before they were cut down by the armed cordon.

Hundreds were scythed down by the hail of bullets shredding through the crowd.

Frost was above it all, watching with horror as men, women and children met one death or another, bullets, or liquid gold.

It was too much to bear; horror on a scale he couldn't imagine if he weren't watching it with his own eyes. It surpassed the horrors he'd imagined second hand seeing photos of the bloodiest conflicts of the last seventy years and more. The inventiveness when it came to causing suffering was staggering. The brutality of it, shocking. The savagery and sheer speed as joy and hope turned to despair, dizzying. It was the perfect act of terror.

And Solomon was going die because of it, the Irishman vowed.

Because he might be helpless here and now, but assuming he made it out of the Square alive he would find Solomon, and he'd be just as cruelly inventive in his vengeance. The dead deserved no less from him.

A man ran past him, shrieking, the side of his face and his shoulder plated in gold, like some twisted cyborg creation.

Steam billowed from the rapidly hardening metal.

As he clawed at his face and shoulder his fingers sank into the gold, and as it set, he could no longer remove them.

It all happened so sickeningly quickly.

The man collapsed and lay there, contorting in death spasms as the molten metal burned through to his brain and finally, mercifully, ended his life.

But Solomon was good to his word: this person died a rich man, shrouded in gold.

A single droplet of molten metal landed on Frost's shoulder, searing through the fabric of his coat and shirt.

He didn't waste time trying to scream, he needed to get out of the clothing before it burned through. The swell of agony from the dying was a chorus of hellish voices. He ripped off his coat and tore his shirt, staring at his shoulder where the single droplet was solidifying, set into the bone. The skin around the wound was raw red and steaming.

The pain galvanized him into action.

Frost pulled his Browning and surged into motion.

He saw a manhole cover, just ten feet away, but with dozens of people crowding around it and rushing across it, trying to get away from the lethal rain he had to shove his way through desperate and dying people to get to it. At the rim, he dropped to his knees, ignoring the punishing blows and kicks of the stampede and jammed the muzzle of the Browning into the small keyhole in the cover and heaved it open.

It took some serious strength, especially with his shoulder screaming at him, but Frost managed to lever up the cover.

He pushed it to one side.

A man with his left arm entirely encased in gold tripped over it and fell to his knees, screaming.

The liquid metal still rained down as the chopper circled, its rotors churning up the air so the stream was more akin to a shower now. A golden arc fell toward Frost's position, burning a cluster of desperate people fighting to escape it. A line of gold seared through the spine of one, cutting like a hot knife through human butter. It was horrific. Frost couldn't look away.

He launched himself down the hole head first, no idea of how deep or what he might land on. It didn't matter, it had to be better than being sliced open by Solomon's gold.

Hands out, he landed on his palms, arms buckling so that his wounded shoulder took the brunt of the impact, and rolled aside just as the liquid metal splashed and sizzled in the thin ribbon of sewage water no more than arm's reach from his head.

Most of the gold ended up on the wall.

Seeing what he'd done, more people climbed down into the hole after him.

Frost was good with that. If it saved a few lives, then his presence wasn't completely in vain.

Painfully, he stood up and moved aside as a man and his young daughter climbed down after him. Ronan swept them out of the way, lifting the girl over the sewage water as another man jumped into the hole.

He didn't collide with the two survivors but landed awkwardly.

Frost heard the bone break.

Ronan grabbed him by the shoulders and dragged him out of the way.

A woman came down next. Her back was spotted with flecks of gold. He couldn't imagine the kind of pain she was in, but she gritted her teeth and moved stubbornly to join the small rabble of survivors huddled to one side of the tunnel.

The next man down wasn't so lucky.

He stumbled on the ladder, missing his footing and fell. As he came down, his head cracked off a metal rung, but it wasn't a bone on metal sound that echoed through the tunnels, it was a sickening metal-on-metal clang.

He landed face first in the sewage water.

Frost moved quickly to try help him, but as he turned the man onto his back to avoid his breathing in the brackish water, he only succeeded in bringing him round. His screams reverberated around the cramped confines of the tunnel. They were harrowing to behold. This was a man who should already be in hell, Frost realised, seeing that most of face was already sheathed in thin patina of gold, both eyes covered like a blind funeral mask, and one side of his neck encased. One side of the man's mouth was free of the hardening gold, meaning his jaw was licked open. His cry of anguish was wretched.

Frost knelt over him.

There was no coming back from this.

The Irishman didn't offer last rights. There was no absolution.

He simply said, "Cover the kid's eyes." And placed the Browning's muzzle against the side of the victim's head that wasn't already gold.

He pulled the trigger.

The sound was impossibly loud in the tunnel.

No one said anything, but they looked at him. They looked at him like he'd just put down a stray dog.

"It was a kindness," he said.

And it was. The man wasn't going to survive. And there was a limit to how much anyone should suffer.

The survivor with the broken leg lay against the far wall, gritting his teeth against the pain. Frost motioned for someone to help him. The kid's father let him lean on his shoulder. The woman and girl stood behind, waiting for Frost to lead them into the darkness.

There was a metaphor in that. He fucking hated metaphors.

"Can't we just wait until the gold cools, then go back up?" someone asked.

Frost shook his head, not sure if anyone could see the gesture. "They aren't cops up there anymore. There's maybe thirty paramilitary, armed with AK-47s, Uzi's and Armalites. We go back up there, they mow us down. We need to get as far away from here as we can, which means using the tunnels."

No one argued with him.

Ronan regarded their terrified faces in the half light. The young girl, lost and confused, the guy with the broken leg, wincing and biting back on the pain each time he so much as shuffled a half-step, the woman with the burns on her back, surprisingly silent despite the obvious pain, the father, trying to assist as best he could. Frost knew he was being hard on them. He was angry, shocked and for once genuinely afraid. But unlike them he had a job to do. He needed the sense of purpose that gave him. He breathed in the foul stench of shit and piss and everything else that made London human, and reminded himself that they'd lost people up there, family, friends, and seen the kind of battlefield horrors that would haunt them every night for the rest of their lives. They weren't soldiers. They didn't carry that same ethos within them his band of brothers did, those two simple words that defined them: soldiers die.

"Okay," he said, picking up his jacket and putting it on. "I'm going to get you out of here. You have my word. I want you to gather behind me, I'll lead the way. We're going home. You with me?"

Together they moved off, Frost in the lead, using the torch from his phone beside the Browning in his hand to light the way. A few of the others took out their phones and used the flashlight app, which helped them see the way.

He kept his pace slow, allowing the injured man to keep up with muffled grunts of pain.

Frost wasn't a fool. Solomon was rigorous in his planning and execution. If Frost could come up with the idea of trying to get people out through the sewers, then the same thought would have occurred to the terrorist leader. Meaning they'd be facing armed resistance sooner rather than later.

Every corner promised death.

But then, Death and Frost were old friends.

FORTY-TWO
PERSONAL JESUS

Konstantin wasn't alone.

Devere's people had cleared out and taken every vehicle with them.

Which meant he should be the last one here. But he wasn't. He knew when he was being watched.

His pursuer was good. They made no sound, but they were there, just at the edge of perception. He wasn't about to make the same mistake twice. That wasn't the Russian way.

Konstantin moved through into a sizeable warehouse with a vaulted steel roof that was attached to the west side of the Devere building. The first thing he noticed in the vast space was a stack of rusty oil drums stacked in one corner. Towards the middle, metal pipes and disassembled shelves lay in a pile like someone was building a bonfire and hadn't quite grasped the idea that the metal wouldn't burn. Konstantin saw a pile of broken wooden crates which would have provided much better kindling. He jogged across to it, using the shattered wood for cover, and kept his eyes on the wide cargo door he had entered through.

He didn't have to wait long.

A man stood in the doorway, caught half in the light.

Konstantin recognized him.

How could he not? The man's face, every last detail of it, was burned into his brain and had been since the moment Pope Peter II died. Then the man had posed as a Swiss Guard to get close enough to the Holy Father to slip the knife fashioned from Iscariot's silver between his ribs.

The crushing defeat still weighed heavily on the Russian's shoulders.

But it was nothing compared with the hunger for revenge that burned in his gut.

He'd seen him again, at the Israeli embassy, bulletproof glass saving the man's life that time.

But this was different.

He was alone with the killer, no tricks between them, no last-minute salvation.

It was all he could do not to make his move.

Patience.

But in his mind's eye he felt the bones of the assassin's neck snap beneath his hands.

Not yet. A few more seconds.

And not before he had wrung out everything, every dirty secret the assassin possessed, and linked it back to Solomon.

The killer was armed. All Konstantin had was his dead guard's nightstick. It was hardly a fair fight. He should throw the nightstick away to give the assassin a chance. A cruel smile crept across the Russian's face at the grim gallows humour. He was going to enjoy this.

Konstantin held his position, gathering a decent sized piece of wood and weighing it in his weaker hand. He studied the assassin's movements. The other man was cautious. He scanned the warehouse for his quarry, and not seeing him, held back. Konstantin waited until the assassin's gaze was almost directly away from his position, then stood up.

He hurled the wood end over end at a distant wall.

Bisch's instincts were good.

He reacted quickly, half-turning toward the sound without totally being sold on it, and raised his piece. The Russian had anticipated the move, and whipped the nightstick out, sending it through a vicious arc at the assassin's back. The slight change in stance meant the stick slammed into his arm, taking the gun clean out of his grip.

Before the assassin could recover, Konstantin was on the move.

He crashed into him like a linebacker sacking a dazed quarterback and sent him sprawling into another pile of broken up kindling.

Before his prey could recover, Konstantin drove a double-fisted slam into the centre of his face. It was brutal bone-breaker of a blow meant to put an end to any thoughts of resistance. The assassin barely got his arms up to protect himself, taking the meat of the blow on his forearms, but such was the savagery of the Russian's follow-up that no amount of desperate blocking was warding the frenzied blows off. His huge fists connected with the killer's cheek, eye socket, nose and jaw, grinding bone and teeth again and again before he was finally bucked clear.

Konstantin scrambled to his feet.

His opponent was fast, despite the beating. He rose, facing down the Russian, and as Konstantin lifted his head, dbarrelled toward him, intent on bringing the big man down.

He came in swinging, body blows aimed at driving Konstantin back.

The Russian blocked four successive clubbing swings, backing up step after step as the assassin advanced.

The onslaught was furious.

Konstantin let the assassin come, taking the beating. He didn't resist. He simply absorbed each fresh blow, eyes locked on the assassin, focussed. His concentration was unnerving. His sheer physical strength daunting. The other man swung again, connecting squarely with his jaw. The Russian barely flinched beneath the impact. Still, more swings came, and he took them, stepping back and back as his body took the barrage.

It was a lie.

Perception.

He let the man believe he was slowly gaining the upper hand, allowing him to land some telling blows, and even as the assassin's fist hammered into his ribcage with enough force to lift the big Russian bodily, Konstantin felt his foot come down against the pile of debris and metal piping in the middle of the room, and stopped retreating.

The assassin doubled down his attack, going at Konstantin with everything he had: feet, fists, elbows, knees.

But Konstantin ducked and swayed, taking them on the bone of his forearm, on the meat of his shoulder, anywhere than minimized the actual impact as he curved and leaned around them, letting his attacker burn himself out.

Konstantin was used to pain, not just experiencing it, or coping with it, but in acting through it.

He dropped low without warning, using his eyes to feign a sweeping attack, which the assassin had to react to. And as he did, Konstantin launched himself forward and upward, cannoning into the other man.

The plate of his skull slammed into the underside of the man's jaw, snapping his head back. His momentum sent the assassin sprawling across the dusty ground.

Without let up, Konstantin grabbed the heaviest metal pipe he could reach and delivered a swing for the fences, sweeping it round in a vicious arc.

His opponent was agile, and already on his feet.

Konstantin faked exhaustion, keeping the pipe low, chest heaving, staring at the man from beneath his heavy brow.

The assassin darted in, landing a one-two combination to the big Russian's shoulder as he dropped it. The pain was intense, a sunburst of black agony. A nerve had fired off. Something was wrong in there. All he could do was ignore it.

The assassin came on again, another snaking right jab aimed at his face.

Konstantin rocked back on his heels, deftly avoiding the clumsy blow.

And again.

And again.

They danced just out of reach, feet scuffing up the dust.

Sizing each other up, feeling out the opponent's weaknesses.

It was only ever going to be a matter of time before one or the other tired and made a mistake.

And Konstantin wasn't about to give the bastard the satisfaction of letting him get the better of him twice in one life time.

The assassin lashed out.

Konstantin let it connect, rolling with the punch, inviting the other man forward.

The man dropped his left shoulder, putting all of his strength behind a wild swing.

Konstantin let it through, taking it in the face. His head snapped back. He staggered back a half-step, scuffing his feet and shaking his head as he looked up, inviting the assassin to try again.

Konstantin said nothing.

He didn't need words.

It was coming.

He could feel it.

And there it was.

The mistake.

His opponent paused just for half a second, caught by indecision and confusion at the Russian's willingness to take a battering, and Konstantin seized that half-second, raising the metal pipe and lashing it round in a savage arc. The killer had misjudged the distance, expecting the Russian's clubbing fist, so his feint only took him into the path of the makeshift weapon in his hand.

He saw it at the last possible second, no time left to react.

The pipe crunched off the side of assassin's skull so hard it decompressed the bone plate, leaving the man with a dent in the side of his head.

The shockwave reverberated through Konstantin's arms and shoulders.

The sound echoed around the empty space like a gunshot.

He went down like he'd been shot. He lay on the floor, one leg, one arm twitching spastically. Drool trickled from his open mouth, pooling in the dust. He was done.

Konstantin cursed.

He'd got too lucky and hit the guy too hard.

Even if he didn't die from the damage he wasn't going to be walking and talking in a hurry.

Konstantin reached down and grabbed the assassin by his collar, dragging him to his feet. The man stared back blankly, the lights barely on, definitely no one at home. More drool spilled down his chin.

He managed a weak gurgling noise in the back of his throat.

"Remember the face of the man who killed you," Konstantin said softly. "Take it with you to Hell and wait for me there. I'll be coming down to put you through an eternity of torment."

He made the same choking noise in response but couldn't make eye contact.

He'd have to live without answers.

The gap between him and Solomon was closing.

It was only a matter of time.

The Russian was patient. He could wait a while longer.

He used the blunt end of the pipe to stove in the assassin's skull. It wasn't about putting him out of his misery or doing the man a kindness. It was about payback.

That was the Russian way.

FORTY-THREE
ALWAYS BELIEVE IN YOUR SOUL

Jude and Shamshi arrived during the aftermath of the attack, forced to confront the sheer horror that had somehow come to pass.

And all he could think was: *This still a long way short of forty days…*

Police had set up a cordon preventing anyone from approaching.

Shamshi flashed her MI-6 credentials and the cops melted away from them. This was technically not her domain, everything about Six's jurisdiction and mission was overseas, gathering intel, fostering foreign contacts, all in secret. But next to a beat cop she was Queen of the Castle and they were content to let her rule.

The bodies they were forced to step over and around on the edge of the square were harrowing enough, flesh ripped apart by sustained automatic fire. Every flagstone was slick and sticky with blood. It pooled and puddled everywhere. All Lethe could think was this is where it had all started what felt like a life time ago with Catherine Meadows, the forensic archeologist, setting herself on fire.

Lethe stopped trying to avoid the blood.

He struggled to hold his shit together.

Beside him, Shamshi, while appalled at carnage, seemed almost detached.

Lethe tried not to look at a little girl lying atop her father, both of them dead, both showing signs of burn damage on their skin. Instead he fixed his gaze on a team of paramedics working their way through the bodies, looking desperately for any signs of life. How they could do it, how they could root around amid all that death in search of life… they were better people than him.

The real horror lay beyond the outer ring. It wasn't about those who'd been cut down as they tried to escape. It was the golden dead. They shone brilliantly in the rising sun, an image of incalculable horror and breathtaking beauty all at the same time. It was unlike anything Jude Lethe had ever seen.

Nevertheless, he was put in mind of Pompeii and its citizens frozen forever in time by the heat of Vesuvius's pyroclastic surge.

The inner-square was still crowded with people, but nobody moved.

There were figures all around him, yet they remained frozen, all still like statues locked in every conceivable pose, and all shimmering in the midday sun, glittering in brilliant gold. It was like walking through the middle of a twisted art installation.

Some of the gilded figures were prone, he saw, reaching out in vain to protect their faces, or gather their children into their arms. Others with their arms outstretched appeared almost to be begging for mercy. So many more had been coated in liquid gold while still on their feet. He saw some, arms raised to the heavens, some simply looking up at the death raining down on them. Some poor souls had been caught fleeing for their lives and would be forever locked in that hideous athletic failure.

A few were on their knees.

One woman sat with her back against one of the stone plinths, itself now partially covered in gold, her golden head in her blistered and burned hands.

One of the dead stole Jude's breath away and broke his heart all at the same time: a man holding a child above his head as a human shield. It was hideous. Sickening. Vile. He couldn't imagine anyone capable of such a thing. And yet here it was. He could only pray it wasn't a father sacrificing his son.

On and on they went.

Statues of people running, panicking, falling, jumping, lying down, covering heads, shielding loved ones, holding on to each other, locked forever in a golden hell.

Only a few were fully encased. Most were half-burned, half-entombed, and somehow those were worse. They offered stark reminders of who the dead used to be.

A golden figure reached out with a real arm, the clothes and skin seared away where the edge of the molten gold had coated the rest of his body. One woman's face was only half covered, the blank expression modelled in the gold in stark contrast to the detailed agony of the flesh.

The reflection coming from the yellow metal loaned the scene an abstract, almost surreal air of unreality. It was never less than painful to look at, so brilliant was the golden glare.

The smell of cooked flesh turned Lethe's stomach. But that stench was one of the few things that helped bridge the disconnect between the horrific reality and the daydream quality that came with walking through

403

the crowd of gold. His brain struggled to process what he was seeing. He didn't know what he was supposed to do with it. How it was meant to fit into his world. And how he was meant to exist in a world where this could happen.

He fell to his knees and vomited noisily onto the gold-plated flagstones.

He felt Shamshi's hand on the back of his neck as he purged himself. She didn't say anything. She didn't judge him. She simply let him know she was there.

He was lost inside the frozen mortality surrounding them.

He couldn't imagine a way of escaping it.

But eventually he rose to his feet. He needed her. He had never felt so hopeless. He wanted to lean on something, to support himself, but everywhere he looked were the golden dead. He couldn't imagine reaching out to lean on one of those. He managed five steps away from the vomit before he sank back down to his knees, broken.

Lethe's eyes stung with tears.

He wiped at them with his sleeve.

He couldn't breathe.

The cloying stench of burned meat was in his throat.

He knew that the carnage of Trafalgar Square would haunt his dreams and fill his waking thoughts for the rest of his life. How could it not? Forget forty days and forty nights of fear. He had walked straight through the gateway into Hell.

He closed his eyes, and still all he could see were golden figures reaching out to him, pleading, screaming, screaming and pleading.

Shamshi helped him up. She let him lean on her as they walked through the golden dead.

And then a terrible, soul-crushing thought formed in his mind: his friends were the kind of people who would run towards a massacre such as this, not run away from it. Koni and Ronan were here. They couldn't have missed Solomon's broadcast. Any one of these shining statues could be one of his friends.

Lethe couldn't help himself, once he'd allowed the thought to take shape in his mind he couldn't banish it. He ran from figure to figure in panic, looking at the gilded faces and the golden clothing for anything familiar, anything that might have been the Irishman or the Russian, and praying he wouldn't find it. The metal coating obscured so many of their heads facial recognition would be impossible, even by loved ones. The tiny, rational part of his brain, told him this desperate search from corpse to standing corpse was fruitless, but there was no way he was about to stop looking. It was a primitive response to trauma.

Shamshi called out for him to stop but he wasn't listening to her voice of reason.

On and on he ran, until he had forced himself to go face-to-face with two hundred, three hundred, four hundred dead, and none of them were his dead.

He had hope.

And that terrified him as he moved on, knowing that the next corpse could be he one that broke him.

And even when he couldn't find them, that didn't mean they weren't here, fused in with the other corpses in the core.

That tiny part of his brain that was still operating rationally fastened on the truth: this was Solomon. This was on him. All of it. Not down to Lethe's failings or Konstantin's exile or anything else. It was Solomon, and he needed to pay for what he had done.

This time, he listened.

Rage consumed him.

No more tears.

He wiped his face.

Shamshi was close to him now, moving to hug him as her own grief caught up with her senses.

She fell into his arms. He held onto her for a moment longer than necessary. She held onto him for a lot longer than that.

Around them, the first responders had finally reached the statues. Men and woman in high-viz jackets carried medical kits as they moved among the dead, like explorers in some alien forest of gold. Their faces ranged from stoic to barely-keeping-it-together to outright heartbreak at the profound beauty and horror juxtaposed in the old Square. But they did their jobs. They went up to every single body, they checked for signs of life beneath the hardened new skin. They lingered with those partially coated by the gold, each time full of hope, each time moving on when it became apparent there was none.

Always with hope.

But the reality was that aside from Shamshi, Lethe, the police and the paramedics, there was nobody left alive in Trafalgar Square.

FORTY-FOUR
SUBTERRANIAN HOMESICK BLUES

Ronan was doing his best not to get frustrated with being their saviour.

They did their best to keep up with him, and he did his best to slow down so they could. He talked to them, offering them some small comfort in the darkness of the sewer tunnels. But mostly that was down to his Browning, not any particular way with words. They saw him as the law. One of the good guys in a world too full of bad guys.

What he needed was evidence of Solomon's men escaping the carnage.

He knew he was leading his survivors toward greater danger.

At some point he'd have to bite the bullet and send these people back up to the surface. It was going to be a bitch for the guy with the broken leg, but as long as they hobbled far enough away from the Square he could hope they'd be safe.

It was all about time.

He was working on the theory that Solomon's men would have left the square by now and were moving to some prearranged assembly point where they could strip off their paramilitary paraphernalia and emerge, blending in seamlessly with the crowds of frightened

Londoners. The question was, did they flee over ground or underground?

Frost raised a hand.

Even though they weren't soldiers they knew what it meant and fell silent.

He caught the faint sound of movement up ahead.

He killed the flashlight app. The others did the same as he motioned for them to take cover. The sewer walls were rounded, long straight tunnels offering no real hiding places. Every hundred yards or so they encountered ladders and manhole covers letting in tiny shafts of light. Some stretches of tunnel were huge, and had platforms at the side, almost like lost underground stations.

They pressed up against the wall.

It was a pointless move that would hardly save them if an active shooter moved into the tunnel ahead. They were lining up for the kill. Broken leg did his damnedest to keep quiet, biting down on the pain as he slumped against the dank sewer wall.

Two tunnels crossed up ahead.

He heard voices, getting louder as they approached. Laughing and talking. It was difficult to judge from the acoustics, but first instinct, they came from the tunnel crossing theirs, not from further ahead inside theirs. He wasn't a huge believer in luck, but with a one in three chance of them coming this way, he was willing whatever devil or deity looked down upon Irishmen sneaking through the sewers of London to throw a little luck his way.

He looked at Broken Leg.

The man was in tears, gritting his teeth. Sweat poured down his face and neck, matting with the lank hair and dirt. Frost could imagine the pain he was in. He'd broken bones before. The worst part was the way the two jagged ends grated upon each other as you forced yourself to move. Keeping still, there was a chance the bones would sit kindly and the pain would subside for a few precious seconds at least.

The little girl clung to her father, eyes closed against the fear.

The father and the woman held up the injured man between them. Everyone in the cramped confines of the sewer tunnel tried to remain absolutely motionless.

Frost held the Browning ready, two hands, braced. He didn't want to waste even a split second of reaction time if he needed to lay down fire.

Three men, all carrying assault weapons, crossed the mouth of their tunnel no more than twenty feet away from where they stood. The voices echoed through the tunnels, effectively drowning out any sounds his survivors might have made.

The deities or demons were on his side. The three men didn't so much as glance in their direction. The three men knew where they were going; meaning they'd walked these tunnels a lot in the lead up to the attack.

Frost waited until their voices faded, then turned to his survivors.

Pitching his voice low, Frost told them, "I need you to go on ahead. Take the left tunnel where those men came from and keep going until you find a ladder. We should be far enough away from the Square. One of you go up and find help, then come back for the others."

They nodded.

"Where are you going?" the father asked.

"I'm going after them. I'm going to make them pay for what they did here today."

Nobody argued with him.

He left them, following Solomon's men into the dark.

*

Frasier Devere received Solomon's call as he walked from the massive helicopter. The deafening engines drowned out the signal, but he felt the insistent vibration against his leg. He broke into a jog across the hardstand back towards his family home.

The crucibles had been ditched into the Rutland Water Reservoir, west of Peterborough.

A charge was placed at the base of each before they were dropped, which shattered them before impact allowing the pieces to sink into the deep waters.

The second helicopter was headed north-east to Grimsby.

Humanity Capital was finished. He knew that. He didn't care. He had made contingencies, going to great pains to divest himself of any involvement in the company.

Devere watched the massive Russian bird lift off again.

He would be suspected of course. He was expecting that, too. He was ready for heavy-handed police to come knocking on his door. And so were his lawyers. He had layers of defence primed and the best legal minds money could buy lined up to defend him.

He was going walk away.

People like him always did.

What he couldn't have explained to anyone was why he'd done it. Why he'd wrecked a company he'd spent his entire life building. Why he'd thrown away half of his fortune just because he wanted a name.

One name.

"The name?" he said when he was far enough away from the rotors to make himself heard.

"Trafalgar Square has never looked more beautiful. You should be proud."

"The name, Solomon."

"Of course. And I do hope you'll appreciate the irony of what I am about to tell you. Your son was killed by Konstantin Khavin."

Devere gripped the phone.

"Say that again."

"Khavin."

"I had him."

"I know."

"Why didn't you tell me? I told you I had him."

"I needed you to hold up your end of the bargain. You did that admirably. Now, all you need to do is wait. Khavin will come to you. He is nothing if not predictable. Be ready. You will only have one chance."

*

Konstantin watched the two policemen as they struggled to lower the body of the assassin.

It had taken ingenuity and effort, but he'd wanted to send a message, and by stringing the corpse from the Humanity Capital sign, twenty feet off the ground, above the entrance to Devere's headquarters, he'd done just that.

The Russian had found a hiding place up on the top floor that offered an unobstructed view of the forecourt and the entrance.

More officers were already inside, searching the building.

They'd find him soon enough.

He needed to split, but the newcomer caught his attention.

Stacia Kanic.

She'd arrived on the scene a couple of minutes ago, taking charge.

He wanted her to see the assassin, and piece it together.

There was a narrative here.

He needed her to understand it.

He wasn't coming out until she did.

Like it or not, he needed the police's help.

Now that Kanic was here, that meant he needed her help, too.

Devere wasn't returning.

Konstantin needed to know where the bastard had gone.

Find Devere, use him to find Solomon and put an end to this.

Personally.

Preferably with violence.

His face throbbed, his eye was completely swollen shut, and his body ached from a thousand bruises slowly flourishing. But pain was good. It meant he wasn't a corpse.

*

Stacia Kanic needed to banish the horrors of Germany from her mind.

The bodies, the rubble, the survivors aimlessly wandering, clothes and faces covered in dust and blood like zombies through a post-apocalyptic landscape. The emergency services stretched far beyond breaking, the roads blocked, the cars abandoned by the wayside as they ran out of petrol. All of it. Every time she closed her eyes she saw more. Her brain conjuring fresh horrors even as it failed to process the first remembered ones.

The guilt she felt as she boarded the British military chopper on the road to Stuttgart, leaving thousands stranded, many injured, all of them exhausted, the expressions of hopelessness and defeat, all of it, she would never stop seeing it.

It would be with her forever, behind her eyes.

But here she was, following orders like nothing had ever happened.

And those orders were to bring down Khavin, permanently if necessary.

That didn't sit well with her, for a lot of reasons. Yes, she was pissed off with the Russian for leading her through his false trail to Bonn, and making her experience the annihilation of the city, but the Russian was complex, the kill order wasn't. It was simplistic. And that warning from Knight to get out, that had festered inside her to the point she felt like she was going all Fox Mulder with the Trust No One thing.

The he dead man was Khavin's handiwork.

The brutality of the caved in skull was all him, as was the neatly written note pinned to the dead man's shirt. "You were looking for the Pope's murderer. This is the assassin." She believed it. She'd known Khavin was innocent for a while now; ever since the Italian police had passed on the identity of the dead Swiss Guard, Alessio Bisch. Khavin should never have been her prey. And yet, even armed with this, Michael Knight was insistent the Russian was subject to a kill order.

She couldn't prove that Knight was dirty, but she damned well believed it.

And that meant she wasn't about to do his grunt work. If Knight wanted Khavin dead he could get his own hands dirty. Though everything she knew about the Russian suggested it'd be Knight in the body bag at the end of that particular encounter.

Her eyes darted from window to window, seeing only reflections in the curved glass. It was an impressive building. Very modern. That kind of ostentatious, look-how-much-money-we've-got-plebs, scar on the landscape. She couldn't see anything inside, but that didn't stop her looking as she cupped her hands around her mouth.

"Khavin!" she called, her voice carrying. "I know you're in there." She knew no such thing. "You can come out. I know you didn't kill Pope Peter. Can you hear me, Khavin? I know you're innocent."

A shiver through the glass of one of the top floor windows caught her attention. The shiver caused the reflected sunlight to dance. Within it, she saw Konstantin Khavin, standing in full view. The big Russian waved at her.

Stacia motioned for him to come down.

She knew it might look like a trap. She didn't know what she could do to convince him otherwise. The last thing she wanted was for him to come out firing.

He backed away from the window.

She waited.

As she waited, a fellow Six agent crossed the lot toward her. He held a tablet. She took the device from him. The image on the screen was a freeze-frame from the scene of the Pope's assassination. She could see Peter the Roman, Khavin and Swiss Guards rushing forward to intercept. It didn't take much to read the body language of the scene. The guard to the Little Father's left wasn't trying to stop the Russian. She used the pinch and zoom to focus in on the guard's face.

It was the face of the man lying dead at her feet.

"You're convinced now?" Khavin called as he walked from the building. He was being escorted by two armed police officers. He looked like shit. One eye was badly swollen, the lids fused together. He was covered in dirt, bruises and blood. His clothes were ragged but he walked tall.

"I am," she replied.

Hunter and hunted stood opposite each other, the dead assassin on the ground between them. This wasn't how she imagined this scene playing out. She only had one thing she wanted to say to the Russian.

"I want my gun back."

Khavin spread his arms wide. "I don't have it" But before she could lose her shit, he promised, "But I can get it. Later."

"I want it back," she said.

"You'll get it. I understand," he said, though he couldn't possibly, even through their shared heritage of violence, he couldn't possibly understand.

"Where's Devere?" she asked.

"He didn't come back here," Khavin said. "He ran."

"There's nowhere he can hide from us," she promised him.

Whether she meant Six, the reach of Her Majesty's Secret Service, or just the pair of them, she didn't make the distinction, and she wasn't sure there actually was one to be made.

*

Lethe and Shamshi sat side-by-side in the police mobile command centre.

Both had been handed steaming hot cups of coffee that had long since stopped steaming. Neither had taken so much as a sip.

He felt disconnected.

He felt lost.

He couldn't read Shamshi's face. Her youth seemed to have drained away leaving the hollowness of sorrow to her features.

There was a computer keyboard on the desk in front Lethe, like the last temptation. He was itching to get back online, but there was that nagging dread now… What if he put out a call and nobody answered?

It wouldn't be long before the officers returned, so it was very much now or never.

Steeling himself, Lethe leaned forward and started tapping at the keys, going through their encryption as though it wasn't there. The police national computer network wasn't exactly DAGDA and a long way from the full functionality and power at his fingertips in the Nest, but it gave him a window to the world. And a shot at finding his friends.

It took less than seven seconds for the first hit.

Somewhere in Europe, a phone rang.

"Now really isn't a good time, mate," Noah told him.

"It's the best time," Lethe told him, so relieved to get an answer. "Where are you?"

"You can't tell? You're slipping. Barcelona."

"What are you doing there?"

"I'm at a Mass."

The line went dead.

Noah Larkin finding religion was the last thing he expected.

Next, a text came in from Orla.

She was on a flight with no ability to call but could use the internet portal to send an SMS. She was due to touch down at Heathrow in a couple of hours. Lethe ordered a car for her and texted back to say a driver would be waiting to bring her to Nonesuch.

"I need to get back," Shamshi said. "I should be with my brother."

"Of course," he agreed. "Family is family, but I need to stay here until I know everyone is safe."

"Will I see you back there?"

"I'm sure you will," he reached out and took her hand. Suddenly all earnest, he said, "Thank you, Shamshi. Seriously. You saved my life getting me out of that place."

She smiled. "I wouldn't go that far."

"Do me a favour, keep them out of here for as long as you can before you go. I'm going to need a few minutes of alone time."

She planted a kiss on his forehead and left him, just as his app lit up on the screen. Another incoming call.

"Lethe?"

"Konstantin! Not dead then?"

"Not yet."

"Where are you?"

"I'm with Stacia Kanic."

"She caught up with you?"

"No. I found her. We are going after Frasier Devere."

"Devere?"

"I need a location."

"I don't have access to the network, but I'll do my best. Give me a few and I'll send through whatever I find."

Another call came in almost before he'd hung up on the Russian.

"Jude," said a voice as he answered the new call.

"Frosty!"

"I need your help," Frost said, without preamble. "I need a schematic of the top floor of the Northumberland Hotel."

"Near Charing Cross?"

"That's the one. Can you send it to this phone?"

"You know I can."

"Are you in touch with the others?"

"For now. Orla's on a flight back to Blighty, Koni's working with Stacia Kanic to bring down Frasier Devere, and Noah's in the grip of a religious epiphany in Barcelona. He's found God."

"Didn't know he was looking for him. What about the old man?"

"I haven't tried. Trying to stay off our new masters' radar now that I'm free."

"You were locked up?"

"In a cage, mate. In a cage. And I'm locked out of our systems."

"Listen to me, Jude. I'm only going to say this once, so try not to let it go to your head. You're our secret weapon, not the machines. Of course, you tell anyone I said that, I'll deny it."

"I won't say a word."

"Good man. Just to loop you in, I followed a bunch of Solomon's goons under Trafalgar Square through the sewers to this hotel. In a minute I'm going to storm the penthouse suite and see if I can convince them to give up their glorious leader."

"I'm kinda piggybacking the PNC, but assuming Shamshi can keep the cops distracted for a while, I should be able to patch into the satellite and get you real time info. I'm glad you're okay, Ronan."

"I know," Frost said, echoing one of Lethe's favourite movie lines of all time.

The line clicked off.

Time to take the fight to Solomon.

*

"Stop fighting me, old man."

Knight dragged Sir Charles's chair backwards down the steps that led down to the herb garden at the back of the manor. The Old Man fought him every step of the way, trying to jam on the brakes and shift his balance to tip the chair.

"I swear, I'll shoot you in the back of the fucking head," Knight threatened.

"Your boss," Sir Charles argued, struggling to catch his breath even as he fought to say more, "said … I was… not… to be… harmed."

"I don't care what that bitch Mendes said. She should never have been put in command. Agency quotas. Promote to fill the politically correct demand. More women in charge, they said. So truly excellent officers, people like me are ignored in favour of incompetents like her. She's weak and indecisive."

"But she is on the right side," Sir Charles managed. The fight had gone out of him. He was powerless to prevent Knight from dragging him towards the shed on the far side of the herb garden.

"You know nothing, old man," Knight snapped.

He let go of the Old Man's chair so that he could wrestle open the door to the shed.

The old hinges creaked in protest.

Clouds of dust billowed up into the air.

Knight returned to his position behind the chair, wheeling it around so that Sir Charles faced the open door. He pushed forward, tipping the Old Man unceremoniously into the dark. He went sprawling across the ground.

"I just need you safely out of the way for a few hours. Sit tight and you'll be back inside the Manor House soon." He slammed the wooden door closed, then took a padlock from his pocket and slipped it through the hasp and snapped it tight.

Before he left, Knight folded up Sir Charles's wheelchair and stashed it out of sight behind the shed.

FORTY-FIVE
UNHOLY, DIRTY AND BEAUTIFUL

Ronan took the lift up to the second-highest floor of the Northumberland.

The floor above that was made up entirely of conference rooms.

He had no idea who might be up there, or how many of them, so he bailed a floor below and headed for the stairs, intending to do some recon rather than going in one-gun blazing.

As he reached the door to the stairwell, his phone bleeped.

"Jude?"

"Yeah, you got an earbud?"

"Nope, I'll have to hang up. What have you got?"

"I see you at the south stairwell. The good news is nobody's waiting for you on the other side, our guards are on the door upstairs."

"That's the good, so the bad?"

"There's plenty of them watching the lift. I make six heat centres. I'm guessing a metric shit-ton of guns. Plan?"

"Take them out one at a time, keep firing until we're at the last man standing, then make him tell me where Solomon is before I put him down."

"A stupendous plan, Frosty, and almost certain to be suicidal."

"The best often are."

"Can I make a suggestion?"

"By all means." Ronan was half way up the stairs to the top floor now.

"Security feed from a building across the way makes it look like they've got the privacy blinds down in the room they're using—first on your left as you go in—there are four other conference rooms up here. I can close their screens remotely. I'm thinking sound the fire alarm, lower the screens, then cut the lights."

"How long will that take?"

"Maybe twenty seconds from the go. Here's the logic, if the alarm goes off they'll assume it's a drill, and even if they notice the screens coming down, they'll just assume that's part of the drill. Means they won't see or hear you coming."

"Okay, kill the lights in here first, give me a few for my eyes to adjust."

"Now you're talking."

Ronan reached the top floor landing. He double-checked the magazine in his gun to make sure it was full. Ten rounds. He needed to make each one count. He checked his pocket for the spare mag – meaning twenty shots, total.

The lights in the stairwell flickered and went out.

A moment later the emergency exit lights died, plunging him into complete darkness.

The muted sounds of people talking came from beyond the heavy fire-door. Six armed killers. Twenty shots. It was a decent kill ratio, but there wasn't much room for manoeuvre.

His breathing was louder than their voices.

He calmed himself.

Focussed.

Centred.

He tried to position as many of his targets as he could by the sound of their voices.

Seconds ticked by.

A minute.

Frost couldn't waste time wondering where the rest of Solomon's people were. There had been a lot more than six surrounding Trafalgar Square.

Right now, his world reduced to these six. Beyond them there was nothing.

Slowly, he started to make out the stair rail and the steps and other features in the grim service stairwell.

As the moments passed, the details of his surroundings grew clearer. It was still dark, but he could at least make out objects and judge distances. Night vision goggles would have been better, but these few precious seconds of adaption time were as good as it was gone to get.

He turned back towards the door and raised his phone.

"Hit it."

The fire alarm went off. It was deafeningly loud in the stairwell. He heard the confused shouting beyond the door. Perfect. Movement with the chaos of voices. Not so perfect.

Seconds crept by with agonizing slowness.

He counted slowly toward eleven, knowing they wouldn't follow the fire drill procedure. By the time he reached six, Lethe said, "Go!" and he moved out.

He pushed open the fire door.

The corridor was in almost total darkness.

Ronan ignored the alarm. He headed for the strained hubbub of voices.

"Someone kill that noise and get the damned lights on."

The man near the lifts barked out the orders.

The side of his face vaporized when Ronan shot him. The sound of the gunshot was lost beneath the shrill alarm, transforming the kill into a weird ballet of blood and bone.

"What was that?"

The idiot leaving the conference room should know better.

He went down from a double-tap, both to the centre of mass. Two blood red roses flowered where his heart opened up. He looked down as his hand went up, not understanding. The cycling wail of the siren was disorientating for both prey and hunter. If a bullet is fired in a hotel and you can't hear the gun discharge, do you still die? Frost thought, watching the man fold. He figured it answered the tree in the forest riddle fairly practically.

Two down. He'd used three of his bullets. Seven left in this magazine.

Shots fired, not from Frost.

They knew he was here.

The question was: did they know where?

Instinctively, he ducked low, using the natural cover over the half-wall outside the conference room to move forward. Always forward. And then, music to his ears: a scream as friendly fire took out one of their own. Well, thank you, darkness, my old friend, Frost thought as more bullets from the automatic rifle strafed the acoustic tiles of the ceiling.

Frost rose, stepping into the doorway.

It took a nanosecond to identify the source of the stray bullets and the screams. A man slumped up against the far wall, beneath the window out onto the city. His face was lit up like a strobe light as more bullets tore into the masonry and empty shells ejected from his gun.

Frost fired a mercy shot.

The disco lights stopped a second later.

Four down.

Five bullets.

Ronan continued moving. Always moving. Always forward.

Back to the wall, he listened through the sirens for the telltale signs of enemy combatants moving around him. Time slowed around him. He was calm. Almost Zenlike. Even with the lack of light and the unknown variables the hotel presented, this was his world. They knew he was here, their eyes would have adjusted now, and even with the cacophony all around, there was nowhere for them to hide from him.

Or him to hide from them.

As suddenly as it had begun, the alarm fell silent, all shrieked out.

The ensuing silence left a horrible tinnitus ringing in his ears that meant the hotel was anything but quiet. He needed to hear through it. He needed to hear every tiny movement.

He'd cleared scenarios like this hundreds of times. It was a regular drill back when he was in active duty in the SAS. They had a murder house set up with hostage situations and all sorts of other scenarios for them to run through. Frost had always excelled at this one-on-many assault. His old CO had taken to nicknaming him the ghost killer, because he could go through a building without being seen, and only heard in the death rattles of his enemies. It was part of his youth and who he had been that he'd never lost, just like Konstantin would never lose the kid who had fled Russia with nothing but the shirt on his back.

The first door was on his right. Further along the corridor there was another on his left. Frost chose left, edging along the wall.

He almost missed the soft rustle of footsteps on the carpet through the ringing in his ears.

He spun into the doorway, Browning at chest height. It was a second entrance leading back to an antechamber, and a subsidiary conference room. There was a decent sized table and half a dozen chairs. It looked like it was primarily used as a break room. He saw evidence of snacks in the bin. The entire floor was a warren of adjustable panels and sliding doors, so the conference rooms could be arranged and rearranged to suit the needs of its occupants. This secondary suit had wide double doors that divided the room in two.

The doors were wide open.

Frost couldn't see what, if anything, was beyond them.

No movement.

No talking now.

Probability said the pair he was hunting had taken cover and would look to kill him as he crossed their line of sight.

They weren't dead, and he hadn't miscounted.

He backed out into the corridor.

He listened for sounds that weren't there.

He moved on, beyond the second door.

He double-checked behind him to be sure no one had moved to come around from his back. The dead man still lay in the doorway.

He moved on, beyond the second door.

His path brought him back around toward the lifts and the first body.

Frost moved fast, a sudden burst of speed across the bank of elevators to another conference room. He hit the ground and slid through the open doorway.

Crouching low, he scanned the room where he was reasonably sure his two final targets were holed up.

Reasonably sure wasn't great. Reasonably could get you killed. He needed certainty where there was none.

In the gloom Frost could just make out the contours of another set of chairs and U-shaped bank tables. There was a whiteboard on the wall. He grabbed the board eraser from the tray beneath it, then moved a chair out into the corridor.

He was thinking as he worked, and working quickly. Frost manhandled the elevator corpse into the chair. The weapon hung from a strap around his neck. Frost jammed the stock into the dead man's armpit and wedged it in place so it pointed straight ahead.

He wheeled his new puppet toward the conference room. It rolled past the door to the antechamber and the dead body in the doorway.

He shoved the corpse forward, doubled over so the body pinned the rifle in place.

It was a stupid idea. It really was. But he was working with what he had, and he couldn't think of anything better right now.

He listened, but they still weren't moving.

It was beginning to annoy him.

Time to fix that.

In one swift motion, Frost jammed the board eraser up against the trigger guard and the rifle exploded into life, firing wildly, round after round through the doorway.

He shoved the chair, rolling it into the room with some force. The chair's wheeled legs rammed into the corpse on the floor, the impact propelling the dead man out of the seat like a crash test dummy.

And still his rifle blazed.

For a heartbeat the illusion was perfect; the momentum brought the dead man to his feet, and in the silence between that heartbeat and the next it looked for all the world as though the corpse was unloading his weapon into the room. Frost sold them the lie.

Two men broke cover, returning fire, their bullets jerking the corpse upright as shot after shot slammed into it.

They emptied their weapons.

Frost was on the move.

He stormed the antechamber, coming in through the alternative door while their eyes were drawn to the twice dead man.

His charge was always going to draw attention; sudden movement was a magnet for the weary eye. It didn't matter. They'd emptied their loads, metaphorically and literally. Frost took out the first as he turned, drawn by the sudden movement. A single shot took him through the temple and buried in behind his eyes. It wasn't pretty. He went down in a sprawl of blood and bone, hitting the conference table hard.

The last man took two bullets, one in each kneecap, taking his legs out from under him, and compounding the agony as he fell to them. His shrieks were desperate, and even as he tried to bring his weapon round to hurt Frost, the mechanism clicked desperately over and over on empty.

Frost walked up to him.

Standing over the fallen man, he pistol-whipped the terrorist, the butt of the Browning cracking brutally against the bone plate.

Two bullets to spare.

He relieved the screaming man of his weapon, kicking it aside.

The blood from the man's ruined knees stained the carpet.

Frost moved to the window and pressed the button beside the light shield, raising the screen to allow the afternoon sun's rays to come flooding in.

He holstered Browning and took the rifle in both hands, flipped it around and struck the window repeatedly with the butt. It cracked on the seventh blow, smashed on the fourteenth. Wind whipped into the room.

He took the time to clear all the jagged shards of broken glass from the frame, chipping them away with the rifle. Splinters fell from a great height down, well short of the mass of evacuees assembled in front of the hotel.

He turned to the last terrorist, who clung stubbornly to consciousness through the screaming pain. Tears mixed with the blood on his cheeks. Frost didn't care. He dropped the rifle and grabbed the man, hauling him up to his feet and making him stand on those ruined knees. His screams were pathetic.

Frost levered him up, dangling him head first out of the window.

He saw people staring up and pointing.

He didn't care.

"One chance. Solomon. Where is he?"

The man caved.

"He's at the safe house."

"Where?"

"I'll tell you, I'll tell you," the man babbled.

"I'm listening," Frost said. "But I'm not hearing a fucking address."

The man spilled his guts, giving Frost the location of a building close to the M25, north of London.

Frost let go.

The man fell.

He pulled out his phone and auto-dialled Lethe as he walked away.

Lethe answered just as he reached the stairs.

"Let there be light," he said in Frost's ear and one by one, racing down to the basement levels, all of the lights in the stairwell came on. Frost descended. Behind him he heard the lift doors chime. He had maybe a minute on them while they tried to work out what had happened. He'd be long gone by then with Lethe's help.

"I need to know where they're coming from. Have you got eyes on?"

"Better than that, mate. I'm coming to you live from the PNC. Current orders are to disengage. I'm ordering them all back out of the building right now. I've transferred jurisdiction to Six."

"Who can't legally act in London."

"They can complain to Mendes" He could hear his friend grinning.

Frost gave him the address of Solomon's safe house.

"Oh, I've got intimate knowledge of that little hellhole."

"Do I want to know?"

"I told you I was in a cage." Lethe didn't offer any more detail.

He didn't ask for any.

"Can you link me through to Koni?"

He continued on down, taking the stairs two and three at a time as he ran, until he crashed out through the fire doors onto the side street behind Charing Cross.

Konstantin's voice came on the line.

"What do you need?"

"Solomon's in London," Frost said.

He came around the corner, deliberately walking away from the assembled crowd.

"I'm a hundred miles away. Need me to turn around?"

"What are you doing? As in, will it wait?"

"Hunting Frasier Devere."

"Why?"

"You saw Trafalgar Square? That was his doing."

Frost turned right, walking down another alleyway between side streets, taking him around the police cordon. Turn and turnabout. He kept walking. It was important he looked natural, relaxed, like the weight of the world wasn't crushing down on him.

"Make that bastard hurt before you kill him, Koni."

"Lethe said you were there."

"I was."

He walked alongside a cop for half a block before turning again. He needed wheels.

"It all comes down to two men. Solomon and Devere. When they are dead then all debts will have been paid in full."

Frost stopped dead on the street.

"What did you just say, Konstantin?"

His mind was back at Nonesuch, at Maxwell's graveside, and Noah handing him the piece of paper, a message from Solomon left at the site of the Cardinals' murders.

"All debts are paid in full," the Russian said, which wasn't quite what he'd said the first time, but which was exactly what had been written on Solomon's message. "It's something I heard in Germany."

"I need you to think, Koni, who said it? Who said that line in Germany?"

The line went quiet for a moment.

"When they were transporting me from the police station. The driver the Old Man sent to collect me. He said it. Why? Is it important?"

"I don't know. Maybe. Look after yourself, big man. I'll see you back at Nonesuch after the shit's gone down."

"You, too."

The line went dead.

He needed to think. He needed to go through everything he knew, every last detail, and he needed Lethe to confirm one, that it wasn't the Old Man who sent that car to bring Konstantin home. He'd called in all sorts of favours, yes, but it was Control who had brought him home.

"Quentin Carruthers," Lethe said, confirming it.

All debts are paid in full.

"Tell me I'm jumping at shadows, mate."

"Knight is rotten. He locked me in that house, the one Solomon is using as a safe house. He pulled Kanic out of Bonn before the quake. He knew Solomon was going to do something. Maybe he's the rot, maybe it stops with him? He could have carried out Control's orders."

"Or it goes much deeper."

"But all the way through Vauxhall Cross to Control?"

"I don't know."

"Jesus, Frosty. They've known each other forever. They've worked together for forty years. They've gone to hell and back together. Do you really think Control could be compromised?"

He wanted to say yes. He wanted to say they locked you in the same house Solomon has taken refuge in. They set up Konstantin. They've been playing us all along, right from day one, because we're off the books, because we can take the fall for them. But all he said was, "The Old Man is back there in Nonesuch all alone."

FORTY-SIX
CONSTANCE CRAVING

Constance Mendes was seriously fucked off.

The world was going to shit around them. They were losing at every turn. It didn't matter what she tried to do, it was always just beyond her, just out of her control. And she hated it.

Knight was being a dick.

He acted like he was running the show and she was an inconvenience. She had been forced to bring him back into line more than once.

Then there was Stacia Kanic.

A week ago she would have said Kanic was one of the best agents Six had. She'd always been fiercely protective of the Ukrainian woman. But feedback coming down the line linked Kanic with Konstantin Khavin, the man she had orders to bring in.

Then there was the fact she'd found those orders, and they'd been changed. The command issued from Control had been to apprehend when it crossed her desk. She'd seen it on Abshir's computer as a kill order. She knew what a kill order looked like. Someone was playing a dangerous game here, using her agent to carry out a kill without her signing off on it. That stuck in her craw.

There was no getting around the fact that the body of the pope's assassin strung up above the doorway of Humanity Capital and the video evidence of the Papal assassination she'd seen very strongly suggested Khavin was being set up to take the fall. So who was doing that? Were they behind the kill order?

And then there was Control.

She felt perpetually off balance, always half a dozen steps behind. And she didn't like it.

Intel was king. It was where they excelled. Normally. But all around her was chaos and conflicting orders. She'd been sending her people off on wild goose chases because of bad intel, and at least once that meant pulling them from leads that seemed promising.

It stank all the way to high heaven.

Or at least Vauxhall Cross.

And as for the so-called Ogmios Team... Where to start?

Khavin was a rogue agent, out of control. Larkin acted like the law didn't apply to him. She had no clue what he had been doing in Rome, or where he was now because the intel she could find on him was endlessly looped media of the priest committing suicide in Saint Peter's Square. Maybe Larkin was rotting in a Vatican cell? Maybe he was dead in a ditch? Maybe he'd found God and joined the holly rollers? Nyrén she knew was returning from Israel. She, at least, had done something useful in preventing the attack at the Dome of the Rock and neutralizing the threat of the Corpse Plane pathogen.

Constance hadn't heard from Lethe since he left Nonesuch yesterday.

Knight didn't seem to be concerned, but she'd read his file. He hardly ever left the Nest since the debacle out in Peru where they'd tangled with a resurrected

Shining Path. He might look like a nerd in his plastic framed glasses, but he was a lethal weapon. He'd been smart enough to lock Abshir out of the majority of the systems here, too, though they'd gained control in the last twenty-four hours. She didn't want to know how. She hadn't seen Shamshi all day. Knight claimed he'd let the young woman go hours earlier, but she wasn't buying it. Something was going on here, she just didn't know what.

And she hated not knowing. It was like one of those Chinese finger puzzles where the more you pulled and tugged at it the tighter the trap's grip on you became.

Then there was Ronan Frost.

What was the Irishman up to?

She rewound and watched again the tourist-shot footage on the tablet, and zoomed the focus up as best she could. She was sure it was Frost up there, hanging a man out of the window for a few short seconds before letting him fall.

It was cold blooded murder.

"We've got an incoming call," Abshir said, looking up from the screen. "It's Frost."

"Patch him through to my mobile phone," she said, before Knight could contradict her order.

Her phone vibrated a second later. "Mendes," she said.

"I need to talk to you." He didn't bother saying who it was. He knew they knew. It was all about economy of effort.

"Where are you?"

"On the move. How many people are on this line?"

"Just us."

"Listen, I need to speak to Sir Charles."

"He's resting in his room."

"Not good enough, Constance. I'm deadly serious here. I think we're compromised. I'm taking a risk now. I'm putting my trust in you. Don't let me down, Constance." She noticed his repetition of her first name. It was a hostage negotiation tactic, build a human connection. "I think Knight is compromised. I need you to make sure the Old Man's safe. Because, believe me, if anything happens to him, all of the king's horses and all of the king's men won't put Six back together again. Am I clear?"

"Be very careful what you say next, Mister Frost."

"You're either on the side of the angels, or you're on the side of the demons, Constance. I'm gambling you are one of the good guys. I'm putting my oldest friend's life in your hands. Don't prove me wrong."

The line went dead.

Constance stared into the middle distance for a long moment, not sure what she was meant to do with that.

"Trouble?"

She looked at Knight. "Where is Sir Charles?"

"In his room."

"Okay. Good. I'm going to go check in with him. See if there's anything he needs."

Knight shrugged. It was a little thing, but something about his indifference bugged Constance. She took the lift up to the ground floor of the manor. The place was eerily quiet with everyone down in Lethe's little nest.

She knocked on the Old Man's door.

When she got no reply on the third time of asking, she tried the handle and opened the door. The room was empty.

She took out her phone and redialled Frost's number.

He answered after a single ring. "Frost."

"He's gone."

"Where is he?"

"I don't know. But he's not here."

"He's not exactly mobile in that chair of his. Find him, Constance, I mean it."

The line went dead again.

It wasn't Ronan Frost she was worried about. It was Quentin Carruthers. If it turned out she'd lost his best friend there would be hell to pay.

Constance dialled Knight.

"Yup," he replied.

"Are you sure you left him in his room?"

"Absolutely. Left him reading a copy of Gibbon's Decline and Fall."

She scanned the room. The only book on the bedside table was one of the romantic poets. Why lie about something so simple? That set her nerves jangling.

"Okay, I'm going out into the grounds to see if I can find him."

"Perhaps he's down by the chapel visiting his friend's grave?" It was reasonable. It had only been a few days since Maxwell had died, after all, and they had been together a long time.

*

Orla breezed through immigration and customs at Heathrow.

With so few operators running at capacity there were few lines, and those that were there moved through the self-service scanners. Her flight into London was only a quarter full, mainly business class. That was the modern world right there, wasn't it? The deal was more important than the risk to their lives.

Her phone rang before she'd cleared the terminal. It was Ronan.

"Listen Orla, I've got a lead on Solomon. Konstantin is going after Frasier Devere."

She saw several drivers waiting for their clients and looked for her name.

"Devere? Did I miss something?"

A tall woman in a crisp black business suit held her name.

"Devere's behind the Trafalgar Square attack. Shit, you were up in the air. I'll let you catch up on the details when you're in the car. I need you to go back to Nonesuch. The Old Man is in trouble."

Orla's heart froze.

"We can't trust Knight. I don't even know if we can trust Mendes or Control. As far as you're concerned going in there, if they're from Six, they aren't your friend."

She knew better than ask for the whys and wherefores. Their life was all about trust.

She followed the driver out into the open air.

The limo was parked up at the curbside.

"Your bag?"

"It's fine," she said, preferring to keep it with her.

The driver held open the door and she climbed in.

They drove slowly through the labyrinth of service roads, following the signs for the M25. Orla gave her the address for Nonesuch Manor, then pulled her phone out again, intending to catch up on the news and send a message to Lethe.

There was no signal inside the car.

She leaned forward, "Any chance I could borrow your phone for a second? I'm not getting a signal on mine."

Instead of answering, the driver raised the screen between them.

It took her a moment to realise what she was hearing: a gradual hiss.

Gas venting into the car.

She saw the curls of smoke rising up from floor level, thickening as they did.

She could already taste the acrid tang in her lungs.

Covering her mouth, she grabbed the door handle and pulled at it, but it was locked.

Thinking fast, Orla lay flat on her back along the leather seats and used the heel of her boots to try and smash through the tinted safety glass. Hammering her heels down again and again, the jarring impact shivering up to her hips as the gas coiled around her face now.

It wouldn't give.

The definition of insanity is trying the same thing over and over that has already failed and expecting the same outcome, but there was nothing else she could do.

She kept on kicking at the glass as it got more and more difficult to keep her eyes open.

She cursed herself for not paying attention.

Stupid.

Stupid.

Stupid.

She had allowed herself to feel safe, being back on home land, and in those few seconds as she'd scanned the waiting signs for her name, she hadn't thought that she might be walking into a setup. The gas swirled around her. Moments later she drifted away.

FORTY-SEVEN
STILL ON FIRE

La Sagrada Familia was still under construction.

It had been twenty years since Noah had last visited the grand basilica of Barcelona. Back then it had been two tall sets of four bell towers with a building site in between. Now, a stunning church had risen from that site, allowing mass to be celebrated under a grand roof where millions of visitors a year gazed up in astonishment at Antoni Gaudi's masterwork.

And it still wasn't complete, even more than a century after breaking ground.

Six additional towers had yet to be built.

Inside, at the rear of the cathedral, Noah and Neri listened to the invite-only Mass. Neri had used his credentials and an element of blagging to get them through the door. They didn't have seats, so they leaned on the back wall and kept quiet. Noah watched from a distance as the Camerlengo—he couldn't think of the man as Pope and couldn't believe he would ever be that—led the Mass. He leaned upon an impressive altar. The man was surrounded by soaring columns. His face was lit by daylight filtered in from high above. The altar sported a huge golden canopy that resembled an elaborate parasol. Noah saw an effigy of Jesus on the cross suspended from the golden canopy. It was a weirdly uncomfortable sight.

His eyes never settled, his gaze darting around the huge space constantly.

Finally, he found who he was looking for: Catalina Sosa.

She stood to the right of the altar, off in the shadows, half-behind one of the floor-to-ceiling columns that ran the length of the basilica's interior.

He nudged Neri and nodded in her direction.

"There she is."

It took the Roman a moment, but then he saw her too.

The Camerlengo delivered the homily, speaking to his congregation in Spanish. Noah wasn't listening. Some sort of ideologue BS, no doubt. Beside him stood the Vatican Monstrance – a blue ring with a mirrored centre, with dozens of golden points fanned around it like the rays of the sun, with a cross at the top and mounted on a gold staff at the bottom. The Camerlengo had brought the exquisite artefact for one reason and one reason only. To tell the faithful: I am the Pope now.

One word in the homily, *paz*, triggered a flurry of activity in Noah's peripheral vision.

Neri saw it too.

He recognized several of the Camerlengo's students as they fanned out around the building's interior.

The place was full to capacity and beyond; standing room only in a building capable of holding ten-thousand. It was hard to make out individual movements, or any significant activity beyond the shuffle of feet and the rustle of cloth, but most under the basilica were rapt, captivated by their holy man's song and dance routine. Noah wasn't most people. He watched as spectators made way for the students. It was natural. They assumed the best from them. How were they to know the truth? It looked natural, like part of the homily, or maybe in preparation for the hymnal to follow.

The students took up their positions. They were at equidistant intervals all around the outer edge of the vast space.

Noah couldn't see them all from where he was, but he didn't need to.

He realised several in his nearest field of vision carried small canisters. Given the Corpse Planes and Solomon's other stunts, his guess was poison gas. They intended to take the whole congregation out. It looked like a suicide attack. The kids had no masks of their own. Just like the Berlin subway.

Noah glanced across at a couple of the local security guards.

Neither appeared to have noticed anything untoward.

He scoped out the exits. The doorways were huge ornamental things, but essentially useless for a mass exodus. The vast majority of worshippers would be dead long before they could escape.

It wasn't looking good.

Beside him, Neri sighed, resigned. "And once again it falls to us, doesn't it?"

"Always, my friend."

"One of these days we won't make it out to the other side."

"Don't worry, this isn't that day," Noah said.

And then he was moving.

There would be a trigger word, something in his sermon, and all of his pet suicide bombers would open their canisters and kill every last person in La Sagrada Familia.

Waiting made no sense.

Every second they waited increased the risk of someone realizing and security intervening.

Which meant Noah had no time to come up with a fancy plan.

He had to do something.

Now or never.

He shoved his way through the throng, moving them forcefully aside as he fought his way to the aisle. He thought for one tantalizing second about simply firing from there, one shot, through the false Pope's heart, and bringing him down at the altar. But there were so many people and killing him wouldn't stop the sarin or whatever other chemical attack his suicide squad was set to launch.

He started walking down the aisle.

"Always the bridesmaid," he said to a woman who looked aghast at his advance.

People were starting to look toward the students, waiting for the grand reveal and wondering what was in the canisters they carried.

Many, he was sure, must have been aware of all of the horrors of the last few weeks, and the threat of forty full days and nights of fear. Congregating anywhere right now was risky, so maybe they were looking for potential attacks?

Noah walked on, moving toward the centre of the huge building, knowing that the trigger word could come at any second.

He looked up down the aisle to the pulpit where the man held something in his left hand, partially obscured behind the lectern where he preached. It could have been a gas mask. It was impossible to tell. He scanned across to Catalina Sosa. She had a canister in one hand and a mask in the other.

She saw him.

He waved, and called out, "You are all going to die!" It wasn't exactly the way he'd intended to introduce himself, but it was effective given they all thought he was the one about to kill them.

People closest to him turned in their pews. A low murmur of discontent rippled through the congregation, not immediate fear, not immediate understanding. They weren't putting two and two together yet and getting sarin gas canisters. Murmurs intensified as he walked toward the false Pope. The preacher stared at Noah Larkin with pure and absolute hatred in his eyes. There was nothing beatific or holy about his benevolence. He was rabid. It was written all over his face.

Sosa took a step forward.

The pair of Swiss Guard assigned to protect the false Pope took several steps forward, looking to shield him, halberds at the ready.

He still spoke, delivering his thinly veiled words of hate that pretended at love.

Noah had a choice.

It wasn't a great choice. There was no good solution here. But he had a choice and he took it.

Noah drew his gun and started to run down the centre of the long aisle, offering a fervent prayer of his own: that no one would shoot him before he got to the holy man.

The reaction was immediate, the panic that swept through the congregation visceral. People screamed, suddenly believing his claims, and recoiled from him thinking he was the one to make good on them. Some scrambled out of the pews, trying desperately to push a way through to the aisle so they could flee. Others ducked down, crouching and in the process blocking their rows before the stampede could ever truly begin.

Sosa broke into a run, heading straight for Noah.

The Swiss Guard gave up on ancient ceremony and discarded their halberds in favour of SIG Sauers, each man aiming at Noah as he ran down the aisle at them. All it needed was one of them to get a clean shot and he was fucked. But panic saved him. Bodies crossed their line of sight as worshippers tried to get out, they ran every which way but toward him.

The guards rushed forward.

The noise was amplified and transformed into something akin to a hellish chorus. It simply would not stop, the sweeps and curves of Gaudi's great basilica making it louder and louder and louder as the panic folded in on itself, echoing in a massive feedback loop.

The false Pope's suicide squad seemed confused as to what to do next, simply let their deadly payloads seep free, or abort their mission and await further instructions.

Across all the noises Noah heard a solid metallic clunk as one canister hit the stone floor.

Noah kept his gun aimed low and continued his headlong race toward the altar.

There was no no coming back from this, whatever he'd told Neri.

In his peripheral vision, he saw Neri wrestling a gas canister from one of the god squad. It was futile but stupidly courageous at the same time; he knew what was in those canisters, and he knew what would happen if even a breath of the toxin leaked out, and still he threw himself at the would-be suicides, wrestling them for the lives of everyone in the damned church.

But he couldn't disarm all of them.

Sosa was twenty feet away and closing fast. Canister in one hand and, he was right, a gasmask in the other.

Seeing the two come together, and their weapons of war, sent a chill through the congregation as panic inherited this particular kingdom of God. Worshippers fought to climb over each other in a desperate need to be away, far, far away.

And still, like a mad man laughing in acid rain, the false Pope stubbornly preached.

His words came faster now, as he stubbornly refused to be silenced.

This was his moment.

Even if he said the trigger words there was no way his eager little suicide children would be able to hear them.

Noah didn't have a shot. Not without risking so many innocents getting caught in the crossfire. And the distance and angle, plus his speed, made the shot exponentially more challenging. Even so, the only thing that stopped him from pulling the trigger was the growing certainty that the false Pope's death would cause his suicide squad to release their poisons. One life for a couple of thousand. The math didn't stack up.

Instead, he raised his gun at a different target.

Sosa was ten feet away when he fired.

Close enough to see the whites of her eyes as the old cliché went.

The bullet hit her in the shoulder.

The impact punched her backwards.

She lost her grip on the canister.

It fell from her hand.

The suicide squad took it as a different kind of signal, that it was over, almost every one of them still holding their canisters gave them up, dropping the gas filled devices and joining the mass exodus.

Almost.

Two still clutched their chemical weapons.

One, Noah thought, was in the grips of terror, muscles seized, and simply couldn't surrender it.

The other, a girl of no more than eighteen, with such a bright future according to her Year Book and the friends she left behind who couldn't believe what she'd done, raised her canister, hand on the release valve to let the deadly toxins free.

Noah didn't hesitate. He didn't care about glittering pasts or wide-open futures. His world reduced to a single second in time, the here and now.

He shot the kid in the neck.

He hadn't meant to deal a kill shot but given the distance it was a miracle he'd hit her at all. She dropped the canister and clutched at her throat. The screaming was overwhelming, echoing around the vast chamber. It wasn't just hers. The shots had let loose the primal fear in all of them crammed into Gaudi's basilica, and given voice they must scream. And scream.

Neri reached the final student and tore the canister from the kid's death grip, so terrified was the young man.

Two Swiss Guard approached Noah now, guns up, yelling at him in German to put down the gun.

Satisfied that the immediate danger had passed, Noah dropped the gun, fell to his knees and interlaced his fingers behind his head.

"Arrest him!" the false Pope demanded. "I want that man in chains!" The PA system carried his rage over the panic. Worshippers showed no sign of calming. They clambered over pews and pushed past each other, still desperate, still terrified.

The Swiss Guard gathered around him.

Noah didn't move.

He wasn't about to give them an excuse.

Catalina Sosa lay bleeding on the floor beside him. This entire section of the basilica was almost empty of congregants now.

"No!" Neri boomed, his voice somehow a match for the huge public address system as he rushed toward the Swiss Guards circling Noah.

He had the kid by the scruff of the neck and dragged him with him down the aisle. It was like watching the weirdest shotgun wedding ever. And it was strange enough that one of the Swiss Guard hesitated, recognizing Neri.

"Kill him!" the false Pope screamed, his voice deranged, distorted by the speakers.

"Hold your fire! HOLD! Detective Dominico Neri, Carabinieri. He is my man. He is polizia!" That stopped them. Neri lifted the shoulder of the student he held, "This boy, along with others like him, was part of a plan to release sarin gas into this basilica and kill thousands." His grip tightened on the student. With his free hand, Neri held up one of the canisters. "Hear his confession."

"It is true," the youth's stammered confession was far too quiet for anyone to hear.

"Tell it to God," Neri boomed, full of righteous fury.

"Yes!" cried the student.

The Swiss Guard had all eyes fixed on Neri, his captive and the potentially lethal canister in the policeman's hand.

Security had reached them now, along with members of the Mossos d'Esquadra, the Catalonian police.

"And who told you to do such a heinous act? Who inspired you to murder? Speak the truth, boy. Now."

The young man didn't hesitate, he raised a trembling hand and pointed immediately to the false Pope still in his pulpit.

The holy man stood stock still for a moment, locked in place. Trapped. Caught.

And then he found his voice. "This is an outrage! He lies! He speaks with the voice of the devil sent in these uncertain times to undo all that is holy! Behold the liar! Do not be fooled!" he yelled into the microphone.

"Liar!" came another voice, and for a moment Noah thought they were defending the false Pope, until he saw another of the suicide squad walk up the aisle, away from the mass of people still trying to evacuate. She carried another of the canisters, which she surrendered to first policeman to reach her, and held out her hands out for them to cuff her. "He gave us the gas. He told us what we needed to do, what needed to happen for the coming of the End of Days. He told us the sinners must die to pave the way for the Messiah, and that only our sacrifice could ensure salvation. He led us. He was our shepherd."

"Who?" Neri said, wanting her to name him in front of everyone.

"The Camerlengo. He killed the Cardinals. He gave the order to kill Peter, the Pope."

The accusation hung there, more powerful than any of them could have hoped.

It changed everything.

The false Pope spluttered out protests of innocence, doubling down on the outrage, until someone cut off his microphone, essentially silencing him. He wasn't going anywhere. The Mossos d'Esquadra advanced on the pulpit, more moved around to cut off his exit at the rear as he tried to leave the dais.

The Swiss Guard made no move to stop the officers, despite their pledge to protect him.

Three men stormed the dais, dragging him down. They wrestled the false Pope to the floor, forcing him to experience the indignity of handcuffs as they hauled him back up again, a false prophet, in chains.

Noah hadn't moved.

He wasn't about to.

Too many itchy trigger fingers.

"Her too," he said, inclining his head in Sosa's direction. "She was the devil's right hand."

The nearest of the Guard hauled her to her feet, causing Sosa to cry out in pain as the wound in her shoulder moved with her arm. They weren't tender about it. They pulled her arms back, forcing her hands behind her back as they cuffed her, and pulled up on the cuffs to inflict maximum pain as they led her from the basilica.

As Sosa passed Noah, she spat at him.

The thick wad of phlegm hit him on the cheek.

Noah didn't flinch.

He just smiled sweetly back at her and said, "You're not the first woman to do that to me, but you're the first I haven't had to pay for the pleasure."

A moment later he felt hands on his shoulders and he was hauled to his feet.

No one was treating him as a hero.

He was cuffed and led away.

It took longer than any of them would have wanted to get outside, even using one of the many side doors. Outside, in the heat of the Barcelona sun, paramedics were fighting their way in the opposite direction, trying to get through the press of bodies and into the church so they could attend to the faithful caught in the stampede.

Some, Noah saw as he passed, were not moving.

All he could think was that it could have been a lot worse.

*

They released him eventually.

Neri spoke to the Mossos d'Esquadra for what felt like hours, haggling like market place traders, before finally an officer came over with the Roman and uncuffed him.

Noah rubbed at his wrists as Neri filled him in.

"You did well my crazy friend."

"I'm not sure about that. We're not meant to make a scene. In and out, no one knows we've been here kind of thing."

Neri smiled at that. "Well they certainly know you've been here," he said, nodding like he'd made the best joke. "The word from Rome is that the Camerlengo has been stripped of his title as pope-elect," Neri lowered his voice, these words just for Noah. "He admitted everything, all of it, including his involvement in the murder of the Cardinals, ordering the assassination of Peter, manipulating evidence to frame your friend… The theft of the Spear, ordering that poor bastard to commit suicide with it, and being the mastermind of the Berlin attack."

"Well that's something. His links to Solomon?"

"Not yet. But our friends here are not adverse to torture, so I have been told, as they are most eager to pin the blame on the deaths of Flight BA0486, *El Avión de Cadáveres*, on someone. The people need it."

Noah nodded. He could understand that. He needed that kind of resolution, too.

"Casualties?"

"Seven killed in the stampede, the kid you shot. Really, we got off very, very lightly. We were lucky."

"Better to be lucky than good," Noah agreed.

Neri clapped him on the shoulder. "Cheer up, my friend! Finally, we have a win. You saved a lot of lives today."

"We saved a lot of lives," he corrected the grizzled old Roman.

The screams of the Cardinals filled Noah's ears again. He would never be able to rid himself of that damned sound.

Neri chuckled. "And at least this time you didn't have to shoot the Pope."

"There is that," Noah said.

The relief didn't last long, as for the second time in just a few long days a nearby television began showing pictures of such unimaginable horror he couldn't wrap his head around what he was seeing.

While the congregation of La Sagrada Familia had got off relatively lightly, a different kind of worshippers who had gathered in Trafalgar Square had not.

"I need to go home," Noah said.

FORTY-EIGHT
CHOOSE LIFE

Michael Knight watched the signal on the monitor as it moved further and further from Nonesuch Manor.

Preparation was king. God was in the details.

He was a meticulous man.

He'd noticed the Old Man's chess board upstairs and recognized the layout as later stages in the Four Knights game, mid-Belgrade gambit. He'd wondered if Sir Charles was trying to send him a message. Four knights, Frost, Nyrén, Larkin and Khavin, all out in the field. It was possible. Quentin Carruthers had warned him the Old Man was sly like that. Well, Control was in for a nasty little surprise.

The tracker he'd placed on Mendes showed her fanning out her search, but still assuming that in his wheelchair the old fool couldn't have got very far. It wouldn't last, but for now she was looking in the wrong direction. Her natural assumption was that he'd left the grounds.

Abshir pointed at a number of dots on a screen above their heads, all converging on a satellite image of a large house.

"Kanic is about to storm Devere's house," he noted. "What do you need me to do?"

Knight stared at the moving dots. "I told you, Kanic has gone rogue. She's joined forces with Khavin. The man they are hunting is innocent and in great danger. I want you to help exfiltrate him.

"Devere?" Abshir said, like he couldn't quite believe the order, but wasn't going to actually challenge it.

"Yes Devere," Knight confirmed.

Abshir turned back to his terminal. "If you say so."

"Alert the ranking officer in situ, this is an unsanctioned mission. I want them out of there. Threaten court martial if necessary."

"We don't have the authority, Sir."

"I know you're not arguing with me, Abshir," Knight said, "Just do what you have to do. Understood?"

"Sir."

Knight summoned the lift that would take him up out of the Nest.

"I have other pressing matters that need my attention. I'll be back in quarter of an hour."

"Sir."

As the lift ascended he felt a vague sense of relief that the most important aspects of what was an incredibly elaborate plan were going well. But with so many moving parts there was still so much that could fall apart and jeopardize everything.

He rushed through the manor, out through the main doors and the glorious stone portico, and headed out into the gardens.

It took him five minutes to reach the herb garden, considerably faster than when he'd had to drag the old fool's wheelchair with him. He retrieved the chair from behind the shed and unlocked the doors. He stepped back as he threw them open, not that he expected Sir Charles to come out swinging, but as with everything caution was the better part of valour.

The Old Man squinted as sunlight flooded the space.

He rested up against a pile of old sackcloth, next to a ride-on mower.

Knight stepped forward.

"Come on, Charlie, time to make your curtain call."

Sir Charles wasn't particularly compos mentis as Knight wheeled him back to the manor house. The shed, in this heat, without water or his precious drugs, was probably overkill. He could have shoved the old bastard in a cupboard and left him there. It wasn't like he could have raised much of a ruckus. Still, the lack of fight was a small perk and he wasn't about to look a gift horse in its big yellowed teeth. It didn't take long to get him into the lift, and down into the Nest.

As the door opened he heard Abshir arguing with the on-site officer.

"Corporal Grace, I say again, Stacia Kanic is to be considered an enemy combatant. Do you read me? Stand down. Continue with this action and you will be considered an Enemy of the State."

The line crackled between them, then a clipped voice came back through the static. "I'm not in the habit of taking orders from a child. Where is Director Mendes?"

"She's indisposed," Knight replied, leaning over Abshir. "This is Captain Knight. Order your men to stand down. You are to take Stacia Kanic and Konstantin Khavin into custody. Is that clear?"

"Crystal. But it's still not happening, *Captain*. I don't take my orders from you, either. I need to hear from Director Mendes or the operation proceeds as planned."

Knight killed the connection.

Knight turned to Sir Charles, slumped over in his wheelchair.

Abshir noticed their guest for the first time. Confused, he asked, "Isn't Director Mendes looking for him?"

"It doesn't matter," Knight replied, brushing the young man's concern off. He was trying to revive the old man, lifting his head and smacking him across the face. When he failed to elicit any kind of response, he lifted Sir Charles and dumped him into a regular chair, then proceeded to tie him to it.

Abshir didn't understand. Nothing was making sense. "What should I do, Sir?" He asked, struggling.

Knight looked at the man. He was a child, basically. A child playing dress-up in an adult world. "Here's what you're going to do, Abshir, new orders. I want you to find the destruct codes for this place."

"For what place? For Nonesuch?" Abshir sounded astonished. "Do you seriously think they've got it rigged to self-destruct?" He shook his head, like he couldn't quite believe what he was hearing.

"We can't afford terrorists of any stripe getting access to this place. You know yourself the power down here. The crawlers and tunnels or whatever you call them that Lethe has burrowed into every system around the globe. We need to bring it down rather than risk being compromised."

"But still…"

"I know the Old Man. He's a wily old bastard. There will be C4 rigged in strategic places. And Lethe is too much of a control freak to need to run around the place trying to set the charges. It's all controlled down here. So, do your job, Abshir. Don't make me regret championing you."

Abshir didn't move. Then he said, "Perhaps we should wait for Mendes?"

"I'm serious, Abshir. Do it now."

There was an edge to his voice that had Abshir moving away from him, fast. The young technician turned quickly to the terminal and began punching in a series of instructions, rooting through Lethe's arcane labyrinth of secrets at the heart of DAGDA, the machine at the centre of the Nest, and there it was, not literally labelled self-destruct, but the purpose of the chain of commands was obvious. He saw on the schematics where the charges were placed. He saw how it was possible to seal off either wing in event of a breach. How it could be used to bring the place down, effectively sealing the Nest in like a tomb. There were half a dozen different sequences beyond the nuclear option. He said as much.

"The whole place comes down. All of it."

"Sir."

"Set the timer. We're getting out of here in five minutes. That's how long this old shithole has left."

"Five minutes," Abshir echoed, like he couldn't quite believe what he was being asked to do, but he did it anyway. "He's coming with us?"

"Of course."

"Five minutes won't give us very long."

"It's all we need," Knight assured him.

*

Outside the gates to Nonesuch Manor, Constance Mendes felt a surge of relief at the sight of a familiar face.

"Shamshi. I was worried."

The girl struggled to smile as she climbed out of the taxi.

"I was in Trafalgar Square," she said, tears filling her eyes.

"I feel for you, dear girl, I do, but grief comes later. I need your help."

The taxi left them.

"Of course," Shamshi said. The girl had surprising strength. Constance found herself liking her more than she'd expected to, all things considered.

"First, a question: are you loyal to Six or to Knight?"

"Six," she said, without question.

Mendes nodded.

"Good. We need to find Sir Charles. He's nowhere to be found. I have a bad feeling about this."

Shamshi nodded. "Knight… is he…?"

She didn't need to say the word compromised. Mendes knew exactly what the girl was asking. She nodded. "I believe so. So, it's you and me. We can't trust anyone else in here. Not even your brother. Understood?"

Again, Shamshi nodded.

"Can you go around to the gardens, double check the chapel and the graveside, see if you can find any sign of him?"

Another wordless nod.

Constance watched her go and then returned to her own search.

*

Jude Lethe had disappeared down a rabbit hole.

He followed the trail left by the malware behind the chip-and-pin attacks in Oxford Street. The kernel change made by the malware exposed the affected systems to takeover from a rogue computer. One machine. That was all it needed to bring down civilization as we knew it. Solomon was the source of the hack. He'd been right from day one, not that this was any consolation. The terrorist leader had used the exploit to seize control of every broadcast network simultaneously, airing his speeches on millions of computers and televisions around the world. Everyone saw him. Everyone heard him. He made his promises. Threats.

He wasn't the Messiah.

He was the ghost in the machine.

He was the herald ushering in the End of Days.

He was many things, but what he wasn't, Lethe swore, was winning.

The sheer reach of the crawler the malware had set up was incredible. It had spread into every exploited system he could imagine. And that was the thing lots of people didn't get, these chipsets had built in weaknesses, often at the insistence of Five and Six, the Secret Services, who wanted backdoor access to any major system so that they couldn't be locked out come the worst-case scenario. And every system he'd checked thus far, from the BBC to the Emergency Services to Six itself, was vulnerable. The backdoors were open. The malware rooted deep into them, leaving everything they protected exposed.

Of course, without the comfort of the Nest and the familiarity of DAGDA he wasn't about to access those systems directly, but he'd learned enough from his exploits to track distinct signatures left within the infected systems. It was akin to finding indicators in a blood sample before the tests confirm cancer.

What staggered him was how the malware had spread so far so fast, and then he realised how they'd done it: the Nest.

It was his fault.

All those scripts and procedures he'd written, all the tunnels and bottles he'd created as little shortcuts to get past firewalls and exploit security, even his decryption algorithms, all of the stuff he used to traverse the dark web in seconds to find out where an illegal arms trade came from, who was trafficking in children, narcotics, endangered species, all of it, all of those creations he wrote, all intended to help him support the team in the field, all of them had been used against him.

Solomon might be inside every computer on Earth.

And that was a fucking terrifying thought.

There was your modern Messiah.

There was your god.

There was your ghost in the machine...

The Metropolitan Police's systems were infected.

The terminal Lethe was working on had those same lines of code in its kernel, ready to allow remote takeover. He had no way of knowing what else it ceded to the intruders. It had taken all of his skill to work around the hack and prevent anything triggering the code. One wrong move, he tipped off the bad guys he was on to them. Do that and they'd shut him down remotely.

He had to regain control of the Nest.

Now.

The problem was it might take weeks.

And the clean-up... that could take years if he had to go from system to system. Even if they stopped Solomon, there was no telling who else knew about this vulnerability and who else might try to exploit it.

Not if, he told himself.

Then it hit him. Like a brick to the side of the head with a note wrapped around it saying, Wake up, idiot! Ralph Henning. The guy with the keys to the internet.

It was there, right in front of him, and had been from the start. Henning and several of his fellow keyholders had been murdered, presumably by Solomon's people.

Why bother murdering them unless they knew about the code?

He tried to think it through. What were the alternatives? Either they had discovered the code and were trying to stop it, or they had been paid to create it in the first place. He didn't see an alternative option. They had the power to cleanse the Internet, essentially, a global reset. And in either instance Solomon was smart to kill them. They were loose ends.

Lethe realised just how lucky he was to be alive.

If it weren't for Shamshi dragging him out of that cage... it didn't bear thinking about.

His phone vibrated.

He picked up the call.

"Frosty," he said.

"I'm at the house. I need eyes."

"I've got you. Two seconds."

Lethe already had a satellite focussed on the house and grounds surrounding it. A quick scan from orbit suggested no life signs inside, which didn't make sense. Not if Solomon was using it as a safe house.

"The good news is, I've got eyes on. The bad news is I can't see shit. Gut instinct, they've shielded it from prying eyes. Solomon isn't an idiot. He knows what we can do."

"Cheers, Jude. Stay with me, okay? Anything pops up, let me know."

"Will do."

A police officer ducked his head into the mobile command unit and told Lethe, "We're moving in ten minutes. I need to shut you down. And yes, I know you're working for that woman from the Secret Service, but we've still got to move."

"Just a little longer, please," Jude called back.

"You've got five. That's it."

Jude turned back to his phone. "Okay, matey, you'd better hurry, in and out, kill the bad guys, no messing," he said. But the device had gone dead.

The terminal wasn't responding either.

Instead, he saw a video looped on the screen.

He tried to kill it, but the system was no longer under his control.

It was only then that he realised what the video was showing.

"Oh shit," he said.

*

Ronan Frost entered the house.

He moved through into a dilapidated hallway, listening for any hint of movement. He moved the Browning from doorway to stairs to doorway checking for anything out of place. Even a mote of dust spinning across his eyeline.

Nothing.

He moved on, just five steps, taking him deeper into the house. The place had a peculiar air about it, like the building itself was dying.

It reminded him of the warehouse. And there was no getting away from what he'd encountered there. Both the big win in getting the hostages out, and the bonus when it came down to shutting down Solomon's counterfeiting operation.

Somewhere nearby, a phone rang.

Frost froze.

It took a moment to isolate the source of the sound; one of the side rooms off the main hallway. The collapsed roof messed with his spatial awareness, shifting the acoustics of the old place. Slowly, carefully, his eyes darting into every corner and every doorway, he moved across the debris toward the source of the sound, ready to put a bullet in the first face he saw.

Inside the room he saw a huge iron cage. It dominated the chamber. The cage door hung open. To one side, over by the far door, he saw an armchair with a side table next to it. On the table was an old-fashioned rotary telephone, its receiver trembling on the hook with every ring. He hadn't seen a phone like that in twenty years. It wasn't hooked up to an answerphone or redirect. It would ring and ring and ring until someone picked it up.

Frost did a circuit, making sure he was alone in the room, no one lurking in the shadows or out of the side door.

There was nobody there.

He picked up the phone, putting his back against the wall so no one could sneak up on him, and scanned both doors, watching as he said, "Yes?" into the mouthpiece.

"Ronan." The voice was unmistakably Solomon. "You don't mind if I call you that, do you? Mister Frost sounds so formal, and I feel like we are old friends now."

"What do you want?" Frost replied.

He used the silence to listen for several things at once— any indication the old phone had been rigged to explode, movement out beyond the door, or an echo on the line that might suggest Solomon was calling him from within the ruined manor.

"I like you, Ronan. Under different circumstances I think we could have been great friends. These days it is very difficult to find real heroes, and I believe you might be one of the closest things we have to a real hero. How does that feel?"

"Honestly? I'm not here for the flattery, Solomon. You called me, I repeat, what the fuck do you want?"

"I want to give you a choice. Think of it as a moral and ethical dilemma worthy of a true hero. You see, I have two people you care about. The divine Miss Orla Nyrén is with me, though I must admit she is feeling a bit under the weather. We were forced to go to rather ugly extremes to subdue her, but rest assured, she is fine. Now, we have just arrived at the luxurious Nonesuch Manor, and I must say your home is simply lovely. I could enjoy living here one day, but I'm getting ahead of myself. Your decision."

Another voice came on the line. "Frost?"

Orla.

"Where are you?"

"That's all you get, I'm afraid. Proof of life. Now you know I'm serious," Solomon said. Ronan couldn't hear Orla any more.

"You said two, who's the other one?"

"I believe you call him the Old Man. I'm having Charlie moved to a secret location as we speak. Now, I mentioned a decision. Think of it as a choice of the future over the past, or nostalgia over common sense. You make your choice, Orla or Charlie, and I'll give you the address. One or the other, you can't save both. And before you get any ideas about calling in the cavalry, Lethe is neutralized. He's not in a position to help. You are blind. There is no one else who can help you. Larkin is still in the beautiful Barcelona, and the Russian is about to kill Frasier Devere, which is just fine by me as he has outlived his usefulness. So, Orla or Charlie, I ask again. One of them is about to go up in a big, beautiful fireball. This began with fire, and it ends with fire. But which one burns is up to you."

"And if I don't choose."

"Well then, I'll choose for you. You have two minutes to decide. If you don't pick up the phone when I call back, they both die. Honestly, I don't care either way. This is about you."

Solomon killed the call.

Frost replaced the old plastic handset. He pulled out his own phone, intending to call Mendes, but there was no signal. His handset was blocked. He picked up the rotary phone again, intending to dial Lethe's number, but there was no dial tone. The phone was dead.

The seconds were ticking down.

He'd wasted fifteen already.

He didn't have time to make it back out onto the road and flag someone down to commandeer their phone, not that there was enough passing traffic, or that he was the kind of helpless soul a traveler would stop to help. No time.

He wouldn't play Solomon's twisted game.

That was all he could think.

And yet, even as his defiance grew, he knew he had to play. A man capable of the slaughter Solomon wrought wouldn't think twice about killing one more person or one less. He needed to think. He had no proof the terrorist had the Old Man, only his word, whereas he knew he had Orla. Frost had one shot, one chance to save one of them, assuming Solomon kept his word. But Orla was the one most likely able to save herself.

He sank down against a wall, wrestling with an impossible decision.

Orla obviously had more years ahead of her. Just in terms of life lived, Sir Charles had had a good run. He knew the old man would tell him to choose Orla, that it was no choice. Likewise, he knew that Noah would never speak to him again if he let Orla die. But Orla would sacrifice herself every time of asking to save the Old Man. That was the bond they all shared. He needed to think like Konstantin. The Russian would be pragmatic. He'd take emotion out of the equation and look at the facts, cold, hard, objective: Orla could take care of herself, he would say. The Old Man needs you to keep him alive.

And then there was the small matter of *that* phrase. *All debts paid back in full.*

Frost was sure Michael Knight was in league with Solomon, whether knowingly or by proxy. Mendes he wasn't sure about, but figured she was their fall guy. But it went higher than either of them. It had to for the sheer breadth and scope of the assaults, and the coordinated nature of the terrors. Someone in MI6 was working so closely for Solomon that he had been indoctrinated with those same teachings. That was all he could think. And it had been weighing on him since he'd first heard that phrase from Konstantin's lips.

The Old Man knew. But who could be so close to Sir Charles? Who could pull the strings like some hidden puppet master making them dance to his tune? One position came to mind. One man who had been threatening to close them down from day one. Control. But did it make sense to believe he was compromised? Quentin Carruthers had been in play for the best part of six decades. He was the quintessential British spymaster.

Surely this malfeasance couldn't go all the way to Control.

But if he was… there was no way Frost could go up against the heart of British intelligence without the Old Man at his side.

Which meant there was only one choice, really, as much as it would damn him to make it.

The phone rang.

Frost picked up the handset, knowing he was about to issue a kill order for Orla.

"I've made my decision," he said.

FORTY-NINE
BIRDS FLY

Kanic's number two eyed the Russian suspiciously.

"We're supposed to, what, trust this guy now?"

Stacia Kanic nodded, heading the argument off before it could get started. "Things change. Get used to it."

The strapping around his face struggled to hold his nose together. It looked like shit and must have felt pretty much the same way.

Konstantin didn't apologize for it. Like Kanic said, things change.

"I'll work with that bastard if I'm ordered to, but that's it."

"Excellent," Stacia said. "We're not here to make friends."

The three of them unshouldered their weapons, checking them over. Behind them, a dozen armed men in black assault gear prepared to move out.

"How do we know he's still inside?"

"Twenty minutes ago we had eyes on," Konstantin replied. "He was in there then."

"A lot can happen in twenty minutes. Why did we lose our eyes?"

Stacia shifted uncomfortably. "Khavin's man lost access to the satellite."

"That's his man. What about our man? We have a whole team of them. To be blunt, why aren't we relying on our own people?"

Stacia held up a hand. "It's a dead zone, Channing. Our men, their man. Makes no difference, they're blind. So, let's go get us a terrorist. Devere's not walking out of there."

"With all due respect," which almost always prefaced a complete lack of any respect in her experience, Channing said, "I don't like this. Not being funny, but did Control clear this?"

"Of course."

Channing stared into her eyes. He breathed deeply, weighing his next words carefully. Finally, the solider said, "I don't believe you."

That surprised her. These men weren't thinkers. They followed orders. She didn't miss a beat. She held his stare. "You saw what happened in Trafalgar Square. Are you in any doubt that Devere was behind the action, soldier?"

"No, but–"

"Nothing matters beyond that first word. That's a direct order. We can argue protocol later, but for the good of country, we go in there united. I have your back, you have mine. Khavin has both of ours. We have his. Understood?"

Channing considered this for a moment. Then said, "We have your back."

He turned and signalled to the assembled soldiers.

"They know we're coming," Stacia said to her team. "We don't know what we're up against in there, so exercise maximum caution. No dumb heroics. I want every last one of you coming out of this alive." She looked to Channing. He nodded. "Okay, let's move in." She gave the signal.

Fifteen armed men moved in as one, rushing the grand house belonging to Frasier Devere. Channing gave another signal and four broke off to go around to right, moving around to the rear of the building, while another four broke to the left, also moving around to the back, while the remaining seven went for the front door.

Konstantin and Stacia flanked either side, while two soldiers brought forward the battering ram.

Two strikes and the door burst open.

She was first in, leading the charge, yelling "Armed police!" as she rushed into the grand hallway. She scanned left and right. Clear. Konstantin moved in behind her.

Twin marble staircases rose organically from the floor on either side, curving around the circular hall. One side didn't reach the second floor.

Two soldiers went up the left side, two headed to the right where a long dining room met the hallway.

That left the three of them, Konstantin, Kanic and Channing.

The trio advanced towards the kitchen area, each covering the other.

She listened for any sign of movement.

Konstantin's hand went up, fist clenched. They stopped. He motioned her, miming throwing a flash bang. She handed him a flash grenade. He primed it, counted to three, then gently rolled it into the kitchen. He counted three more off on his fingers, then the three of them took cover as intense flash of light burned up the inside of their eyelids. Konstantin gave the signal, and they rushed into the kitchen to find two men down on the kitchen floor, blinded and reeling.

Stacia shot one of them dead as Channing grabbed the other.

"Where's Devere?" he demanded, spittle flying into his captive's face.

"Upstairs."

Konstantin glanced up towards the ceiling as gunfire erupted from somewhere above their heads.

Channing looked at her for orders. "Secure him," she said.

He bound the man with zip ties to the wrists and angles, trussing him up like a pig as she and Konstantin left the kitchen. They returned to the hallway as one of their soldiers came tumbling down the grand staircase. He hit the ground hard, neck broken. It didn't matter. He was dead before he started to fall.

More of her people converged on the hallway, drawn by the gunfire above.

Stacia led the way, Konstantin two steps behind her, as they ascended. The centre of the marble stairs was worn flat from the shuffle of generations of feet fetching and carrying for rich masters.

They reached the landing.

All was quiet.

Another one of their men lay unmoving on the landing. A pool of blood thickened around his torso.

Stacia motioned for the others to fall back, taking up defensive positions.

"Give it up!" Stacia called. "We have the numbers. You're not walking out of this unless you come out with your hands behind your head."

The immediate response was a burst of gunfire, which left her in no doubt as to what the likelihood was of a peaceful resolution. Chunks flew out of the drywall near Stacia's head. "Body bags all round it is then." She ducked down, using the heavy balustrade as partial cover.

Konstantin returned fire.

She couldn't see if he'd identified targets or was firing blind.

On the far side of the curved landing several doors led off into the upstairs rooms. They could have been in any of them. Or all of them.

She broke cover, keeping low as she moved along the length of the banister.

There were regular gaps in the framework, plenty wide enough to allow a lot more than bullets through. Movement was a calculated risk, but staying where they were left them as sitting ducks if Devere's men moved around to isolate them. She'd already lost two of her team. She wasn't about to let the rest be picked off like tin cans in a shooting gallery.

She gestured to Konstantin: *You and me.*

He nodded, reading her intent.

They moved together, the soldiers behind them laying down covering fire.

A bullet took a piece of banister out five inches from Konstantin's head. The big Russian didn't so much as flinch. No recoil. No change of position. The shooter had tipped his hand. She'd seen the muzzle flare and knew which doorway the prize waited behind.

She gave the signal.

They crossed the landing to the door, taking up position either side.

Konstantin held up a hand, meaning: *Stay there.*

He backed up to the previous doorway.

She read his mind. She'd seen the doorway inside, between the two rooms—presumably an en suite bathroom shared with the adjoining room.

She bought him time, firing off a couple of rounds into the bedroom to keep the shooter focussed on her.

He replied with a volley of three wild shots that threatened the light fixtures.

What should have been a fourth was greeted by the click of an empty chamber and the unmistakable sound of a magazine being ejected.

That was his cue.

She stepped into the doorway just as the Russian wrenched open the adjoining door. One shot. Centre of mass. One dead man lying on a very expensive carpet.

It wasn't Devere.

"Where the fuck is he?"

Channing moved into the room behind her.

"No sign of Devere. Two of ours dead. The place is clear."

"That doesn't make sense. Search the grounds. Tear the house apart. He isn't fucking Houdini. Find Devere."

"Yes Ma'am," Channing said, and he left the room.

She looked at Konstantin, the reality sinking in. They'd missed Devere. Somehow.

The Russian wasn't listening to her.

He held a finger to his lips: *Quiet*.

She heard it then; a creak. Overhead.

"Let's bug out," Stacia said, slightly louder than before. Making sure her voice carried. "He's not here."

"He's got to be in the grounds," Konstantin agreed, playing along.

They moved back into the hallway.

The attic trapdoor was in the ceiling above the middle of the landing.

"No way we're opening that without him hearing," Konstantin whispered.

Stacia kept her voice down also. "We can always light up the attic from here," she suggested.

"Tempting. I pull down the door, you start firing?"

Stacia moved to the other side of the hatch.

473

She raised her gun.

Ready: she nodded.

Khavin made a jump for the hatch, pushing it up to disengage the auto-lock. As he landed lightly on the balls of his feet, the access hatch came down, a steel ladder automatically dropping in stages, with a series of loud ratchetting sounds.

She took a step back and opened fire, spraying bullets into the dark opening above.

No screams. No answering fire.

She ducked back out of line of sight.

Still no noise came from above.

Konstantin held out his hand. Stacia handed him the last of her stun grenades. He activated it but didn't immediately throw it. He counted down again, and at the last possible moment rose up one foot on the metal ladder and hurled the grenade through the hatchway into the dark space above them.

She closed her eyes.

The blinding flash was immediate and brutal, the answering cry of pain visceral.

Whoever was playing Anne Frank up there was blind.

Gunfire ricocheted around the confines of the attic, thundering into the wall behind Konstantin, through the plaster, into the timber frames, roving wildly across every wild inch of space. The Russian moved fast, no thought for personal safety. He was up through the hatch in seconds, as disoriented bullets went everywhere. One bit in the floorboards by Konstantin's head as he stepped out into the dark.

The *click click click* of the gunman's rifle was music to his ears.

"Drop it," Konstantin called into the darkness. "Or I drop you."

Without the muzzle flash he couldn't see the shooter's position, and the sun through hatchway was lighting him up like bonfire night, but that wasn't helping a blind man. The effects of the flash bang were going to take time to clear. He was good.

Konstantin heard the man's gun drop to the floorboards.

"It's down," the shooter said.

There was a shuffle of boots as he moved forward.

Konstantin could just see him, a darker shape emerging from the gloom.

He grabbed the shooter and forced him to half climb, half fall down the ladder into the light.

He landed awkwardly, missing the last steps and sprawling in a heap at Stacia's feet.

Konstantin descended after him.

Stacia grabbed a handful of the man's hair and dragged his head back.

"Devere?" she asked.

Konstantin looked down at the face of Frasier Devere.

"Humanity Capital is finished. You're finished," Konstantin told him.

"I don't care. None of that matters. I just want you dead. I want you to pay for what you did to my son."

"Your son was a parasite. He got exactly what he deserved. Believe me. It could have gone a lot worse for him." Konstantin said.

"Fuck you," Devere spat back, defiant.

"That's not how this works. For what you did to those people in Trafalgar Square this is where I fuck *you*."

Stacia reached for her cuffs. "I'll take him in," she said.

"You think he deserves a trial for what he did? I don't. I think he deserves the same fate, dying face down in a pool of his precious gold," Konstantin said, bluntly.

A flash of fear crossed Devere's face then. Just for a moment, and then it was gone. "Solomon will finish you all," he said. "He has already won. You're just too stupid to see it."

"You ever notice how bastards like this wet themselves when they're done?"

"Khavin," Stacia warned him. "I need to take him in."

"No," the Russian said. One word. Terse. To the point.

The fear returned.

"I know things. I can—" Konstantin silenced him. A crushing right hook to the temple. It was like the bolt from a stun gun. Devere went down and didn't move.

"I don't like grasses," Konstantin said.

"You're a strange, strange man," Stacia told him.

The Russian just nodded.

FIFTY
NOBODY'S HERO

The whole think reeked of a setup.

His emobile phone was blocked, no signal in or out.

He'd followed Solomon's instructions to the letter. The conference centre he'd just broken into was eerily quiet.

The entrance hall led to a long corridor, with signs up advertising a tech conference due to take place next week. He saw windows into offices and smaller conference rooms all along one side, and at the end he saw the double doors out onto the main floorspace.

Frost had no backup and no communications.

But that wasn't going to stop him.

He was on a clock.

Each second one more than he could really afford to take.

His shoulder ached like hell from the single drop of molten gold that had fused to his bone, and his lungs were tight, still suffering the aftereffects of smoke inhalation. It wasn't a good day.

He was walking into the lion's den.

There was no point trying to hide his presence.

Solomon knew he was coming.

Even so, old habits died hard.

Frost crept along the half-dark passageway, Browning in hand, conscious of every little noise around him.

Buildings were never truly silent, new or old, there was always some kind of life in them be it the creak of settling boards, the clang of a pipe or rumble of water through the cisterns and boilers. Always something.

He pushed through the double doors, stepping out onto the main trade floor.

He kept close to the wall with its industrial design of exposed steel, in the thicker shadows, surveying the giant floorspace. It was like a giant warehouse. The exhibition floor would normally host stalls and booths offering the latest in tech, sporting goods, comic books, or whatever exhibiters were trying to flog to the masses. Between trade shows it was more or less empty. A few packing crates stood abandoned around the area, but he wasn't looking at those. There was a raised dais in the centre of the vast space, and on it, a chair. Someone was in the chair, their back to him, shrouded in darkness. Around the foot of the dais Frost saw what looked like barrels. Explosives, he assumed, given Solomon's promise of fire.

No doubt the chair was rigged to blow if he tried to extricate the person sitting there.

Beyond the figure, he realised, was a massive television screen, like the kind they used at sports events to capture the action replays for the crowd who couldn't have possibly seen it in real time. The display was dark.

Frost kept his back against the wall, circling the perimeter.

He could hear his breathing loud in his ears.

Every footstep seemed to echo for eternity.

"Ronan?"

The voice came from the chair.

Orla.

Solomon had lied to him. Of course, he'd lied to him. He'd chosen to rescue the Old Man. He'd made all the rational choices about who he needed at his side if he was If he was going to take this fight to Vauxhall. And Solomon had known that. He'd played him.

"Yes," he said. "You okay?"

"Been better."

"Alone in here?"

"Haven't seen or heard a soul since I came around."

"And that's a bomb?"

"You're getting good at this."

"Pressure plate? Any sort of remote timer on you?"

"I don't think so, but don't trust me, I can't see half the platform from here."

"Well we'll just have to hope I don't blow us both up then," Frost said, climbing onto the dais. It took him a couple of seconds to cut through the bonds restraining her.

"What happened?"

"I was gassed in the back of a limo. Not my finest hour."

In front of them, the television came to life, the sudden brightness of the image enough to throw the entire hall into half-light.

Solomon looked down on them.

"Ah, Ronan, you truly are so very, very predictable. It's hardly a challenge."

"Where is he?"

"Shaking hands with St Peter," Solomon replied. "Not that I expect the old bastard to get in, his soul is so tainted by the things he's done."

*

"That's it. That's the signal. Start the countdown."

Abshir stared open mouthed at Knight.

"This makes no sense."

"I have my orders and now you have yours."

Abshir keyed in the code initiating the shutdown. "Five minutes. I'll help you with him."

Abshir rose and moved to get Sir Charles's wheelchair. The old man was awake now. Groggy but awake.

"What do you think you're doing?" Knight asked Abshir.

"I'm getting his chair. We can't carry him."

"He stays here."

"What? You can't be serious. That's… that's murder."

Knight walked over and called the lift. "I am very serious. You are welcome to stay here and burn with the old bastard if you wish."

Sir Charles told the young hacker, "You should go."

"You see?" Knight said. "He's absolving you. Clean conscience. No stains on your soul. Now let's go."

Still shaking his head, Abshir moved the wheelchair beside Sir Charles and started to work at the bonds tying him.

"Step away from him," Knight said, a chilling calm coming over his voice. They'd already wasted thirty seconds arguing. He didn't have time to cajole the boy into coming, so if they both had to die here, so be it. He really didn't care.

Abshir worked the first tie lose.

"Last warning."

"Fuck you, Knight. I am not going to leave him here to die. You'll have to shoo –"

Knight put a bullet in his skull.

Abshir fell across the Old Man.

"You really are a vile contemptible little man," Sir Charles spat, his hand going to the dead boy's head where it lay in his lap.

"And you can shut the fucking fuck up, you sanctimonious bastard," Knight sneered. "Your relevance is done. You're a footnote in history. Now think happy thoughts. Four minutes until bye-bye. He stabbed at the lift call button several times, but the door wasn't opening.

"It's not coming," the Old Man said, quite reasonably. Like it was obvious.

"What?"

"The manor is on lockdown."

There was a moment, a glimpse of fear, as Knight realised what that meant. But he refused to believe it.

"The sequences young Abshir found, they were built by Lethe to my specifications. This is my house. My family home. It explains so much about your psyche that you believe I would simply run. That isn't how this works. A captain goes down with his ship. I am the captain, Nonesuch is my metaphorical ship. "I don't fear death. I never have. But you? Are you afraid?"

Knight stared at the old man.

He dashed over to the passageway leading to the stairs, a minute gone. More. He needed to get out of there while he still had time. Knight heaved on the door, but it was sealed. He didn't hesitate, he stepped back and fired several shots into the lock plate, then into the hinges, and tried to kick his way out, but the door was not giving.

"The irony here, I'm sure you will appreciate, is that if anyone was going to be able to save you from yourself it was young Abshir. And you killed him."

Knight abandoned the door and crossed the room, intending to take his frustration out on the Old Man.

He pistol-whipped Sir Charles with the butt of his service weapon, drawing blood and breaking old brittle bone.

"Just shut the fuck up. I'm trying to think."

Sir Charles licked at the blood gathering in the corner of his mouth. "Why break the habit of a lifetime?" How long has it been now? Two minutes? Three?"

"If you don't shut the fuck up I'll put a bullet in your fucking face."

"Be my guest. There's not much difference between dying now and dying in ninety seconds."

Knight pressed the muzzle up against the Old Man's temple.

"Go on," Sir Charles said. "Better men than you have tried and failed. Do it. Pull the trigger. Eighty seconds. A minute. It's all the same to me."

Knight hit him again, but there was nothing, not even personal satisfaction to be gained from pulverizing the Old Man's skull. He turned his back on him, and went back to Abshir's console, trying to wake the machine. Not that he had even the rudimentary skills needed to crack whatever code was counting down his life in seconds.

"Wouldn't it be nice if it talked? Imagine that wonderful deep voice, maybe Morgan Freeman, saying ten, nine, eight." The Old Man smiled. "I'd quite like that. A soothing voice to listen to for the last few seconds."

*

The drone buzzing overhead was the first clue that something was very wrong.

It hovered over Nonesuch Manor, high up, as though taking aerial shots of the grounds.

Why was it up there?

Who was piloting it?

Constance Mendes stared up at the aircraft. It wasn't part of any security detail she'd ordered. It looked to be military grade. One of Lethe's toys, maybe?

Shamshi joined her at the portico. She stood beside Sir Charles's Daimler.

"No luck?" Constance asked, already knowing the answer.

Shamshi shook her head. "One of ours?" She pointed up at the drone.

"No."

"What's it waiting for?"

"I am damned if I know," Constance Mendes said, looking from the manor house, then back at the drone.

The aircraft backed off, retreating over a hundred feet from its previous position.

It was pure instinct. She didn't think about what she was doing. She grabbed Shamshi's arm and half-pulled, half-dragged her across the gravel drive out of the main arc of the courtyard and along the driveway back toward the gates.

Every fibre of her being told her to run.

The explosion was all-consuming.

The shockwaves were immense. It felt as though the ground collapsed from under them. The entire world was on fire. The air full of heat. The concussive impact was deafening. She heard nothing outside the seconds of detonation, one after another after another in a chain. She didn't fall, she flew, unspeakable force driving her on, and where she'd been running her feet no longer felt the solidity of the ground beneath them.

She came down hard, sprawling and tumbling, grit and gravel biting into her skin as she tried to brace herself.

Shamshi was beside her.

Mendes looked back slowly, the searing heat scorching her eyes as she struggled to focus on the conflagration.

She he couldn't look away.

A huge fireball rose into the sky, burning bright, licks of flame lashing out as the flames grew out of thick, black smoke. It only took seconds to blot out the sun and the sky.

She pushed herself up to her hands and knees.

The world around her grew dark.

The flames lit her face.

Ash and soot rained down over the grounds of the old manor.

She couldn't move. She couldn't think. She was trapped in a no man's land of indecision and shock as the fires raged. The inferno tore through the house. So much was already destroyed.

Smoke clouds roiled like thunderheads.

The air was thick with ash, making it hard to breathe.

The heat was like nothing she had ever felt before.

Mendes didn't move. She didn't try to stand. She didn't trust herself.

The sky would return. Daylight would take hold once more. But for now it was like something out of Dante's nightmares.

Parts of the manor house still stood; sections of the façade, the arc of the arboretum's high windows, but much of the stuff behind the façade was simply gone, consumed, and all that remained was rubble. Gone were the statues and the fine art. Gone were the relics and the vast wealth of knowledge. All that remained was dust and ash, and even that threatened to blow away on the black winds.

There was a massive wound in the forecourt. The Old Man's Daimler was gone, swallowed by the black maw of destruction, meaning if they hadn't run they would be dead now. That drone had saved her life. She moved up to the edge, and saw the twisted chassis and the heat-warped steel. She still couldn't hear anything beyond the tinnitus ringing through her skull, but her other senses more than made up for it in terms of delivering the horror.

Shamshi stood beside Constance, clutching her arms around herself as though they could somehow anchor her to normality, keeping her safe.

Every part of Mendes hurt but she barely noticed.

She couldn't take her eyes off the ruin of Nonesuch Manor.

It was gone.

As though to emphasize that thought an entire section of unsupported wall teetered and collapsed in a rush of sound and dust.

Anyone in there was gone. There was no way anyone could have survived. Even in a blast-proof box like Lethe's Nest, they didn't stand a chance against the sheer explosive power of the blast.

She moved around the crater, walking toward the ruin. She still couldn't get close, the heat was so intense. She couldn't take her eyes off the debris and realised she was cataloguing the devastation, anything recognizable from any part of the house gave an idea of just how devastating the blast had been in that area, helping her build a picture. But the truth was it was a pointless exercise; so little of worth had survived in anything approaching a recognizable state. Most of what remained was reduced to rock dust and rubble.

Seeing two deeper craters within the devastation, marked by rings of ash, she figured the explosions had begun underground and pushed the entire frame of the old building up and outwards, hence the collapse.

It was purely guesswork, but she'd just walked out of one disaster zone, and had a decent idea how upwards pressure could devastate a structure.

Flames still raged in various parts of the devastation, consuming anything and everything that would feed them. They would burn for a while yet.

Beside her, she realised Shamshi was screaming into the wreckage, and it was only when she turned and saw the shapes of her lips and really heard the name of her lost brother for the first time that she realised what the girl was going through. Her anguish was gut-wrenching. She grabbed at Shamshi now, trying to hold her back. Trying to stop her from getting down on her hands and knees and digging through the rubble even as it burned. The human cost of what they'd just witnessed hit home hard.

Shamshi fought against her, but she wasn't letting go.

In the end, the poor girl broke down and allowed herself to be held.

Her weeping was wretched.

Nonesuch Manor was gone. Abshir was dead. Knight too, and Sir Charles if he'd still been in there.

It would be days before they could get at the bodies and know for sure.

But one thing Constance Mendes did know: she had failed.

*

Orla was on her feet.

Frost stood beside her, struggling to process what he saw on the big screen.

The drone footage of Nonesuch Manor disappeared as a huge fireball engulfed the screen. For too long there was nothing. Smoke. Flame. Ash. It took too long to clear. Too long before they could see the devastation.

No one was walking away from that.

Orla's eyes were full of tears.

He had never seen her cry.

He stared at her, his brain refusing to accept the truth of his own eyes.

"Charles," Orla breathed.

"Maybe he wasn't in there," Frost said. It was wishful thinking.

"He was in there," Solomon's voice confirmed, like some twisted narrator talking over the sickest nature documentary.

Frost stared at the screen.

He felt cold.

Twisted up inside.

This wasn't how it ended. Not for Sir Charles Wyndham. Not in fire. Not a bomb. Not after how they'd met. Not after what had happened to him. Not a bomb.

He walked up to the screen, with no idea if Solomon had some sort of webcam watching them, but he made sure his face was right up close to the glass as he promised, "I am going to kill you for this." He didn't raise his voice. He didn't swear or wave his gun around. He just stared at the screen and promised Solomon he was a dead man.

It was something he'd learned from the Old Man; sometimes less is more.

He didn't need to rage.

On the screen, they watched as the drone flew lower, the camera turning to take in the sheer scale of the devastation. He felt no sadness for the old building. It was just stone. It could be rebuilt. But his friend. His mentor. He couldn't. He couldn't allow that grief to form. Not yet. Everything had its season and soon enough it would be the time to lament. He saw Constance Mendes and Shamshi Yasin holding each other in the middle of the screen. Battered but alive. They were two less deaths on his soul. The girl was sobbing.

"Her brother," Orla said, joining the image to the reality behind it.

Mendes took out her gun and aimed it at the drone.

A second later the screen went blank.

"Was Jude in there?" Orla asked.

He didn't have an answer for that, so he said nothing.

"Mister Lethe is quite safe," Solomon promised. "He's here with me."

Two words echoed around the vast space. "Sorry Frosty."

The voice was unmistakably Jude Lethe's.

"Jude? Where are you?" Orla called.

"That would be telling," Solomon said.

Frost heard something. A mechanism. It took him a moment, the shadows of the trade floor masking the movement, but some sort of curtain was being drawn back beneath the big screen.

He hadn't even realised it was there until it parted.

Solomon faced him,

Alone.

Unarmed.

Frost didn't hesitate. It was pure instinct. He moved forward immediately, striding toward the terrorist. He fired shot after shot in Solomon's direction.

Some went wide.
Some.
Others hit their mark.
Frost kept on firing until his gun was empty.

FIFTY-ONE
FIELDS OF FIRE

Constance took Shamshi by both shoulders. She held her at arm's length. She looked into her eyes.

"Listen to me, girl. Nothing has changed. We can't mourn now. We are different, people like us. We need to do our jobs. That means you need to do what you are good at. You're my only hope."

She looked back defiantly.

"What do you need me to do?" Shamshi asked, voice strained, tears staining her cheeks.

"Find out where that drone was broadcasting to. They were watching. They knew what was going to happen. That means whoever murdered your brother is on the other end of that signal."

Shamshi nodded.

This was something she could do.

Together the two women walked to where the drone had crashed after Mendes's bullet took out one of the rear rotors. It had come down in the woodpile over by the pagoda. Constance hauled the heavy frame out of the wood, and turned it over to Shamshi, offering up access to the guts of the machine, including the camera.

Shamshi took out her phone and hooked it up via USB3 to the drone's control box.

*

Ronan Frost knew that his bullets weren't hitting Solomon, but that really didn't matter. His rage drove him forward, and step after step he fired off every last round in a second magazine.

Solomon did not fall.

By rights he should have died a score of deaths in the last twenty seconds.

And even now, Browning emptied, Frost didn't stop firing.

He kept walking forward, squeezing the trigger.

But eventually he stopped.

He had no choice in the matter.

His gun arm dropped.

He stood there, halfway between the dais and Solomon.

The terrorist's body was distorted by twenty imperfect circular fractures in the bullet-proof glass where Frost's bullets had hit repeatedly. The glass wasn't perfect. The other man got lucky. Two or three shots in close proximity and the membrane that held the glass together would have ruptured, then he would have ended the bastard. But he hadn't seen the glass.

Solomon shook his head and smiled, like he was dealing with an errant—and as he'd said already—utterly predictable child.

"You really must do something about your anger management issues, Ronan."

Frost ejected the magazine and reached for his last one.

He froze as more curtains moved aside, and armed men and women emerged, fanning out quickly around the trade floor to surround Orla and Ronan.

They stayed at the periphery of the room, rifles held at the ready. A threat.

Frost was done with threats.

Solomon motioned for him to drop the Browning. He did, reluctantly. But he wasn't kneeling or raising his hands. He stood there, his eyes locked with Solomon's, knowing that if he could just get his hands on the man he'd break him in two. He didn't need guns to end a man's life. But with the screen between them that wasn't happening.

Orla moved forward, standing just behind his shoulder.

He did not look at her.

One of Solomon's men stepped forward, dragging Jude Lethe with him.

He held the muzzle of Desert Eagle to Lethe's head.

It was overkill.

From point blank range a bullet from a beast like that would leave, quite literally, nothing of Lethe's head behind.

The soldier pushed Lethe around, until, on his knees, he was in front of Solomon, a penitent man awaiting his judgment. The bulletproof shield was between Frost and his friend. The shooter didn't take the gun off Lethe.

Frost's mind ran through the options.

Not that there were many to play with.

But he had Orla.

As good as the others were or weren't, they weren't Orla Nyrén.

Even unarmed, they were a force to be reckoned with.

But surely Solomon knew that? He seemed to know everything about them.

Frost saw something in Solomon's right hand. He couldn't make out what. As though sensing his curiosity, Solomon opened his hand as though offering it up.

The Spear of Destiny.

It was the same weapon the priest had used to take his own life in Saint Peter's Square.

"History is with us. You see, thanks to Father Francesco's sacrifice, the world is now very much aware of what this is. It is a weapon of the light. The three of you will die today, believe me, but your deaths will be majestic. They will be symbolic. Shedding your blood, the great defenders of the realm, Ogmios, the god meant to stand against the Antichrist at the end, has fallen. And fallen to such an ancient and powerful relic. Killed by the blade that killed their precious Christ, a mirror to the silver of Iscariot that took their Little Father. It is beautiful in its simplicity, really."

"And what, you are the Antichrist in this scenario?"

Solomon shook his head. "It doesn't have to be me. Like I told the world, I am not the Messiah. Neither am I the antichrist. I am simply a vessel of the truth. The people must decide. Even now, in this enlightened age, people are inherently simple. They care deeply about the gods that they worship – and this is what is leading humanity to its own destruction. Whatever god they adore, a religious one, a financial one, a two headed god of fork-tongued politicians, it doesn't matter. They are all the same. They are all of them vulnerable. All will fall. That was my promise. And now it is time I deliver on it. Today all of your gods die."

"Nice speech," Frost said. "Deserves a more receptive audience."

"What I don't get," Orla said, "Is what killing us will achieve, even with the Spear? Nobody knows who we are. We are ghosts."

Surprisingly, the answer came from Lethe. He was shaking his head, struggling to find the right words. "I saw a video... It was part of the malware infection, rooted into every system, the one they tested with the chip-and-pin attacks a few days ago. You need to understand... Almost every screen in the world is showing the same video."

"Jude?" Ronan asked.

Instead of answering, the screen above their heads came to life again.

"People of the world," the giant Solomon on the screen said. "I make this promise to you. Each of you can be a *Chassid*. Each of you can talk to God. You don't need money, you don't need your failed religious leaders, you don't need your corrupt politicians.

"Instead, you can be like my disciples.

"Every great visionary has those closest to him, those he trusts with his great plans. I want you to know them so you can look to them as your example, allow them to show you the Way as I have shown them the Way. They have chosen me to be the Messiah and I am humbled beyond words, but I am not a fool. There are forces aligned against me. The truth is that I could die tomorrow. What then? What of our great truth?

"For our work to continue, for this world and all its people to be redeemed, we need more examples to follow. Let these brave men and women be your examples."

Frost could only stand and watch as then the picture changed.

"First, my right hand, my weapon of truth, Konstantin Khavin," said Solomon, as the picture on the screen changed. "You will recognize him, of course as the killer of Petrus Romanus. Konstantin took the head off the unholy beast that has failed so many of you over and over again. And not only that, on my word he struck at the heart of Humanity Capital, the epitome of corporate greed and money worshipping in our Neo Liberal world. The man behind Humanity Capital has stolen, quite literally, billions of pounds from you. Billions." The images were police photos from Miles Devere's apartment. They focussed on the blood on the corpse, showing Devere from every angle imaginable, and all of the damage the big Russian had done to him. And then the images shifted, and showed Konstantin going up against his father. They were in the house. Photographs of Kanic and Khavin moving through the Nottingham mansion. They showed Devere on his knees, and in three rapid fire frames, showed Konstantin's hammer blow that took him down. "Frasier Devere had to pay for his financial crimes. The loss of his son was only the down payment on his guilt. Khavin was my collector. He is the scourge of the wealthy and the shameless. He is my red right hand. Look to Konstantin. Follow him. Turn on those who steal from you. Humble them. Take back what is rightfully yours."

The image switched to the familiar streets of Rome. He could see Noah in the centre of the shot. "This is Noah Larkin, Disciple of Solomon. Here you see him, blood on his hands, emerging from the Vatican after the death of the Cardinals. This was his work. He is my greatest achievement. He instigated the purge of the unrighteous. He is my plague on earth. He is my wrath. None can stand against him." The images shifted to Gaudi's chapel in Barcelona, Noah in the aisle, gun raised, yelling in the face of the false Pope. "My loyal servant, Noah, doing God's work, purging this Earth of corrupt and fallible men."

495

Frost just stood there, powerless to do anything but watch as the images changed again. All he could think was that these images were going out on every screen, in every home.

"Orla Nyrén," Solomon continued. "Disciple of Solomon." An image of Orla strung up naked in a supermarket basement, battered to the point of death, violated, faded into one of her lying on the Rock within the Dome, followed by film of her being dragged away by Israeli police. "She failed at the Dome of the Rock yesterday. Today it must fall, for we must build a Third Temple for the glory of our Lord and His kingdom here on earth. Others need to take her place and keep fighting."

Ronan turned to Orla and saw steel behind the tears. He wished that he could read her mind.

*

Stacia Kanic answered her phone, switched to talk via her headset and shouted to be heard over the roar of the helicopter's engines.

"I don't think you should be talking to me," she said.

"Where are you?" Constance Mendes's voice, despite all the other noise, was loud in her ear.

Stacia hesitated.

She didn't know who she could trust.

Was Mendes in with Knight?

"I'm in a chopper heading back to London."

"Knight is dead," Mendes reported.

Stacia wasn't sure how to handle this news.

"That might not be the worst news you could have given me," she said after a beat. "He was corrupt.

Either he'd infiltrated us, or he'd been corrupted, but he was working with Solomon. I can prove it."

"I know," Mendes said. "I worked it out. Too slow. But I worked it out."

"The thing is, how do I know you're not one of them?"

"I can prove I'm clean, Stacia," Mendes said.

"How?"

"I can tell you where Solomon is. He sent a drone to record the explosion."

"You're getting way too far ahead of me now. Explosion? What are you taking about? What explosion?"

"Nonesuch Manor. Knight was inside when it was destroyed. Abshir too. It looks like we lost Sir Charles Wyndham, as well. No one can find him."

"Shit shit shit shit shit," Stacia said, and saw Konstantin studying her face. He couldn't hear what Mendes was saying, but he didn't need to know she was delivering bad news. She didn't want to be the one to tell him his friend and mentor was dead.

"I brought down the drone. Shamshi got access to its control systems and tracked it back to a point of origin. It was being guided via satellite from a conference hall in Southeast London. I'm sending you the exact location. Look, I'm being honest with you here, Stacia. I don't know who else to trust. This thing goes higher than me, I'm sure of it. Knight wasn't working directly for Solomon. He was reporting to someone at Control."

That echoed her worst fears. Could they truly have been compromised all the way to the very top?

Mendes continued. "Khavin is with you?"

"Yes."

"Good. You are going to need someone you can trust. Despite everything you have been told, I truly believe you can trust him with your life."

"I do," she said, like she was accepting some weird sort of marriage proposal.

"It's going to take numbers. How many have you got with you?"

"Three in this chopper, five more in a second. The rest of the team are bringing Frasier Devere in by car."

"That will have to do."

"How many people are we talking about?"

"Frost reported dozens of shooters at Trafalgar Square. He took out several in a follow-up action, but we have to assume Solomon still has plenty of men he can call on. Stop him. I need to find out who he's working with inside Six."

Stacia peered out of the window. "I'd say we're about ten minutes away."

"Make it five."

Stacia laughed, but Mendes had already killed the connection.

Her headset switched back to the helicopter's internal comms.

"Mendes?" Khavin asked.

She nodded.

"Any news from my people?"

"Some," she said, knowing that lies weren't going to help either of them.

*

"Ronan Frost." Solomon's voice called out to every screen and network on the planet. "Disciple of Solomon. You might recognize the scene. This is Threadneedle Street. It is the night before. The calm before the golden storm. Frost is my mastermind. The Irishman, with a history of provocation and attack against the homeland, was behind the robbery that saw the bullion broken out of the Bank of England's vaults, and ultimately, the attack on Trafalgar Square." Images of Ronan standing before the shattered Bank filled the screen, followed by a series of images putting him at the scene in Trafalgar Square. There was even a shot of him ducking down the manhole into the sewer as the molten gold flowed from the sky.

It was all circumstantial of course, Solomon very much a master of lies, but who was ever going to let the Irishman explain himself after this?

"Jude Lethe. Disciple of Solomon. No system is safe from Lethe," the commentary continued. "He controls the devices you are watching this video on. How did you think I was talking to you? He is my voice and so much more. He can do anything with a machine. He has already stolen your data, obtained your credit records, your browser history. He knows you better than you know yourself." The images on the screen were various shots of Jude sat in front of a computer, one at the shop in Oxford Street, another in the Police mobile command unit near Trafalgar Square. Nothing in them presented a shred of evidence to support the notion that Lethe was a bad guy in this scenario. But that didn't matter. Show the people what they wanted to see, you got them believing what you want them to believe. It was guilt by association.

"Stacia Kanic," the commentary continued. "Disciple of Solomon." Video of the MI6 operative in a field, pumping water into a valve set into the ground. There was something about the footage that felt wrong, then Frost spotted a black dot in the sky, a bird, flying backward somehow, and he realised that the footage had been reversed.

But that wasn't what was important.

Solomon had given them an unexpected ally.

She'd turned on Knight. That meant she was as much an enemy of Solomon as they were. He just had to find a way to use her.

"Kanic can be seen here pumping tons of water into an underground waste water facility just outside the city of Bonn last night. It was these actions that led directly to the tectonic displacement that devastated that city. Contrary to what you might have heard this was no wrath of God. Bonn isn't a modern Gomorrah. It was just an example of the dedication of my disciples. Proof that the will to do it really can move mountains." There was no hint of irony in the man's tone. Frost wanted to crush him. Not just kill. Crush.

"And finally," Solomon's narration promised, as an image of a youthful Sir Charles Wyndham, taken just days before the bombing that left him paralyzed came up on the screen.

"Don't you dare," Frost whispered, but of course he dared, the broadcast had already gone out. It had cycled through however many loops on its endless cycle of repeats.

"Sir Charles Wyndham," Solomon's voice said, as the picture moved to a more recent one of the Old Man as he was today. "Disciple of Solomon."

"Fuck you," Orla said, so much passion in those two words, in the way that only good old-fashioned Anglo-Saxon vulgarity can truly express. Of all Solomon's vignettes of lies and misdirection, corrupting the memory of their friend was by far the most egregious.

"Sadly, this great man is no longer with us, but in his time he was a fierce fighter for our cause."

That was it.

Nothing but a still photograph.

No evidence, no video footage, nothing.

Banal words. Lies. There was nothing because there was nothing. Anyone who knew the Old Man knew that. They had to. Frost was livid. His anger barely kept in check. He clenched and unclenched his fist, visualizing the first sledgehammer blow rupturing Solomon's nose, then the second and the third and the forth driving him to his knees, and more raining down until there was nothing recognizable of the man's ruined face, only gristle and bone.

But he didn't come up swinging.

There must have been fifty guns on him.

He wouldn't have got to within swinging distance.

He closed his eyes, focussing on the fire within him. He summoned all of the patience and street smarts growing up in Belfast during the Troubles had instilled in him. He was a scrapper. A survivor. If Solomon didn't kill him here every last breath in his body would be dedicated to undoing the man and all of the crimes he had perpetrated in the name of his unholy terror.

"Now is the time," Solomon urged his faithless. "Rise up. Challenge those whose corruption has betrayed our world. Challenge those whose false gods betray our brothers and sisters. Challenge those who have found the wrong kind of truth in money. Challenge our leaders who have been bought. Challenge all who have lost their way. Let my children show you the way. Continue the work of my Disciples. Prove yourself worthy to be my disciples. That is my war cry to you, my people. Become a *Chassid*!

"Soon the world will see what we are willing to do for their Messiah as we enter the End of Days."

The screen went blank.

Frost stood there. He didn't move. He didn't say a word. He simply stood there. He focussed on the rise and fall of his chest, and the deep Zenlike serenity of his breathing. He was the eye of the storm. He was the calmness at its deadly heart. He was the single most destructive force in the universe, gathering his strength, feeding off the fear and desperation all around him. He was the primal force in the ancient prophecies that faced down the antichrist. He was Ogmios.

And he wasn't alone.

Orla was beside him. Lethe was on the other side of the glass in front of him. Three aspects of the same ancient Celtic deity. The Old Man had chosen their name for a reason, and it wasn't because of his obsession with all things arcane, it was because he knew that when it came down to it these people, his children, would stand up. They would fight. And they would die fighting if that was what it took.

Frost was ready to die.

He hadn't realised it until that moment.

But he was.

He was at peace with who he was, with all that he had done. There were no great laments or regrets. He had lived his life. And if this was it, then so be it. He would make them pay heavily for his life. That was all any soldier could do; sell his life at a cost the enemy wouldn't want to pay.

Three steps.

He could do it, he realised. He could cross the gap between them, moving through the bullets, but he still wouldn't be able to reach Solomon to tear his eyes out. Not while the glass was between them.

Three steps.

It was nothing.

All he had to do was take the first one. The others would follow. Wasn't that what Solomon had promised? He half smiled at the irony of it, the shift in his expression catching Solomon's eye.

"I'm thinking about killing you," he told the terrorist.

Before Solomon could answer, he heard the gunfire.

It was distant, coming from outside, but it was unmistakable. And it was obvious from Solomon's face that it wasn't part of his twisted plan. The amusement dissolved, replaced by confusion.

He motioned to one of his goons.

"Find out what's happening. Take as many with you as you need. We don't need them here. Ronan can fantasize all he likes about killing me, he wouldn't get two steps before they cut him down. That's just the cold reality," he said, seeing Frost's smile.

"I'd only need one step," the Irishman promised.

The goon nodded and signalled two men to stay behind while the rest of the squad moved out with him.

Frost watched them go.

Only leaving two gunmen behind to guard them was arrogant. Even so it was still bullets versus bare hands. But it was still essentially three against four, though he couldn't imagine Solomon getting his hands bloody in a fair fight.

Solomon was visibly wound up.

He paced back and forth for a few moments.

"He lied to me," Solomon muttered suddenly, seemingly coming to a realisation. Frost didn't care who'd done the lying, he'd happily shake their hand. The enemy of my enemy and all that. "You." Solomon motioned to the man with a gun to Lethe's head. "Go get our friend. I think we need to remind him of our arrangement."

The man put his Desert Eagle in Solomon's hand, then left through the gap in the curtain.

Solomon pointed the massive gun at Lethe.

"It would be so much easier if I just put a bullet in you now."

"Easier for who?" Lethe said, not looking up. "Not me, that's for sure."

Frost chuckled.

"I don't know what you think is so funny, Ronan, but I'm glad you are enjoying yourself. It is important to take pleasure from the small things in life, like final breaths."

Frost wasn't listening. He was calculating distances, angles and probabilities in his head, working through a dozen alternative ways the fight played out from the first blow to the last. In more than half of them either him, Lethe or Orla, didn't walk away. In most of those it was Lethe who didn't make it. He needed better. He needed a way to utilize the bulletproof shield Solomon had hidden behind, and turn it to his advantage, which meant working the angles to move at least one of the shooters around, out of position.

No.

He needed to be smart.

He needed to use what he had to hand.

Hand.

His smile spread, and he launched himself at the screen, no intention of going for Solomon. He lied. He needed two steps to reach what he needed, not one. When he did, Frost hammered his fist directly into the middle of the web of damage his bullets had wrought. He hit it so hard he felt it shiver beneath the impact.

Solomon instinctively backed off before he remembered Frost couldn't reach him.

Frost didn't care. He slammed his fist into the same spot, the cracks spidering around the impact. It wouldn't hold forever. One, two more blows and it would shatter. But that wasn't why he was taking his anger out on the bulletproof screen.

He was drawing the guards to him.

And it worked like a charm.

The two men left their position, coming for him, rifles raised.

"Back off," the nearest growled.

Frost thought about trying for one final clubbing blow, the glass was barely held together by the film, but he restrained himself. He backed off two steps, arms raised. He took two more steps, not looking back to see where he was going. The Irishman had decent special location awareness. He knew that another couple of steps would put him within striking distance of the gunman. And that was why he'd beaten his fist bloody on the bulletproof glass.

Orla saw what he was doing.

She mirrored his movement, stepping closer to her guard, but he was watching and took a step backward, jabbing the muzzle at her. The message was blunt. Stand still.

Solomon wasn't watching either of them.

His agitation increased at the staccato rattle of gunfire from outside. This burst was more intense than the last and sustained.

There was some serious action going down outside the conference centre.

He couldn't enjoy the thought of the cavalry out there for long, because Lethe's guard returned, bringing with him another prisoner. It was obviously the man Solomon had accused of lying to him.

He walked like a broken man.

He didn't look up until Solomon took hold of his jaw and lifted his head to look him in the eye before he asked him why he had lied to him.

Frost knew the man.

It was Control.

Quentin Carruthers.

FIFTY-TWO
I JUST DIED IN YOUR ARMS

Konstantin fired two short bursts at the enemy combatants as they threw themselves behind any cover they could find. He had them pinned down outside the huge plate glass doors that were the entrance to the conference centre.

More armed men and women came out of the building. There were too many entrances for them to cover them all. Within minutes the area outside was flooded with the enemy. It was easy to see several choke points and vulnerabilities in the layout. It wasn't ideal ground for a battle, too many angles and blind spots, too many places the hostiles could advance on your positions, too easy to be isolated. And with only eight of them, isolation was a killer.

A fresh hail of bullets scattered asphalt and flakes of paint as they pinned Kanic's squad down.

This was only ending one way, the Russian realised.

He knew he was reacting emotionally to the news of Nonesuch, and that emotion in any situation that wasn't sex was a mistake, and even then it wasn't the safest course of action as it left you vulnerable, and vulnerability was weakness, but he didn't care. For once he was going to obey his heart not his head.

"Cover me," he told Kanic.

"Don't get yourself killed, Khavin. I still want my gun back."

There wasn't a great deal she could do, but she tried. She lifted her head and shoulders above the line of the vehicle and laid down several bursts of covering fire while Konstantin sprinted, head down, arms and legs pumping furiously, away from the conference centre. He didn't care if she thought he was running away. She could think what she wanted. He covered the hundred yards to where the chopper had set down after being damaged by gunfire upon their arrival. The sprint took him out of the line of fire.

Thick smoke billowed from the engine as the rotors slowed their spin. Solomon's men had done some serious damage to the bird on its approach. They were lucky to be alive. Konstantin ran toward where the pilot was battling keep the engines cool as the turbines idled. The body had taken some structural damage. There were scar lines of bullet holes through the shell. The pilot pulled the pin on a hand-held fire extinguisher and used the foam to cool the belly and in turn the engine down. It was all he could do to keep it running.

Konstantin came up behind him.

"Stand back."

The pilot seemed confused, and then understood.

Konstantin opened the door.

"It's not safe."

Konstantin smiled. "It doesn't need to be."

He climbed into the seat behind the control yoke.

The motor was not in great shape, but all he needed was enough lift.

He opened the throttle. In response, more smoke billowed from above his head. It didn't take much for the cabin itself to grow hazy as the filters were overloaded. Konstantin put the oxygen mask on, opening up the airflow as he forced the rotors up to speed. A terrible whine came from the motor.

He pulled back on the stick and the chopper lifted into the air.

Not far, a few inches at first in a jerky motion before it bounced down again.

A warning buzzer sounded, half of the dashboard lighting up.

More smoke gushed from the wounded motor.

He pulled back on the stick again, taking her up.

It was a battle to get any real altitude; whatever was wrong with the engine it was fundamental. He didn't need much for what he had in mind. At twenty feet, Konstantin tilted the chopper forward and accelerated away from the building, and towards Stacia Kanic and the conference centre.

As he came around the corner he saw that his allies were completely pinned down, unable to retreat, almost surrounded, with Solomon's men fanning out on either side like a pincer. Konstantin's ailing helicopter buzzed low over their heads. Bullets slammed into the fuselage, tearing through the metal. The Russian willed the bird to fly. And keep flying. He fought to keep the nose up to protect the engine overhead and the tail rotors at the back. All it would take was one bullet in the wrong place and he'd crash down burning into his own people.

Sustained fire came from several directions.

The first shells ricocheted off the windshield, but it couldn't hold against the barrage, finally shattering. A heartbeat later, the downdraughts battering him back into the bucket seat, a single round punctured the chair beside him. Another shot took him in the arm, just below the elbow. The pain was instantaneous and savage. The force of the impact chipped off a piece of bone as the bullet exited. There was blood. A lot of it. But best he could tell it had missed the major axillary artery. That didn't mean that it didn't hurt like fuck, but he could still control the stick, and that was all that mattered. A few seconds longer. That was all he needed.

The chopper was between Solomon's followers and Stacia's people. It came down to inches. There was maybe fifteen yards between the two forces. That was nothing. Still the hail of fire rained up at the bird. He heard the weirdly dull thunk of the shell puncturing the fuel tank. It wasn't like movies, it didn't go up in a fireball. Critical systems flashed warnings. The helicopter was going down and there was nothing he could do about it.

But that was what he wanted.

He battled the stick, screaming through the pain, to keep the bird on target. Every nerve down his right side shrieked out as he fought, muscles tense as the blood spilled. The sheer amount of blood was too much. Maybe the shell had nicked the main artery? He felt himself going lightheaded and his heartrate accelerating as the first few seconds of system shock kicked in. "Not yet," he said through gritted teeth, but whether those words were to the helicopter or the reaper, it was impossible to distinguish, but to both the message was the same. He wasn't going anywhere.

At the last possible second Konstantin wrenched the stick, momentum tipping the whole aircraft forward. The rotors pitched, fully exposed to the men on the ground. It was like a wounded animal offering up its throat; they couldn't resist. The stood their ground and fired, unloading everything they had into the helicopter, even as the realisation that the mad Russian had brought the bird on a suicide mission.

Some tried to run then, too late, while others stood frozen with indecision and terror as the shattered rotors scythed through their ranks, slicing limbs, heads and bodies indiscriminately. Konstantin Khavin had unleashed the beast and the beast didn't care what side you fought on, what flag you honoured. It was going to be fed.

Blood arced across the broken glass of the cabin's side door was the Russian yanked it open, ready to bail.

The deadly blades chewed their way through everything in their path, sparking and buckling on the ground as the blades were twisted out of the couplings at the rotor. The mechanical screams of the beast drowned out any screams of the dying.

He counted down in his head, now or never.

Three.

Two.

One.

And bailed, throwing himself out of the side door to the ground as the helicopter skidded away from him across the car park into the huge plate glass doors of the conference centre.

Fuel lines leaking, rotor blades cannibalizing the bird, electrical sparks misfiring, it took five long seconds of silence before the deafening explosion tore through it, the concussive wave barrelling Konstantin from his feet before he'd even managed to half-stand.

Stacia's people seized the advantage he'd bought them.

It was carnage.

He didn't stay to watch it.

He trusted the woman to do her job.

Biting down on the pain, he drew the Glock. It could have been worse, he told himself running across the hardstand; it had taken his mind off his fractured eye socket. He could hardly feel *that* at all.

He couldn't get in through the main doors.

All he could see there was smoke and fire from the wreckage.

It was hard to breathe, the air was so thick and hot in his lungs.

Racking the slide, he stumbled towards the nearest entrance that wasn't on fire.

FIFTY-THREE
PRAYER FOR THE DYING

"Just kill me," Quentin Carruthers said. There was no strength behind his words. "I'm tired of living."

Solomon stared down at the man who had been Control.

He was on his knees.

He looked exactly like what he was—a frail old man—for the first time in all the years that Frost had known him.

"I almost feel sorry for you. After all these years we've known each other, Quentin, what in the world possessed you to think you could lie to me?"

Quentin said nothing.

"I'm talking to you."

Still, Quentin said nothing.

"Do you think he," Solomon looked at Frost, "will save you? He hates you. Just look at his face. He blames you for this. He blames you for what happened to his friend. He isn't your salvation."

"Like I said, dear boy, just kill me and get it over with. You win. You're the big scary Messiah, and I'm just the queer old soul who couldn't stop you."

"Stop me? You helped me every step of the way, and you know it." Solomon turned to Frost. "We go back, Quentin and I. All the way back to his time in Jordan in the '80s. We danced many a dance, this old queen and I. Ask yourself this, how did I ever become Akim Caspi? How did a man like me fill the shoes of a dead man without setting off a million alarm bells? Quentin, that's how. He wanted a man inside. He wanted a puppet to dance to his tune and play that region for the best interests of his meddling country. Do you have any concept of what my people have been through at the hands of your so-called Empire? I was born into a world where it was perfectly all right to test chemical weapons on Yemenite civilians. I was born into a world where the Palestinian Liberation Organization were driven out of Jordan by Hussain and Fatahland was born. I was born into a world where on the holiest of all days the Syrians and Egyptians tried to wipe my people out. We have had to fight for every day of our existence. Do you know what one of my first memories is? The battle to reclaim the Old City from the Jordanians, during the Six Day War. What kind of childhood is that? Do you know what I remember most about those weeks? The song, Jerusalem of Gold. My life as I knew it changed forever on October 5th 2004, with the Days of Penitence. That was the day Akim Caspi was born, or should I say resurrected. There was a vote that day, more meddling politicians deciding the fate of my land. The United Nations Security Council were demanding an immediate end to military action in the Gaza Strip, and that my people should withdraw. The British abstained. But the blood was already on their hands. My friend here came to me with a proposal. He promised me I could be a part of ending this conflict forever. So, of course, I said yes. I was to infiltrate the Jabalia refugee camp and assassinate Abed Nabhan, the local Hamas leader. Nabhan was responsible for the death of several children with his Qassam rockets. I was only too happy to play executioner. It was my first act in my new life as Akim Caspi, servant of the British Empire. And I was loyal. So very, very loyal."

"That's not how it was," Quentin said, talking to Frost, not the terrorist. "Yes, I helped him become a new man. He was an asset. I placed him within the IDF during the Palestinian conflict. I used him. I built a relationship. I worked him. But only so far. Solomon was my asset. But he wasn't loyal. He was driven by a hatred for everything the West represented. I should have known just how dangerous he was, even back then. But he was mine, and I thought I could control him."

Frost's head was spinning. He didn't know who, or what to believe, in what felt like a falling out amongst thieves.

"Ever the liar. How do you keep all the lies you tell straight in your head?" Solomon asked. "Do you even believe your own lies?"

"I used you, Solomon. A direct line to the most dangerous man in the world since Bin Laden? I wouldn't have been doing my job if I didn't try and exploit it. It's simple really. For all your complicated plans you were blind to what was right in front of you: me. When we learned that Schnur was Mabus, and there was a mysterious figure lurking in the background I knew it had to be you. It didn't take a genius to work out you had compromised at least one of my agents, and they had sold out Grace Weller. The problem was that I didn't know who. I needed to do my job. I am a rat catcher."

"You never know when to stop lying, do you? You sold out your friends. You sold out him, and his people," Solomon turned on Frost. "And now, you're trying to turn again, wriggling like a worm on a hook.

You are a pathetic little man. Do you think your friend Charlie knew just how much you'd betrayed him?"

"He knew how things had to be. He was a practical man."

"That's a nice way of rationalizing your betrayals. I'm sure it helps you sleep at night."

"What have you done?" Frost found his voice, finally.

"What I had to," Quentin said. "I told Charles, I warned him, I told him your Russian had part of a message, and that message was that there were rats inside Six. Rats dancing to his tune." He looked up at Solomon. "I worked out it was Knight, but couldn't tell if it stopped with him, or if the infection was more pernicious."

"The messages? You deliberately wanted Konstantin to consider all debts paid in full because that was what Solomon had told Noah in Rome? That was your puzzle?"

Despite everything, Quentin found it in him to smile. "Perhaps you really are as clever as the Old Man always believed you were, Ronan," Quentin said, one arm clutched around his belly, shielding himself from discomfort. The gesture was so obviously unconscious it betrayed the fact he'd taken a beating before being dragged out before him. "Do you remember your lessons? There is no such thing as a coincidence, meaningful or otherwise, in this life. I was sure he would pick up on it, and given our last conversation, know what to do." He shook his head sadly. "Pity the old fool didn't listen. We might have been saved this. As it is, you give your life to your country and if you're an old queen like me people still rush to think the worst of you. I am sorry I failed you, Ronan. It won't mean much, but I am sorry. I lost good people in this mess. And I hate the idea of losing more."

"This is all very touching," Solomon said, "but answer me this, Control: if you aren't with me, what are you doing here?"

"I made a mistake," Quentin said.

"That you did, and quite frankly, I'm bored with you now."

He put the gun to Control's head.

"Take this thought with you to the grave," Solomon said. "I played you, and that means you died a traitor to everything you believe. It's tragic, really."

He pulled the trigger.

The shot was so much louder than it should ever have been, engulfed in a huge explosion outside. Solomon looked down at the gun in his hand as though trying to understand how it could have delivered such biblical wrath, then up as he realised there were screams out beyond the hall's main doors.

The screams were cut short by more gunfire.

Frost reacted.

He launched himself at the nearest guard, slamming his fist into the man's face, and as his head snapped back doing it again. There was less force behind the second blow, lacking the momentum of the first, but it didn't matter. It was a crunching blow. The gun in his hand went off, a single shot into the web of bulletproof glass that finally failed to live up to its name. The shield between them and Solomon shattered.

Orla took her man down, a roundhouse kick to the face sending him sprawling across the floor as he failed to get out of the way.

Frost wrestled his man for the gun.

"Stop or Lethe dies!" Solomon yelled.

Frost didn't stop.

In his peripheral vision he saw Lethe drive his elbow into his man's face.

He had to trust the kid could handle himself.

They all had to trust each other.

His guy wasn't giving up the gun. Both of them fought over it, not giving an inch. Frost didn't have time for this. He slammed his head forward, driving the thick bone of his forehead into the soldier's face. The impact was sickening. The fight went out of the other man. He wrested the rifle from his hands, twisting it sharply, and delivered another crunching blow with the weapon's stock, driving the butt into the man's face once, twice, three times, until he went down, blood where his face had been. And twice more to stop him moving.

Immediately Ronan snapped the rifle round into a firing position, looking for Lethe.

Orla had her opponent up against the wall, using his rifle to crush his windpipe.

He took two shots. The first jerked the terrorist's head back, the second left a hole in his neck where his Adam's Apple had been.

Lethe was on the floor, unmoving.

He saw the blood.

For one sickening second Frost thought he was dead.

He rushed over to Jude, dropping to one knee. His eyes were closed and he was bleeding from a blow to his head, but there were no holes in him, which was a major plus. "You with me?" he asked, putting a hand on his friend's shoulder. Lethe just grunted. That was enough.

Orla joined them.

"Where is he?"

"Exit stage left," Lethe said, nodding toward the curtains.

He pushed the heavy drapes aside and saw glass double doors behind them.

He saw Solomon and he saw the gun, but it was already too late.

His first instinct was to protect the others.

He took a bullet, a punch in and through his chest as he threw himself sideways, crashing into Lethe, and taking him to the ground as the door exploded in a rain of glass shards. He felt the cuts against his skin, face, hands, some stinging at his neck. But even a thousand cuts weren't going to kill him.

The hole in his chest might, though.

He rolled to his side, as Solomon fired again, this time aiming down. Lethe scrambled away. Frost had never seen the kid move as fast in his life.

Solomon's wild shots weren't meant for him now.

Orla.

She was moving too fast for him to keep up, running wide.

Frost came up firing to buy her precious seconds.

She disappeared from Solomon's line of sight but that didn't stop him from unloading a barrage of bullets into the wall where she had been. The masonry wept. And then silence.

He was out of bullets.

Orla stepped back into view, walking remorselessly forward, not rushing, not wild, but with the kind of calm only someone used to taking lives could muster. She closed the gap between her and her prey while Solomon fought with his weapon.

Lying on his side, Ronan saw something in the darkness of one of the side rooms. A small red dot, like the scope from a sniper's rifle settling on its kill.

He tried to tell her.

The words wouldn't come.

She stepped in close, driving blow after blow in a wail of fists that Solomon simply couldn't defend himself against. She ripped the rifle from his grasp, and with ruthless efficiency turned it on him, using the stock to stove in his nose, driving the gristle back into the bone of his skull.

Solomon went down.

Orla stood over him, breathing hard.

He lay there smiling up at her through the ruin of his face.

Smiling.

He was smiling.

He tried to pull something from his pocket.

Orla reached down, vicelike grip closing around the other man's wrist.

He was weak.

She pried the dagger-like spear tip from his hand.

Too late, he realised what she intended to do. Frost tried to warn her, to stop her, the light, she'd stepped into the light... But he couldn't find the breath to form words. The world threatened to swim away from him. The pressure in his chest threatened to tear him apart. It was unbearable.

Orla plunged the sharp end into Solomon's neck, twisting it, her expression one of almost bliss as the arterial spray from his punctured jugular slashed across her face.

"That is for my friend," she spat, driving the glittering spear head into the centre of the dying man's face with such force the entire cartilage around his nose collapsed in on itself, opening a sinkhole into him.

And still Solomon smiled, even as he was dying.

"I'm ready for my close-up," he managed, though it was more of a gurgle of sounds than actual words.

Orla looked up.

Through the nearest doorway she saw a camera on a tripod, the red light indicating it was filming. It was focussed on the corpse and the woman who had made it, and the religious artifact glittering where Solomon's nose should have been.

The Spear of Destiny.

Lethe stood in the doorway, hands on knees, struggling to catch his breath. He looked at her, at the spear tip, and at the corpse. "You just killed the Messiah, with the spear that bled Christ." He pointed at the camera. "And half the planet saw it happen live."

"He's not the Messiah," she said.

"No. We just made him a martyr. And that's all he ever wanted."

*

The paramedics covered Quentin Carruthers body, and wheeled him out of the conference centre on a gurney.

Frost still didn't know what to think. It was a tangled web, no getting away from that, but maybe they had misjudged him? He'd not wanted to believe that Control was the spider at the centre of the web, betraying the Old Man, selling out Konstantin, when the reality was he was the opposite, and in his dying declaration he'd given Frost a reason not to believe. He preferred this reality where Quentin was loyal to the Crown, and had tried to warn Sir Charles that his own people were compromised. It was believable. The problem was the all the best lies were believable, and Control was one of the very best liars in the espionage game. But he had no reason to believe Solomon and plenty of reasons to need to believe Quentin, so that was what he was going to do.

The pain in his chest was incredible.

He was dying.

His grip on consciousness slipping. It was so tempting to just let go.

But not yet.

He felt the pressure on his chest but couldn't open his eyes.

Or were they still open and he just couldn't see out of them?

For a moment Frost thought he saw the Russian's dour face staring down at him.

He tried to focus on it, but it was gone.

Of course, there was no reason for Konstantin to be here. Maybe God had a sense of humour and had sent a lookalike to shepherd him over to the other side?

So instead he clung on to Quentin's defence: he had tried to get word to the others, linking Solomon to Six and Michael Knight, and Knight had made it impossible for the Russian, and with Konstantin on the run the two ends of the message never got put together. If it was a lie it was a very good one, because it was a tragedy on the smallest scale when set against all of the other acts of fear perpetrated in the name of this unholy terror, but it was still a tragedy. Two good men were gone. It was an ending. Without Sir Charles, without Control, they were finished.

He just wanted to go back to Nonesuch, to go home again.

But the one great lesson everyone learned in their lifetimes was that no matter how desperately you wanted to, you could never go home again.

FIFTY-FOUR
THE RAIN KING

Noah was feeling good.

It was a peculiar feeling. It had been a while since the world had gone his way. It was very different to the last time he'd come home.

His mobile wasn't working, so he found a payphone and called Nonesuch.

It didn't even ring.

He tried Lethe's personal number but that didn't work either.

Neither did Ronan's.

He'd worry about that in the morning.

Noah was bone tired.

He felt like he might finally be able to sleep through a night, for the first time in a long time.

Since beating seven shades of shit out of Jordan Walker, he realised, and thinking about him meant thinking about Margot, and thinking about Margot meant picking the phone up to call her.

She was the one surefire way to guarantee a decent night's sleep.

She didn't pick up.

It wasn't unusual. She was probably on the clock.

He'd just go around to her place, wait his turn, bring some booze. They could drink and sleep and screw, and for once in his life all would be right with the world.

He'd earned that much.

He'd deal with real life tomorrow. No one was going to be waiting on him to save the day. And the last place he wanted to go back to right now was Nonesuch, with the three fucking stooges in residence. Mendes, Kanic and Knight, they sounded like a backstreet law firm.

He walked out of the ferry terminal, looking around for a taxi, thinking he'd ride back to London, pick up the Austin Healey and then drive round to Margot's, with a brief pitstop at the off-licence for a drop of the good stuff. Push the boat out. They were worth it.

He realised he was being stared at.

The man leaned against the wall by the side of the terminal doors.

He wasn't moving. He made no show of doing anything, just staring.

It gave Noah the creeps.

He didn't like being stared at. It was ruining his good humour.

Noah decided to take the direct approach.

He walked straight at the man, and before he could get out of the way, pushed him hard up against the wall, hand locking around his throat.

"What are you staring at?" Simple. To the point. Noah kept his temper in check.

"I know you."

"No, you don't."

Noah didn't let him go.

"I do. I saw you somewhere."

"Where?"

"I dunno. But I know you."

"So, what's my name?"

"I don't know."

Noah let him go.

"You don't know me," he said.

As he looked around, he saw a family had joined the line at the taxi rank.

The mother was looking at him.

Not looking.

Staring.

Shit.

What fresh hell was this?

Noah turned and pushed past the family to the front of the line as a taxi pulled up. He jumped in the back, giving the address of the lot where he'd left the car parked.

The driver kept glancing in the rearview mirror as he drove out of the ferry terminal.

Noah turned his head towards the window and kept it there.

He had no desire to waste his good mood on small talk.

*

Nowhere in the world felt more like home to Noah Larkin than behind the wheel of his Austin Healey. He drove across London to Margot's apartment, not caring about the lights that didn't go his way. He was content to listen to some of his favourite tunes and just enjoy winning for once. The deep-voiced singer was telling him how with a nail and a tear, she carved her name on his heart. He liked that. It was simple but emotive, and put him in mind of a morning after with Margot lying beside him, drawing a heart across his chest with her red-lacquered fingernail. It was one of the most intimate moments of his life, even if it wasn't love.

They had a rule, the two of them, that he was never to disturb her in person.

He had to call first.

He tried again, but got no response.

Noah parked up outside her apartment block, and checked his phone. There was no network carrier, he realised, which explained why he couldn't reach anyone.

He should have picked up a burner at the docks.

He noticed another stranger looking at him. It was really getting to be an issue.

Maybe it was because they'd seen him in that mobile phone footage of the priest's suicide in Saint Peter's Square? That had been broadcast all over the world a dozen times over. See a face in a film often enough, even in the background, and you're going to think you recognize the man. It's only natural. That had to be it.

He buzzed for Margot's apartment and waited.

No answer.

He buzzed again and waited some more.

Still no reply.

He called another apartment, explaining he'd forgotten keys. The lady who answered buzzed him up.

Noah headed up the stairs.

The carpet had seen better days but it was clean. And most of the bulbs on the stairwell were still lit, though there were a few pockets of gloom along the ascent.

The light in the hallway on the fourth floor flickered with an electric buzzing sound. It illuminated and then hid the yellow tape across the doorway of apartment 402.

Yellow tape.

Noah pounded up the last few stairs to reach the door, then tore away the Police tape across it, trying not to let the darkness in.

The door was closed but not locked.

He pushed it open.

He didn't want to go inside.

He didn't want to cross the threshold and make it real.

As long as he was out here, on the landing, she was alive, she was with a client, she was in a bar, she was getting drunk or getting fucked, both of which she excelled at. But once he stepped across the threshold and walked into the darkness there was no room for make believe.

Noah went inside.

He walked from room to room, like he was checking the place was clear. He'd already seen the only thing he needed to, but he kept looking. The apartment was empty but for a few pieces of thrift shop furniture, an old square TV from the '90s and a few oddments of clothes and makeup strewn around a bed and dresser in the bedroom.

He returned to the lounge.

The ratty old sofa in front of the TV was stained red.

A spray pattern decorated the wall behind.

Margot's blood.

There was so little of her left in this place, just a few smears of blood and a few old clothes.

He needed to hurt someone.

Noah returned to the front door.

He checked the lock plate. There was no sign of damage, meaning she had let the killer in.

She had died sat on her sofa, not the bedroom. The blood spatter suggested a knife wound rather than a bullet. Messier. You come into the lounge to talk. It's intimate in a different way to the bedroom. It didn't fit the idea of an angry punter. That would have been in the bedroom or the hallway as regret kicked in. This was different. Whoever came here did so with the sole intention of ending her life.

Jordan Walker.

Margot's tout.

Revenge for Noah's lesson.

"I should have just killed the cunt," Noah said, then sank down onto the blood-soaked sofa as grief threatened to overwhelm him. He didn't move for the longest time. The lyrics of that song went through and through his mind. *It's the kindest, gentlest things that tear you apart.*

There was part of the song that really rang true, where the singer admitted it was against his nature to untie the heroine from the rails, and yet he did it this time. He opened himself up. Made himself vulnerable. And with a nail and a tear she carved her name on his heart.

That was Noah and Margot. That was who they were to each other. That was what he had lost, the one woman he'd untie from the rails as the train bore down on them.

The anger came easily to him then.

He left the apartment, careful to close the door.

*

Jordan Walker had hired himself some protection since the last time Noah was here.

It wouldn't save him.

Noah watched the *Wet Dream* from a distance, marking two heavies standing guard on the boat.

They were clearly visible even at night – but then that was the point.

They were a deterrent.

He watched them, and the longer he watched the more convinced he was that they were worthless, nightclub bouncers at best, debt collectors at worst.

Their being here was good news.

It meant Jordan Walker was *in*.

Noah moved naturally, looking for all the world like a man taking a stroll by the canal. As he approached the two men on the path eyed him suspiciously.

He kept his face turned away from them.

It was dark enough that they shouldn't recognize him, even assuming Walker had provided a description.

He kept his hands in his pockets, so they wouldn't see he was wearing gloves.

"Evening, boys," he said as he drew level with them.

One nodded. The other said nothing.

They didn't take their eyes off him.

"I feel like I should apologize," he said.

"What the fuck are you going on about?"

In answer, Noah jumped down onto the deck of the boat, taking the largest of the two down with a swift throat punch, then swinging his body around to block his partner's attack.

The second guy went for a gun.

That was unexpected, but not necessarily a problem. It wasn't like they could shoot him in the middle of London.

He grabbed the would-be shooter by the hair and smashed his head into his partner's face. The brutal impact sent him over the side. That should have been the end of it, but like a fucking horror film the guy wouldn't stay down. He came back up over the side as Noah was trying to deal with his partner.

He saw the canal-soaked man rise up above the stern, gun in his hand, and realised the idiot was going to shoot.

Survival instincts took over.

He hauled up the half-conscious man from the deck and barely got him around, between him and the shooter, before his partner put six rounds into him, causing Noah's human shield to dance like a motherfucker.

Noah charged the shooter, arm around the corpse's neck to keep himself covered, and as he ran, he pulled the dead man's gun from its underarm holster. He didn't need six shots.

He dumped both bodies in the water.

He turned towards the door to the cabin, ready to put a foot through it for the second time. There was no element of surprise this time.

He hesitated before striking the wood.

The shotgun blast tore into the door, spitting splinters and shot.

In the aftermath where there was a shocking absence of sound, Noah heard the distinct pump action reload.

There was no second shot.

He shouldn't have dumped the corpses in the water.

Still, Walker was a jacked-up bundle of fear, getting that second shot out of him wasn't a challenge. Noah took a shoe off and tossed it in through the open door like a grenade.

Walker wasted his shot on nothing. A heartbeat later Noah was through the door and on him, smashing the pimp across the face with the butt of his borrowed pistol.

He grabbed Walker's shotgun and tossed it out onto the deck.

"You and me, we need to talk," Noah said, standing over the cowering man.

The scarring was red and angry, the entire right side of Walker's face was a mess. Huge pits and troughs scored his skin and a network of scar tissue rendered him unrecognizable from one side. The web of ruined tissue continued down his neck.

"You can't touch me," Walker said. The right side of his mouth drooped, lips refusing to move in tandem with his left. His speech was slurred.

"Watch me," Noah said.

He grabbed Walker's shirt with one hand and made a fist with the other, drawing it back behind his head.

"Fuck you, Noah Larkin. Just fuck you. Yes. I know you. I know who you are. I know what you did. I've seen Solomon's videos. I know what you are. And you're fucked. Those guys outside you killed. I didn't hire them. They're my protection. They're police."

Noah's blood ran cold.

"You don't get protection. Not from me." Noah said.

"You won't kill me."

"You broke your promise."

He raised the borrowed gun and put a round through Walker's forehead.

The pimp shit himself as he died.

It was fitting.

Noah dropped the gun. He didn't need it anymore. There was one less arsehole in the world.

He'd deliberately not brought his own weapon so ballistics wouldn't link the killing to him. The police would have a long list of suspects, no doubt, and he was almost certainly first on the list. But it had to be done.

Now he needed to disappear.

FIFTY-FIVE
WHERE THE ROSE IS SOWN

Dawn broke over the remains of Nonesuch Manor.

The morning mist on the grounds conjured the illusion of smoke still rising from the ruins. She felt hollow. This place had been her sanctuary. After Jenin it had been her salvation. Her home. But a home wasn't the bricks and mortar, no matter how noble they might be, or the kind of history they might possess, it was the people inside it that made it a home.

Konstantin and Orla worked side-by-side digging a second grave beside Maxwell's.

It really was a beautiful spot, even with the scars where the manor house had been. The boating lake, the pagoda, the herb gardens, it was so absolutely English. She remembered a story the Old Man had told her about Sir Walter Raleigh's oak, a venerable old tree in the grounds, supposedly planted by the great man himself when he returned from his search for the Lost City of Gold. It was a nice old story, but she had no idea if it was true. Still, the shadow of the tall tree would just reach the grave when it was stretched to its thinnest. That was something. She thought the Old Man would have appreciated that, resting in the shadow of so much history.

Orla did nothing to hide the tears.

This work was meaningful.

It was meant to hurt.

She jammed the shovel into the earth and lifted clear more worms.

Beside her, Konstantin laboured in silence. Sometimes she wished she could read his mind. He had taken the Old Man's death hard. They all had. But Konstantin wasn't the kind of soul to open up when it hurt. He simply dug. But every now and then he was forced to stop, wincing in pain before he forced himself back to it. His eye must hurt, but the pain from his arm must have been excruciating. A bullet to the elbow that had nicked the bone as it exited? How could it not be? But he was stoic and determined, and nothing, no amount of pain was going to stop him from doing his duty. That, more than anything, was the essence of the Russian.

The sun was low in the sky. It was still early.

She couldn't look at the broken stones.

They represented so much of what was lost.

She didn't know what she was going to do beyond the next hour. She wasn't sure it mattered any more. All of them were wanted, if not by the police then by the crazies Solomon had inspired. To half the world they were the disciples, the ones who would continue their Messiah's work. To the other half they were the ones who brought down and murdered the Messiah. Either way, they had painted targets on their backs for the faithful and the faithless. All of his scheming, all of the fear and the promise that all their gods would die, and really it came down to one man who knew how the world worked, and how best to undermine their faith in it. Gold.

She heard the car approaching.

She saw Jude Lethe's Civic coming up the long curving stone driveway toward the ruin.

He parked a short walk from the graveside. Orla watched as he helped Frost out of the car. The Irishman leaned on the younger man as they walked towards her. It was obvious he was in serious pain. He had no business being out of hospital. He'd taken a bullet to the chest that had missed his heart by a couple of inches. If his reactions had been a fraction slower he wouldn't have made it. He'd been in theater for six hours as the surgeons battled to save his life. And here he was. She shook her head at the sheer stubborn pigheadedness of the Irishman. She couldn't help but love him for it.

They joined her at the edge of the empty grave.

"I told him to stay in the hospital," Lethe said. "But you know what he's like, even getting shot through the heart isn't going to stop him."

"It wasn't the heart," Frost said.

"Of course not, you don't have one of those." Lethe grinned.

And for a moment it was almost as though the world hadn't ended. That things were as they were always meant to be, them, here, a family.

"Anyone heard from Noah yet?" Ronan asked.

"Say his name and the devil appears," Orla said as a green Austin Healey turned in through the stone gates at the bottom of the winding driveway.

"I'm not looking forward to telling him," Orla said.

"No one is. But he's a big boy. It's not like he'll go off the rails and do something stupid," Frost said. No one laughed, because they knew that was exactly what he'd do.

Noah parked up alongside Lethe's Civic. He killed the engine but didn't get out of the car. He seemed to be listening to the end of a song. She liked the way he did that. It reminded her of being a lot younger, when music mattered so much. She missed those days. Sometimes she thought about the choices not taken and wondered what kind of life she would have had if she hadn't seen that small advert in The Times promising exciting opportunities for a language expert. On such small things lives pivot.

She raised a hand in greeting as Noah finally got out of the car.

He nodded but didn't say anything. He simply breathed in deeply, taking in the full extent of the ruin and what it meant for them as a family. He saw the second hole in the ground. Again, he didn't comment on it. He watched Lethe as he returned from his car with a hospital-issue wheelchair.

"What happened to you?" he asked Frost as Lethe helped him sit. There was something symbolic about it, the first of their number in a chair, presiding over the funeral of their spiritual father and friend, Orla thought.

"I got shot," the Irishman replied, tapping his chest.

"Careless," Noah said.

"I've had better days," he agreed.

"And lucky you, you'll have plenty more," Lethe said, resting a hand on Frost's shoulder which earned another wince. "Gold," he said, "from Trafalgar Square."

"So, you got shot, burned and wound up in a wheelchair? I'm not sure we should let you out of the house anymore."

"Solomon is dead," Konstantin said from within the open grave. "It is over."

They had a body. They had his DNA. His fingerprints. The truth behind who he was wouldn't stay secret forever. They'd be able to name him and strip him of his mystery. But she wasn't sure it mattered anymore whether he was an Eitan, Elijah, Ari or a Tamar. He was dead. Did putting a name to the face of his terror really help? Would the world look him any differently if he was called Duane or Cletus? And on an Intelligence level, getting a name and knowing how exactly he tied in to the Israeli Embassy that they would offer protection and smuggle out his pet assassin was a can of worms Six wasn't willing to open. Not yet, at least. It was a political hand grenade. If DAGDA and the Nest had survived Lethe could have found a lot more than just a name now that they knew he was one of Control's assets. There would be documentation. They'd just been looking in the wrong place.

"And now we're gathered to bury the bastard here?"

Nobody answered.

Orla couldn't look at him. She was going to have to tell him. She could feel the thickness in her chest, the tears threatening to fall again.

Konstantin finished digging and stabbed the earth with his shovel.

"Speaking of wheelchairs, where's the Old Man?" Noah asked. "It's not like him to miss a party."

Orla couldn't do it. The words wouldn't come.

"He was inside," Lethe said.

There was a moment, the silence in between being told and it becoming reality, when they just remembered what the Old Man meant to them. They were intimate memories, truths they would never share.

Noah broke the silence. "So, the old sod went down with his house? He'd have appreciated that," Noah said.

And that one did earn a grim chuckle from Frost, because it was absolutely true. The Old Man would have appreciated it.

"So, this is what winning feels like, huh?"

Frost nodded.

"Can't say I'm much of a fan," Noah said.

Orla walked over to him and gave him a hug.

It wasn't much, but it was obvious he needed it.

"Okay, more of a fan," he said, not letting go.

That earned another chuckle. There was an easy comradery between them. They were family, even without the blood.

Konstantin moved over to a black body bag, almost invisible where it lay resting against the heat-scarred shrubbery. He lifted it effortlessly, the frail form sagging in his arms. He carried the body of Sir Charles Wyndham over to the grave.

"A little help," he said, setting the body down.

He knelt at one side, and with Noah's help lowered Sir Charles Wyndham into the pit.

"Anyone want to say something? It feels like we should say something," Lethe said, but looking around the faces it was obvious no one did.

"The Old Man was the one for speeches," Frost said. "I'm not. I'll just say that he saved my life, he gave me purpose, and I wouldn't be who I am today without that grand old bastard. And I am going to miss him. I'd like to think that he's done enough good that wherever he ends up he gets to be someone's guardian angel."

"Mine, preferably," Noah said, "Because I mean, let's be honest, I've burned through about half a dozen in the last couple of weeks." That earned a wry smile from the Russian. "I saw that, Koni. I'll get a laugh out of you yet."

Noah knelt down to gather up a handful of dirt and tossed it into the grave. He stepped back to let Lethe do the same. Frost leaned in the chair, dragging his fingers through the dirt to get a handful, which scattered across the plastic body bag like black rain. Konstantin solemnly gathered up his own offering and cast it into the grave.

Orla took a flower from the garden and leaned down to lay it over the Old Man's heart.

"Always got to go one better," Noah said, but he was crying and smiling at the same time.

She held his hand. It was a simple intimate gesture, her offering him some of her strength.

"You're hitting on me now?" Noah said, "I'm not sure that's appropriate, all things considered."

And that did it, Konstantin let out a short bark of laughter that had them all laughing.

"Told you," Noah grinned.

"Where do we go from here?" Orla asked what they were all thinking: what happens now?

Nobody had an answer to that.

Konstantin, ever the practical one, took up his shovel again and started filling the grave with dirt.

Nobody else could bring themselves to help, but he didn't seem to mind.

"I have to go away," Noah said, suddenly. "Best you don't know why. What you don't know can't hurt you."

"Mendes has promised protection, but I'm not sure what good it will do," Frost admitted. They were all painfully aware of the situation. With Control dead and Knight's treason exposed, Vauxhall was in uproar. It would be a long time before things settled into a normal routine, and even if Secret Service Mandate 7266 hadn't been rescinded their position in this was only ever going to be that of scapegoat. They operated outside the law. They were outside the security of the State machinery. Deniable when the shit hit the fan. In other words, the perfect scapegoats. Finally, they were worthy of their own preferred nickname—not Crucible, not Forge Team, not Ogmios—The Lost Cause. It had never felt more appropriate.

"Shamshi?"

"She's fine," Lethe said, and when they looked at him, confused, he shrugged and managed a shy smile. "She's been staying at the flat in town with me for a few days."

"Shamshi and Lethe, sitting in a tree, *kay eye ess ess eye en gee*," Noah said, but his heart really wasn't in it.

Lethe just shrugged.

The world really was changing.

"You thinking about rebuilding?" Orla asked Frost.

"I don't know. The money is there. The Old Man was nothing if not practical. I got a package this morning, all the necessary paperwork, deeds, entitlements, codes for accessing the funds and offshore accounts. His Last Will and Testament was in there, too. So, maybe one day we'll put this place back together again, but not today."

Orla nodded. It made sense. They all needed space and time to grieve in their own ways.

"It won't last forever," Lethe said. "They'll forget us. They always do. Soon enough anyone who does remember it will just say 'Oh, that? Fake news.'" It was the mantra for the age. Don't believe the truth of your own eyes. Don't believe the evidence of your own ears. Everywhere people were being bombarded by the notion that the truth they thought they understood couldn't be trusted. Maybe he was right. Maybe there would be a day when people didn't think of the five of them as *those* people. But until then it wasn't as though they could put out the truth. That was the nature of this new world they were living in, people believed whatever they heard first and would steadfastly refuse to open their minds to other possibilities. They'd been burned. What happened next was down to whatever people wanted to believe.

The truth had no place in their futures.

"Have you thought about where you'll go?" she asked.

No one said anything, though obviously they had their own ideas as to what happened next.

She could well imagine Konstantin just disappearing to pop up in crisis zones across the world wherever and whenever he was needed, like some sort of taciturn super hero. Noah, she figured, was in trouble. Again. So, after they hugged and said their goodbyes she assumed he was off to some remote safe house where he could lay low until the whisky nightmares had him moving again. Lethe was in love, that much was painfully obvious. But what about Shamshi? She'd just lost her twin. That was going to damage the girl in ways he couldn't image while they were caught up in a tangle of sweaty sheets trying to decide if they were each other's tomorrows or if this was just grief and the very physical response to loss. In Orla's experience sex and death were intrinsically linked, sex being the single most powerful way to prove you were still alive. Would it go beyond that? For Lethe's sake she hoped so. He deserved good things.

As different as they were, she could imagine good lives for her friends. Better than the ones they had been living for the last few weeks.

Frost said, "Actually, I was thinking I might write a book," which was the last thing she imagined him doing. No, she looked at him in his wheelchair and realised for the first time just how much he looked like an old man.

And in that moment, she saw his future.

THE END

www.ingramcontent.com/pod-product-compliance
Ingram Content Group UK Ltd.
Pitfield, Milton Keynes, MK11 3LW, UK
UKHW021322180426
11947UKWH00017B/1386